Praise for *Bloody River Blues* and Jeffery Deaver

'The best psychological thriller writer around.'   *The Times*

'If you want thrills, Deaver is your man.'   *Guardian*

'The twists and turns from devilish Deaver will have you burning the midnight oil, then using it to set fire to the candle you'll be burning at both ends until you finish this . . . This is the perfect accompaniment on a winter's night, curled up on the sofa with a glass of your favourite tipple.'   *Sun*

'No one is better at narrative misdirection. Just at the point you think "That's impossible!" Deaver demonstrates the exact opposite.'   *Evening Standard*

'Jeffery Deaver is grand master of the ticking-clock thriller.'
Kathy Reichs

'Deaver is a master of manipulation himself; his skillfully constructed plots are devilishly tricky to track and impossible to solve, just the way we like them.'
New York Times Book Review

'Jeffery Deaver is a master at crafting intricate crimes that are solved through guile, tenacity and sheer creative genius. And Lincoln Rhyme is one of a kind.'   Harlan Coben

Also by Jeffery Deaver

Mistress of Justice
The Lesson of Her Death
Praying for Sleep
Speaking in Tongues
A Maiden's Grave
The Devil's Teardrop
The Blue Nowhere
Garden of Beasts
The Bodies Left Behind
Edge
The October List

The Rune Series
Manhattan is My Beat
Death of a Blue Movie Star
Hard News

The Location Scout Series
Shallow Graves
Hell's Kitchen

The Lincoln Rhyme Thrillers
The Bone Collector
The Coffin Dancer
The Empty Chair
The Stone Monkey
The Vanished Man
The Twelfth Card
The Cold Moon
The Broken Window
The Burning Wire
The Kill Room
The Skin Collector
The Steel Kiss

The Kathryn Dance Thrillers
The Sleeping Doll
Roadside Crosses
XO
Solitude Creek

A James Bond Novel
Carte Blanche

Short Stories
Twisted
More Twisted
Trouble in Mind

JEFFERY DEAVER

BLOODY RIVER BLUES

HODDER

First published in Great Britain in 2001 by Hodder & Stoughton
An Hachette UK company

This Hodder paperback edition 2016

5

A CIP catalogue record for this title is available from the British Library

Paperback ISBN 978 1 473 63198 4
eBook ISBN 978 1 848 94183 0

Typeset in Fairfield LH by Palimpsest Book Production Ltd,
Falkirk, Stirlingshire

Printed and bound by Clays Ltd, Elcograf S.p.A

Hodder & Stoughton policy is to use papers that are natural, renewable and
recyclable products and made from wood grown in sustainable forests.
The logging and manufacturing processes are expected to conform to
the environmental regulations of the country of origin.

Hodder & Stoughton Ltd
Carmelite House
50 Victoria Embankment
London EC4Y 0DZ

www.hodder.co.uk

For Monica Derham

"All you need for a movie is a gun and a girl."
    – Jean-Luc Godard

1

All he wanted was a case of beer.

And it looked like he was going to have to get it himself.

The way Stile explained it, "I can't hardly get a case of Labatts on the back of a Yamaha."

"That's okay," Pellam said into the cellular phone.

"You want a six-pack, I can handle that. But the rack's a little loose. Which I guess I owe you. The rack, I mean. Sorry."

The motorcycle was the film company's but had been issued to Pellam, who had in turn loaned it to Stile. Stile was a stuntman. Pellam chose not to speculate on what he had been doing when the rack got broken.

"That's okay," Pellam said again. "I'll pick up a case."

He hung up the phone. He got his brown bomber jacket from the front closet of the Winnebago, trying to remember where he'd seen the discount beverage store. The Riverfront Deli was not far away but the date of his next expense check was and

Pellam did not feel inclined to pay $26.50 for a case even if it had been imported all the way from Canada.

He stepped into the kitchenette of the camper, stirred the chili and put the cornbread in the small oven to heat. He had thought about cooking something else for a change. Nobody seemed to notice that whenever Pellam hosted the poker game he made chili. Maybe he would serve it on hot dogs, maybe on rice, but it was always chili. And oyster crackers. He didn't know how to cook much else.

He thought about doing without the beer, calling back Stile and saying, yeah, just bring a six-pack. But he did the calculation and decided they needed a whole case. There would be five of them playing for six hours and that meant even a case would be stretched pretty thin. He would have to break out the mezcal and Wild Turkey as it was.

Pellam stepped outside, locked the camper door and walked along the road paralleling the gray plain of the Missouri River. It was just after dark, an autumn weekday, and by rights ought to be rush hour. But the road dipped and rose away from him and it was deserted of traffic. He zipped his jacket tight. Pellam was tall and thin. Tonight he wore jeans and a work shirt that had been black and was now mottled gray. His cowboy boots sounded in loud, scraping taps on the wet asphalt. He wished he had worn his Lakers cap or his Stetson; a cold wind, salty-fishy smelling, streamed off the river. His eyes stung, his ears ached.

He walked quickly. He was worried that Danny – the script-writer of the movie they were now shooting – would show up early. Pellam had recently left a ten-pound catfish in Danny's hotel room bathtub and the writer had threatened to weld the Winnebago door shut in retaliation.

The fourth of the poker players was a grip from San Diego who looked just like the merchant marine he had once been, complete with tattoo. The fifth was a lawyer in St Louis, a hawkish man with jowls. The film company's L.A. office had hired him to negotiate property and talent contracts with the locals. He talked nonstop about Washington politics as if he had run for office and been defeated because he was the only honest candidate in the race. His chatter was a pain but he was a hell of a good man to play poker with. He bet big and lost amiably.

Hands in pockets, Pellam turned down Adams Street, away from the river, studying the spooky, abandoned redbrick Maddox Ironworks building.

Thinking, it's damp, it may rain.

Thinking, would the filming in this damn town go much over schedule?

Would the chili burn, had he turned it down?

Thinking about a case of beer.

"All right, Gaudia is walking down Third, okay? He works most of the time till six or six-thirty but tonight he's going for drinks with some girl I don't know who she is."

Philip Lombro asked Ralph Bales, "Why is he in Maddox?"

"That's what I'm saying. He's going to the Jolly Rogue for drinks. You know it? Then he's going to Callaghan's for the steak."

As he listened, Philip Lombro dipped his head and touched his cheek with two fingers formed into a V. He had a long face, tanned. The color, though, didn't turn Lombro bronze; he was more silvery, like platinum, which matched his mane of white hair, carefully sprayed into place. He said, "What about Gaudia's bodyguard?"

"He won't be coming. Gaudia thinks Maddox is safe. Okay, then he's got a reservation at seven-thirty. It's a five-minute walk – I timed it – and they'll leave at quarter after."

Ralph Bales was sitting forward on the front seat of the navy-blue Lincoln as he spoke to Lombro. Ralph Bales was thirty-nine, muscular, hairy everywhere but on the head. His face was disproportionately thick, as if he were wearing a latex special-effects mask. He was not an ugly man but seen straight on his face, because of the fat, seemed moonlike. Tonight he wore a black-and-red striped rugby shirt, blue jeans and a leather jacket. "He's on Third, okay? There's an alleyway there, going west. It's real dark. Stevie'll be there, doing kind of a homeless number."

"Homeless? They don't have homeless in Maddox."

"Well, a bum. They've got bums in Maddox," Ralph Bales said.

"Okay."

"He's got a little Beretta, a .22. Doesn't even need a suppressor. I've got the Ruger. Stevie calls him, he stops and turns. Stevie does him, up close. I'm behind, just in case. Bang, we're in Stevie's car, over the river, then we're lost."

"I'll be in front of the alley then," Lombro said. "On Third."

Ralph Bales didn't say anything for a moment but kept his eyes on Lombro. What he saw was this: a hook nose, kind eyes, trim suit, paisley tie . . . It was odd but you couldn't see more than that. You thought you could peg him easily as if the silver hair, the tasseled oxblood loafers, polished spit-shine and the battered Rolex, were going to explain everything about Philip

Lombro. But no, those were all you could come up with. The parts and the parts alone. Like a *People* magazine photo.

Lombro, who was calmly looking back into Ralph Bales's eyes, said, "Yes? Do you have a problem with that?"

Ralph Bales decided he could win the staring contest if he wanted to and began to examine the swirl of hair on the back of his own hand. "Okay, I don't think it's such a good idea, you being there. But I told you that already."

"Yes, you did."

"Okay, I still don't think it's a good idea."

"I want to see him die."

"You'll see pictures. The *Post-Dispatch*'ll have pictures. The *Reporter*'ll have pictures. In color."

"I'll be there from seven-fifteen."

Ralph Bales was drumming his fingers on the leather seat of the Lincoln. "It's my ass, too."

Lombro looked at his watch. The crystal was chipped and yellowed. Six-fifty. "I can find somebody else to do the job."

Ralph Bales waited a moment. "That won't be necessary. You want to be there, that's your business."

"Yes, it is my business."

Without response Ralph Bales swung the car door open.

That's when it happened.

Sonofabitch . . .

A thud, the sound of glass on glass, a couple of muted pops. Ralph Bales saw the man – a thin guy in a brown leather jacket – standing there, looking down, a sour smile on his face, a smile that said, *I knew something like this was going to happen.* Foamy beer chugged out of the bottom of the cardboard case, which rested on its end on the sidewalk.

The man looked at Ralph Bales, then past him into the car. Ralph Bales slammed the door and walked away.

The man with the rueful grin said, "Hey, my beer . . ."

Ralph Bales ignored him and continued along Adams.

"Hey, my beer!"

Ralph Bales ignored him.

The man was stepping toward him. "I'm talking to you. Hey!"

Ralph Bales said, "Fuck you," and turned the corner.

The tall man stood staring after him for a moment, his mouth twisted and indignant, then bent down and looked into the window of the Lincoln. He cupped his hands. He tapped on the window. "Hey, your buddy . . . Hey . . ." He rapped again. Lombro put the car in gear. It pulled away quickly. The man jumped back. He watched the Lincoln vanish. He knelt down to his wounded carton, which was pumping beer into the gutter like a leaky fire hydrant.

Maddox Police Department Patrolman First Class Donald Buffett watched the last of the beer trickle into the street, thinking that if that had happened in the Cabrini projects on the west side of town you'd have a dozen guys lapping it out of the gutter or knifing each other over the unbroken bottles.

Buffett leaned against a brick wall and watched the guy – Buffett thought he looked like a cowboy – open up the case and salvage what he could, like a kid picking through his toys. The cowboy stood up and counted what looked to be maybe twelve, fifteen surviving bottles. The cardboard box was soaked and disintegrating.

Buffett had expected him to take a swing at the man who

stepped out of the Lincoln. There was a time, before the service, before the academy, when going for skin was what Buffett himself would have done. He watched the cowboy lining up all the good bottles in the shadow of a Neuman furniture warehouse, hiding them. He must have been planning to go back to the store. He dumped the box in the trash and wiped his hands on his pants.

Buffett pushed off from the wall and walked across the street.

"Evening, sir," he said.

The cowboy looked up, shaking his head. He said, "You see that? You believe it?"

Buffett said, "I'll keep an eye on them, you want to get a bag or something."

"Yeah?"

"Sure."

"Thanks." He disappeared down the empty street.

Ten minutes later, the cowboy returned, carrying a plastic shopping bag, which held two six-packs. He also carried a small paper bag, which he handed to Buffett.

"I'd offer you a Labatts but they probably got rules about you being on duty. So it's a coffee and doughnut. A couple sugars in the bag."

"Thank you, sir," Buffett said formally, feeling embarrassed and wondering why he did. "Didn't have to."

The cowboy started to pick up the beers and loaded them in the shopping bag. Buffett did not offer to help. Finally the cowboy stood up and said, "John Pellam."

"Donnie Buffett."

They nodded and didn't shake hands.

Buffett lifted the coffee into the air, like a toast, and walked off, listening to beer bottles clink as the man headed toward the river.

At seven-twenty that evening, Vincent Gaudia looked down the low-cut white dress of his blond companion and told her, "It's time to eat."

"What did you have in mind?" she asked breathily, smiling tiny crow's-feet into the makeup that was laid on a few microns too deep.

Gaudia was addicted to women like this. Although he viewed them as a commodity he tried not to be condescending. Some of his dates were very intelligent, some were spiritual, some spent many hours volunteering for good causes. And though he did not pursue them for their minds or souls or consciences he listened avidly as they spoke about their interests and he did so with genuine curiosity.

On the other hand, what he wanted most from this girl was to take her to his co-op, where he would tell her to shut the hell up about spirit guides and climb onto her hands and knees, then he would lift her garter belt with his hands and tug on it like reins. He now eased a strategically placed elbow against her breasts and said, "For the moment, I'm talking about dinner."

She giggled.

They left the Jolly Rogue then crossed River Road and walked up Third Street, toward downtown Maddox, past foreboding warehouses, storefronts filled with blotched and decaying used furniture, groundfloor offices, dingy coffee shops. The woman squeezed closer to him against the cold. The chill air reminded Gaudia of his boyhood in Cape Girardeau, when he would walk home from school shuffling leaves in front of his saddle shoes, working on a toffee apple or Halloween candy. He had pulled some crazy stunts at Halloween, and he could not smell cold fall air without being stirred by good memories. Gaudia asked, "What'd you do on Halloween? When you were a kid?"

She blinked then concentrated on her answer. "Well, we had a lot of fun, you know. I used to dress up mostly like princesses and things like that. I was a witch one year."

"A witch? No way. You couldn't be one if you tried."

"Sweetheart . . . And then we'd go for tons of candy. I mean, like tons. I liked Babe Ruths, no, ha ha, *Baby* Ruths best, and what I'd do sometimes is find a house that was giving them out and keep going back there. One Halloween I got twelve Baby Ruths. I had to be careful. I had a lot of zits when I was a kid."

"Kids don't go much anymore. It's dangerous. Did you hear about that guy who put needles in apples?"

"I never liked apples. I only liked candy bars."

"Baby Ruths," Gaudia remembered.

"Where're we going? This is a creepy neighborhood."

"This is a creepy town. But it's got the best steak house in the state outside of Kansas City. Callaghan's. You like steak?"

"Yeah, I like steak. I like surf and turf." She added demurely, "But it's expensive."

"I think they've got surf and turf there. You want surf and turf, order it. What you want, you can have."

Ralph Bales stood on the street corner, in the alcove of Missouri National Bank, watching the couple stroll under a dim street-light, three of the four bulbs burnt out. The girl was glued on to his arm, which probably was more a plus than anything, because if Gaudia was carrying a weapon she'd tie up his shooting hand.

Philip Lombro's dark Lincoln Town Car, boxy as an aircraft carrier, exhaust purring, sat across the street. Ralph Bales studied the perfect bodywork, the immaculate chrome. Then he looked at the silhouette of Lombro behind the wheel. That man was crazy. Ralph Bales could not understand his wanting to watch it – watching the act of the shooting itself. He knew some guys who got off on doing people, got off on it in some scary sex way. He sensed, though, that this was something Lombro felt he *had* to do, not something he *wanted* to do.

A voice fluttered over the cool air – Stevie Flom, Ralph Bales's partner, was doing his schizoid homeless routine. "There's what it is, I mean, there's *it!* I read the papers . . . I read the papers I read them forget what you read forget what you read . . ."

Then Ralph Bales thought he heard Stevie pull the slide on the Beretta though that might have been his imagination; at moments like this you heard noises, you saw things that were otherwise silent or invisible. His nerves shook like a dragster waiting for the green light. He wished he didn't get so nervous.

Tapping, leather soles on concrete. The sound seemed very loud. Tapping and scuffing along the wet, deserted sidewalk.

Giggling.

Tapping.

Light glinted off Gaudia's feet. Ralph Bales knew Gaudia's reputation for fashion and figured he would be wearing five-hundred-dollar shoes. Ralph Bales's shoes were stamped "Man-made uppers" and the men who had made those uppers had been Taiwanese.

The footsteps, twenty feet away.

The murmur of the Lincoln's exhaust.

The beating of Ralph Bales's heart.

Stevie talking like a crazy drunk. Arguing with himself.

The blonde giggling.

Then Stevie said, "A quarter, mister. Please?"

And son of a bitch, if Gaudia wasn't stopping and stepping forward with a bill.

Ralph Bales started across the street, holding the Ruger, a huge gun, barrel-heavy in his hand. Then: the woman's shrill scream and a swing of motion, a blur, as Gaudia swung her around as a shield putting her between him and Stevie's. One pop, then two. The blonde slumped.

Gaudia was running. Fast. Getting away.

Christonthecross . . .

Ralph Bales lifted the heavy gun and fired twice. He hit Gaudia at least once. He thought it was in the lower neck. The man stumbled onto the sidewalk, lifted a hand briefly, then lay still.

Lombro's Lincoln started away, accelerating with a sharp, gassy roar.

Silence for a moment.

Ralph Bales took a step toward Gaudia.

"Freeze!"

The scream came from only five feet away. Bales almost vomited in shock and the way his heart surged he wondered if he was having a heart attack.

"I mean *you*, mister!"

Ralph Bales's hand lowered, the gun pointed down. His breath flowed in and out in staccato bursts. He swallowed.

"Drop the weapon!" The voice crackled with a barely controlled hysteria.

"I'm dropping it." Ralph Bales did. He squinted as the gun fell. It didn't go off.

"Lie down on the ground!" The cop was crouching, holding his gun aimed straight at Ralph Bales's head.

"Okay!" Ralph Bales said. "Don't do anything. I'm lying down."

"Now!"

"I'm doing it now! I'm lying down now!" Ralph Bales got on his knees then lay forward on his stomach. He smelled grease and dog piss.

The cop circled around him, kicking the Ruger away and talking into his walkie-talkie. "This's Buffett. I'm in downtown Maddox, I've got a 10-13. Shots fired and two down. Need an ambulance and backup at—"

The Maddox police and fire central radio dispatcher did not find out exactly where Donnie Buffett needed the backup and ambulance – at least not at that moment. The cop's message ended abruptly when Stevie Flom stepped out of the alleyway and emptied the clip of the Beretta into his back.

Buffett grunted, dropped to his knees, and tried to reach behind him. He fell forward.

Ralph Bales climbed to his feet, picked up the Ruger. He walked over to the unconscious cop and pointed the big gun at his head. He cocked it.

Slowly the heavy blue muzzle nestled itself in the cop's damp hair. Ralph Bales covered his eyes with his left hand. His heart beat eight times. His hand tensed. It relaxed. He stepped back and turned away from the cop, settling on one head shot for Gaudia and one for the blonde.

Then, as if they were a couple of basketball fans eager for some beers after the game, Ralph Bales and Stevie Flom walked briskly to a stolen black Trans Am with a sporty red racing stripe on the side. Stevie fired up the engine. Ralph Bales sat down in the comfortable bucket seat. He lifted his blunt index finger to his upper lip and smelled sour gunpowder and primer smoke. As they drove slowly to the river Ralph Bales watched the aura of lights rising up from St. Louis, to the south, thinking that all he would have to do now was take care of the witness – the guy with the beer – and that would be that.

2

Yellow light fading in and out, going to black, black to yellow, motion, shouting, more blackness, deep deep pain, can't breathe can't swallow . . . The fragments of yellow light. There they go, slipping away . . . Don't leave, don't leave me . . .

Donnie Buffett focused for a moment on Penny's terrified face. Pale and framed with dark hair. The sight of *her* terror terrified *him*. He reached for her hand. He passed out.

When he opened his eyes again his wife was gone and the room was dark. He had never been so exhausted.

Or so thirsty.

After a few minutes he began to understand that he had been shot. And the instant he thought that, he forgot everything – Penny, the sickening loose feelings in his back and guts, his thirst – and he concentrated on trying to remember something. One word. A short word. The one word that gave purpose to his entire life.

The Word. What is the Word? He slipped back into uncon-
sciousness. When he woke again he saw a Filipino nurse.

"Water," he whispered.

"Rinse and spit," she said.

"Thirsty."

"Rinse and spit." She squirted water into his mouth from a
plastic bottle. "Don't swallow."

He swallowed. He vomited.

The nurse sighed loudly and cleaned him.

"I can't feel my legs. Did they cut my legs off?"

"No. You're tired."

"Oh."

*The Word. What the hell was it? Please, dear Mother of our
Lord, let me remember . . .*

He fell asleep trying to remember the Word and when he
awoke a short time later he was still trying to remember it.
Sitting across from him were two men in rumpled suits. When
he looked at them he smiled.

"Hey, he's smiling." The man who said this was blond and
square-jawed.

"Yo, Donnie," the other man said, "I won't ask how you're
doing, 'cause your answer's gonna be: what a dumb-ass question
– I feel like shit." He was dark-complected, with short, slick hair.
He looked at Buffett with real affection. He gripped Buffett's
hand warmly.

"They got me from behind. There was another one behind
me."

Bob Gianno, the dark-complected detective, continued, "The
mayor's coming down to see you. He wants to wish you
luck."

Luck? Why do I need luck? I've been lucky. I don't need luck. What I need is to get out of this bed.

Buffett's lips were rising and falling.

"What's that?" Richard Hagedorn, the blond detective, leaned forward.

"Why can't I . . ." He shook his head and said indignantly, "I had my body armor on."

"He got you below it. That's what they said at the press conference."

"Oh." *Press conference?* There was a press conference about *me?*

Gianno said, "We met your wife, Donnie. She's really pretty."

Buffett nodded blankly.

The detective continued, "Guess you know why we're here. What can you tell us about the hit?"

The periphery faded fast, dissolving again into a million black dots. Yellow light, white light. His organs seemed to shift. Floating. He felt deep pain that was all the more terrifying because it did not seem to hurt. He tried to remember the word. *The Word. The WORD. The answer lies in the Word.*

"I . . ." His voice ended in a rasp. He inhaled hard.

"Maybe we should—" Hagedorn began but Buffett wiped sweat away from his face with the blanket and said, "All I saw was one perp. Cauc, balding, dark hair. Back was to me, I didn't make the face. Thirty-five maybe." A pause. The air hissed in over the dry tissue of his mouth and burned like alcohol on a cut. "Make him five ten, eleven. Weighed one ninety. Wearing a dark jacket, shirt, jeans, I think. I don't remember. Had a big gun."

"A .44."

"Forty-four," Buffett said slowly. "The other one, the one shot me . . ."

"You make him at all?"

Buffett shook his head no. Then asked, "Who was the hit?"

"Vince Gaudia and some squeeze."

"Man," Buffett whispered reverently. "Gaudia." He closed his eyes and shook his head. "Peterson's gonna be pissing red."

Hagedorn said, "Hell with Peterson. *We're* gonna get the scumbag that did you, Donnie."

Buffett said, "I didn't see the third one, either."

"Third one?" Hagedorn asked. He and Gianno exchanged glances.

"The guy in the Lincoln."

"What Lincoln?" Gianno was taking notes.

"Dark Lincoln. It was parked across the street. I didn't get tag numbers or make." Buffett coughed. "I want some water."

Hagedorn went into the john and got a glass.

He handed it to Buffett, who hesitated then said, "I might puke."

Gianno said, "I seen worse than cops barfing."

Buffett didn't puke, though, and he handed the empty glass back to Hagedorn with triumph. "Best thing I ever had in my mouth."

The men laughed; there was no need to say aloud any of the three punch lines that materialized simultaneously in three different minds.

Gianno asked, "The guy in the Lincoln. Was he get-away?"

"No, he drove off by himself. Maybe it was somebody who had to ID the hit."

"Naw," Gianno said, "everybody knows what Gaudia looks like. He's a cover boy. Well, *looked* like."

Buffett said, "Well, maybe it was the guy who hired baldy."

"Some big fish? I wonder. Donnie, you got any idea who was inside?"

"No, but I saw a guy who did."

"There's a witness?"

Buffett told them about the beer incident. "This guy was talking to the driver, saying something."

"Fantastic." Hagedorn smiled.

Gianno turned to a blank page in his notebook. "What's he look like?"

Buffett was about to give them a description, and that's what did it. The Word came back to him. The magic *Word*.

Buffett beamed. He whispered, "Pellam."

"Tell him?" Gianno asked and looked at Hagedorn with a frown.

"His name's Pellam." The smile on Buffett's face glistened and grew.

"You got his name?" Gianno nodded enthusiastically. "He live around there?"

"Dunno." Buffett shrugged, which sent a stab of pain through his neck. He remained very still for a moment, frozen as the pain slowly receded.

"We'll find him," Gianno said reverently.

The smile slipped off Buffett's face as he tried to shift his leg and found he was unable to. The sheet, he guessed, was tucked in too tightly. He absently pulled at the bedclothes and smacked his thigh. "Gotta get the circulation going. I've been on my butt too long."

"We're gonna go find this guy, Donnie." Gianno slapped his notebook shut.

"One thing," Buffett said, "you know witnesses. When it's a hit like this? He's gonna get amnesia. Bet you any money."

Gianno snorted. "Oh, he'll talk, Donnie. Don't you worry about that."

Apparently some trouble with the chili.

The beer and whiskey were gone completely, but the whole pot of chili was pretty much untouched.

Danny and Stile remained behind in the camper after the other poker players had left and they helped Pellam clean up. Danny, with his thick nose, twenty-nine-year-old's smooth complexion, and shoulder-length black hair, resembled a Navajo warrior.

"What'd you do to the chili?" Danny said to Pellam, crinkling his nose, then emptied some ashtrays into a trash bag. Although he often said blunt things to people they rarely took offense.

The chili?

Stile slipped Labatt's bottles into another bag and twirled his bushy mustache. Although Pellam was descended – so the family story went – from a real gun-slinger, Pellam thought Stile was dead ringer for the ancestor in question, Wild Bill Hickok. Stile was lanky and had a droopy Vietnam vet mustache the shade of his dark blond hair. He reflected, "I remember this western I worked on one time . . . I forget whose. I was falling off a cliff. I think it was an eighty-foot cliff . . . and the compressor broke, so they couldn't inflate the air bag as much as the unit director wanted to."

"Hm," Pellam muttered, and stepped into the kitchenette to

look at the chili. He'd eaten two bowls, piled with onions and slices of American cheese. Seemed okay to him.

"No," Stile reflected. "It was a hundred-and-thirty-foot cliff."

Bored again, Danny said, "Got the point." An Oscar-nominated scriptwriter, Danny sat in deluxe hotel suites in front of an NEC laptop computer and wrote scenes that sent people like Stile off hundred-and-thirty-foot cliffs; he was not impressed.

Stile: "Man, there we were in the middle of this desert, in a very Native American frame of mind, you know what I'm saying?"

What's wrong with the chili?

Pellam tried another spoonful. Yup, burned. It reminded him of Scotch, the smokiness. But there wasn't anything *wrong* with it. It could have been intended, as if he had tried a new recipe. If it tasted like mesquite, for instance, nobody would have said anything, except maybe "Damn good chili, Pellam."

He piled dishes in the tiny sink, rinsed some of them in the dribble of the water from the faucet.

"Anyway, when I landed I went down so far, my belt loops made an impression in the mud beneath the bag."

"Uh. That happens sometimes," Danny said lethargically.

To air out the camper Pellam opened the front door. Chili smoke was only part of it. The lawyer from St Louis had been lighting one cigarette after another. Pellam had noticed that midwesterners did not seem to know this habit was bad for you.

Danny and Stile argued about who had the riskier job – Stile falling off high cliffs and Danny having to pitch his stories to producers and development people. Stile said that was an old joke, and tried to convince Danny to go base-jumping with him sometime.

"To Live and Die in L.A.," Stile whispered reverently. "Awesome scene. The jump from the bridge."

Pellam, still at the front door, squinted. He saw a large, boxy shadow in the grass not far from where the camper was parked. What was it? He squinted, which didn't help. He remembered seeing that area in the daylight – it was a field full of crabgrass and weeds. What would be sitting in the middle of a lousy field this time of night? Funny, the shadow looked just like . . .

The shadow began to murmur.

. . . a car.

It accelerated fast, spraying dirt and stones, nosing quickly out of the grass, grinding the undercarriage as it went over the sharp drop to the highway.

Probably lovers, Pellam thought. Necking. He could not remember the last time he necked. Did people still do it? Probably in the Midwest they did. Pellam lived in Los Angeles and nobody he'd ever dated there necked.

It was only when he turned back to the camper that he realized that the car had not turned on its lights until it was far down River Road; because of this, the license plate was not illuminated until it was too far away to be read. Odd . . .

"Wish I'd seen it," Danny said emphatically.

"Was just a car," Pellam muttered, glancing toward the disappearing taillights.

The other two stared at him.

"I meant," Danny said, "the base jump off that bridge."

"Oh."

Danny thanked Pellam for the game and the company but not the chili. After he left, Stile stepped into the kitchenette and began doing the dishes.

"You don't have to."

"Not a problem."

He washed everything but the chili pot.

"Man, black-bottom chili. You're on your own there, buddy."

"I got diverted on my way back from the store."

Stile asked, "How long *you* in this hellhole of a town for?"

"Till shooting's done. Tony's reshooting every other scene."

"He does that, yup. Well, if we're here next week, come over to the Quality Inn for a game. I've got a hot-plate there and I'll whip up Philly cheese steaks. With onions. By the by, I'm getting the Hertz tomorrow. You can have your bike back then."

Stile had been in town three weeks and had already burned out the transmission of his rental car. Rental companies should ask for occupation and not rent their vehicles to stuntmen.

Pellam walked him to the door. "When you got here, d'you see a car parked over there?"

"Where? There? That's just a mess of weeds, Pellam. Why'd anybody park there?"

Stile stepped outside, inhaled the air. He whistled a Stevie Wonder tune through his gunslinger mustache as he walked in long strides to the battered Yamaha with the rack dangling precariously from the back fender.

"Was it him?"

"I couldn't tell."

"He get a look at the car?"

"If I couldn't tell it was him how could I tell if he got a look at the car? And if you cracked that transmission case, boy, you're paying for it. You hear me?" Ralph Bales was speaking to Stevie Flom. They had abandoned the Pontiac and were in Ralph Bales's Cadillac, Stevie driving.

Flom was twenty-five years old. He was north Italian blond and had gorgeous muscles and baby-smooth skin. His round face had never once been disfigured by a pimple. He had slept with 338 women. He was a cargo handler on the riverfront though he took a lot of sick days and for real money he ran numbers and did odd jobs for men who had the sort of odd jobs few people were willing to do. He was married and had three girlfriends. He made about sixty thousand a year and lost about thirty thousand of it in Reno and at poker games in East St Louis and Memphis.

"Drive," Ralph Bales instructed, looking back at the camper. "It's like he was looking at us."

"Well, was he?"

"What?"

"Looking at us?"

"Just drive."

The night was cloudless. Off to their left the big plain of the Missouri River was moving slowly southeastward. The same water that had looked so muddy and black yesterday, when he was planning the hit, tonight looked golden – lit by the security floods of a small factory on the south shore.

Ralph Bales had thought that locating the witness would be easy. Just find the store where he'd bought the beer and trace him from there.

But he'd forgotten he was in Maddox, Missouri, where there was not much for the locals to do except be out of work and drink all day, or do muscle labor for Maddox Riverfront Services or stoop labor for farmers and drink all night. Ralph Bales, checking the yellow pages, found two dozen package good stores within walking distance of where he'd collided with the witness as he climbed from Lambro's car.

So they'd ditched the Trans Am, sent the Ruger to sleep forty feet below the choppy surface of the Missouri and sped home to change clothes then returned here in Ralph Bales's own car. He had shaved off the mustache, donned fake glasses, a rumpled Irish tweed cap, a pressed blue shirt open at the neck, and a herringbone sport jacket. Pretending to be an insurance company lawyer representing the cop who'd been shot, he walked from store to store until he finally found a clerk who remembered selling a case of beer to a thin man in a bomber jacket at around seven that evening.

"He said he's got a camper parked over at Bide-A-Wee."

"It's that . . . What is it?" Ralph Bales asked.

"You know, that trailer park? By the concrete plant?

"One thing," the clerk had warned solemnly. "Don't ask him for a part in the film. He don't take to that."

Film?

Ralph Bales and Stevie had then cruised down to the river and parked in the weedy lot outside Bell's Bide-A-Wee. They could look through the camper's small windows, but Ralph Bales had not been able to see clearly if it was the beer man or not. Then the door had opened and Stevie had gotten it into his head that he was calling in a description of the car to the cops and had burned out of there, Ralph Bales shouting, "Be careful with the transmission case," and Stevie Flom not paying any attention.

They now cruised through the night, at fifty-five m.p.h. even, away from Maddox.

"Tomorrow morning, let's pay him a visit."

"But maybe he'll give the cops a description of you tonight."

Ralph Bales considered this. He shook his head. "He doesn't even know about the hit. Christ, he had a party going on in there. A guy's a witness to a hit, he isn't going to have a party. I mean, wouldn't you think?"

Stevie said he guessed and put on a Metallica tape.

At seven the next morning they started with the sledge-hammers on the Winnebago door.

The interrupted dream was about old-fashioned cars driving slowly in circles around a movie set. Someone kept asking Pellam if he wanted a ride and he did but whoever asked didn't stop long enough to let him get in the car. Pellam had grown very bored waiting for a car to pick him up.

It wasn't a great dream, but at least he was asleep when he was having it and when the sledgehammers started he became awake. Pellam sat up and swung his feet over the edge of the bunk in the back of the camper. He found his watch. Pellam had often been up at seven but he had rarely *wakened* at that hour. There was a big difference between the two.

The hammers pounded.

He stood up and pulled on his jeans and a black T-shirt. He looked in the mirror. He'd slept in one position all night – on his stomach like a baby – and his black hair had gone spiky. Pellam smoothed it and rubbed at the welts that the crumpled sheet had left across his face. He went to see who was swinging hammers.

"Hey, dude," Stile said, walking into the kitchen past him. "I was sent to collect you."

Pellam put a kettle on. Stile stood beside the camper's tiny dining table, still covered with cards and Pellam's meager winnings. He looked at the chili pot and tapped the black crust with his fingernail. He foraged in the miniature refrigerator. "You got zero food in here."

"Why are you here?" Pellam mumbled.

"Your phone. It's not turned on." Stile found an old bagel and broke it in half. He lifted the other half toward Pellam, who shook his head and dropped two spoonfuls of instant coffee into a Styrofoam cup. "Coffee?" he asked Stile.

"Naw. I got my wheels. You can have the cycle back. It's in the trunk. There's a little teeny dent on the fender. Otherwise it's in perfect condition. Well, it's muddy. Well, the rack, too."

Pellam poured water into the cup and sat heavily on the bench. Stile told him his hair was all spiky.

"What are you doing here?" Pellam asked again as he smoothed his hair.

"Tony needs you. He's like apoplectic – is that the right word? – and you shut your phone off."

"Because I wanted to sleep later than seven o'clock."

"I been up for an hour." Stile did tai chi at dawn. He ate the bagel thoughtfully. "You know, John, I got to admit I was a little curious why you're working for Tony."

Pellam took three sips of scalding coffee. That was something about instant. It tasted terrible but it started hot and stayed hot. He rubbed his thumb and index finger together, designating money, in answer to Stile's question about Tony.

Stile's grunt equaled a shrug, as if he suspected there was more to it. On the other hand, Stile was a senior union stuntman and even at the Screen Actors Guild's contract minimums, would be well paid. But he was also a stand-in for one of the leads, and because of this and because of his experience, his agent had negotiated an overscale contract. He understood all about the motives for being attached to a big-budget project.

"Well, Herr Eisenstein has summoned you and I'm delivering the word." He finished the bagel.

"He tell you what's up?"

"He wants to blow up an oil refinery. For the final scene."

"What?" Pellam rubbed his eyes.

"I swear to God. He's going to build this mock-up of an old DC-7 and tow it behind a chopper, then –" Stile mimicked a plane diving into the stove "– Ka-boom . . ."

Pellam shook his head. "He's out of . . . You son of a bitch. You eat a man's last bagel and you rag him all the while you're doing it and here it is not even dawn."

Stile laughed. "Damn easy to pull your chain, Pellam. Up and at 'em. Rise and shine. Our master calls."

Bell's Bide-A-Wee contained two tents, the Winnebago, which was parked in the row closest to the road, and a Ford Taurus, from whose trunk a yellow motorcycle protruded.

The camper was surrounded by unoccupied spaces dotted with short galvanized steel pipes and junction boxes for utility hookups that stretched away toward the river like slots in a miniature drive-in movie theater.

Stevie Flom had turned off River Road and driven a half block through a stretch of boarded-up one- and two-story houses and stores. He had started to park nose-out in an alley between two deserted shops. Ralph Bales had told him not to get fancy – just parallel park on the street and read the paper or something – only leave the engine running.

Ralph Bales walked down to River Road. It was morning, but he saw lights on in the camper. Then he saw a man's silhouette walking around inside. Ralph Bales stepped into a phone booth, whose floor was covered with the tiny blue cubes from its four shattered windows. Three tall weeds grew up through this pile. He picked up the receiver with a Kleenex and pretended to talk while he studied the camper.

He looked beyond the Winnebago to the river. This morning it looked different still – not silver-gray, not the golden shade of last night. Now the surface had a rusty sheen to it, mirroring a redness in the sky that came, Ralph Bales believed, from garbage pumped into the air by refineries outside of Wood River, across the Mississippi. The wind was steady and it bent grass and weeds on the riverbank but hardly lifted any ripples from the ruddy water, which plodded southward.

Ralph Bales remembered a song that he hadn't thought of for years, a sound-track song from twenty-five years ago, the Byrds' closing number in *Easy Rider*. He heard the music in his head clearly but could not recall the lyrics, just snatches of words about a man wanting to be free, about a river flowing away from someplace, flowing to the sea . . .

The door to the camper opened.

Yep, it was him. The beer man, the witness. He was followed by a tall, gangly man with a droopy mustache. Together they stepped to the back of the Taurus and wrestled the motorcycle out of the trunk.

The Colt appeared from under Ralph Bales's coat, and he looked around him slowly. A mile away, a semi downshifted with a silent belch of smoke. A flock of gray birds dotted past.

In the middle of the muddy river a scarred and patchy tug fought its way upstream.

The two men were talking, standing together over the cycle. The mustached man pointed to what looked like a dent in the mudguard, then he jiggled the chrome rack. The beer man shrugged, then wheeled the motorcycle toward the road.

Ralph Bales was waiting for the friend to get in the Taurus and leave but then decided he should kill both of them. He lifted his Colt and rested the square notch of the sight on the beer man's chest. The silver truck approached. He lowered the gun. It roared past, engulfing the men in a swirl of papers and dust.

Ralph Bales lifted the gun once more. The road was empty now. No trucks or cars. Nothing between him and his targets thirty feet away from the phone booth and its floor of shattered glass.

3

He climbed onto the battered, muddy yellow motorcycle and fired it up, then gunned the engine several times. Pulling on a black helmet, he popped the clutch suddenly and did a wheelie, scooting a precarious ten feet before the front tire descended again to the street. He skidded to a braking stop and returned to his mustached friend.

Ralph Bales steadied the gun with his left palm and began to apply the nine pounds of pressure required to release the hammer.

The beer man pulled on dark-framed sunglasses and zipped up his jacket – for one slow moment he sat up completely straight, perpendicular to Ralph Bales, offering a target that was impossible to miss.

At this moment Ralph Bales lowered the gun.

He squinted, watching the man sit forward and tap the bike into first gear with his toe. It skidded away on River Road with a ragged chain-saw roar of the punchy engine. His friend shouted at him and shook his fist, then leapt into the Taurus and, with a huge spume of dust and gravel, roared over the curb and chased the cycle down River Road, laying down thick tire marks.

Ralph Bales eased the hammer down onto an empty cylinder and slipped the gun into his pocket. He looked up and down the road, then turned, jogging back into the murky shadows of the riverfront streets. He walked up to the Cadillac. He rapped on the driver's window.

"Jesus, I didn't hear it!" Stevie shouted, tossing the paper in the backseat, the sheets separating and filling the car. He flipped the car into gear. "I didn't hear the shot, man!" He glanced through the rear window. "I didn't hear it!"

Ralph Bales casually flicked his fingers toward Stevie.

"Let's go!" the young man shouted again. "What do you mean? What are you doing?"

"Move over," Ralph Bales mouthed.

"What?" Stevie shouted.

"I'll drive."

Stevie looked back again, as if a dozen Missouri Highway Patrol cars were racing after him.

Ralph Bales said, "Put it in park."

"What?"

"Put the car in park and move over," he responded with exasperation. "I'll drive." He climbed in and signaled and made a careful, slow U-turn.

"What happened?"

"Have to wait."

"You didn't do it?"

"Excuse me?" Ralph Bales asked with mock astonishment. "You just said you didn't hear any shots."

"Man! Scared the living crap out of me. I mean, *bang, bang, bang*, on the window. I thought you were a cop. What the hell happened?"

Ralph Bales didn't answer for a moment. "There were a bunch of people around."

"There were?" They now drove past the deserted campground. Stevie protested, "I don't see anybody."

"You wanted me to do it right in front of a dozen witnesses?"

Stevie swiveled around. "What was it, like a bus drove past or something?"

"Yeah. It was like a bus."

Samuel Clemens once stayed in the town of Maddox, Missouri, and supposedly wrote part of *Tom Sawyer* here. The Maddox Historical Society implied that the caverns outside of town were the true inspiration for Injun Joe's cave, despite evidence – and the assertion of a more credible tourist board (Hannibal, Missouri) – to the contrary. Other claims to fame were pretty sparse. In 1908 William Jennings Bryan gave a speech here (standing on a real soapbox to do so), and Maddox was cited by FDR in a Fireside Chat as an example of towns decimated by the Depression. One of the now defunct metalwork mills in town had the distinction of fabricating part of the housing used in what would have been the third atomic bomb dropped in World War II.

But these honors aside, Maddox was essentially a stillborn Detroit.

Unlike Jefferson City, which sat genteel and majestic on gnarled stone bluffs above the Missouri, Maddox squatted on the river's muddy banks just north of where the wide water was swallowed by the wider Mississippi. No malls, no downtown rehab, no landscaped condos.

Maddox was now a town of about thirty thousand. The downtown was a gloomy array of pre-1950 retail stores and two-story office buildings, none of which was fully occupied. Outside of this grim core were two or three dozen factories, about half of them still working at varying degrees of capacity. Unemployment was at 28 percent, the town's per capita income was among the lowest in Missouri, and alcoholism and crime were at record highs. The city was continually in and out of insolvency and the one fire company in town sometimes had to make heartbreaking decisions about which of two or three sim-ultaneous blazes it was going to fight. Residents lived in decrepit housing projects and minuscule nineteenth-century bungalows hemmed in by neighbors and uncut grass and kudzu, amid yards decorated with doorless refrigerators, rusted tricycles, cardboard boxes. On every block were scorched circles, like primitive sacrifice sites, where trash – whose collection the city was often unable to undertake – was illegally burned.

Maddox, Missouri, was a dark river beside the darker rust of storage tanks. Maddox was rats nosing boldly over greasy, indestructible U.S. centennial cobble-stones, Maddox was wiry grass pushing through rotting wooden loading docks and BB craters in plate glass and collapsed grain elevators. Maddox was no more or less than what you saw just beyond the *Welcome To* sign on River Road: the skeleton of a rusted-out Chevy one-ton pickup not worth selling for scrap.

But for John Pellam, Maddox was heaven.

A month earlier, he had just finished scouting locations in

Montana. He had been sitting outside of the Winnebago, his brown Nokonas stretched out in front of him and pointing more or less at the spot where George Armstrong Custer's ego finally caught up with him. Pellam had been drinking beer when his cellular phone had started buzzing.

He hadn't more than answered it before the speaker was barraging him with a story about two young lovers who become robbers. A machine gun of facts, as if the caller and Pellam were resuming a conversation cut short minutes before by an ornery mobile phone. Pellam believed the name of the man with whom he was having this animated talk had passed his way a moment before, but he'd missed it in the onslaught of words.

"Uh, who's this again?"

"Tony Sloan," the surprised, staccato voice fired back.

"Okay." They had never met. Pellam knew Sloan, of course. But then, so did everyone who read *Premiere* or *People* or *Newsweek*. A former producer of TV commercials, he had directed last year's *Circuit Man*, a computer sci-fi political thriller, a megahit that had snagged Oscars for best special effects and best sound and had grossed thirty-six million dollars its first weekend against a total budget of seventy-eight million.

Pellam had seen the first two of Sloan's films and none of the rest. He preferred not to work for directors like Tony Sloan – special-effects directors, he considered them, not people directors – but that day in Montana he had listened to the man with some interest, for two reasons. First: After his recent hit Sloan could write very large checks to those he hired and never be questioned by his studio. Second: Sloan was explaining with a gravity surprising for a child of television that he wanted to make a movie with some meat on it. "Artistically, I want to expand. A *Badlands* tone, you know what I mean? Minimal. Essential."

Pellam had liked *Badlands* and his favorite films were minimal and essential. He felt he should hear Sloan out.

"John, I've asked around. People say you been all over the country. They say you're a walking site catalog."

Perhaps not. But Pellam did have many scrapbooks filled with Polaroid snaps of quirky, cinematic locales just right for the sort of feature film that Sloan was describing. Moreover, Sloan had less location experience than most directors because his flicks were usually soundstage setups and computer graphics transfers. To make his movie he'd need a solid location manager.

"Keep talking," Pellam said.

"They're bank robbers," Sloan was explaining. "Young bank robbers. It's a vehicle – for like Aidan Quinn and Julia Roberts before she was Julia Roberts. I don't want to go with anybody who's been on the cover of *People*. Nobody bankable. It's got me scared, but I need to make this change. Between you and me I'm suffocating under the system. You know what I'm saying?"

Pellam did and he told Sloan so.

"They're not understood, this couple. They're angry, they're disaffected—"

Listening to Sloan back then, Pellam had seen what he believed were the Black Hills. They weren't black at all, but were dark blue. They were very far away, but in the awesome, undisturbed sky towering above, they looked both regal and unsettling.

"It sounds vaguely familiar, Tony."

"I know, you're thinking *Bonnie and Clyde*," Sloan said.

Ah, right. That was what Pellam had been thinking.

"This's different," the director continued. "It's called *Missouri River Blues*. You hear about it? Orion was kicking it around a few years ago before it was belly-up time. These characters are *real*. They live and breathe. Dunaway and Beatty were . . . Dunaway and Beatty. What can I say? Good movie, one of my primal influences. But I'm going *beyond* it. Okay, Ross, that's the boyfriend, he's in prison and going crazy. He's going to kill himself. He can't take it anymore. We open on these incredible shots of a lock-down. That's when . . . See, in prison—"

"When they close up the maximum-security cellblock for the night."

"Right. How'd you know that?"

"Tell me about the film, Tony."

"I've got the DP working on a special micro lens. Angles on the insides of the locks and bars clanging shut. It's beautiful. So we get a sense of confinement. Everything closing around him. Well, Ross escapes, and he and Dehlia—"

"Dehlia?"

". . . he and Dehlia drive around the countryside, robbing armored trucks mostly. They're highwaymen, modern highwaymen. Ross's driven by his fear of the lock-down. She's driven by the social convention that forces women to be homemakers. Claustrophobia. The script plays off the risk of freedom versus the fear of imprisonment. Which is worse? Prison with its security, freedom with its dangers?"

"It sounds a lot like *Bonnie and Clyde*."

"No, no, the characters are all different. Also the freedom of love versus its confinement. Oh, and the kids're concerned about the environment." He added significantly, "This's the early fifties. They're concerned about A-bomb testing."

"A-bombs," Pellam said. "That's very socially conscious." Sloan completely missed the irony and Pellam asked, "Set in Missouri, I presume?"

"Medium-sized town," Sloan said. "The postwar boom has passed it by. That sort of town."

"*Bonnie and Clyde* was set in Missouri," Pellam pointed out. "Part of it anyway."

"It's not like *Bonnie and Clyde*," the director said icily.

Pellam flipped through his mental Rolodex of locations he knew in the Midwest. "I did a job in Kansas a few years back. Small town on a river. How's Kansas?"

"I want Missouri. The title, you know."

Pellam asked, "Could you tell Kansas from Missouri?"

"I grew up in Van Nuys. I can't tell Ohio from Colorado. But that's not the point. I want Missouri."

"Got it."

Sloan now paused. "The thing is, John, I've got some timing problems here."

The tail of the sentence wagged silently.

"Timing."

"You know, I've had nothing but headaches with the project. You know the *Time* article about me? Last year?"

"I missed it," Pellam said.

"When they called me the 'High-tech Visionary'?"

Pellam said that whatever they had called him, he'd still missed the article.

"I mean, Sony or Disney would have written a check for the GNP of France if I'd made the sequel."

Son of Circuit Man, Pellam thought, then reconsidered. He said, "*Circuit Man Rewired*."

"Ha, John. Very good. Very funny. But *Missouri River*? It was a battle to get the green light. It's an action film, but it's a *period* action film, and it's an intelligent period action film. That scared people."

Perhaps competing with Kurosawa and Altman and John Ford – and Arthur Penn, the director of *Bonnie and Clyde* – scared people, too.

"So what are you saying, Tony?"

"I'm saying that I'm in a bind. I got the go-ahead yesterday and I need locations in two weeks, absolute maximum."

Pellam laughed a laugh that terrifies producers and directors. It means: Not only are you asking the impossible but I don't need the job nearly badly enough to put up with the crap I know I'm going to have to put up with to do what you want.

"Six," Pellam said. He was, in fact, ready to leave that night – just as soon as the Black Hills turned truly black and he finished his beer. But two weeks was impossible to find sites for the hundreds of setups in a full-length feature.

It was the moment when one of them would say, "Four weeks" and they would shake hands, remotely, on the compromise.

Tony Sloan said, "You find me locations in two weeks and I'll pay you twenty-five thousand dollars."

Pellam felt heat flow from his black hair down into his throat. He believed his skin was flushed. "Well—"

"Thirty-five."

Thirty-five thousand?

"I'm a desperate man, Pellam. I'm not going to bull-shit you."

After a pause, Pellam asked, "Tony, tell me, does a Texas Ranger track them down in the end and machine-gun them to death?"

"It is a goddamn different movie, Pellam."

"Deal. Express Mail the script to me care of Kansas City GPO."

Four days later, Pellam drove over the city limits into Maddox, Missouri, braked the Winnebago to a stop, and knew he'd just earned himself some big money.

> *MISSOURI RIVER BLUES*
> *SCENE 34 – EXTERIOR EVENING, STREET IN FRONT*
> *OF BANK*
> *MEDIUM ANGLE ON Ross and Dehlia, dressed up*
> *as if they were "out for an innocent stroll." They are*
> *supposed to be casing the job, but Ross is introspective.*
> *He stops.*
> *ANGLE ON REAL ESTATE OFFICE, ROSS'S POV*
> *CU OF LISTING SHEETS OF ONE-FAMILY HOUSES*
> *ANGLE ON Ross's face*
> *ANGLE on Dehlia's face, looking at him:*
> *TWO SHOT OF both of them.*
> ROSS
> *There was a time when I needed to be an outlaw. But*
> *it's different now. (CLOSE ON his face.) Since you and*
> *me've been on the road together, lover, it's all different.*
> *Now I've got you and I want to be part of the world we've*
> *been looking in on. Looking in on from the outside for a*
> *long, long time.*

The bank-robbing lovers in the film come upon a small midwestern river town filled with abandoned factories and characters whose lives have been ruined by rampant capitalism. They decide to make one last heist then follow the lead of all the returning World War II veterans: buy a house in the 'burbs and raise babies.

More than even minimal or essential movies, Pellam loved good movies. He was not convinced that *Missouri River Blues* was a good movie. The script contained a number of time bombs – long speeches, shoot-outs, car chases and stylish camera directions. But a script is merely a promise. What Sloan would make of it, nobody, perhaps not even Sloan himself, could know at this point.

It was not Pellam's job, in any case, to career-counsel visionaries. He did what he'd been hired to do. He read the script ten times got a sense of what it was about, did his outline of the scenes, blocked them out, consolidating similar ones to minimize travel between locations. Then he clocked seven hundred miles on the Winnebago as he threaded through Maddox and environs, shot sixty packs of Polaroids, met with the mayor and the city's insurance company then wrote up his report and shipped it off.

Within a day Sloan and the director of photography flew to St Louis and drove north, where Sloan approved most of the locations. They jetted back that night to finish casting.

For the next week Pellam helped the key grip with site preparation and deciding what cranes and other equipment would be needed for the shooting. Sloan and the cast and crew had arrived in a swirl of frenzied excitement. Grip trucks, camera cranes, Winnebagos, location vans. This movie was bigger news in Maddox than FDR and William Jennings Bryan combined.

As on most sets, the atmosphere was boisterous in the first few days of shooting. Pellam had had some fun. Because scouts are often first on the scene, newly arrived personnel ask them for tips on places to eat and things to see. A young hotshot actor, playing one of Ross's gangsters, asked Pellam bluntly where he could get laid and how much would it cost.

Pellam thought for a bit, then remembered an ad he had seen not long after he arrived in Maddox. "It'll be cheap but you've got to drive a ways." He gave the actor elaborate directions that sent him ten miles into the boonies. He returned an hour later, fuming, and stormed onto the set, where Pellam and the crew greeted him with high-pitched squeals and calls of *soo-eee!*

Pellam had sent him to the St Charles County Hog and Ham Museum.

But that had been a month ago, and now the time for jokes was over. *Missouri River Blues* was badly overschedule and vastly overbudget. The producer from the studio financing the film had sent a representative – Sloan referred to him, openly, as "the stoolie" – to goose things along. The problem, in Pellam's view, was that while Sloan could entice performances from characters fighting to the death with lasers or changing themselves into charges of electricity he did not know what he wanted in less apocalyptic scenes: love, betrayal, friendship, longing . . . So the introspective scenes were gradually replaced by more shoot-outs and chases and extreme close-ups of guns being loaded and dynamite bombs being assembled and armored truck locks being picked or blown apart.

And all the while Sloan shot more and more film. He averaged ten thousand feet a day – almost two hours worth of film from which to distill out about two minutes of real screen time.

"It's an asshole picture," the lean, balding key grip complained to Pellam. Meaning the movie was not being made here, as it was filmed, but would be cut and pasted together at the back end of the whole process – in the editing room. Desperate Tony was shooting as much footage as he possibly could, out of which he would hammer together his movie. ("Hitchcock didn't work that way," the grip whispered.)

After principal photography started Pellam thought that he would have plenty of time on his own. The bulk of a location manager's work would normally be finished at this stage. He had merely to oversee paying site rentals on schedule and keep track of permits and insurance binders. But more and more frequently he found himself waiting for calls from an increasingly anxious Sloan – such as this morning, which summons now had him racing at seventy miles an hour through the bleak and abandoned streets of Maddox, Missouri, which might have been a businessman's nightmare but was at least a motorcyclist's dream.

———◆———

4

P ellam put a twelve-foot skid mark from the curb to the catering table on the set of *Missouri River Blues* and hopped off the Yamaha only to find the dusty Ford Taurus braking to a stop six inches from his thigh.

Pellam shrugged and Stile emerged from the Ford out of sorts. He had lost the race because he had stopped for a red light that Pellam had ignored.

"Didn't know we weren't playing by the rules," Stile grumbled, wandering off toward wardrobe. "I'll gitcha next time."

Pellam walked to the scaffolding that rose above that morning's setup.

Tony Sloan was a hawkish man, muscular, very lean in the face, which was why he sported a black beard. He was wearing blue jeans and a faded green T-shirt. His black hair, dusted with gray, was pulled back in a short ponytail. Occasionally he talked frantically. Other times, not at all. His eyes, perhaps reflecting his thoughts, would either dart about or lift slowly and hover before descending momentarily onto the face of the person he was speaking with.

These eyes now landed hungrily on Pellam.

"John, gotta get that phone fixed. Listen, I've been rethinking the ending. I want them to get that house, you know." He fidgeted with his beeper.

"Ross and Dehlia?"

"I've got an image of what they should have. I can see it. You find me one? A fifties sort of house. You know, a bungalow maybe." Sloan's gaze rose, did a few slow circles, and returned to Pellam, who was trying to recall the most recent ending for the film.

"That's instead of what?"

"The bus depot," Sloan answered. "We don't need the bus depot anymore."

"Okay. That's easy. You want a house. You want to do interiors there?"

"I don't *want* to, no." Sloan's voice was exasperated. "Why would I want to?"

"I didn't mean *want to*, Tony. I meant are you going to?"

The eyes rose. "I *want* to build a set. On a sound-stage. I don't want to have to cram all the damn equipment into a twelve-by-fourteen-foot living room. But I don't have any choice."

"You want a bungalow with a twelve-by-fourteen living room."

"Well, I *want* bigger. If you can get me bigger."

"I'll—"

The voice was very close to Pellam's ear. "Excuse me." He started in surprise.

They turned.

"One of you John Pellam?"

Pellam smiled a greeting.

"I'm Detective Gianno, this's Detective Hagedorn. With the Maddox Police Department."

Pellam saw ID cards and gold badges and immediately forgot their names. An Italian detective, dark-complected and short. And a WASP detective, blond, athletic, tall. He had a very square jaw. Pellam smelled after-shave. Something dry. He had been close to cops a few times in his life and could not recall smelling after-shave on a law enforcer.

Sloan said, "What's this all about?" His eyes now alighted on the Italian detective's and remained fixed.

The cop asked in response, "Who're you?"

"Tony Sloan." When they registered no response the detective added, "I'm the director."

The WASP turned away from him. "If you'll excuse us we'd like to talk to Mr Pellam here."

"If there's some problem, I'm in charge of—"

"There won't be a problem, sir –" he glanced at Sloan as if he were a nagging panhandler "– if you'd just give us a few minutes alone with Mr Pellam here."

Sloan gave him an astonished glance then turned to Pellam, who shrugged. "I'll get you that house, Tony."

The director wandered off to a motorized camera crane, a Chapman Apollo, the boom extended and the camera platform nearly ten feet above the ground. Sloan paused in the shadow of the boom and glanced back at the two men now standing on either side of Pellam. Several grips and gaffers noticed Sloan's frown and stopped what they were doing to watch the three men.

The WASP stepped closer. The scent of lime was very strong. "The *Post-Dispatch* did a story about this film." He spoke with the same stilted formality that marks conversations between cops and civilians all around the world.

"It's a crime movie? About bank robbers?" The Italian detective said this as if people would not think of breaking the law if movies didn't put the idea into their heads.

"Armored car robbers," Pellam corrected.

"We've never had a movie made in Maddox," the detective added solemnly. "I hope you portray the town in a good light. We've had our share of trouble but that's not our fault."

"No, it isn't," said the WASP.

"What exactly," Pellam asked, "do you want?"

"Last night there was a shooting. We're wondering if you could give us some information about it."

"Around here?"

"It happened on Third, near the river."

He tried to remember if he had heard anything. He couldn't recall but with the tape deck playing and the Cardinals on TV and the noise of five men playing poker, a lot of sound outside would get missed. Pellam shook his head. "I'm sorry. I don't think I can help you." He started to walk away.

The WASP detective put a firm grip on Pellam's shoulder and laughed in surprise, like a schoolteacher insulted by a student. "Hey, hey, hold up there a minute. We're not through yet."

Pellam shrugged the hand off and turned around. "I can't help you."

"Well, we think you can, sir. A policeman was shot and critically injured and two people were killed. Vincent Gaudia and a Miss Sally Ann Moore."

"I'm sorry. That doesn't mean anything to me."

"People are killed and you don't care?" the WASP asked. His hands, palms up, rose at his sides.

"I don't mean that. I just mean I don't know who they are."

The Italian was saying, "The car? The Lincoln? Does that ring a bell?"

"No. I . . . Oh, wait. There *was* this guy got out of a big car, maybe it was a Lincoln. I didn't really notice. I'd bought some beer. He bumped into me."

"Could you describe him?"

"Was he the guy who was killed?"

"Description?"

"Not too tall, stocky, balding, a beard or mustache, I think. Mid or late thirties."

"Race?"

"White."

"Any scars or markings?"

"I don't remember any."

"What was he wearing?"

"A jacket, I think. Jeans. Dark mostly."

"He was alone in the Lincoln?"

"No. There was somebody else. They drove off after a while."

"They?"

"Well, *he*."

"Could you describe him?"

"I didn't see him."

The detectives didn't exactly exchange glances but their eyes swung like slow pendulums toward each other.

Sloan called, "Pellam, you gonna get me that house, or what?"

The Italian detective called back, "This is official police business, mister."

Oh, brother. Pellam cocked his head helplessly at Sloan and said, "They're just asking me a few questions."

Sloan continued to stare for a moment, eyes no longer flitting with artistic distraction but now boring angrily into the cluster of men from the shadow of the crane.

"The thing is, Mr Pellam," the Italian cop continued, "the officer who was shot . . ."

"He was shot a number of times in the back," his partner said.

"God, that's awful."

". . . said he saw you talking to someone in the car. He—"

"*He* was the one got shot? That policeman? Danny? What was the name?"

"Donnie Buffett."

"That's terrible. Yeah, I was talking to him. Is he going to be okay?"

"They don't know," the Italian cop said.

In the thick silence that followed they stared at him. Pellam felt guilty under these gazes. "I didn't see him. The driver, I mean. I looked. I looked into the car but I wasn't really talking *to* him. I was just saying things. It wasn't like a conversation."

"How did you know it was a man?"

Pellam didn't speak for a moment. "That's a good question. I don't really. I just assumed it was."

"You seem pretty sure it was a man," the WASP said. "You said *him*."

"I was assuming it was a man."

The Italian cop said, "It'd just be kind of strange, wouldn't it, you're standing a few feet from someone, not to at least see what they were wearing? What their sex was? Whether they were black or white?"

"I don't know what's strange or not, but that's what happened. It was night—"

"Adams is lit up like Gateway Park," the Italian cop said.

The WASP detective looked at his partner. "All those car accidents. That's why they put in sodium vapors."

"There was glare," Pellam said. "That was one of the problems. On the windows. I was blinded."

"So the fact it was *night* wasn't the problem," said the WASP. "I mean, you said it was night as if you meant it was too dark to see anything. But now what you're saying is it wasn't dark at all. It was too *bright*."

"I guess," Pellam said.

"What kind of Lincoln was it?"

"Black."

"What *kind?*"

"How do you mean?"

"Town Car? Continental?"

"I didn't notice. I wish I had but I only remember it being big and black."

"You're sure it was black?"

"Well, it was dark. Navy blue maybe."

They asked about license plates, dents, scratches, damage, bumper stickers . . .

Pellam couldn't help them.

The cops fell silent.

"Do you think I'm lying?"

"It's just kind of strange is all we're saying."

"What's strange?" Pellam rocked on his boot heels.

"Being so close and all and not seeing anything," the WASP said. "That's strange."

"It was dark." Pellam tried to sound as frustrated as they were.

"And there was a lot of glare," the Italian added. Sarcastic? Pellam couldn't tell.

"Officer Buffett said he saw you talking to whoever was in the car."

"I told you, I wasn't having a conversation with him . . . or her." Pellam saw, in the distance, the curtain in a window of Sloan's van pull aside for a moment. A black gap was visible and in that gap Pellam imagined he could see the two tiny, paranoid eyes of an impatient visionary director. He said to the WASP, who though bigger seemed more reasonable, "Look, I'm very busy just now. This is a bad time for this."

The blond cop just repeated, "Officer Buffett said you were talking to the driver. What are we supposed to think about that?"

Pellam sighed. "I was mad. I was just talking to let off steam. I don't remember what I said. I was muttering."

"Why were you mad?"

"The guy I told you about, the one who got out of the car, bumped into me and I dropped a case of beer."

"Why did he do that?"

"It was an accident. He didn't do it on purpose."

"If it was an accident," the WASP asked slowly, "why were you so mad you were talking to yourself?"

The Italian cop offered, "'Muttering,' you said."

"Okay, that's it. I've got nothing more to say." Pellam started away, tensing his muscles, ready for another vise grip.

Neither cop followed, but the blond said, "There's two dead people and a cop shot in the back."

His partner offered, "People sometimes get scared. They don't want to volunteer, to be witnesses. You don't have to be worried. We can protect you."

"I didn't see anybody get shot. All I saw was some guy who nearly knocked me on my ass."

"We're more concerned with the person in the car. We think he's the one who ordered the hit."

"Sorry. Now, if there's nothing else . . ." Pellam lifted his hands like a TV preacher confronted with more sin than he can absolve.

"Will you at least help us do a sketch of the man you saw?"

"Yes. Sure. But not now."

The WASP cop shifted his weight like an impatient college boy. He was no longer reasonable. "He's not going to cooperate."

"Cooperate?"

The WASP said to his grimacing partner, "Let's go. He's a GFY." The cops put their notebooks away.

"What's a GFY?" Pellam demanded.

"An official term we use about reluctant witnesses."

"I'm not reluctant. I didn't see anything."

When they got to the perimeter of the set, the Italian cop turned suddenly and said, "Look, mister, a lot of local people cooperated with you so you could shoot this damn movie here. They aren't going to be too happy to hear you're not so cooperative in return."

The WASP cop waved his arm. "Aw, he's a GFY. Why bother?" They walked off the set.

In Sloan's trailer, the curtain fell closed.

The indictments against him read:

Counts 1–2: Conspiracy to sell controlled substances.

Counts 3–32: Criminal federal income tax fraud.

Count 33: Conspiracy to interfere with civil rights.

Count 34–35: Perjury.

Count 36: Extortion.

Counts 37–44: Criminal violations of the Racketeering-Influenced Corrupt Organizations Act.

Peter Crimmins did not exactly have the words memorized but this – the paraphrase – he knew, the essence of the government's case against him.

Crimmins (the name was his father's impulsive recasting of Crzniolak) was fifty-four. He had a body like a pear, a face like a potato. His hair was combed forward in bangs, Frank Sinatra style, over his high forehead, on which a single dark mole rested above his left eyebrow like a misplaced third eye. He was presently sitting in his office, which overlooked the parking lot of his trucking company and, through windows in the opposite wall, a large room filled with gray desks, filing cabinets, overhead fluorescent fixtures and a dozen office workers who appeared simultaneously bored and anxious.

Peter Crimmins had a thousand business decisions he should be making but it was the words of the indictment that kept running through his mind.

And they made him furious.

Oh, several counts were nonsense and had been thrown in

by an eager runt of an assistant U.S. Attorney. The civil rights
thing, ridiculous. Conspiracy, ridiculous. The drug counts were
absurd. He had never sold an atom of any controlled substance.
The extortion, well, that was somewhat true but only a little.
But what infuriated him were the counts that were accurate –
the RICO charges.

Peter Crimmins thought of himself as a blue-collar philoso-
pher and had decided that there were simple rules in life
you could figure out without anyone's help. Not the Ten
Commandments, which were a little too simple-minded even
for a good Russian Orthodox like him to buy. But rules like: A
man's dignity should be respected, take care of those who cannot
take care of themselves, do your duty, support your family, don't
hurt anyone innocent . . .

You live your life by those rules and you will do just fine. So
here he was, doing his duty, supporting his family, not hurting
anyone (anybody innocent, at any rate), making a living, going
to church occasionally – and what happens? He runs smack
into another set of rules. And these rules made no sense to
him at all.

They were pure idiocy.

The problem was that they were collected in Title 18 of the
United States Code. And if you happened to break *these* rules,
people would come after you and try to put you in jail.

But what was the most frustrating of all was that he was
wrestling with these forty-four indictments solely because of a
single mistake, which was that he had hired a maniac, Vincent
Gaudia, now deceased, gunned down the day before.

The two men were contrasts. Crimmins had noticed this
immediately, at their first meeting, in a German restaurant

in Webster Groves, Missouri. Crimmins was unflashy. He had years of experience as a labor negotiator before he left the union and opened his own business. He drank vodka in moderation and smoked Camels and wore boxer shorts and white shirts and combed his hair with Vitalis every day and he loved playing pool and boccie with friends he had known for years. He was faithful to his wife of thirty-three years and he served on the planning and zoning commission of his suburban hometown. Crimmins was a controlled man, a disciplined man, a *solid* man.

Gaudia, on the other hand, was a man controlled by his appetites. He wanted women's bodies and wet food and sweet drinks with straws. Gaudia's primary organs were his tongue and his penis.

Still, Crimmins had been in business long enough to know that other people's weaknesses can be your strengths.

He had noted Gaudia's lusts and hired the man immediately because Gaudia was more than a minor hood with a busy tongue. He was one of the best-connected people in eastern Missouri and southern Illinois. Crimmins checked around and got a feel for the labyrinthine network Vince Gaudia was hooked into. It was inspiring. The pipeline did not reach to Washington and, curiously, Gaudia could not fix a parking ticket in St Louis. But hundreds of those in between – court clerks, judges, councilmen, county executives, banking commissioners, administrative agency workers, in St Louis, Jeff City and Springfield – were all snug in his pocket. And his skills went beyond knowing who. They extended to *how*. He had a feel for the ethics: who would take a case of J&B but resent a gift of money, who would take a junket, who a job for their kid, a P&Z decision reversal, a co-op in Vail.

Gaudia was an expert at bartering and the product he dealt in was influence.

Crimmins, who had established the most complicated and high-volume money-laundering operation in the Midwest, decided Vince Gaudia could make a major contribution to his company.

The match looked heaven-sent and although they were temperamental opposites, Gaudia and Crimmins hit it off extremely well. Crimmins's laundering was making bold inroads into Kansas City and he had an eye on Chicago. He pioneered the use of not-for-profit organizations as money-laundering vehicles and was probably the only person in the world, certainly the only Christian, who cleaned money through both an Orthodox synagogue in University City and a Nation of Islam mosque in East St Louis, both unwitting coconspirators. Crimmins's business, with Gaudia as his lieutenant, would have become one of the major profitable enterprises in the metropolitan area if it were not for the coincidental occurrence of two things.

The first was a network TV news exposé – *60 Minutes*, no less – about a problem in the office of the U.S. Attorney for the Eastern District of Missouri. There had been a string of bungled drug cases. Well, putting bad guys away is not easy, and the good guys get cut a lot of slack from judges but these slipups were so egregious – and so lip-smackingly exposed on nationwide TV – that the attorney general himself took action. He called the U.S. Attorney for the Eastern District, Ronald Peterson, and brought him to Washington for a talk about the botched prosecutions. Peterson kept his job by a thread and returned from D.C. with a renewed sense of devotion to put away people like Peter Crimmins.

The second coincidence was that Vince Gaudia slept with the wrong woman.

He would not have described her that way, probably. She was a sullen brunette with long, icy red nails and disks of green eyes. She talked in a little-girl singsong voice that made his mind glaze over instantly but forced his cock to attention just about as fast. They had only one date, during which they became wildly drunk and made love for four hours. She claimed later that he proposed she come live with him in his riverfront co-op. Gaudia did not remember saying that. Nor, when she finally tracked him down after a week of not returning her phone calls, did he remember her name.

She apparently had a much better memory than he did, however, and in a letter to U.S. Attorney Peterson, described almost verbatim many of the secrets a drunken Vince Gaudia had shared with her.

U.S. Attorney Peterson saw a chance to redeem his career and wired an FBI agent, who posed as an administrative hearing judge. He met with Gaudia in a bad Italian restaurant near the Gateway Arch. After a little soft-shoe the agent accepted five thousand dollars in exchange for agreeing to overlook an EPA violation by one of Gaudia's clients. One minute later Gaudia was arrested and about an hour after that a deal was struck: In exchange for a probation plea recommendation Gaudia would hand over Peter Crimmins's balls on a fourteen-karat gold plate.

But now Gaudia was dead as a rock and Peter Crimmins knew that U.S. Attorney Peterson had yet another count he wished to add to those forty-four indictments: Crimmins's murder of a government witness.

Crimmins was lost in thought about this situation when the outer door to his office opened and his lawyer entered. They shook hands and the man sat. The lawyer was beefy, with an automatic pilot of a smile that would kick in at any time for no seeming reason. He played tennis on powerful legs and drove a Porsche. He said things like, "Pete, my man, I'd look at that deal with a proctoscope." And "As your counselor and as your friend I'd advise you . . ."

Crimmins had never told the man he was his friend.

The lawyer now asked bluntly, "Where were you Friday night?"

"What are you asking?"

"I gotta know, Pete. Were you with anybody?"

"You think I *killed* Gaudia?" Crimmins asked.

"I don't ask my clients if they're guilty or not. I want to establish your alibi, not your innocence."

"Well, I'm telling you," Crimmins said. "I didn't kill anybody."

The lawyer tightened the titanium knot of his silk tie. "Did you hint to anybody—?"

Crimmins raised his voice. "I didn't do it."

The lawyer looked sideways and clearly did not believe this denial. "It's not what *I* think. It's what the U.S. Attorney is going to think. And I'll tell you, with Gaudia gone, Peterson's got you by a lot less short hairs than he did two days ago."

Crimmins knew this, of course. "You think the indictment won't stick?"

"Peterson's a whore pup. Your conviction is his ticket to D.C.

He believes in his soul you killed Gaudia and he's going to turn you fucking—"

"I don't like those words you use," Crimmins muttered.

"—inside out. Your case gets thrown out, he's going to lose his media defendant."

"There are plenty of defendants to go around."

The lawyer was losing patience. "But he wants *you*. You're the one he told the world he was going to get. You're the one he had. He'll be a bitch in heat. Mark my words."

"This is selective prosecution." Crimmins believed he knew enough law to be a lawyer himself.

"I've got your closing statement all prepared, Pete. I don't need to hear your version of it."

Why was Crimmins putting his life – well, his liberty and pursuit of happiness, at least – into the hands of this slick man with a resonant belly and a vicious backhand?

"*If* – for the sake of argument – you had to have an alibi—"

"I—"

"Humor me, Pete. If, if, *if* you had to have an alibi for the time that Gaudia was shot, would you have one?"

Crimmins did not answer.

The lawyer sighed. "All right. What I'm going to do is ask around some. See who knows what. See what Peterson's going to do about this. I've got some friends're cops. They owe me. Supposedly there's a witness nobody's found yet."

"A witness?"

"It's just a rumor. Some guy who saw the shooter."

The lawyer stood up. "Another thing: They think the getaway car was a Lincoln."

Crimmins was silent for a moment. He said softly, "I drive a Lincoln."

"A dark-colored Lincoln is what they said."

Peter Crimmins had selected Midnight Blue. He found it a comforting color.

The lawyer walked to the door, pulling his short-brimmed hat on his bullet-shaped head.

"Wait," Peter Crimmins said.

The lawyer stopped and turned.

"This witness. I don't care what you have to do. What it costs . . ."

The lawyer was suddenly very uncomfortable. His hand went to his belly and he rubbed the spot where presumably his sumptuous breakfast was being digested. "You want me to—"

"Find out who he is."

"And?"

"Just find out," Peter Crimmins whispered very softly as if every lampshade and picture frame in the room contained a microphone.

5

"**H**e's lying," Donnie Buffett said into the telephone.
Detective Bob Gianno said, "No doubt about it."

"What he did," Buffett continued, "he bent down and looked into the car from just three feet away . . . No, not even. One foot away. If he says he didn't see anything he's lying."

Gianno said, "All he's gotta do is talk and the case's a grounder. Nothing to it. A hose job."

Buffet said, "You'll keep on him?"

"Oh, you bet, Donnie boy. You bet."

They hung up. Buffett's stomach was growling regularly but he didn't feel hungry. They were giving him something from a thick plastic bag, a clear liquid that dripped into his arm. Maybe glucose. He wondered if that was a good idea, because glucose was sugar and before the shooting he had been meaning to lose a few pounds.

He thought about the doughnut and coffee Pellam had brought him. Was it just last night? Two nights ago? It could have been a week. Why was Pellam lying about seeing the killer's partner? Afraid probably.

The door pushed wider open and a doctor came into the room. He was a compact man, about forty, with thick black hair. Trim, with muscular forearms, which made Buffett think that he was an orthopedics man. Buffett loved sports, all kinds of sports, every sport and he knew jock docs; they were always in good shape. He pulled a chair close to the bed, sat down and introduced himself. His name was Gould. He had a low, pleasing voice.

"I guess I met you before," Buffett said. "You operated on me?"

"I was one of the neurosurgeons, yes."

Gould lifted the chart from the rack and flipped it open. He skimmed it, set it down. He leaned forward and, with a penlight, looked into Buffett's eyes. He asked the policeman to watch the doctor's finger as it did figure eights then to extend his arms and touch his nose.

Donnie Buffett did as he was told.

The doctor said, "Good." Which did not mean good or anything else, then he asked, "How you feeling, Officer?"

"Okay, I guess. My shoulder stings."

"Ah." He examined Buffett's chart again and he examined it for a very long moment, it seemed to Buffett.

"Doctor . . . ?" Buffett's voice faded.

The doctor did not encourage him to continue. He closed the metal cover of the chart and said, "Officer, I'd like to talk to you about your injury, tell you exactly what happened, what we did. What we're going to do."

"Sure."

"You were shot in the back. Several slugs hit your bullet-proof vest. They were small – .22-caliber – and shattered right away. A third bullet hit the top side of the vest. It was deflected but it grazed your scapula, your shoulder blade. That's the pain you feel there. It's a minor wound. We removed the bullet easily. There's some risk of sepsis – that's infection – but the odds are that won't happen."

Gould was taking out a pen, a fancy gold and lacquer pen, and was drawing what looked like the lower half of a skeleton on the back of a receipt.

"Donnie, three of the bullets hit you below the vest. They entered here, that's where the lumbar region of the spinal cord joins the sacral region. One shattered and stopped here." The pen, top replaced, was now a pointer. "The other two lodged in your intestine but missed the kidneys and bladder. We removed all the pieces of lead. We've repaired the damage with sutures that will absorb into the tissue. You won't need any further surgery, unless we have a sepsis situation."

"Okay," Buffett said agreeably. He squinted and studied the diagram as if he'd be tested on it later.

"Donnie, the bullet that shattered – it entered your spinal cord here."

Buffett was nodding. He was a cop. He had seen death. He had seen pain. He had *felt* pain. He was totally calm. His injury couldn't be serious. If it were he'd be hooked up to huge machines. Respirators and jet cockpit controls. All he had was a tube in his dick and an IV that was feeding him fattening sugar. That was nothing. No problem. He felt pain now, a wonderful pain that ran through his legs, playing hide-and-seek. If he were paralyzed he wouldn't be feeling pain.

"Donnie, we're going to refer you to a Dr Weiser, one of St Louis's top SCI neurologists and therapists. SCI, that's spinal cord injury."

"But I'm okay, aren't I?"

"You're not in a life-threatening condition. With upper SCIs, there's a risk of respiratory or cardiac failure . . . Those can be very troublesome."

Troublesome.

"But your accident was lower SCI. That was fortunate in terms of your survival."

"Doctor, I'll be able to walk, won't I? The thing is, my job, I'm a *cop*. I have to walk." He lifted his palms as if he were embarrassed to be explaining something so simple.

"Uhn, Donnie," the doctor said slowly, "your prognosis is essentially nonambulatory."

Nonambulatory.

"What does? . . ." Buffett's throat closed down and he was unable to complete his question. Because he *knew* exactly what it meant.

"Your spinal cord was almost completely severed," Gould said. Buffett was looking directly into his eyes but did not see any of the intense sympathy that was pouring from them. "With the state of the art at the present time I'm afraid there's nothing we can do about it. You won't walk, no."

"Oh. Well. I see."

"Officer, you're very lucky. You could easily have been killed. Or it might have been a quadriplegic situation."

Sure, that's true.

Gould stood up. The chart got replaced on the bed, the doctor's nifty pen went back into his shirt. "Dr Weiser is much more competent to talk about your injury than I am. You couldn't ask for a better expert. A nurse will be coming by to schedule an appointment later." He smiled, shook Buffett's hand. "We'll do everything we can for you, Officer. Don't worry about a thing."

It was several minutes later that Donnie Buffett said, "No. I won't," and only then realized that the doctor was no longer in the room.

Philip Lombro had this habit. He would polish his shoes at least twice a day. He kept a big horsehair brush in his desk at work and a smaller pig-bristle brush in his attaché case, along with chamois squares. Sometimes he would polish the shoes three, four, five times in a single day. He used Kiwi a lot. His favorite, though, was Meltonian. *Crème à chaussures*.

He had no obsession over the shoes themselves – he owned only seven pairs – and he did not have a foot fetish. (He was not even sure what a foot fetish was or what somebody with a foot fetish did.) What he liked was shiny shoes and the process of getting them that way. Putting your feet into newly polished shoes was a regal feeling.

This morning he sat in the office of Lombro & Associates in downtown Maddox and absently ran the brush over his oxblood wing tips.

The office was in the shadow of a huge redbrick building that had started life as Maddox Omnibus and Carriage Company and had become, through the generations, Maddox Electric Automobile Company, then the Maddox Clutch Company, and recently the Maddox Machinery Division of Fujitomo Limited.

Several stiff brush bristles became dislodged from the brush and fell to the floor. Lombro bent down and picked them up, then flicked them into the waste-basket. He wiped his fingers with a spit-moistened Kleenex. Outside the window, a piece of newspaper floated past and vanished. Lombro stared at the sides of the Maddox Omnibus Building. Lombro remembered, from ten years ago, the *Reporter* photo of a young man who killed himself by jumping off one of the factory's huge smokestacks. Wearing a suit, he had died crumpled in the roof of a delivery truck. It enfolded him like a blanket.

This was what the Maddox Omnibus and Carriage Company Building signified for him: death. And this thought, in turn, led to Ralph Bales.

Lombro had met Ralph Bales at the wedding of his sister's daughter. Lombro, never married, regretted that he'd never been a father; nieces and nephews in St Louis area became surrogate children. He doted, he spoiled them, he took them on outings. He was more astonished than their parents to see them become adults. When his brother-in-law could not pick up the tab for the girl's wedding Lombro himself paid for the function.

One of the guests had been Ralph Bales and what caught Lombro's attention was that Ralph Bales had brought a gun to the wedding.

Late in the evening, Lombro, standing at the urinal in the men's john of Orsini's restaurant, was aware of someone entering behind him and going into a stall. He then heard a clunk of something falling and glanced under the door. A hand was quickly retrieving a pistol. Lombro washed his hands quickly and left the men's room. He waited outside, hiding behind a plant, to catch a look at the intruder. A few minutes later Ralph Bales emerged, slicking back his thinning hair with damp hands. Lombro didn't know what to do. A friend of a friend on the groom's side, Ralph Bales had been invited, true, so he probably was not a robber. On the other hand, Lombro felt responsible for the safety of his four hundred guests.

Finally, after an agonizing half hour of indecision, Lombro had walked up to Ralph Bales and, as the children were cutting the cake, struck up a conversation. He learned that Ralph Bales had grown up in St Louis. He was orphaned young – as Lombro had been – and had made a career of various riverfront jobs. They talked careers, real estate, making money, losing money. Ralph Bales mentioned, vaguely, unions and shipping companies and waterfront services and Teamsters. He lived in a house not far from Lambert Field. He enjoyed working in his garden. Lombro did, too, he said, though he hated the sun.

Ralph Bales said he loved the sun.

Lombro was satisfied that the man represented no danger and said good-bye. Ralph Bales touched him on the arm in a special way and offered his card. "You say you're in real estate," he said with ambiguous significance. "If you ever need any security consulting, let me know."

So the card, *Ralph Bales, Consultant*, was filed away in Lombro's Rolodex. He thought he might have a need for a consultant at some point.

A month ago, he had.

And now, as he put the shoe brush away in his bottom drawer and vacantly watched the papers blowing outside the windows of his office, he foresaw that the transaction that arose out of that wedding might have been the only serious mistake he had ever made in his life.

"Okay, kind of a problem," Ralph Bales now said.

Philip Lombro listened, his head immobile, eyes moving slowly around the face of his visitor.

"He snuck up on us, the cop."

Lombro said, "There was nothing you could've done?"

Ralph Bales was deferential to clients. He didn't roll his eyes or sigh. He said, "No, he came up out of the blue."

Lombro opened his desk. He pulled out a thin envelope containing $25,000. He handed it to Ralph Bales.

Ralph Bales said, "Thank you."

Lombro nodded.

Neither man seemed grateful, or pleased, by the exchange.

"How much of a problem is it?" Lombro sounded reasonable. Men like him tend to stay calm when they have problems.

Ralph Bales chewed on the thin lip that was cut into his round, padded face. "Well, you don't want to shoot a cop. Whatever happens, you don't want to do that."

Lombro's eyes settled on Ralph Bales's naked upper lip. He realized the moustache was gone.

"I'm not being, you know, cute," Ralph Bales continued. "The cops don't get mad when you kill a DA witness because witnesses are scum. When the cops get mad is when you shoot a cop."

"And?"

"And there's some things we have to do."

"Such as?"

"Okay, we've got to find the guy that saw us."

"Who?"

"The guy walked into me when I got out of the car. The one with the beer."

Lombro lifted one ankle to his other knee and touched his heel absently then rubbed it.

"He saw me," Ralph Bales said. "And he saw you."

"They might not find him, the police."

"No, that's—"

Lombro continued an argument that seemed to reassure him. "Why would he volunteer? Why would anyone do that?"

"He might not," Ralph Bales agreed. "But some people are funny. They do weird things."

Lombro said, "The way you're talking, it sounds like you've decided something."

"Excuse me, it isn't really a decision. I mean, we don't have a choice, okay?"

Hit Man Shoots Cop in Back. The newspaper sat prominently on Lombro's desk. Ralph Bales had been wrong. There was no photo of Vince Gaudia's body. Just the shot policeman's wedding picture.

"I don't like this at all."

"With all respect, Mr Lombro, when you –" he looked for words that weren't too incriminating "– take on a project like this there are potential downsides. Okay? Like you buy a building and find out it's got termites or something. It just happens. You can't run away from it."

"The woman, too. You killed the woman."

"Stevie tells me that was an accident. Gaudia pushed her in front of him."

Lombro was nodding. "I don't care much about her. She knew the kind of bastard she was getting involved with."

Outside the window a blackbird settled on the top of a brick facade. The bird's nervous, glossy head flicked about. It shot into the sky in a gray streak.

Ralph Bales said, "We did the job for you and there was a glitch. But the fact of the matter is, I don't live here and Stevie Flom don't live here but you do. And so this glitch, it's sort of your problem."

Lombro considered this speech unemotionally. "What are you proposing?"

"I can drive out of here now and you can take your chances. Or you can pay me to take care of this guy, too."

"No, absolutely not."

"Then . . ." Ralph Bales let the word float through the room like a puff of cigarette smoke. "There's another option."

"What? Go on."

"Maybe I could find him. Threaten him. Scare him a little."

"Would that work?"

"It usually does. But I don't want to do it. It's a lot riskier than just, you know, taking care of him."

"You want more money. Is that what you're saying?"

"Yeah, that's what I'm saying. It's just a question of risk. Ten thousand and he's gone. Twenty thousand and I find him, put pressure on him."

"Twenty?"

"What do you want me to say? Nineteen ninety-five?"

Lombro did not speak for a moment. He gazed at the newspaper, then closed his eyes and flipped his hand forward in a gesture of frustration. "All right." He looked at Ralph Bales. "But I want your word that you won't hurt him."

Ralph Bales frowned. "You didn't say you didn't want him hurt."

"I mean," Lombro said, "you won't *kill* him, will you?"

Ralph Bales nodded and, looking straight at Lombro, said, "Of course not. I told you I wouldn't." He had found that when you look somebody in the eye, they will believe anything you tell them.

The car cruised past the camper slowly. By the time Pellam was out of the kitchenette and at the window it had turned off of River Road and was gone. He remained at the window, looking out through the blinds, which he now noticed could use a good cleaning.

Maddox offered no night parking and Pellam was forced to keep the camper in this pathetic trailer park. The owners, Annie and Fred Bell, advertised fifty hookups and during some prior vacation seasons they might all have been used. But that would have been before the cement plant went in next door and gouged out five hundred yards of idyllic riverfront grassland, replacing it with bunkers and steel docks. The Bide-A-Wee trailer park was currently occupied by John Pellam's Winnebago and two clusters of tenters who were obviously – and understandably – tired of the picturesque view of Ochner Cement & Stone and were packing to leave.

At first Pellam had not much cared about the emptiness. But that was before he was a witness in a murder case. Well, a sort-of witness. Now he wished for a little more anonymity. He looked at his watch. It was only 11:00 A.M. but he had already seen or heard four – no, make that five – cars slow as they cruised past the trailer court. He suspected the occupants were not checking out the Bide-A-Wee for upcoming vacation sojourns in Maddox but were more interested in him.

Another car now stopped directly in front of the trailer. It was a beat-up old sedan, its fenders attached with gaffer tape. The driver was a shadowy form behind a grease-stained window. The condition of the car told him that this was not the cops come a-calling again.

Pellam, who had been hacking away at the impossible crust of burnt chili, dried his hands and walked to the front of the Winnebago. He opened a map compartment beside the front door. This tiny space *did* contain maps, probably thirty of them, all limp and seam-torn. It also contained a Colt Peacemaker .45-caliber pistol. It had a steel barrel and rosewood grips. He lifted the gun out and thumbed open the cylinder cover.

Pellam put the pistol on half-cock, loaded five of the six chambers, then eased the hammer down on the empty slot. He slipped the gun into his waistband, pulled on his bomber jacket and left the camper, striding toward the car.

Why did everybody in Maddox have somber cars?

The driver – Pellam did not recognize him – was a man of about forty with a square face, eyes staring evenly at him. Pellam had hoped that he would see Pellam coming to confront him and burn rubber to escape.

The man shut off the engine and got out.

Pellam's hand casually went to the zipper of his jacket.

The intruder was huge. He slammed the door with a loud bang. He kept staring at Pellam. Then he started across the street. He had a crew cut and folds of skin hung over his eyes.

Pellam unzipped his jacket and stood by the roadside. His

hand rested on his belt and he rubbed the buckle. With an index finger he touched the wood grip of the gun.

When the man reached the shoulder of the road, twenty feet away, he stopped. Looking straight into Pellam's eyes, he said, "You need any young men?"

Pellam squinted and cocked his head.

The man repeated, "Young men?"

"I'm sorry?"

"Look," the man said stiffly, "I know you hear that a lot of folk aren't happy to have you all in town because you're saying things about Maddox in your movie that aren't so nice. Well, you won't hear that from me. I don't feel that way at all."

"Uh-huh, good."

"Now," the man continued his recitation, "my boy Larry's seventeen and was most recent in a play. I mean a serious play without music. *I Remember Mama*. He was good – I'd say that even he wasn't my son – but he'd be top-notch in a movie where you get to say your lines over and over again and they take the best one. I mean top-notch."

"Well, sir, I don't do any casting."

"He'll do it real reasonable. You know, just to get his foot in the door, so to speak. Could do manual labor, too, till an acting part comes 'round. He's strapping."

Pellam shook his head.

"He's taking classes."

"Sorry." Pellam zipped up his jacket. "I wish I could help out but I can't."

The man stood, shoulders drooping and face bright red. Behind him was a decrepit house that at one time was a marvel of Victorian excess. It had been abandoned halfway through a futile make-over. He said in a stiff voice, "I've been out of work three years now. Was a deckhand for a inland tow company. I'm about at the end of my rope."

"I'm sorry."

"I don't want sympathy. I'd work if there was any work but there ain't. Larry's 'bout the only chance we've got for some income."

Pellam shook his head. "Wish it were different."

"Sure." The man stood for a moment longer. "Thanks for your time." He turned silently and walked back to his car. He looked at the camper, then started the engine. Pellam watched the car roll away, followed by the bubbling sound of a rust-shot muffler.

He trudged back to the camper, disarmed himself and hung up his jacket. He returned to the kitchenette.

A half hour later he was sitting at the tiny table, flipping through his Maddox location file, which was filled with Polaroid snapshots. As Tony Sloan had requested he'd taken a number of shots of empty houses – nearly every other house in certain parts of town – and he had narrowed the bungalow search down to four: two of them cute and two run-down. He was checking the addresses against a tattered map of Maddox.

That was when he heard the hesitant footsteps on the gravel walk. Pellam's hands froze on the report.

Had Larry's dad returned for another audition?

Pellam stood and walked to the rear of the camper, peering out. No, it was a different car. A dark red sedan.

The sort the Italian and the WASP detectives would drive.

It turned out not to be the two cops, however. Without knocking, a dark-complected man in his mid-thirties stepped inside and looked around, orienting himself. He wore a trim, double-breasted charcoal gray suit and reflective blue sunglasses.

He said, "I know what you're hoping for but give it up. You're not getting out of here." The door swung shut and he slowly pulled his sunglasses off and slipped them into his breast pocket.

———◆◆◆———

6

P ellam pursed his lips together. He shook his head.

"What?" the intruder asked.

"It's 'I know what you're thinking. But it's too *late*. You're not getting out of here.'"

"No." The man frowned. "I'm sure." He propped a briefcase on the driver's seat and opened it.

"Anyway, I've decided to cut the dialogue. Do it in visuals. Want coffee? It's instant."

A script appeared from the briefcase and the man began thumbing through it. "Aw, no. Pellam. Don't cut it. It's a great line. 'But give it up.' It's very – what's the word? – anachronistic. Oh, you're right." He read the script carefully. "The line's gone."

"Take a pew," Pellam said and put the kettle on the flame.

Marty Weller easily settled his lanky frame into the dining banquette. A yoga practitioner, he possessed the sort of physique that could comfortably handle a camper environment. He had an airbrushed tan and muscles in places where only a Nautilus machine could put them. Where his trimmed eyebrows ended above his nose there appeared California creases – two short, vertical furrows, the result of a lifetime of squinting. "Tea. Herbal." He tapped the script. "I must have been thinking of the first draft. Or the second. Or one of them. You rewrite a hell of a lot, John."

"Lipton?"

Weller looked about, as if he might spot a box of Celestial Seasonings chamomile hidden nearby. "Okay," he said with reservation. Then: "Honey?"

"Domino."

"Well, this *is* middle America." Weller smiled slyly and asked, "So?"

"Yes?"

"You know what I'm asking. What's the scoop? On *Sloan*."

Independent producer Marty Weller was as much a gossip sponge as anyone in Hollywood – though he was not sufficiently powerful to use much of the gossip he absorbed. He had done a string of offbeat films that were lukewarm hits. This opened doors for him but did not automatically get his pictures made. Still, gossip about Tony Sloan, while not particularly useful to Weller, was platinum gossip. One wanted it the same way one wanted Taittinger or beluga.

Yet Weller's presence here in small-town Missouri now reminded Pellam of L.A. protocol and, cognizant of his obscenely large fee, he recalled the rule: Assume anything you say, even in strictest confidence, will immediately be transmitted to the *Hollywood Reporter* and attributed to you. Pellam gave Weller a diluted version of the film's production woes.

"Word is he's cindering in the upper atmosphere," Weller said with a frown that did nothing to mask his delight.

Pellam shrugged. "Okay, Marty, don't keep me in suspense. Go or no go?"

Weller picked up the battered black-covered script he had just misquoted. The title was *Central Standard Time*. "We're close, John. Damn close. I've got maybe eighty percent of the financing in place." He fell silent for a minute and riffled the pages. In his former life – which in Hollywood meant only a few years ago – Pellam had both written and directed independent films. *Central Standard Time* had been the film he'd been working on when his career had been derailed in a big way.

No one had been interested in the property until immaculately tanned Marty Weller had appeared on Pellam's doorstep and told him, with as much sincerity as a Hollywood producer could muster, that he was going to get Pellam's "vision" turned into a dark arthouse classic.

Finally, he said delicately, "There were some questions about what happened before." He looked up uncomfortably. "You were actually in production?"

"We were two weeks into principal photography."

Weller did not look up but intently read what happened to be the blank back cover of the script. "When he got sick, you mean."

Got sick. Pellam said, "That's right."

Tommy Bernstein – the leading man in *Central Standard* and Pellam's best friend – had not "gotten sick" at all but had died of a cocaine-induced heart attack during principal photography, which had brought the production to a halt and Pellam's life as he'd lived it to a shattering conclusion.

Weller was flipping through the script and sending a stale breeze up into the air. "Somebody . . . I'm just explaining why it's taking so long. This is bullshit, I know. But somebody talked about a jinx."

Pellam laughed. "Like the *Exorcist* stories, that old crap?"

"People are more superstitious about money than about their lives. More producers *fly* on Friday the thirteenth than write checks, you better believe it."

"Well, nothing I can do about that."

"And you directing, that's still carved in stone?"

Pellam noted that the cautious tone in the man's voice was not going away. He said firmly, "Yep."

"The thing is, John . . . Well, you've been out of the loop for a long time."

"I direct or they don't get property. It's a deal-breaker."

"And they're saying if they don't get to pick the director, leads, and DP, we don't get the money. They'll—"

"Mexican standoff."

"They'll let you coproduce. I think they'll even go gross points since you wrote it."

"Producing means nothing to me—"

"It means a shitload of money is what it means. Look, John, the budget is seven million." He tapped the script. "It's got 'film noir cult classic' written all over it. We're going to shoot in black and white, for God's sake. This is going to make money. It cannot *not* make money—"

"Marty," Pellam said patiently.

Weller's momentarily wide eyes shrank to a more sober size.

"Forgive me, I know not who I bullshit. Okay, think about this alternative: Can you get up two hundred, two twenty?"

"What if I can?"

"We cut back to four million, finance it ourselves, shoot with unknowns, and pucker up at the sight of every distributor's backside. You can direct."

Pellam realized the teakettle was filling the small kitchen with steam. He made himself coffee and Weller a cup of tea, while he was mentally adding a second mortgage on his house, selling his old Porsche and adding in the fee for *Missouri River Blues*.

"One twenty, one fifty, maybe I can do."

Weller performed his own calculations. "I'd have to make some phone calls but I think if you come in with that, we can get it done. For that, you can direct but you don't get points. You'd work for scale and maybe have to kick some back."

"I want this film made. I've never wanted to get rich."

"You always were a crazy sonofabitch, Pellam." Weller sipped the hot tea, holding it inches above the table and lowering his mouth to the rim. "I should tell you one thing, though. Never rains but it pours. Paramount's interested in a property I optioned last year. Terrorist hijacking thing. Cliché, cliché, cliché, I know. Mea culpa. Budgeted at forty-five. It's not going to happen but I've still got to go to London to meet with some people about it."

"What if it *does* happen?"

"I want to do *your* film, John." For a moment the passion beneath the silken tan seemed real. In his obscure way Weller was explaining that he would rather be a producer who was a cult artist and rich than one who was commercial and excessively rich.

Hollywood, Pellam knew, is a crucible of trade-offs.

"Next step?" he asked. He took a sip of coffee then poured it out. His gut was wound up. Not often is one offered the opportunity to direct his own picture and to go hopelessly into debt at the same time.

"I leave tomorrow night for London. Let me get on the horn now and see what I can do. But I give you my word, if we can work it, I'm doing *Central Standard*. It'll be a bitch, but I'd tell Paramount so long, bye-bye. I don't care how many effing zeros they wave in my face. Does that shock you, John? Does it?"

It did, but Pellam said, "No, Marty, it impresses me."

The bungalows wouldn't work. The interiors were too small for a Panaflex and lights and actors all at the same time. Sloan had wanted a complicated tracking shot where the camera on a doorway dolly starts in the yard and follows a character's point of view into the living room. But he finally agreed with Pellam and the key grip that the scene would have to be edited together. They would shoot the exteriors of the bungalows (the most decrepit of the four) and the interiors in the parlor and living room of a two-story colonial next door.

Pellam left Tony Sloan barking instructions to the gaunt key grip, whose resilient humor from the first several weeks of shooting had vanished completely under the weight of tasks like this one: completing in six hours a setup that would normally take two days. Pellam hopped back on his cycle and drove to the bank that held the deeds on both houses. The banker, wearing a pastel green suit, had carefully read the standard location release and signed it, accepting the six-hundred-dollar check with an air of embarrassment.

"Most money them houses've made in two years."

"Times're rough round here, looks like."

"Yessir, that they have been. I just wish this recession would hurry up and get done. We'll get through it, though."

Pellam returned to the bike and fired it up. As he drove through town he noticed a car following, keeping the same distance behind. Two people in the front seat, he believed. Pellam made two unnecessary turns. The car took the same route. He braked the cycle to a stop and pretended to look into a storefront window of dusty antiques while the driver of the car stopped and pretended to look at a map. Eyes still scanning the window of the store, Pellam suddenly popped the bike into first and squealed away from the stop, turning down a narrow walkway between two deserted buildings, a space just wide enough to leave about an inch on either side of the handlebar grips. He could touch neither the front brake nor clutch without leaving knuckle skin on brick.

When he emerged from the alley he braked to a fast stop and saw the car was skidding to a halt at the far end of the alley. Pellam made a sharp turn down a one-way street and aimed toward a strip of brown river. After he had driven for a block he felt a strong sense of déjà vu and slowed, dropping down into first gear. The car was nowhere around him and, guided by instinct, he turned right and parked. He was on Third Street, next to a series of low factories and warehouses.

From here he could see what had at one time probably been Maddox's budding riverfront scene. Now it contained only empty storefronts, uninspired antique stores, bars and Callaghan's Steak House.

This was also the place where Donnie Buffett had been shot.

Pellam noticed something beside his booted foot. Bloodstains, he believed, though they may have been nothing more than antifreeze or chocolate milk.

"*I'll keep an eye on them, you want to get a bag or something.*"

"Yeah?"

"Sure."

"Thanks."

Pellam parked the bike and found a phone booth. The phone worked, which surprised him. Upon calling directory assistance, he also was surprised to learn that the address he sought was only a block away.

Pellam did not care for the smell of the place.

Something about antiseptics, that sweet cheap-perfume smell of chilly stuff that gets dabbed on your skin before they cut or stick.

Also the design was depressing: aluminum, bright vinyl, linoleum. For some reason, orange was very popular. Orange and purple. Pellam had been in old hospitals, where you really got a sense of *Medicine* – dark woodwork and brass and pale green. As if somebody were discovering anesthetic or penicillin behind one of the gold-stenciled doors.

Maddox General was like life and death in K Mart.

Pellam signed in. The nurse pointed him down the hallway. Pellam walked past a cop stationed at the head of the corridor. He eyed Pellam carefully. "Hold up there, sir."

"I'd like to see Officer Buffett."

"You're the witness." The cop's stony face remained immobile; his eyes painted Pellam up and down.

"I just want to see how he's doing."

"Open your jacket."

"I—"

"You want to see him, open your jacket."

Pellam opened his jacket. The cop frisked him roughly and motioned toward Buffett's room.

On the TV was a game show. The sound was low; everything but the loudest applause was inaudible. The reception wasn't very good and there was a thick band of distortion through the center of the screen. The host and the contestants were smiling a lot.

Buffett wasn't.

"How you doing?" Pellam asked and identified himself.

"I remember you."

Pellam walked to a gray chair. He stood as if deciding whether or not to sit. "I brought you this." He put a book, a recent best-seller, on the table. "It's a mystery. I don't know if you like them."

Buffett kept staring at him.

Pellam cleared his throat. The silence filled in again. He said, "I didn't know if you'd like a bottle. What d'you drink anyway? Beer?"

"I got shot in the back."

"I heard. How you feeling?"

"How do you think I feel?"

Silence again. Pellam decided there wasn't going to be any lighthearted banter and joshing. He stood back from the chair and crossed his arms. "Look. I'm sorry about what happened. But I'd like to ask a favor. Your buddies in the police department, a couple detectives particularly, are giving me a pretty hard time. You know, following me. They think I saw this guy who was in the car—"

Buffett, eyes on the TV screen, blurted, "Well, you *did*."

"I didn't see him," Pellam said evenly. "I know you think I did. But I didn't."

Buffett kept staring at the tube. His eyes were dark, agitated. He licked the corner of his mouth with the tip of his tongue. This made him seem like a cornered animal. "How could you help but? He was in the front seat."

"There was glare."

"The hell there was glare."

Pellam's face flushed. "You think I'm covering up something? I'm not. I described the guy who bumped into me."

"Oh, that's mighty brave of you. *I* saw him. We don't need *his* description. Anyway, he's rabbited. He was just the hired gun and he's back in Miami or Chicago by now."

"Do you think they paid me off?"

"I think you're like everybody else. You don't want to get involved."

Pellam sighed. "I better be going."

"I think when you look in the front seat of a car, you fucking see somebody. I think when you *move* your mouth, you're *talking* to somebody!"

"I wasn't—"

"You saw him! I saw you look right into his face."

"If you saw so damn much why the hell didn't *you* see him?"

"How much did they pay you?"

"I didn't—"

"Listen, mister," Buffett blurted viciously, "you're gonna

have cops on your ass every minute of the day! They're going to stay on you. They're not going to let you crap until you tell—"

Pellam waved his hand in frustration and walked to the door.

"You son of a bitch!" Buffett's face was livid, tendons rose in his neck, and flecks of spittle popped from his lips. His voice choked and for a moment Pellam feared he was having a heart attack. When he saw that Buffett was simply speechless with rage he himself stormed out of the door.

And walked squarely into a young woman as she entered.

"Sorry," he muttered.

She blinked and stepped aside timidly. "Oh, I'm sorry."

The woman was thin, blond, late twenties, dressed unflashy, like an executive secretary, looking shy and embarrassed. Pellam assumed she was the cop's wife and thought he was lucky to be married to someone so pretty. He also thought she was going to have to put up with pure hell for a long, long time.

She said, "I'm looking for Dr Albertson."

Pellam shook his head, shrugged and walked past her.

In the hall he heard Buffett shouting to him, "Sure, so just leave. Just like that! Go ahead, you son of a bitch!"

The voice faded as he proceeded down the corridor. The cop on guard said something, too, something Pellam didn't hear, though from the snide smile on his face, he guessed it was no friendlier than the cop's farewell. Then he was at the elevator, kneading his hands and feeling his jaws clench with anger. He punched the down button seven times before he realized it had lit up and the car was on its way.

A woman's voice startled him. "I'm sorry. I didn't mean to barge in."

He glanced back and saw the blond woman walk up, looking at the floor indicator.

Pellam's mouth tightened. "No problem."

"He looks familiar." She glanced back up the corridor.

"Who?"

"Well, your friend. The man in the room you were just in."

"Don't *you* know him?"

She explained that she didn't. She was looking for her mother's doctor and the nurse had sent her there. She nodded toward the room. "Who is he?"

Pellam said, "He's the cop, the one that got shot."

"Oh, sure! The *Post-Dispatch*. They ran his picture. What's his name?"

"Donnie Buffett."

"He's your friend?"

Pellam waved his hand. "What you heard back there . . . I don't think you'd call him much of a friend."

The elevator arrived. They both stepped in. Behind them stood a man in a dressing gown, his hand grasping a tall IV bag on wheels like a chrome hat rack.

"The doctor's left for lunch already." She grimaced. "I was supposed to meet him here about Mother. Now I've got to come back in an hour."

"Your mother's a patient?"

"Hysterectomy. She's fine. Well, she's complaining nonstop but that means she's fine."

The elevator, slowly filling with her fruity perfume, arrived on the ground floor. "So," he said as they walked outside into the cool air of the spacious lobby.

"Well."

"My name's John Pellam."

She took his hand. "Nina Sassower."

They walked out the front door of the hospital and Nina surveyed the street. She had a great profile; the lines of her face were . . . What came to mind? Unencumbered.

Then he smiled ruefully to himself. *Unencumbered.* Too much movie talk, too much artistic vision. No, she's *sensuous*, she's *pretty*. She's *sexy*.

Pellam looked at his watch. He had a lot to do and not much time to do it in – getting the insurance binders for the bungalows, running his daily check on the dozens of shooting permits to make sure they hadn't expired during this elongated filming schedule, calling his bank in Sherman Oaks about the mortgage to finance his own film, *Central Standard Time*, seeing what other markers he had that he might call in – and all the while dodging cops.

What he did, though, was none of these things. Instead he asked, "You interested in lunch?"

And, as it turned out, she was.

At three that afternoon Pellam was in the camper, about to ride to the set, when his phone buzzed. He snagged it and propped it between his shoulder and his cocked head as he pulled on his leather jacket. "'Lo?"

"Dinner tomorrow."

"Okay. Is that you, Marty?"

"Here's the deal. You ready? . . . Telorian."

Pellam did not speak for a moment. "Are you sure?"

"Ugh. Am I sure?" Weller repeated sarcastically.

Ahmed Telorian. The fifty-year-old Armenian-Iranian investor (after the hostage thing he began calling himself "Persian") had grown to love American movies as much as he loved making millions from electronic component sales. Telorian and his wife had bought, gutted, and renovated an old theater in Westwood. They had turned it into a cult stronghold, in which they showed oddball films, many of them film noir, John Pellam's forte.

Telorian and Pellam had spent an evening together several years ago, drinking and talking about Claire Trevor and Gloria Grahame and Robert Mitchum and Ed Dmytryk. They argued vocally and with white knuckles around their thick glasses of ouzo.

The reason for that meeting several years ago was Telorian's other avocation – producer of low-budget films. He had read Pellam's *Central Standard Time* and was interested in optioning it. This happened to be at a time when Pellam had not wished to have anything to do with film companies, except location scouting. A generous offer of option money was rejected and Telorian had huffed away from the meeting. Pellam had not thought about him since then. He now felt his pulse increase a few tempos as he asked, "He's in Maddox?"

More likely to see Elvis hustling for a table the Hard Rock Cafe.

"He happened to be in Chicago. My secretary tracked him down. You kind of blew him off a few years ago, he says."

"I blew everybody off a few years ago."

"It's not like he's taking it personally. Not *too* personally. He still thinks *Central Standard* can be a hit. He's got to be home day after tomorrow but I got him to agree to stop over in St Louis to talk to you."

"What does he feel about me directing?"

"Not a problem. He just wants to know how you'd do it. Times aren't as flush as they used to be. He's interested in hits. He doesn't mind a grainy film. But it has to be *hit* grainy film. Got it?"

"When's his plane get in?"

"Whenever he tells his pilot to land. Meet us at eight at the Waterfront Sheraton. Lobby bar. You know where it is?"

"I can find it."

"About forty, fifty minutes from Maddox."

"He's got the treatment? The script?" Pellam asked.

"He's got everything. All you need to bring is as much Tony Sloan gossip as you can dig up."

In the floral-wallpapered entryway was a white Formica table. On it rested a Lucite pitcher filled with plastic flowers. To the left, through an arched doorway, was a parlor. The furniture in the rooms was mostly 1950s chain store – kidney-shaped tables, blond wood chairs, wing-backs and love seats upholstered in beige, a lot of plastic. Plastic everywhere. In the corner of the parlor was a young woman in a white blouse and black pedal pushers, struggling through a Chopin étude. A young, muscular man in brown slacks and yellow short-sleeved shirt leaned against the piano, smiling at her and nodding slowly.

"When I first saw you, you know, it was the night of the dance. It was—"

"I remember." She stopped playing and looked up.

"It was hot as in-line block. You were across the room under that Japanese lantern."

"That lantern, it was the one that was busted."

"Sure, it was busted and the bulb shone through that paper and covered you in light. That's when I knowed you was the girl for me." He put his hand on hers.

A heavyset man appeared slowly in the doorway. He lifted a Thompson submachine gun. The couple turned to him. Their smiles vanished.

"No!" The woman screamed. The man started forward toward the assailant. The gun began its fierce rattling. Pictures, vases, lamps exploded, black holes popped into the wall, bloody wounds appeared on the bodies of the couple as they reached toward each other. As the magazine in the submachine gun emptied and a throbbing silence returned, the couple slowly spiraled to the floor, their slick, bloody hands groping for each other's. Their fingers touched. The bodies lay still.

None of the fifteen or so sweaty people standing in the room around the immobile, bloody bodies said a single word. No one moved. Most of them were not even staring at the couple but were looking instead at the bearded man in jeans and green T-shirt who leaned against a reflector stand, his red eyes dancing pensively around the room. Tony Sloan paced over the spent machine-gun cartridges. He was shaking his head.

The man in brown sat up, wiped blood off his nose, and said, "Come on, Tony. It works."

"Cut," came the shout from behind the camera.

The bloody actress jumped to her feet and slapped her sticky palms on her hips. "Oh, Christ," she muttered viciously.

Sloan stepped closer to the carnage, surveying it. He spat out, "It *doesn't* 'work.'"

The machine gunner pulled cotton out of his ears and said, "What's he say?"

The actress grimaced. "He says it doesn't work."

The killer shrugged.

Sloan motioned to Danny the script writer and the assistant director, a young blond woman in her early thirties. The three of them huddled in the corner of the room, while wardrobe and grips spread out onto the set, cleaning up. "We gotta shoot it outside," Sloan said.

The assistant director's golden ponytail swaggered as she nodded vigorous approval.

"Outside?" Danny sighed. According to the Writer's Guild contract, he was paid a great deal of money every time he revised *Missouri River Blues*. The fun of making that money, however, had long ago worn off.

"It's not, you know, dynamic enough," Sloan mused. "We need a sense of motion. They should be *moving*. I think it's important that they *move*."

Danny pulled *his* earplugs out. "If you remember the book and if you remember the shooting script, they escaped. *I* didn't kill them in the first place."

The director said, "No, no, no, I don't mean that. They've *got* to die. I just think they should get killed outside. You know, like it suggests they're that much closer to freedom. Remember Ross's fear."

"Fear of the lock-down," the assistant director recited, shaking her stern blond ponytail. It was impossible to tell if she was speaking with reverence or sarcasm.

Danny wound his own ponytail, the color of a raven's wings, around stubby fingers, then touched from his cheek a fleck of red cardboard from the blank machine-gun shells. He looked as exhausted as Sloan. "Tell me what you want, Tony. You want them dead, I'll make them dead. You want them dead outside, I'll make them dead outside. Just tell me."

The director shouted, "Pellam? Shit, did he leave?"

Pellam, who had not been wearing earplugs but had been sitting on the front hall stairs thirty feet away from the shooting, stood up and walked into the living room. He dodged bits of pottery and glass and stepped over two arms assistants in protective gear who were removing several of the explosive gunshot-impact squibs that had failed to detonate.

Sloan asked him, "What about a road?"

"Why do you want a road?"

"I'd like them to die on a road," Sloan said. "Or at least near a road."

The actress in pedal pushers said, "I don't want to get shot again. It's loud and it's messy and I don't like it."

"You've got to die," Sloan said. "Quit complaining about it."

With a bloody finger she pointed to the cartridge of film the assistant photographer was pulling off the Panaflex camera. "I'm dead. It's in the can."

The director stared at the ground. "What I'd like is to find a road going through woods. No, a field. A big field. Maybe beside a school or something. Ross and Dehlia are planning one last heist. But it's an ambush. The Pinkerton guys stand up in the window suddenly, out of the blue—"

Pellam began to say something.

"Will you stop with that *Bonnie and Clyde* shit already, Pellam?" Sloan snapped. "This'll be different. Everybody *thinks* they're going to get shot – I mean, the audience is thinking *Bonnie and Clyde*. They're thinking they've seen this before. But uh-uh. Here, the kids get away. Maybe the guns don't go off and—"

Danny said, "*Neither* of the guns go off? There are two agents."

"Well, one gun jams and the other guy misses."

"So now you want them to live?" Danny asked brightly.

"No, no, no. I want them to escape then get killed, maybe in a freak accident. I've got it! They drive into a train."

The actress said, "If I don't get shot again I don't mind."

Pellam said, "Somebody else did a train crash ending. Who was it? That's very seventies. Elliott Gould might've driven a car into a train once. Or Donald Sutherland. *Sugarland Express*." He wondered why he was getting so riled. *Missouri River Blues* wasn't *his* movie.

The stoolie from the studio, a young man with curly hair not tied in a ponytail, lit a cigarette and said to no one in particular, "You know what it costs to rent a train?"

Sloan started to speak, then reconsidered. He said, "I could go with a tractor-trailer maybe."

Pellam said, "Why don't you rename the film and call it *Daughter of Bonnie and Son of Clyde?*"

Danny slapped Pellam's palm, five high.

The director ignored them. "Daniel, rewrite it and let's get John a copy. I want it to look like they're going to get blasted but then something happens and they escape and there's a freak accident."

Exasperated, Danny said, "What? What happens? Tell me. Give me a clue."

The director said, "Surprise me. I want it like Man can't touch them, but Fate can. Fate or nature, or some shit."

Pellam asked, "You want any particular kind of road?"

"A road . . ." His eyes began to fly again. "I want it near the river and I want a big field on one side. I want the car to careen into the river."

The river: Pellam grimaced. It was often impossible to get permits for scenes like that nowadays – no one wanted gas and oil and random car parts filling up their bodies of water. Many of the car crash setups were guerrilla shots – without a permit, in and out before the authorities found out, the evidence left at the bottom of the river or lake. Pellam guessed that if Sloan insisted on launching Ross's Packard into the Missouri River, it would have to be a guerrilla shot.

Sloan said, "I'm going to look at rushes." He hurried toward the door. Before he could leave, though, the sound of arguing voices rose from the hallway. A security guard was backed onto the set by two tall men in light gray suits. They walked steadily toward him, speaking low and pleasantly but insistently. One of the men looked at Pellam. He said to his partner, "That's him." They turned from the flustered, red-faced guard and strode onto the set.

"Hey, hey, hey," Sloan said. "What is this?"

"John Pellam?"

Before Pellam could answer, Sloan said impatiently, "This is a closed set. You'll have to leave."

One said in a high, contrite voice, "I'm sorry for the intrusion.

This won't take a moment." He turned to Pellam. "You're John Pellam?"

"That's right."

Sloan looked at Pellam with a mixture of perplexity and anger in his face. "John, who are these guys? *What's* going on here?"

Like the cops the day before, these men ignored Sloan and said to Pellam, "We're with the Federal Bureau of Investigation." IDs appeared.

And like the day before, when the cops had shown up, everyone on the set stopped working and turned to watch.

"I'm Special Agent Monroe and this is Special Agent Bracken. Would you mind stepping outside with us? We'd like to ask you a few questions." The agents ignored the bloody actress. Perhaps they had seen a lot of machine-gunned bodies in their day.

"About what?"

"A crime you may have been a witness to. If you have a few minutes now?"

"I really don't."

"Yessir," Bracken said. Monroe, with his razor-cut hair and tidy mustache, looked like an FBI agent. Bracken was scruffy and had a wrinkled suit. He looked like a thug. Maybe he worked undercover. "It won't take long."

"He's very busy," Sloan said. "We're all very busy."

Bracken spoke to Pellam, as if *he* had uttered this protest. "Well, sir, the thing is, if you continue not to cooperate we'll have to take you to St Louis and—"

Sloan strode over to them. "I don't know what this is all about, but you can't just walk in here. Go get a warrant or something. John, what the hell is going on here? What are they talking about?"

"Well, we can get a warrant, sir. But that'll be to arrest Mr Pellam here—"

"For what?"

"Contempt and obstruction of justice. Now, if that's how you'd like us to proceed . . ."

"Jesus," Sloan whined, closing his eyes. He sounded more upset than Pellam. "Talk to them, John." He waved his hand fiercely as if scaring away a bee. "This is *not* a problem I want. You understand me?"

"Maybe if we could just step outside, Mr Pellam," Monroe said. "It shouldn't take long."

Sloan lifted impatient eyebrows at Pellam and told the agents, "He'd be happy to."

———◆———

7

Pellam preceded the two agents out of the house, past a row of location vans, dollies, and generator trucks, then down the street. They kept motioning him along the sidewalk, away from the curious eyes of the cast and crew and the crowd of locals, who stared with fascination at the equipment and occasionally waved – some timidly, some like relatives – at the cast.

One middle-aged man pointed at Pellam and whispered something to the woman by his side. Their faces seemed to darken and they stared, unsmiling, as he walked out of sight behind a row of shaggy hedges. When he turned, as directed, into an alley between two empty houses he could glimpse the couple again. They still stared with apparent hostility, and several others had joined them.

Halfway through the alley, which Pellam thought led to the agents' car, the two men stopped, one on either side of him.

"We can talk here."

"Here?" Pellam stepped back to put some distance between him and the agents. He brushed against the brick wall of one of the houses. He turned and found himself hemmed in.

Pellam turned back to Bracken. "Couldn't we—"

"Shut up," barked the unscruffy Monroe.

Bracken pointed a stubby finger at Pellam's chest and pushed him hard against the wall. "We know he got to you. We know he's pulling your dick." Though they both shaved, Bracken had done the sloppier job of it. He smelled of sweat. No after-shave for these boys.

Grim-faced, Pellam waved his arm in the air and started toward the mouth of the alley. "You can go to hell."

Two huge fists suddenly grabbed his shoulders and slammed him back into the wall. His head bounced against the window, which cracked under the impact.

"We're not getting through to you," Monroe said.

An unlicensed pistol in his waistband, Pellam did not want to be frisked. He lifted his arms unthreateningly, palms outward. "Why don't you just tell me what this is all about."

"A witness to a federal crime who refuses to testify or who fabricates testimony known to be false can be guilty of contempt, obstruction of justice and perjury." Bracken wore a thick gold bracelet on his hairy wrist, which seemed unbecoming on an agent of the federal government.

"As well as conspiracy if a link can be shown between him and the primary perpetrator."

Bracken lowered his face into Pellam's. "I'm talking about if you haven't got the balls to tell us what you saw that night we're looking at you as an accessory."

"Are you arresting me?"

"No, sir."

"Then this is harassment. I think it's time I called my lawyer."

Bracken took him by the lapels again and shoved him back against the wall. Pellam remembered to keep his head tilted forward so he wouldn't break any more windows. "We know you saw Crimmins in the Lincoln and we want you to identify him."

"I don't even know who you're talking about."

"The man who's paying you off? You don't remember him?"

A surveillance photograph appeared from Monroe's pocket. It had been lifted from a videotape and the time and date were visible in the right-hand corner. The picture showed a heavyset man with a broad, Slavic face and receding hairline. His mouth was open and he was turning his head to speak to an unseen person walking behind him.

"I've never seen him."

"Look again, Pellam. That's Peter Crimmins."

"I do not—"

"Look *again*, Pellam," Monroe said. "He's the man who was in the Lincoln. He's the man responsible for the death of Vincent Gaudia and for the shooting of a Maddox policeman. He's the man you saw. All we need is your confirmation."

"I can't confirm what I didn't see."

"You're not going to cooperate?" Bracken barked.

"This *is* cooperation – listening to you two. In fact, it's beyond cooperation. I'm leaving."

It had been a long, long hour.

Peter Crimmins was sweating. His Sea Island cotton shirt

was wet in the small of his back and under the arms. The sweat would bead on his chest hair, and when he moved, would press, cold, against the skin. Sweat was gathering too in the deep folds of fat where his waist met his chest. It trickled down his back.

Crimmins knew that at any time he could have asked the agents to leave and then they would either have to let him go or arrest him. But if they arrested him – which they might easily have done – that meant he would have to have his friend and counselor present.

That was something Crimmins didn't want. So he had consented to the questioning. He waved the men into seats in his office, sandwiched between the parking lot and the room of dark desks, and rested his fingertip on the mole above his eye. The barrage of questions lasted for an hour. They were handsome black men and looked more like recent business school graduates than federal agents. They seemed like many of Crimmins's clients (both the legitimate ones and the less so) – clever, polite, reserved.

But underneath: the personalities of a Midwest dawn in January.

One asked the questions. The other alternated between staring calmly at Crimmins and taking notes.

"Could I ask you where you were last Friday night, sir."

He hated the *sir*. The way it fell like a fleck of spit off the end of the sentence showed their contempt for him. But what could he do? That was an old rule in negotiations – never say anything that can be quoted against you later. If he later claimed harassment, the agent would say, *I never called him anything but "sir"* . . . *Look at the transcript.*

"I was at my office most of the night."

"Until when?"

"About ten. Quarter to, maybe."

"By yourself?"

"Yes. My secretary leaves at five-fifteen every night. I stay late a lot of times."

"Is there a guard?"

"We got guards, sure. But I didn't see any of them that night when I left."

"Is there any way of confirming your whereabouts?"

"You really think I killed Vince Gaudia?" Crimmins asked, exasperated.

"Is there any way of confirming it, sir?" the agent repeated.

"No."

"Do you own a Lincoln?"

"Yes. And a Mercedes wagon. A diesel."

"What color is the Lincoln?"

Crimmins rubbed the bump of his third eye. Why did they hate him so? "Dark blue. But you know that already, don't you?"

"What's the license number?"

He gave it to them

"Where was that car on the night we've been talking about?"

Crimmins was hungry. He had bouts of low blood sugar. If he didn't eat regularly – sometimes five meals a day – he would have attacks. He thought with some pleasure that Vince Gaudia never got to eat his last meal the night he died. "I drove it into the city."

"And parked it where, sir?"

"The place I always park it. The garage near the Ritz."

"And that's a Lincoln Continental?"

"I told you that already."

"Actually, no. We don't know what model. Is it a Continental?"

"It's a Town Car."

"Now tell me again where you were on that night."

Crimmins asked, "Where I was sitting, you mean?"

"You were in your office, you claim."

"I'm not claiming. I was there. I *told* you that. Didn't he write it down? I saw him write it down."

"Why wasn't your secretary there?"

"She leaves about five-fifteen every day. I told you that too."

The interview went on and on and on and the agents picked over every word that Crimmins said.

Finally the men stood. They flipped their notebooks closed and gathered their raincoats. Suddenly they were gone.

He now sat at his desk, staring at the familiar nicks along the side, running his finger over them, feeling the bulge of his gut against his belt.

The phone rang.

His lawyer was on the line. Crimmins decided not to tell him about the visit from the FBI. It had been worse than expected, but if he told the lawyer, the man would have a tantrum that he had spoken to the agents alone. But the issue didn't come up; the lawyer wanted to talk, not listen.

"Pete, I've got some news. Call me on a safe phone, will you?"

Crimmins grunted and hung up. He walked downstairs and up the street to the Ritz Carlton parking garage. Without proffering a ticket, he nodded to a young attendant, who scurried off to retrieve the Lincoln. Crimmins looked at it sourly as it rolled up. He gave the boy a bill then got inside and drove out onto the broad street. He lifted the receiver of the car phone, the number of which was changed so frequently that he was 95 percent sure it was a secure line.

"News, you said." Crimmins drove leisurely, well under the speed limit.

"The witness," the nonfriend and counselor said.

"Yes."

"The witness to the Gaudia hit."

"I *know* that's what you mean. What *about* him?" Crimmins snapped, angry because there was a 5 percent chance the line was not secure.

"I found him."

"How?"

"I called some favors in."

Called in favors? Nonsense. Nobody owes a leech any favors. "Who is it?"

"A man with this movie company that's up in Maddox."

"Movie company? I never heard about a movie company."

"They're shooting some gangster film up there." His voice was bright with an irony that Crimmins didn't wish to acknowledge.

"Well? Tell me about him."

The man said, "They know he saw who was in the car. Both Maddox police and the FBI. So far, he's been too scared to testify."

"What did he see?" Crimmins asked slowly.

"They're sure he saw the driver," the lawyer said, then added, "There's something else I should tell you. I heard from somebody in the Justice Department that Peterson's going after him. He's going to jump on this guy with both feet. He's going to jump on him until he burns you."

A sigh. "What's his name?"

"John Pellam."

"Where's he staying?"

The lawyer hesitated – perhaps at Crimmins's sudden interest in details. Then he said, "He's got a trailer. You know, a camper. He parks it different places but mostly he's staying at the old trailer camp by the river in Maddox. Near the cement plant."

"I thought that was closed."

"Maybe for the movie people they opened it."

"It's deserted around there, isn't it?"

Now the hesitation grew into a long silence. The lawyer managed to ask, "Why do you want to know that? Tell me, Peter."

Crimmins said, "I don't need anything more from you for the time being."

"Line it up for me, Nels," said Ronald L. Peterson, the U.S. Attorney for the Eastern District of Missouri.

He sat in a large office, done up in functional sixties design. The furniture was expensive. The desk was solid teak, but you could not tell by looking at its top, which was covered with a thousand pieces of paper. On the bookshelves, filling three walls, were dark, wilted volumes. *Moore's Federal Practice Digest. Federal Sentencing Guidelines. Federal Rules of Civil Procedure.* Case reports, law reviews, *ABA Journals.*

Young Nelson, sandy-haired, solid, a purebred preppy, opened a file stuffed full of scraps of yellow foolscap and began pulling out sheets and organizing them.

Peterson, forty-four, was wearing a Brooks Brothers navy suit, about one-fifth as old as he, a white shirt, a yellow tie with black dots on it (a summer model technically, but this was his good-luck tie, having been around his neck when he put seven Cosa Nostra leaders into prison, and so he wore it when – as now – he felt he needed luck). Peterson was a solid man, with thick hands and a smooth face. Balding. A roll of belly and midriff that showed taut and pinkish under the thin white shirts he always wore. He was the sort of man whose face revealed exactly the boy he had been at thirteen. And in other ways, too, he was much the same then as now: confident, vindictive, smart, determined, prissy. And manic.

Ronald Peterson's approach to this job, as well as his approach to the practice of law, was characterized by an almost charming simplicity. He was the chief U.S. lawyer in a major judicial district for the same reason he had worked in the Justice Department for the past nine years: because he thought that people who did bad things ought to go to jail.

Years ago, in law school, troubled about what kind of practice to go into, Peterson had heard one of his Harvard Law professors say that the best lawyers make the worst judges. Meaning that the practice of law provides its own morality – lawyers do not need to make terrifying judgments about right and wrong; they just apply the rules. This observation was an epiphany for him, and that summer he took a job as an intern in the same U.S. Attorney's office that he now headed. He had been applying the simple rules ever since. He went about this task with the devotion of a fundamentalist Shi'ite – with whom he shared a sense of righteousness and an ecstatic appreciation of the abstract.

The man who was the focus of Peterson's present *jihad* was Peter Crimmins. This campaign actually had less to do with the infamous *60 Minutes* program skewering his office than one might think. No, what Peterson resented so much about Crimmins was what the prosecutor had identified as a serious problem in America – a legitimate businessman's cool, conscious decision to move into illegal activities. Crimmins, like the insider traders whom Peterson also loathed, had simply found the profits at his trucking businesses not up to his greed and had expanded into money laundering and other crimes as if that were the next logical step in market expansion.

Nelson, an assistant U.S. Attorney, had reviewed all the sheets of foolscap. He looked into his boss's adolescent eyes. "It's dicey." His voice stopped abruptly and he immediately regretted the word. Peterson continually told his people not to give soft assessments. He wanted specifics. Yeses and nos. Peterson was renowned for his temper tantrums. But today he was not in the mood to beat up anyone for casual lapses like this. He drank more of his coffee and asked, "What do we know about Crimmins the night of the hit?"

"He denies it all but hasn't got an alibi. We didn't have a tail on him. But there were no phone intercepts in or out for two hours on either side of the shooting. He does have a Lincoln."

"Match?"

"Circumstantial. Both the getaway and Crimmins's are dark-colored. But there's no tag or other ID. Not yet."

"Crimmins's got that bodyguard, doesn't he?"

"Yep. But he doesn't match the ID of the gunman."

"What about earlier wiretaps?" Peterson wondered. "Was there a *syllable* that might be taken to suggest Crimmins was ordering a hit? Was there some talk of *accidents?* Anything about, oh, *cleaning house?*"

There had not been, Nelson reported, as he stroked his young, pink cheek, under which several teeth seemed to chew nervously on his tongue. He added, "But you know how tough surveillance has been. Crimmins makes half his calls from the park and his car phone . . ."

A serene Peterson spun in his functional 1960s chair and licked a smear of coffee off the side of his cup. Losing the star witness on whom he had pinned so much hope had been such a blow that it transcended simple rage. Besides, a measure of such anger as Peterson might feel had no target other than himself – for acquiescing to Gaudia's flippant request to keep the U.S. Marshals out of his hair.

The U.S. Attorney breathed slowly as he looked out over the city. But would Crimmins really have been present at the hit? Why? Maybe they had been meeting. Maybe Crimmins was trying to cut a deal with Gaudia and the talks had turned sour.

Peterson patted his thighs. He was on a diet. (One of the things that irked him was that he looked like Peter Crimmins, only Crimmins had more hair.) His head turned slowly but powerfully as if it were geared at a very low ratio. "What about the witness? What's his name? Pellam?"

"The cops aren't sharing anything with us."

"Pricks," Peterson spat out. He slapped his leg, feeling the fat reverberate. "One of theirs gets shot and the mayor and commissioner sit on the witness. You know why they do that. For the *Post-Dispatch*. That's why they do it. Who's on him?"

"Monroe and Bracken. Roasted him good. But he's not talking."

"You're sure he got a peek?"

"Yep. No way he could've missed him. Impossible."

"I think it's a pay-off."

"I think so, too," Nelson said, though he in fact did not. What he believed was that Crimmins had said simply, "If you talk, I'll kill you."

And Pellam had been struck dumb.

Peterson said, "Move on it big. Find out everything you can about him."

"Who, Crimmins?" Which Nelson realized to his dread was an immensely stupid question. He said quickly, "Oh, you mean Pellam."

"Uhm."

"Then tell them, Monroe and Bracken . . ." Peterson mused absently gazing at a wind-up toy on his desk. "Have them beat him up."

"What?" Nelson whispered.

Peterson's eyes flickered and landed on his assistant's troubled face. "Figuratively," he added casually. "*Keep on him*, I mean. You knew I meant that, didn't you?"

"Figuratively," Nelson said. "Sure, I knew."

———— •※※• ————

8

Pellam realized suddenly that he had known Nina Sassower for twenty-four hours and had no idea what she did for a living.

"I'm unemployed actually," she said in response to his question. She was blushing and suddenly appeared very embarrassed. Pellam told her that he'd been in films more than ten years and the majority of that time he'd been unemployed.

They were walking through what was left of down-town Maddox. They had finished lunch and were moving, at Pellam's tacit guidance, away from the park where Tony Sloan was choreographing the murders of two Pinkerton men who stumble on Ross's hideout; Nina's narrow eyes darted uncomfortably at the sound of the gunshots. They were make-believe but still troubling. Pellam touched her arm to direct her toward the river.

Today she wore a bulky orange V-neck sweater. The matching orange skirt was billowy and a brisk wind snapped it like a ship's sail. Her shoes were tan and she carried a raincoat that was the same shade. An improbable outfit on Santa Monica Boulevard, but in Maddox, Missouri, it was quite becoming.

When they had put some distance between them and the gunfight, she relaxed. "Before I got laid off, I was a school counselor, grade school."

Pellam had taken those tests. His teachers, in the Catskill town where he grew up, were encouraging, but the tests revealed he had relatively little aptitude for any of the listed careers. (Because Pellam liked to read, the counselor suggested, "Book salesman." Because he liked to go to movies, the man offered, "Usher, then with hard work, theater manager.")

"Not a *guidance* counselor – more of a therapist."

"A psychiatrist?"

"Psychologist. But budget cutbacks . . . Illinois, too. All over the country, I guess."

"Surprised they even have schools left in Maddox."

"Well, I really live in Cranston, which isn't as bad off as here. Closer to St Louis. But we still aren't doing well. Anyway, I guess if you're the one laid off, it doesn't matter if unemployment is one percent or twenty."

"Guess not."

They looked straight down this broad street and saw the gray slab of river a quarter mile away. Despite a heavy network of overhead power and telephone cables, the street seemed very nineteenth-century – like a deserted frontier town's. It would look perfectly natural for the road to be filled with muddy mule teams and drovers and ponies and river workers slogging through the muck toward the docks. Pellam noticed a couple of scabby, atmospheric buildings, right out of 1880. "Let me take some snaps. Hold up a second."

A battered Polaroid camera unfolded and he took four pictures. He stuffed the undeveloped, moist squares into his shirt, then continued on, Nina beside him.

"Are those for your movie?"

"Not the one they're shooting now. I have a catalog of buildings and places that directors might want. Keeps me from reinventing the wheel every time I get a call."

"You work for the studio? Or do you have your own business?"

"Free-lancer. Like most everybody here. Nowadays the studios just finance and distribute. Everybody else is hired as an independent contractor. Used to be different. In the thirties and forties the studios owned your soul – if you had a soul, that is."

She didn't laugh but seemed to be memorizing this lesson in Hollywood enterprise, and so he decided not to make a casting couch joke. Not yet. He turned back to the old buildings and Nina watched him take more pictures.

"What's that?"

"Your catalog of locations."

Pellam stored the binders in a file box under his bed in the camper. He said, "That can be arranged."

They continued up the street.

"Let's go in, can we?" Nina nodded at a store. Although Pellam was extremely aware that he owed Sloan a big field, he said sure. They walked into a huge warehouse, filled with scavenged relics from buildings. Nina said she was interested in columns and mantelpieces. They found a couple of scabby wooden columns, stripped down carelessly; you could still see blotches of paint and nicks and the scorch marks from the blowtorch. Nina liked them but thought at four hundred each, they were too pricey. Pellam agreed. He also did not think they would fit into his California contempo bungalow on Beverly Glen. "And dangerous," he added, "in the camper."

She smiled at this, then stopped in front of a dark, flaking mirror, framed in ancient oak. She flicked her hair with her fingers.

Pellam asked, "Tell me about yourself."

She blushed and gazed at a brass coal bucket with a face embossed into it.

"A cherub," Pellam commented, not pushing the deflected question.

"I always thought that was a cigar. Like the kind Clint Eastwood smoked in those Italian westerns."

"Isn't that cheroot?"

"Could be. I'm always getting things mixed up."

After a pause she said in a dogged voice, "So, tell you about myself. Well." She had apparently steeled herself for the response. "You'll probably find it pretty boring. I grew up in Maddox. Went to Mizzou – that's the University of Missouri – in St Louis, studied English lit, which gets you nowhere. I got a job in a library and didn't like where it was going. So I got a master's degree in psychology. Then moved over to Cranston, nice safe distance from Mom and, at the time, Dad. Hobbies? Astrology, shiatsu—"

Massage? He thought quickly. Was it too early in their courtship to make a thigh reference? Probably. He opted for back. He said, "I have this problem in my back." Then added, "My *lower* back."

She parried with feigned disappointment. "I don't do lower backs."

"You specialize. I see." He waited what he thought was the proper amount of time. "No boyfriend?"

"Boyfriend." She considered and he wondered if she was tailoring a lie. "There's this guy I see off and on. A lot off and not much on. You know how it is. When I was younger I dated a lot but, I don't know, something about me – I was kind of a jerk magnet. What rocks those boys crawled out from under . . ."

"Ever been married?"

"No. You?"

He was a veteran, Pellam admitted.

"See, I'd rather not get married than be married and have to go through the pain of divorce."

"Well," Pellam said, "without pain, there's no appreciation." They both considered that while they stared at a ninety-dollar spittoon. He said, "You're thinking that was a stupid thing to say."

Nina was nodding. "Uhm, yeah, I think it was." She laughed and they paused at bins filled with old albums, selling for fifty cents each. Pellam liked the scratchy sound of LPs. He didn't own a CD player. He sunk a lot of his listening money into records. When he got home he'd record them on cassettes for the tape deck in the Winnebago. He began going through the jazz bin. "You like music?"

"Oh, yeah, music is the best," she announced, and looked over his shoulder at the album cover he was reading.

"Who's that?" she asked.

"Oscar Peterson." *Who's that?*

"Sounds familiar."

"Oscar Peterson," Pellam said again.

"Uh . . . I'm kind of into soft rock, you know. Light FM. It's relaxing."

Oh.

"It's jazz," he said.

"Like Stevie Wonder?" Nina asked sincerely.

"Sort of," Pellam said. "They use the same notes."

Outside, the voodoo of Tony Sloan's paranoia caught up with Pellam. He explained that he had to get back to work. When he leaned forward to kiss her cheek, to say good-bye, she responded with firm pressure on his hands and even leaned into him. A semihug. He glanced down and got a clear vision of the plunging neckline of her sweater. He was staring at her pale skin when they separated and she caught his downward-looking eyes. He said quickly, "I was admiring those earrings. They're interesting."

"A present," she said, perhaps choosing not to believe him.

He slipped on his sunglasses and smiled. "You interested in searching for a field with me sometime?"

Nina nodded. "Sure. I'd like that." She touched his arm and looked serious. "But I'd like to say something."

The boyfriend who wasn't *a boyfriend. The girlfriend who was a girlfriend. I don't like men with film companies. Lips that touch liquor . . .*

"Yup?"

"I want to tell you why I picked you up."

"How's that?"

"I mean, not that I don't like you."

"No."

"See, I heard that when the film company came to town they were hiring people. I mean, it's not the *only* reason I started talking to you."

I see.

"Is there any way I could get a job?"

Well, he should have known. This was hardly the first time it had happened. She must have seen the flicker in his eyes. The Ray-Bans were not all that dark.

"I'm sorry." Her eyes went straight to the ground. "I shouldn't have asked. It's just—"

"I don't mind."

"It's just that I've been out of work for six months. I haven't even been able to find a job waitressing."

He touched the incredibly soft orange alpaca over her muscular arm. "The thing is, shooting's almost over. All the extras have been cast and they don't make much money anyway."

"No, no, no." Her face had turned pink. "I wouldn't want to *act*. I don't even like movies. I think they're stupid."

She doesn't like movies?

"Oh." *Everybody likes movies* . . . "Well, what did you have in mind?"

"I don't know. I see so many people in town from your company . . ."

Thirty-seven cast members from Hollywood. Sixty-two local extras. Seventy-one L.A.-based crew members, sixty-seven from St Louis, twelve stuntmen, eight drivers, two producers, two caterers, two animal wranglers, one stoolie from the Coast, one high-tech visionary director.

One location scout.

"Is there," Pellam asked, "anything you can do?"

Nina considered this for a minute. The blush was gone and so was her bashfulness. He suspected that beneath the wan Julia Roberts face was a ball-buster of a school counselor. "I can't really do anything other than coach girls' gymnastics and talk to students."

Pellam squeezed her arm again. "And," he said, "you can make yourself beautiful."

She sniffed a laugh. "You're flirting."

"No, I have something in mind," Pellam said. Then he added, "In addition to flirting."

> *MISSOURI RIVER BLUES*
> *SCENE 180A – INTERIOR DAY,*
> *ROSS'S GETAWAY CAR, cont'd*
> > *ROSS*
> *When I first saw you, you know, it was the night of the dance. It was—*
> > *DEHLIA*
> *(holding wounded arm) I remember.*
> > *ROSS*
> *It was hot as a in-line block. You were across the room under that Japanese lantern.*
> *ANGLE ON Dehlia, hair flying in the breeze. She looks back with* LOVE *in her eyes.*
> > *DEHLIA*
> *(gasping) That lantern, it was the one that was busted.*
> > *ROSS*
> *Sure it was busted and the bulb shone through that paper and covered you in light. That's when I knowed you was the girl for me.*

"Ouch. That's terrible. Don't read anymore, Pellam." Stile and Pellam sat on a river bluff overlooking the Missouri.

Pellam was looking down at the revised script. He recited emotionally, "'You was the girl for me.'"

"Pellam," Stile said, wincing. "Please."

"That's what they say just before they skid into the river. Don't you think that's purty? The hole in the lantern's a metaphor for freedom."

"You know what's a metaphor? To keep the cows in. In this case –" Stile nodded toward the script "– it's where the bullshit is."

"I'll bet in the final scene the cops find the car but not the bodies." Pellam flipped to the end and read. "Damn damn damn, I'm right. Gimme five."

Stile and Pellam slapped palms and the stuntman limped over to the Yamaha. He had spent the afternoon getting shot with a .45 at close range and tumbling down a flight of stairs. Thirty gunshots and fifteen falls. Then Sloan had changed his mind and decided Stile should fall through a window after getting shot. But the stunt coordinator insisted they postpone the scene till tomorrow and gave Stile the rest of the day off. He had joined Pellam and together they spent the afternoon driving around on the cycle looking for Sloan's big field. "Who was that squeeze I saw you with?"

"Nina Sassower." Pellam joined Stile at the cycle.

"Well, that's a name and a half. I haven't seen her around."

"That's because this is her first day on the set. I got her a job doing makeup. She's pretty good at it."

"She's also pretty good at kissing and throwing her arms around you."

It was true, she had been.

"Casting couch is one thing, Pellam. If you get laid 'cause you got somebody a job as a makeup artist while I fall out of tall buildings and have to content myself with ring around the rosy at night there is no justice in this world."

Pellam was not, however, thinking of Nina Sassower and her embracing arms. He was obsessed with getting the field. The houses and buildings for the film had been easy, Maddox's economic condition being what it was. The field was another story. It needed a border of dense trees, a road, a river, and a school in a stand of bushes. Also a small cliff for the dramatic crash.

The best they had found was a small overhang beside a weedy pumpkin patch. To reach the bluff for its dramatic fall, Ross's Packard would have to crash through deep thickets of forsythia and juniper and maple saplings.

"Very vegetative place, this Missouri," Pellam observed, "and oddly short on fields."

"I still don't see why you're working for Sloan. Even a whore's got principles. Sort of oil and water is what I'm saying."

Pellam wiped beads of dew off the face of his Casio. Six P.M. He had to meet Marty Weller and Ahmed Telorian in two hours. "Let's have a beer, call it quits." He sat in the saddle of the Yamaha. Stile pocketed the Polaroid and climbed on behind.

The wind rose up in sudden chill bursts. The rain had mostly stopped but the streets were flecked with its aftermath – bits of bark and branches – and the air was very damp. A dog with fur spiked by an earlier down-pour walked up to them, sniffed belligerently then fled as Pellam kicked over the engine. They sped onto the asphalt.

"I called Hank," Pellam shouted over the roar, referring to the card-playing attorney retained by the film company. "He said there's nothing I can do about it."

"Those FBI guys, you mean?"

"They can interview whoever they want, they can stop production, they can look at all our permits. They can go to Delaware and Sacramento and look at everything the company's ever filed."

"Wooee, Tony's gonna roast your nuts, boy."

"He'd just fire me is what he'd do," Pellam said.

"I don't think he can fire you for not testifying. I'll bet you can sue him if he tries."

"Yeah, right."

Pellam motioned toward the river. A mule team of barges slapped through the water beside them. The wind was up and sailors were huddled on the pushing tug. Deckhands stood on the front of the barge, wearing orange vests and speaking into walkie-talkies – presumably to the captain, who stood, three football fields behind, in the pilot house. He wore a suit and tie.

Stile watched it and shouted, "I love riverboats, yessir. Eighteen fifty-three. The *Altona* made the run from St Louis to Alton in one hour and thirty-five minutes. See the lights? That's Alton."

"How do you *know* this stuff?" Pellam shouted back over the rattle of the engine.

"Nobody beat that record for a while. Well, the *Robert E. Lee* could've, of course. Or the *Natchez*. Watch the curve there."

Pellam looked back at the road just in time to make the curve with a skid that didn't even make Stile flinch. They turned off River Road and shot toward downtown. The lights were gassy and brilliant in the mist. "See," he shouted to Stile, "glare everywhere. How could I see anything?"

Pellam pulled into the discount package store and killed the engine.

They walked into the green-neon-lit store, went to the cooler, and began fighting it out over Canadian or American beer. Pellam lost the toss and Stile snagged a six-pack of Bud, plunking it down into Pellam's hands. "Gotta take a leak."

Pellam paid for the beer and wandered outside. He opened a can and sat on the Yamaha, sipping. He looked over at the flat black strip of the river.

He softly whistled a few bars from "Across the Wide Missouri."

The siren remained silent until the car was directly behind him then it burst into a huge electronic howl. The spotlight came on simultaneously. Pellam was so startled, he dropped the beer, spilling a good portion on his jeans. "Goddamn!" He spun around and looked at the car. The doors were opening and two men were coming toward him like G-men about to gun down Dillinger.

The WASP detective and the Italian detective. Oh, no . . . Them again.

"Look what you did," Pellam lifted an arm, showing them the drenched Levi's.

The Italian cop ignored the spill and grabbed Pellam's arm. He cuffed his wrist.

Pellam stared at the silver chain. "What—"

The other wrist got cuffed, too.

"—are you doing?"

"You have the right to remain silent. You have the right to an attorney." It was the Italian detective speaking.

"If you can't afford one," his partner took over, "one will be appointed for you. If you waive your right to remain silent, anything you say can and will be used against you in court."

"Do you understand each of these rights?"

Pellam thought they somehow knew about the unregistered .45 that was sitting below his butt in the toolbox of the Yamaha.

"I—"

"Do you understand these rights?"

"Sure, I understand them. What am I being arrested for?"

The WASP cop said, "Sir, we take drunk driving very seriously in our community."

Pellam closed his eyes. He shook his head.

"We'll have to give you a Breathalyzer test," the Italian detective said.

The WASP said, "But I'm afraid we don't have it with us."

The Italian said, on cue, "We better take him downtown."

"What's going on here?" Stile, chewing on a piece of beef jerky, walked out of the store.

"I'm—" Pellam began.

"Just stay out of this, mister," the WASP cop said ominously to Stile.

"—being arrested."

"For what?"

"For bullshit," Pellam called. He looked at his watch. It was six-twenty. "Look, I have a very important meeting at eight. I can't—"

"Quiet."

"No, look, I've got to meet a man in St Louis—"

They roughly dragged him to the squad car and, with a furry Italian hand on his head, pushed him inside.

Pellam called, "Stile, you gotta make a call for me. You gotta call Marty—"

"All right, that's enough out of you." The door slammed shut. Pellam kicked the front seat furiously.

"He's a hairsbreadth away from resisting," the Italian cop said to nobody.

"Where's the station?" Stile asked. "I'm coming down there."

The cops climbed into the front seat. One of them said, "It's in the phone book. Look it up."

They drove off leisurely, leaving Stile with a strip of beef jerky in one hand and five cans of beer in the other.

9

"Listen," said Ralph Bales.

Stevie Flom was listening.

"Okay, the man is not happy."

They sat in a chain restaurant on Big Bend Boulevard in St Louis. Stevie drank decaf. Ralph Bales was drinking tea, bleached by two wedges of lemon. It was All You Can Eat Don't Be Shy Spaghetti Night. Around them, fat families sat hunched over mounds of food.

"Not very happy at all."

Stevie was a punk and rarely gave a shit who was happy and who was not, except that this particular unhappy person owed him a lot of money.

"So it's my fault?" Stevie said, his voice shrill. The table rocked as he leaned forward and he whispered, "What, I was supposed to let a cop take you out?"

Ralph Bales held a finger to his lips. "*I'm* not complaining. Lombro isn't, you know, rational. He thought you should've shot the cop in the leg or something so they wouldn't be so concerned about it. Not the back."

"Yeah, right, shot him in the leg. Like it's night and I've got a pussy gun and I shoot him in the leg and he feels a little bee sting and turns around and explodes my head with hollow points. Bullshit. I mean, bullshit!"

The men did not know each other well. They moved in different circles. Ralph Bales was older, fifteen years. He was well connected on the riverfront and probably could have been more of a mover except he ran into some trouble in Chicago, working for the Giancana family. Some money that was supposed to find its way from Cicero up to Oak Park had not made that short journey. Ralph Bales remained alive to pay it back, out of his salary, but his name was suspect in Chicago ever after. So he returned broke to his hometown of St Louis and found his way into riverfront services and cargo and trucking and finally became a consultant.

Ralph Bales had in fact been doing some security consulting when he met Stevie Flom. A mutual friend needed some partners to help some expensive Scotch fall off a truck and to move the cases after they touched down. The job went smoothly, though Ralph Bales had been irritated by arrogant Stevie. He found, however, that another person resided inside the young man – Desperate Stevie, who had worked up such incredibly large debts giving his money to casinos and to poker players and to the skirts he humped (nightly, it seemed) that he would do whatever he was told to, provided he was paid for it.

"It's my fault, you're saying. Suddenly it's all *my* fault!"

"You're not listening," Ralph Bales said. "I'm just telling you."

The weather was cold and wet but Stevie wore a sleeveless tank top. He had good muscles; he liked to show them off.

"We've got to handle Lombro—"

"*Handle* him," Stevie exploded again, though the detonations were softer because he was lifting his coffee to his lips. "What the hell does that mean?"

"First, what it means is we don't get paid."

"Don't get paid?" Back to the high decibels. "Lombro was in the audience too! He should've been looking out for heat, he shoulda honked the horn or something. Fuck!"

Several parents, worried about their chubby offspring, glanced ominously toward the table.

Ralph Bales leaned forward. "Look . . ."

"'Listen, look.' You sound like a crossing guard."

"This man is nobody to fool around with."

"Well, *you* look. I'm out five thousand dollars. Which – I've been asking around, all right? – and I find is pretty on the low side for a hit."

Ralph Bales had told Stevie that Lombro was paying them ten thousand – not twenty-five – to split between them. He looked at the young man with steely eyes. "Who've you been talking to?" he asked in a menacing voice.

Stevie stopped exploding. He looked down at his cup and poured more cream into it. "Nobody. I mean, I was just asking around, you know. But I didn't mention anything specific."

Ralph Bales sighed. "Jesus. Don't say anything to anyone ever. Anything. Anyone. Ever. Lombro has connections you wouldn't believe."

"Deals . . . connections." Stevie rolled his eyes. He was

speaking softly now, though. The look in Ralph Bales's eyes had spooked him.

"Okay, here's the arrangement. We take care of the witness and Lombro'll pay us everything, plus twenty-five percent."

"Well, why didn't you just finish it the other day? By the river? We could've waited."

"Okay, think about it," Ralph Bales said slowly.

"Well . . ."

"Think about it."

Stevie was too cool and too much of a punk to show admiration, but his smile blossomed. "I get it. You wanted to, like, goose Lombro for more money."

"*You* just, you know, go ahead and *do* things," Ralph Bales lectured. "I thought it out."

"Twenty-five percent?" Stevie tried to figure the numbers. What was one quarter of five thousand? Fifty percent is twenty-five hundred. Then half of that? He got lost.

Ralph Bales said, "Means you walk away with close to seven thousand bucks. Not bad for two days' work."

Close to seven? Stevie smiled. He didn't want to but he grinned.

Ralph Bales smiled, too. "Hey, does your buddy Ralph take care of you right? Okay?"

Stevie said, "I guess it's all right. When?"

"When what?"

"When do we do it?"

"Well, I was thinking about that. I think we ought to wait a day or two. Make Lombro think that we're earning the money. I'll call him from time to time and tell him we're close. Like, we've almost found him but we aren't sure."

Another grin of near admiration on Stevie's face, aimed down into the beige coffee. Then it faded and Stevie said, "But what if, you know, the asshole decides to talk to the fucking cops, what if—"

"Excuse me, gentlemen." A shadow loomed over them. A large man, his gray hair close-cropped, muscular shoulders in a starched plaid shirt, gazed somberly at the men. He looked exactly like an undercover detective. Ralph Bales's doughy face burned and he felt the exact spot where his Colt rested on his hip. His hand eased toward it as he scanned the three or four dozen families surrounding them. His heart began to pound and it pounded faster when he saw Stevie Flom looking up at the man with a belligerent grin on his face.

Oh, man . . .

Grim-faced, the man said, "Like to ask you a question."

"Would you now?" Stevie tossed the words at the tall figure. "What'd that be?"

Don't do anything stupid, Stevie . . .

"I got my children over there." He nodded toward a nearby table. "Would you mind watching your language a bit? I don't know where you're from but we don't talk that way around here."

Stevie's grin vanished and his eyes flared. His hand disappeared under the table, where he undoubtedly had his .25.

Oh, Jesus, Lord . . .

Ralph Bales's face popped out in sweat. He leaned forward suddenly, reaching for Stevie's arm.

But the young man's hand emerged with his napkin. He wiped his mouth carefully and said, "I'm mighty sorry, mister. Been a hard day. Terrible trouble on the job."

"That's all right now. For myself, I don't care. It's the kids I was thinking of."

He turned away. To his back Stevie commanded, "Wait."

The man turned.

Stevie paused a moment, then said, "My friend, he'll apologize to you, too." Grinning, he looked at Ralph Bales, who held Stevie's eyes for a minute, then said to the gray-haired man, "Accept my apologies."

"Surely do."

The swing of the car door. The reflection of a streetlight hitting him in the face. The momentum of the case of beer as he tried to grab it. The heavy crash of glass on glass. The grimacing face of the half-bald guy, saying, "Fuck you." Bending down and looking in the car, seeing himself in the window of the car, the beer hemorrhaging at his feet . . . The Lincoln pulling away.

That's what Pellam told the detectives.

One thing he couldn't tell them was the one thing that could have gotten him sprung instantly and on the way to the meeting with Marty Weller and their potential partner – the description of the driver of the Lincoln.

How far away was the Sheraton? Pellam wondered. How long would it take to get there? Forty minutes, he seemed to recall. Not that it would matter at this point. The time was now nine-thirty.

He sat in a small room in the Maddox police department. Across an unsteady table were the two detectives. This tiny room, like the rest of the office, stank of age: old wood, Lysol, mold, sour paint. The walls were sickly green, and shaded incandescent bulbs hung down from the cloudy, grimy ceiling on black wires. In the main office of the station were a dozen desks. Only two of them were occupied, and only three others showed any signs that they were used.

The drive to police headquarters seemed to take forever. Pellam now decided he shouldn't have told them about his meeting; he was sure the cops had intentionally driven ten miles out of their way to take him to the station and make sure he'd be late.

When he'd been led in, cuffed and scowling, the four cops in the room looked up with eight resentful eyes. The Italian detective had crouched down in front of a cabinet, opened the doors and begun pulling things out, a Sears catalog, empty flowerpots, a shotgun in a plastic bag, stacks of memos. "Nope. Can't find it. Charlie, where's that Breathalyzer got to?"

"Dunno."

They had searched for a few minutes more, but it was a halfhearted exploration and they couldn't locate the machine. "We're going to have to get one from the Highway Patrol. Shouldn't take more'n an hour. You'll have to wait here till we do."

When they'd said that, the time had been 8:05.

"It is absolutely vital I get to my meeting," Pellam had growled.

"Well, when people get arrested they don't always get what they want."

"I. Am. Not. Drunk. Book me or release me."

This had prompted them to take Pellam into the tiny canister of a room where he now sat. They asked, as long as they had some time, what did he remember about the Gaudia hit. They told him he could make a phone call if he'd give them one fact – just one – about the man in the Lincoln.

"This is a setup."

"Well, whatever you want to call it, it's all completely legal," the WASP said indifferently. "So why don't you just put on your thinking cap?"

He gave them the story one more time and then said, "I want to see my lawyer."

"That's it? That's what you told us before."

"My lawyer," he said.

"You aren't being charged with anything. We can't charge you with anything until you take the Breathalyzer test. You just—"

"I want a lawyer."

"You just'll have to wait." The Italian cop was angry at Pellam's impatience.

The WASP cop looked like he had an idea. "Maybe as long as he's here, he could do that picture."

"I don't know," Pellam offered. "I'm probably too drunk."

"Ha. Give it a shot, why don't you?"

He tried to do an Identikit composite of the man who had knocked into him. As he spoke, he gazed blankly at the words on the Suspect Description form. *Hair, kinky, afro, fade, cornrows, caesar, processed, scar, tattoo words only, tattoo unknown type, limp, pimpled, pocked, harelip, left-handed, bushy eyebrows, muscular, stocking cap, cowboy hat, applejack, turban* . . .

No one was impressed with his composite drawing and the cops decided he was still being recalcitrant.

The *H* cop said, "You know, nobody's come forward. You're the only one who can help."

Pellam was trying to remember their names. Who was the *H* cop? *Hilbert, Hanson, Hearst?*

". . . we've done a tag check—"

"Tag?" Pellam asked.

The Italian cop, the *G* cop, said, "License plates on other cars in the vicinity that night."

"Oh. Your supervisor? I want to see him right now."

The WASP continued, ". . . and it came up zip. We've got no other witnesses."

Hellman, Harrison?

The *G* cop asked somberly if Pellam knew how many people were killed annually by drunk drivers. Pellam didn't know if he was supposed to answer or not.

Hagedorn! That was it. Now he just had the *G* cop to worry about. *Giovanni?*

Pellam said wearily, "Let me talk to my lawyer."

"You can't talk to a lawyer," the *G* cop said.

"I have a right. It's in the Constitution. Confront my accusers." Which Pellam regretted immediately. He sounded prissy and obnoxious – like the bald, spineless CIA director Tony Sloan had cast as the villain in his first movie. The cops looked at each other, then back to him. They seemed to be rolling their eyes, although their pupils didn't move from his face.

The *G* cop said, "That's only if you're the defendant."

"If I'm not a defendant then what am I doing here?"

"Not very much," the *G* detective said bitterly. "Not very much at all."

Pellam slammed his open palm on the desktop. It hit with a sound that surprised even him. The cops blinked but neither of them moved. "Are you going to arrest me for standing nearby a motor vehicle and having a sip of beer or not? If you can't find the killer . . ." Pellam felt his heart sprinting. "*You* can't find any leads, so you're blaming *me*."

"Hey—"

Through clenched teeth Pellam said, "You go to your boss and you say, 'It'd be open and shut, except there's this witness who hasn't got the balls to help us. He's a GFY.' Whatever the hell that is."

Hagedorn said, "Is somebody paying you off?"

The Italian cop said, "That's a crime, sir. A serious crime. And you'll do hard time for that."

Pellam knew about *good cop, bad cop* from some films he'd worked on. This was a variation: *bad cop, really bad cop*.

Another officer, a young uniform, stuck his head in the door. "Can't find that Breathalyzer anywhere. Sorry. And MHP don't have one to spare."

"Well, this is your lucky day, Pellam."

"I've spent three hours in this hellhole. That's not lucky."

"Well, sir, you could've been in our lockup all these three hours, which is a lot less pleasant than here."

Pellam walked past them into the main room. He asked the desk officer, "Was there a guy here? Tall, blond hair, mustache?"

"Yeah, but he left. Sorry."

"He left sorry," Pellam's voice rang out in a singsong.

"We had a little mix-up. My fault. I heard them boys talking about the Highway Patrol and, not seeing you, I thought they'd taken you there. I sent your friend to the troop HQ. It's over on I-70 a good piece. Forty, fifty miles or so." The voice added unemotionally, "Sorry about that."

Pellam closed his eyes and rubbed them. "Could you give me a ride back to my camper?"

"Afraid not, sir. Since you're not a suspect or a witness or anything that'd be against regulations."

"Well, could you call me a cab, at least?"

"Cab?" the officer laughed. He was joined by chuckles from other cops in the room. "The last time Maddox had a cab company was in, what was it, Larry?"

"Oh, I'd guess it must've been—"

"That's okay," Pellam said, "I'll walk."

"To your camper?" one cop called. "Say, that's a long walk."

Another said, "Couple miles, easy."

10

H e found a pay phone outside a closed deli and finally got the front desk.

Yessir, Mr Weller had waited in the lobby until nine, then left with another gentleman. They were going to dinner. Would this be Mr Pellam by any chance?

"Yes. Did he leave a message for me?"

Weller had. Pellam was to meet him at the Templeton Steak House at nine-thirty.

An hour and a half ago.

"Where is that?"

According to the young man's blithe directions, it was a half hour from Maddox.

"I'm calling from a pay phone. You wouldn't happen to have their number, would you?"

"Well, I do. Were you thinking of having the steak?"

"What?"

"I was wondering if you were going to eat there or if you

were going to meet Mr Weller. Because if you were going to meet Mr Weller, he was leaving the restaurant at ten-thirty. He had an eleven o'clock flight out of Lambert Field."

"He's checked out?"

"That's right. Believe he mentioned a trip to London."

Pellam sighed. "And the other gentleman? Mr Telorian."

"I believe he was flying to Los Angeles tonight. I should say, sir, Mr Weller was pretty anxious to see you. He asked a number of times at the desk if you'd called."

Pellam was staring at the number pad on the phone.

"Hello?" the pleasant desk clerk asked.

"Still here."

"Don't be too fast to pass up Templeton's. For my money, best T-bone in the county. You still want that number?"

Pellam declined.

He dug another quarter out of his pocket, made a call and sat down on the curb.

A half hour later the headlights of Stile's Taurus swept around a curve, and the car braked to a stop beside him. It was the first car he had seen on this road all night.

"What you're experiencing is called phantom pain."

"Like Ghostbusters," Donnie Buffett said.

The woman smiled.

Buffett shook his head as he laughed at his own tiny joke. Mostly, though, he was studying her. All right, she was a doctor *and* she was a woman. Well, Buffett knew better than to think it was weird that Dr Weiser, this famous SCI specialist, wasn't a man. But he could not get over what *kind* of woman she was: young, early thirties, a sleek, pretty face, short, punky auburn hair, a pug nose, a chin dimple. Fingernails painted glossy white. Lipstick red as a stop sign. Under a white lab coat was a silk blouse printed with red and green and blue geometric shapes. And – in addition to dark stockings and black ankle boots that had hooks, not eyes, for the laces she wore a black leather skirt. Almost a miniskirt.

When she'd entered the room, the woman had stuck her hand out, firmly shook his, and said, "Wendy Weiser. Your SCI doctor. You're the cop, right?"

Buffett had cocked his head, brushed off the surprise, and said, "Hope you don't mind if I don't stand up."

"There you go," she had said. "Today's men. No chivalry to speak of."

Then Weiser had plopped down in a chair and started right off talking, flashing her green eyes at him. She repeated a lot of what Dr Gould had said. She didn't use the word "nonambulatory," though her message was no better than his.

She explained the pain he had been feeling in his legs was common in SCI trauma and was called "phantom pain." That's when he had made the Ghostbusters comment.

Now, as Buffett studied her outfit, Weiser suddenly hopped up. She strode to the door and swung it closed, then returned. "There are rules, but . . . what's life without risks, huh?"

"I'm a pretty safe man to be in a closed room with, wouldn't you say? I mean, I can't exactly chase you around the room. When I get a wheelchair you better watch out."

"You and me, we'll race someday." She examined him with a curious smile. "Sounds like the gunman didn't get your sense of humor."

"Hey, Doctor." Buffett looked overtly grave. "If you're

gonna help me I'm gonna help you. I'm gonna teach you to speak cop."

"I say something wrong?"

"Shooter."

"I'm sorry?"

"Not gunman."

"Oh. You don't say gunman?"

"On TV they say gunman. We say shooter. Or perp."

"Perq?"

"*Perp*etrator. Perp."

"That's great." Her eyes widened. Buffett did not for a minute believe this enthusiasm but he appreciated it anyway. She added, "I'll have to use that sometime. Perp. Would a perp also rob somebody? Like a burglar?"

"Yup. Perp equals bad guy."

"So my ex-husband is a perp."

"Could be," Buffett said. "And, while I'm giving you a lesson. He doesn't shoot. He smokes them. Or dusts them. Or he lays the hammer on somebody. And if he kills them, he offs them or ices them or whacks or does them."

"You have to learn all this in cop school, huh?"

"It's more your postgraduate work."

"Officer . . ."

"Donnie."

"And I'm Wendy. Everybody calls me Wendy." She looked at him with mystified, amused eyes. "Donnie, I've got to say that most people aren't quite so chipper after they've been through what you have."

He waved his arm vaguely toward his feet, signifying his injury. "This goes with the job description. You're not willing to accept it you don't sign on in the first place. Doesn't mean I like it."

Could he really call her Wendy? She was a *doctor*. Then again, she was wearing earrings in the shape of tiny hamburgers.

Weiser opened her purse and took out a pack of cigarettes; a lighter was stuffed efficiently into the Cellophane wrapper of the pack. "You mind?"

"No."

She asked, "You want one?"

"No."

"Don't tell," Weiser said.

"I don't work vice." Buffett realized he hadn't shaved since he had been in the hospital. He guessed he looked like shit. Well, that was *her* problem. He didn't have to look at himself.

Weiser pulled the gray chair closer, inhaled deeply on the cigarette several times. She crossed her legs and bent down to stub out the cigarette on her boot heel. She dropped the butt in her pocket.

"Evidence," she said. She straightened up, put both feet on the floor.

"Doctor—"

"Ah . . ." She cocked an eyebrow.

"Wendy," he corrected. "It seemed so real."

She raised an eyebrow.

"The pain."

She stood up and opened the window, to air the room out, and returned to the chair. He felt the cold air on his arms and face. But he didn't feel it on his legs. She said, "It's both psychological and physiological. Amputees have the same sensation. It's real in the sense that pain is a subjective experience and what you're experiencing is just like any other pain. But it's phantom because you aren't feeling a pain response to stimuli at the nerve endings. Say, wasn't your wife going to be coming by?"

"She was. A while ago. She'll be back tomorrow." He tried to picture Penny Buffett and Wendy Weiser chatting at a barbecue or PBA picnic. It was impossible to imagine this scene.

Weiser nodded. "Well, next time. This is mostly a social visit, Donnie. We've done a lot of tests and we're going to do a lot more. I'll be talking to you more specifically about the results of those tests in the next couple days. What I'd like to do now is just talk with you about your injury in general."

He looked away. She shifted her chair casually so that she was closer to his line of vision. He glanced at her and he felt compelled to hold her gaze.

"I want to tell you what I'm going to do, as your doctor, and talk to you about what you're going to do for yourself."

"Fair enough."

She said, "First, I want to do something I don't do with all my patients: I'm going to tell you what's going to be going on in your mind over the next several months. This is sort of like – what's that they say on Wall Street? – insider information. Normally this is what we doctors keep in mind as we work with our patients but you seem like somebody who's got a good handle on himself. You look skeptical. Donnie, I've had SCI patients that won't even let me in the room for the first month after their trauma. I've had vases thrown at me. See this scar? It's from a dinner tray. I've had patients who don't seem to see me. They watch TV while I'm talking to them. It's as if I'm not even in the same room. They don't acknowledge me, they don't acknowledge their injury. You're in a different league from them."

"I can't ignore a woman in a leather skirt. It's in my genes or something."

"I think we're going to be a great team." She then grew serious. "There are several stages of recovery – I'm speaking of emotional recovery – in a trauma like you've experienced. The first is shock. It's numbness, emotional blockage. It's similar to what happens to the body with physical injury. Shock insulates the patient. That can last up to two or three weeks after the incident. I'm amazed but you seem to be out of this stage already. That kind of snappy recovery is rare. I'd guess you're already in phase two, which is realization of what's happened. You'll start feeling anxiety, panic, fear. A real bummer."

"Bummer."

"My daughter's language."

"You have a daughter?"

"Twelve."

"Don't believe it."

She deflected this with a polite smile. "What you're going to experience is that you're not real *present*. We say that you'll be, quote, unavailable psychologically."

"And what would your daughter call it?"

Weiser considered. "'Zoned out,' probably. A defense mechanism because you're going to start to feel awful. But with you, I have every reason to believe that it'll be short-lived."

She pronounced it with a long *i*. *Short-liiived*. That sounded weird so he figured it was probably right. He also guessed that between the punk earrings was a very, very smart brain.

"So that was the second phase," he said. "What's the third quarter going to be like?"

"What we call 'defensive retreat.' You're going to believe that you can cure yourself. Or that you've come to accept your injury and it doesn't bother you. You'll miss therapy sessions, you'll do everything you can to avoid thinking about the accident. Oh, by the way, you'll probably become an insufferable son of a bitch. You'll want to blame somebody for what's happened. You'll have a lot of anger in you."

"Kid I knew got hurt once, bad. We was diving off the docks, and this kid from the neighborhood—"

"Which is?"

"Alton."

"No kidding," Dr Weiser said, "I'm from Wood River."

"Ha, Land of Lincolners in the Show Me state." Buffett snorted.

"When I was married – he was a professor at Wash U – we lived in Clayton. God, I was glad to get out of there, move back to the country . . . You were telling me about this friend of yours?"

"Just a kid. He dived in the water . . ." Buffett wondered if *dived* was the right word. *Dove?* He wished he'd said *jumped*. ". . . and you know how high some of those piers are. He hit a board he didn't see. We got him out right away so he didn't drown but what happened was he went blind. He hit the back of his head or something. He tried to beat me up. He said I should've seen the board. He accused another kid of pushing the board under him. Finally he moved away. He never came back or called."

He wondered what the point to the story was. He looked for

something concluding – something to tie it into what she was saying – and fell silent.

Weiser said, "We're used to behavior like that. It's part of recovery. You may get some of it right back from me. I grew up with three brothers. I've got kind of a short fuse myself sometimes." She retrieved her cigarette from her pocket and broke away the crushed part. She lit it again and drew three times then went through the extinguishing routine once again. "The fourth phase is where we get the work done. You're going to come to understand what's happened. The defenses – whether it's anger or denial or rationalization – will crumble and you'll confront it."

"I never did understand that word. *Confront*. Like *deal with*. Those aren't words that mean a lot to me."

"You're not there yet so you can't expect them to. You'll be in heavy-duty physical therapy throughout this phase. Finally . . . You're looking skeptical again. Are you listening? The final phase is the coping phase. In effect, you accept what's happened and you reorganize your life around the way you are."

Buffett laughed again. "Yeah, yeah, I'll be able to play the violin after the operation."

Weiser's smile faded and she leaned forward. For an instant he was wholly unnerved by the eye contact but was compelled to return her gaze. He felt electricity between them. His scalp bristled and his heart suddenly pounded like a snare drum.

He felt a twitch of pain. Well, phantom pain. When he spoke, it was not his own voice that he heard but one that was lower and more mature and calmer. "Doctor, I don't want you to think I've got a swollen head or anything but I'm a survivor. I don't lose. At anything. Ever. Getting into the police academy, getting onto the varsity basketball team, yeah, even at five ten. Everything I've ever set my mind to do, I've done. Well, what happened to me is crap, sure. But I'm alive. I got friends. I got family." His right hand curled into a fist. "And I'm going to get through this."

Weiser sat back, her pine green eyes neither cautious nor inspirational, but immensely pleased. It seemed as if by delivering his monolog he'd passed a test of some sort. "It's going to be a real pleasure working with you, Donnie."

They shook hands and made an appointment for their next session.

When the door closed, Donnie Buffett exhaled slowly and said a short, silent prayer of thanks. If Weiser had turned inches to the right she would've seen the hypodermic syringe that a harried orderly had accidentally left on the bedside table just before the doctor entered the room – the syringe that had been virtually the only thing in Buffett's thoughts during the doctor's entire visit. He gripped the head of the bed with his large hands and tightened his ample biceps. He moved up one inch. Sweat broke out. Another huge flex, another inch. He felt as if he were dragging the weight of ten men with him. He reached for the syringe.

No, not yet. Six inches to go.

He inhaled deeply and gripped the bed once more. Another inch, then another.

He kept at it, two more inches, closer and closer. A half inch. He paused for a minute, wiping the slick sweat from his eyes and feeling his heart slam fiercely from the immense effort. Donnie Buffett figured this exertion was good. It was perfect. Because when he injected the air into his vein, the course of his racing blood would speed the bubble straight to his heart and jam it stopped like a swollen piston, sending his whole body to join his legs in a sleep that was cold and deep and forever.

"Howdy." John Pellam stepped into the hospital room.

He startled the cop, who dropped something on the floor.

"Hell," Buffett snapped. "You scared me."

"Sorry." Pellam walked past the flowers, looking around. Dozens of bouquets, wreaths, plants. Pellam wondered if the nurses got irritated, having to water all this foliage.

A pale, pretty face appeared in the doorway. Pellam motioned her in. "This is Nina. Donnie Buffett."

She said hello.

"How you doing?" came Buffett's muffled voice. He was contorted sideways, bending down trying to pick up something from the floor, struggling. His face was red and slick with sweat.

"You okay?" Pellam walked around the bed. Buffett was reaching for a pen he had dropped . . . No, not a pen, a syringe.

"Here, I'll get it." Pellam bent down, retrieved the needle, and stepped over to a plastic box that said *Used Syringe Disposal Only*.

"No!" Buffett shouted.

Pellam paused, and he and Nina looked at the cop curiously.

"I've got to give myself a shot."

"You?" she asked. "Don't the nurses do that?"

Buffett stared at the needle for several seconds. He cleared his throat. "I'm, you know, a diabetic. I can give them to myself."

Pellam shrugged. "It was on the floor. I'll ask the nurse

for a clean one." He dropped it in the disposal box. "I don't mind."

Buffett's eyes clung to the disposal box, looking heartsick. Pellam reached for the nurse call button. Buffett barked, "I'll do it myself later."

"No trouble."

Buffett snatched the button away from him. "I said I'd do it myself."

A difficult silence arose. Nina and Pellam simultaneously asked him how he was feeling, and he answered, "Fine. I'm fine." More silence. Nina turned to the flowers, examined them and refilled several of the vases with water. Buffett seemed angered by this but he said nothing and she didn't seem to notice that he was out of sorts.

Pellam studied Buffett for a moment and decided he looked pretty good, all things considered. Apart from the red face and sweat, he seemed to be a healthy man lying in bed. The only evidence of injury: He was dressed in a white, blouselike gown speckled with small, pale blue dots.

"Something you wanted?" Buffett asked.

Pellam did not know how to respond. He wasn't expecting this constant level of hostility. He said the first thing that came into his mind. "You need anything?"

"No. I'm doing fine." When the silence filled the room again Buffett relented and made conversation. "I get kind of bored, you know. I got TV." He motioned broadly at the old set as if they couldn't spot it themselves.

Pellam said, "I guess I came by, one of the reasons, I was a little hotheaded the other day."

Buffett was being forced to apologize and he didn't want

to. He watched a silent CNN news broadcast for a moment. Tankers unloading in some foreign port. Pellam was just starting to wonder if the cop would clam up and that would be that. He was glancing at Nina when Buffett said, "I started it. You were just, you know, reacting. All this . . . It's got me kind of shook up."

"I read in this magazine one time," Nina said. "*Glamour*. No, *Mademoiselle*, I think. That if you have a serious accident, it's like you're a whole different person for at least six months afterwards." She abruptly stopped speaking, perhaps worried that Buffett would think he was doomed to a half year of mental anguish.

But Buffett was laughing. "Well, it's got me a shitload of flowers. You want any, go right ahead."

Nina shook her head. "Oh, I couldn't, no."

Buffett glanced at Pellam. "And the mayor came by to visit me. Which isn't as exciting as, say, the mayor of L.A., since our guy also has the Buick dealership out on 104. He's that kind of mayor, you know." There was a manic edge to Buffett's voice. Maybe he was being cynical, maybe he was really impressed that the mayor had come to visit him. Pellam couldn't tell. Buffett broke the silence that followed this by saying, "It's just so damn boring. TV sucks, you know that?"

"I don't own one," Pellam said with more enthusiasm than he intended. "I've got a monitor, but it doesn't receive. It's just hooked up to a VCR."

Buffett sighed and began clicking the gray box of the remote control through a series of stations. An old movie came on. He shut the set off. "I should probably get some sleep. I'm still in shock. No, really. Spinal shock, it's called. Not like, ha, normal shock. Sleeping's a good thing."

The script in Pellam's mind now called for the cop to ask what he had come here to ask: Could Buffett please call up his detective buddies and ask them to stop ruining his life.

But he couldn't ask. Pellam wondered what stopped him. He believed it was not the fact that Pellam was going to leave in a moment with a pretty woman beside him and go back to his job. Nor was it Buffett's face, which no longer looked so healthy as Pellam had thought – mouth hanging loose, eyes darting, filled with a fear that he perhaps thought he was concealing.

No, what stopped Pellam was simply that he stood and Buffett lay.

As simple as that.

"We better be going," Pellam said. "Just wanted to stop by."

"Yeah." Buffett nodded. "Good seeing you."

"What do you read?" Pellam asked. "I'll bring you a magazine next time I stop by."

"I don't read. I don't like to read." The mystery that Pellam had brought on the first visit sat prominently unopened under the bedside table.

"You got any hobbies?"

"Yeah, I got hobbies."

"What?"

Buffett looked from the square of the TV screen to the box where Pellam had pitched the hypodermic needle. "Basketball, softball, jogging, and hockey. Those're my hobbies."

*   *   *

At the main desk of the hospital, downstairs, Pellam remembered that he had met Nina when she was visiting her mother. He now asked if she wanted to see the woman.

She shook her head. "I visited her this morning. Twice a day is a little much. She can be a dear, but . . ." They stepped outside. The day had grown overcast and chill. She asked, "Your parents both alive?"

"Just my mother. She lives in upstate New York. I don't see her that often. We run out of things to talk about after three days."

Nina took a scarf from her pocket, a long one covered with blotches of brilliant green and yellow. She began to tie it around her neck. He watched the flimsy cloth cover the pale skin at her throat.

She said, "I'm really enjoying that job you got me. Everybody's really nice."

"Making movies is fun at a certain level. You get much higher up than location work or makeup and it's a pain in the ass."

"The only yucky part is special effects. All that fake blood and those gunshot wounds." She closed her eyes and shivered. "Why does Mr Sloan make such violent movies?"

"Because many, many people pay money to watch them."

"Why," she asked, "are you looking around so much?"

"Am I?"

"Yeah. It's like you think somebody's following you."

"Naw. Always working. Looking for locations. In fact, that's where we're going right now. Find a big field. I need the help of a local."

"I'm not a local, remember. I'm from Cranston."

"You're more local than I am."

"Is that the reason you want me to come along?" A faint smile on her frosted pink lips.

"Well, scouting isn't as easy as it looks. I sense you're a natural at it."

"Me?"

"I need a big field next to the river. And a road running through it. How would *you* go about finding one?"

"Well, I don't know. I guess I'd just drive along a road beside the river until I found a field."

"See what I mean. You're a born location scout."

They both laughed.

"All right. But I have to be back at seven. I've got a call then. See, I can talk movie. *Call.* Oh, I didn't want to ask on the set but what's the difference between a gaffer and a grip?"

"The most-asked question in the movie business. Gaffer's an electrician and lighting guy. Grips are workmen who do rigging and other nonelectrical work."

They approached her car.

"Another question."

Pellam preempted her. "The best boy is the key grip's first assistant."

"No," Nina said, tossing him the keys. "I was going to ask if you knew any casting couch stories."

Peter Crimmins was a member of the Ukrainian Social Club in St Louis.

He could easily have afforded to join the elite Metropolitan Club or, although he was a bar-sinister Christian, the Covington Hills Country Club. Yet this was the only social organization he belonged to. The club was in a shabby, two-story building, greasy-windowed and grimy, nestled between vacant lots filled with saplings strangled by kudzu. The inside, smelling of onions and cigarette smoke and mold, was one large room, filled with broken tables and chipped chairs. The club seemed locked in a time warp dating to the year it had opened – 1954.

This afternoon Crimmins was sitting at a table with Joshua, his driver and security chief. They drank tea that had been brewed in a cheap samovar. There were four or five other men in the club who would have liked to sit with Crimmins but who tended not to when Joshua was with him. The bodyguard's presence made them uncomfortable. They, of course, knew all about Crimmins. They read the *Post-Dispatch* as well as the *Ukranian Daily News*, which reported, respectively, on his criminal activities and on his social, ethnic, and professional endeavors. The latter did not interest them in the least; any fool can give away money. But a successful criminal is hot stuff. So they sat around him, basking in his dangerous presence. Crimmins gave them status. John Gotti had gone to his social club in Little Italy in New York; Peter Crimmins went here. They believed the nearby streets were safer because of him.

Crimmins and Joshua had been drinking tea for ten minutes when a broad-shouldered man wearing a blue denim jacket and jeans entered. His shirt was dirty. He was squat, though he moved with a certain elegance. Crimmins did not approve of the common clothes, but this sort of man might be a foreman or carpenter in addition to being what Crimmins was now hiring him for.

Joshua said, "Tom Stettle. Mr Crimmins."

"How do you do, sir." Stettle's eyes swung one way then the other, settling on Crimmins's mole of an eye for a moment.

"Stettle, is it?"

"Yeah," the voice said. "Yessir."

"Sit down."

He did. The Samsonite folding chair creaked under his weight. Crimmins let the silence run up for a moment. Rather than feeling uncomfortable, Stettle grew more at ease and gazed back at Crimmins pleasantly.

Finally Crimmins said, "Joshua talked to you?"

"Yessir."

This was not the safest way, meeting Stettle face-to-face. The identification issue later, if it all went sour, but Crimmins liked to see the people who worked for him. You could have a better conversation with someone when you knew what he looked like. You could pick up on his mannerisms, match them to his words. That helped you decide if he was telling the truth, if he was dependable, how much he could be bought for.

"You've been following him? Pellam?"

Stettle nodded.

"The police have been, too, I know. Have you seen anyone else? Anyone from Peterson's office?"

"Some. Off and on. It's funny. It's like, hey, we got the budget for it today but not tomorrow. They're not there more than they're there."

Crimmins had an urge to remind the man that he was making fifteen thousand dollars for this job. But he said nothing. Another of his basic rules, like providing for the family, was: Don't jerk leashes until you need to.

"Stick with him."

"This being the country, pretty much, it's harder, you know what I'm saying? In the city, with a lot of people around, there are more ways to get away, like cabs and subways. You can set up things a lot faster." The measured and respectful tone of Stettle's reply made Crimmins feel comfortable. He was pleased that Stettle was giving a frank appraisal. Crimmins himself would have guessed it was easier to do this sort of thing in the country.

"All right. Keep at it. Joshua knows where to get in touch with you?"

Both men nodded.

"Thanks for stopping by. You want some tea? Some pastry?"

"No, sir."

Stettle left the club, glancing around him with studious eyes. Crimmins supposed he was surveying the shoddy paneling job and thinking he could do better.

Crimmins said to Joshua, "Is he good with it?"

"With what?"

Crimmins forgot that some people did not think as quickly as he did. "A gun."

"That's not really the question. All's I know is he's got one and he doesn't mind using it. Maddox's got a mandatory sentencing thing and a lot of guys have a problem with that. He doesn't."

Crimmins rose and poured both Joshua and himself two more glasses of tea.

11

"*S'il vous plaît, est-ce que vous avez un* . . . guest, *Monsieur Weller?*"

The crackling of the eight thousand miles of cables and airwaves filled the phone.

"*Non, monsieur.*"

"Well, *est-ce qu'il a une réservation?*"

The crash behind Pellam nearly made him drop the cellular phone. He spun around. He saw the fist knock on the camper door again. Pellam leaned forward and looked outside with a sinking heart. *Them.* For some reason he could remember the names of the FBI agents more easily than he could those of the Italian cop and the WASP cop. Bracken and Monroe.

"Just a minute!" he called. "I'm on the phone." More knocking. "Just a minute. I'm on the *phone* to Paris. *Répétez? S'il vous plaît* . . . He's not? Okay. I mean, *merci.*"

Damn.

Marty Weller had left London six hours ago, supposedly

bound for Paris. He was not, however, at the Plaza Athenee – where he always stayed (or where he *told* everyone he stayed) – and Pellam had no idea where he might be. Pellam was trying to make nice for the missed appointment with Weller and Telorian.

He dropped the phone in its cradle and opened the door. He nodded solemnly but did not invite them in.

"How you doing, sir?" Monroe said.

Silence.

Bracken, looking much less scruffy today, asked, "Mr Pellam, you mind if we come in?"

"I think I would mind that, yes."

"It won't take very long."

Pellam asked, "I really don't—"

"We'd just like to ask you a few more questions. Our discussion—"

"Discussion?"

"—the other day wasn't very productive."

"Last night I told the cops in Maddox exactly what happened. For the second time. Maybe the third. Don't you people talk to each other?"

Monroe remained as pleasant and persistent as a door-to-door salesman. "We apologize for the other day. We've been under incredible pressure. You know how it is."

Pellam waited a few seconds and said, "Come in."

Inside, both agents sat on chairs, scooting forward to keep their posture perfect. The cuffs of their light-colored slacks were hiked high above their ankles. It was funny, Pellam thought – they didn't have the frisky presence of the city cops. There was something anonymous about them.

They complimented him on the tidiness of the camper and Bracken said enviously he hoped to get a Winnebago himself one day. Drive up to Minnesota for muskie and pike.

So far the game was *good cop, good cop.*

"The fact is Maddox hasn't been cooperating with us. They don't much care for federal officers."

Wonder why.

"We'd really appreciate it if you could tell us whatever you can remember. You've got to understand, Mr Pellam, Mr Gaudia's death means that two years of work could be in jeopardy."

Pellam wanted to reward them for being polite. He told them the facts one more time. In as much detail as he could remember. The beer, the Lincoln, the guy who bumped into him, bending down and looking through the window, the car pulling away, the cop. Pellam was getting pretty good at telling the story by this time.

The agents were unemotional. No eyes were rolled, much less lapels grabbed and windows broken. They just nodded and did not complain. And they didn't call him a GFY either. They just asked questions.

Finally Pellam realized that they had been here for an hour. He was growing bored. He felt like a hooked pike. He almost mentioned this to Bracken the fisherman.

"Tell us again . . . just one more time. Promise, just one."

"Okay. Once more." Pellam recited the story.

Monroe wrote it down. Pellam wondered what they were getting paid and how much tax money was being spent to record an incident of car window glare.

Then they began to ask questions that seemed to have nothing to do with the killing. Why was he going to get so much beer? Tell them about this poker game, would he? Did he know who Vincent Gaudia was? Had he ever seen the policeman before?

"No."

"Was it true that you gave something to the policeman just before the shooting?"

"Well," Pellam said, "I did."

"You seemed surprised just then. Why were you surprised?"

"When I gave him the bag?"

"No. Just now. When we mentioned it."

"Well, I didn't think anybody knew I gave him anything." Their eyebrows perked. "And what was it?"

"You think it was a bribe?"

"We'd just like to know what it was."

"It was a doughnut."

"A doughnut?"

"Whole wheat," Pellam offered. "It seemed healthier."

"Yessir."

More questions, another half hour passed.

"Did the driver," Bracken asked, "have a cup caddy?"

"Are you serious?" Pellam asked. He looked at his watch.

Finally they stood up, in unison, as if his answer to their question ("Did you know Vince Gaudia before he was killed?" "No.") was the exit cue.

He walked them to the door. They thanked him for his time then Bracken turned to him and said, "You weren't thinking of leaving town soon, were you, sir?"

There was something in the tone. He was not a bad cop yet but he was no longer a good cop either. "I'm staying until the film's finished. But—"

"How long will that be?"

"A week, tops."

"Well, you should know – we have an intelligence report that Peter Crimmins – the main suspect in the Gaudia killing – has been speaking to associates out of state. Chicago, we think."

Pellam didn't know what to make of this news bite.

"That often happens," Bracken continued, "when a mob boss is going to hire some muscle. They don't like to use anybody local."

"Oh."

"I just say that so you'll know to be careful."

"Right. Well, I appreciate you telling me that."

As they walked out the door, Monroe thanked him again and added, "You know, sir, we have men at all the local airports."

"All the airports?"

"Amtrak, too."

And they left him to wonder if that meant they'd be looking for hit men or that Pellam himself should book a seat on Greyhound if he wanted to escape the long tentacle of the law.

The nurse noticed his bloody thumbnail.

"What?" she asked. "Whatsat?"

She was Filipino, short and broad. She had kind eyes but the wispy mustache and broad purple lips made her face look dirty, which in turn gave her an impression of cruelty or, at best, indifference.

The nurse pulled two clear plastic gloves off a roll. She put them on and lifted his hand, studying the red stain distastefully.

"I don't have AIDS," he said miserably.

She held his hand in a solid grip and twisted it as she examined the digit. God, she was strong. He detected a meaty smell coming from her.

"Where you do it?"

"What do you mean?"

"Where you stick yourself?"

Abruptly she yanked the sheet and blanket off of him and began with his midthigh, probing her way up, turning him, pushing his numb legs. Buffett thought of dough. Bread dough, kneading it. This made him want to cry.

"I'm all right. Could you just leave me alone, please?"

"You make it worse. You people make it worse."

Fingers he could not feel were searching along his skin. He closed his eyes. He made it a test – even now, in his humiliation and anguish, he tried to sense the fingers. He thought he could tell where she was probing but when he opened his eyes, her hands were not near where he had imagined her touch. He couldn't feel a thing . . .

Then she saw the tissue, stuffed in his boxer shorts. She lifted it out, the wadded Kleenex, blotched with dark blood. Buffett's face burned. Sweat broke out on his face.

The nurse's cruel or indifferent mouth tightened. She dropped the Kleenex into the wastebasket and bent and spread apart his pubic hair. She studied the small gash next to his penis. It wasn't long or deep but it had bled a lot. The hair was matted and there was a red stain on the catheter.

The nurse sighed then took short, shiny scissors and trimmed the thick hair back. She washed the cut and put gauze over it, then taped the gauze to the spot with white adhesive tape. She pulled the gloves off and threw them out.

"I'm sorry," he said. "I just . . ."

Her dark lids lowered knowingly. "You wanted to see if you could feel something." Her tongue clicked. "People like you . . . You make it worse. You make everybody's job worse."

Buffett watched her go. His eyes then slipped to the medical waste box, where his precious syringe had been. He looked up at the blank TV screen, hands in his lifeless lap, and stared at the ceiling, waiting for tears that never came. Finally he reached up and in fury began tugging at a jump rope, which was hung over a traction bar above his bed. After he had spent the entire morning – 7:00 A.M. to noon – having tests done Buffett had asked an orderly to rig a rope over the bar so he could work on his arms. He would grip the handles hard, pulling against himself, first letting the right arm be the weak one, then the left. The orderly watched him with approval. "Man, I ain't gonna arm-wrestle you."

Buffett now began the workout again. He was counting down from sixty. When he exercised, he always counted down, rather than up, because it was harder to quit if your goal was to reach zero.

Fifty-eight, fifty-seven, fifty-six . . .

If you *did* quit before you got to your goal, that was the worst. Something terrible would happen.

Like, for instance, the Terror would get you.

Forty-seven, forty-six, forty-five . . .

Sweating.

Pull, pull, pull.

On thirty-three Wendy Weiser strolled into the room.

"Hey, Donnie."

"Yo, Doctor."

"How you feeling today?"

"Nifty." Buffett kept a nifty smile on his face.

Phantom pain, phantom smile. Fair enough, huh?

She pulled up the chair in that way of hers and dropped into it, like she was sitting on her boyfriend's lap. He thought of it as charming. He was not quite sure if that word fit or how someone can sit charmingly but that's what he thought. He had been here two or three days now and he'd had five dreams about her already. Sometimes, when he was awake, he fantasized about her, he thought about the way she sat down, the way she kept her legs spread slightly when she sat, the way she slouched, which hid the shape of her breasts, the way her panty hose would rustle, the lab coat would fall . . . He did not let the fantasies get beyond that point.

Dr Weiser was the only thing that troubled him about killing himself. He hoped she wouldn't be the one to find his body.

"You want something to drink?"

"Scotch. Glenfiddich. Aged twelve years. Neat."

Snappy Donnie, snappy jokes.

"OJ?"

"I'll pass."

She opened his chart. "I see we've got you lined up for more tests over the next couple days. There still isn't much to report. Spinal shock is slowly subsiding."

Weiser then did some poking and probing of her own and went through the same neuro exams that Gould had done a few days before. When he touched his nose she said, "Good," the same way Gould had, and though he wished her version meant something more than his, it clearly didn't. She made a notation on his chart, sat back then lit a cigarette.

"You cut yourself," she said.

He nodded, avoiding her eyes. He pushed a dangling handle of the jump rope out of the way.

"I . . ." His words stopped.

"I know how anxious you are to find out about your recovery," she said kindly. "But until the shock subsides, all you can do is hurt yourself doing something like that. You could get a bad infection. Hospitals are filthy. They're full of bacteria."

"Sepsis," Donnie whispered desperately.

"Sepsis." She studied him for a moment then said, "You want to know about sex."

"I want to . . ." He nodded, then confessed, "I wanted to see if I could feel anything. Down there."

She told him it was too early to know much. But she agreed to tell him a few things. Weiser added, "I don't have much time now. I'm going away for a couple days."

His heart choked. She was leaving him.

The Terror at least was pleased at this news and pawed Buffett mercilessly as he sweated and clung to the gingham jump rope.

"Where you going?" he asked, to take his mind off the Terror's maul.

"I have a place at Lake of the Ozarks."

"You married?"

"I'm divorced."

He remembered she had mentioned that.

Weiser added, "I have a boyfriend."

"I go down there some. Horses. A lot of horses, I remember . . . And trees." A vague memory came to him, then vanished.

"Unfortunately, Donnie, there are no short answers to the sexual aspects of SCI."

"'Aspect' . . . You doctors use funny words." For an instant his facade cracked. She paused as she noticed the blip of anger in his face. His smile returned.

"You worry about it a lot?"

"What the hell else is there to do?" He grinned. "I stare at Vanna White's tits all day long."

Weiser laughed. "We know from the location and nature of the trauma that you won't be able to walk again, Donnie. At least not with the state of the technology now. But sexual dysfunction is still an open question in this stage of your recovery."

Dis function, dat function . . .

Buffett was hugely disappointed in her. She was bullshitting him. Partnership? A good team? Crap.

"Even in the worst case there's a lot we can do."

As she talked his thoughts wandered. Down at her summer place, how often would she fuck her boyfriend? Would she tell him about Buffett? Would she lie underneath him and whisper to him that she had spent the morning talking about pricks and come to a eunuch? Would that make her boyfriend hump her harder?

". . . *two concerns. The act of intercourse. And second, siring children . . . Now, a man . . .*"

She probably made love to her boyfriend four, five times a week. She probably had shuddering orgasms, she probably took him into her mouth . . .

". . . *two types of erections. Reflexogenic and psychogenic. Reflexogenic are caused by some stimuli to the genitals, the penis, of course, primarily, but also to the prostate or bladder. You don't need your brain to participate in order to have this kind of erection.*"

Ping. Sweat sprang to Buffett's skin.

The Terror was having a ball.

Buffett's armpits itched. He felt sweat appearing where it never had before – his cheek, his ears, the backs of his hands. Jesus God Almighty, his wrists were sweating! As if the moisture were crawling out of his flawed body, escaping.

"You wake up in the morning with an erection, that's reflexogenic. Psychogenic is the type of erection in response to fantasies, visual stimuli – thoughts that turn us on."

Weiser paused to ask, "Are you okay?"

"Hot in here."

She stood up and opened the window. She turned her back to him, and the silk skirt was taut against her butt. He saw the outline of her panties.

Donnie swallowed.

She sat down again. Lit a cigarette, drew on it deeply three times, then crushed it out.

"I'll give you an exam. We'll find out if your lesion is upper-motor neuron or lower-motor neuron. If it's upper, you'll be able to have reflexogenic erections . . ."

What is she talking about?

"If it's lower-motor neuron, that will mean your sexual activity will be what we call areflexic . . ."

"Psychogenic?" Buffett tried to concentrate. He hated words like that, big words, Doctor words. The Terror ate them up. They gave the Terror strength – ha, a hard-on! It stirred and stepped over his pain, the phantom pain, the betraying pain, and slid into his gut. Then the Terror moved through his chest. Buffett clenched his teeth and tightened his stomach muscles to keep it from oozing into his heart, where he knew it would kill him.

He kept his eyes locked on to hers and he pulled at the jump rope hard. Arm wrestling with the Terror.

"There are four possibilities. You could be complete or incomplete reflex, or complete or incomplete areflex. The most severe is complete areflex – that means no reflex activity and no brain involvement."

Here is Donnie Buffett, six feet away from a beautiful woman, with sparkling green eyes, talking to him about hard dicks . . . He glances down at the small, motionless bump at his groin and feels the Terror dig an inch closer to his heart.

"Usually, in the case of gunshots, the lesion isn't complete. In the case of areflexic patients with incomplete lesions, three-fourths of them have intercourse, and more than half have ejaculations and orgasms."

But I'm not going to be one of them. A girl in a tight leather skirt talks to me about coming and I can't feel a thing . . .

"It may not be necessary – it probably won't be – but you might want to consider a prosthetic."

Buffett thought that meant artificial leg.

". . . There are a couple different kinds of penile implants."

The Terror was really up for this, carousing, squirming, swimming on its fucking back. The sweat poured. Buffett swallowed.

"Now, on the question of siring children, spinal injury generally results in a decreased sperm count, but many people without SCI have problems conceiving, and there are a number of techniques . . ."

A son? What about a son?

And, that was it – bang, the Terror got him.

Donnie Buffett shook like an antelope in a lion's jaws.

Her eyes were narrowing a little, squinting, as he wiped the sweat off his face. "Donnie—"

He looked at her and swallowed. "I'm sorry." He tapped his shoulder. "I've still got a hell of a lot of pain. You know, where I got shot here. It's really a bitch sometimes."

"Do you want something for it?"

"No, I just get these twinges. Makes me sweat like a pig. Keep going." A smile. "Please."

He could say that only because he was dead. The Terror's fangs had shredded his heart. He was gone. He was as polite as a corpse at the wake.

She continued for a few minutes then offered some conclusion. Something cheerful, something snappy. He nodded and had no idea what she had said. She said she was sorry she had to leave. They'd talk again soon. He thanked her. Looked her right in the eye and said, "This's been real, you know, reassuring. I appreciate it." They shook hands. Buffett told her to have a nice weekend.

When she was gone he picked up the phone and called Bob Gianno at the Maddox police station. They talked about nothing for a while and when Buffett could wait no longer he asked the detective for a phone number. There was silence for a moment and then Buffett heard the numbers. He memorized them. He asked Gianno, "This is one of those cellular phones, right?"

"Yeah, it's in his Winnebago."

"And I just call it like a regular number?"

"That's all you have to do."

------◆◆◆------

Through his closed eyes, Donnie Buffett was aware of a shadow over him. He hoped it was not Penny.

He particularly hoped it wasn't her parents.

The nurse changing the urine bag would have been okay.

The nurse changing the Foley's wouldn't have been.

He was pleased to see that it was John Pellam.

Buffett said, "Hey, chief, it's you."

Pellam nodded and walked into the room.

"You got more flowers. Looks like a nursery."

"Yeah. I don't like flowers so much, you know. She said she didn't want them, that girl of yours. But you ought to take some to her. What's her name? Tell her you bought 'em."

"I'm glad you called. I was going to stop by."

Buffett waved to the chair. "Why? You in the mood for more abuse?"

Pellam laughed.

"I was feeling bad, you know. I was a real shit."

"No problem," Pellam said.

"I kind of go crazy. I didn't—"

"I understand. You doing okay?"

Buffett nodded, and laughed. "I'm fine. I was, I think the doctor called it, 'resisting.' I was resisting what happened to me. If you go with it you feel better."

"Good."

"A little therapy. I'll get a wheelchair. There're a lot of laws. Wheelchair access. Go to the Cardinals games, they gotta have ramps. You can get practically anywhere."

"I saw they have sports for . . . you know." Pellam was hesitating, maybe not sure whether to say "paraplegics" or "handicapped." What he said was, "Wheelchair sports. I saw it on the ESPN."

"Yeah, basketball. Wheelchair basketball. And some guys do the marathon. I guess you can coast downhill. Man," he said, smiling, "that's me – doing a marathon sitting on my ass. Hey, you want something to eat?"

"Thanks a ton. Hospital food?"

"Naw, I got some good stuff here. Ruffles, dip. Cookies."

Pellam shook his head. Buffett ate half a cookie and stared into the Cellophane bag for a moment. He rolled the top of the bag tight. Set it on a tray.

Pellam did a tour of the greenhouse by the window. He said, "So how long you been on the force?"

"Close to seven years."

"You say that? Force?"

"Sure, you can say that."

"And you walked a beat, like in the old days?"

"Some neighborhoods aren't so good anymore. Maddox's really gone to the dogs. So you make movies?"

"Not me. I just find locations."

"How'd you get into that?"

"Fell into it, I guess. I like to travel."

"You meet any Hollywood honeys? You must, huh?"

"I stay clear of the Coast. Not my scene, really."

"Then why're you in movies?"

"Why're you a cop?"

Buffett shrugged.

"Oh, I forgot." Pellam lifted the stained bag he carried. "It's beer. Can you drink it?"

"Hell, yes, I can drink it."

Pellam sat down on the sturdy gray chair. They opened two cans and drank them down. "You know," Buffett said, "all these guys I work with? Mean sons of bitches some of them, it's like they turn into pussies when they come to see me. They bring me flowers. They bring me magazines. Nobody's brought me any beer. A lot of guys don't come. I think they're nervous or something about seeing me, about what they're going to say."

Pellam stood up and slipped two fresh cans in the water pitcher next to the bed. He filled it with cold water. The lid did not close completely. "If you got a spacey nurse, maybe you can get away with it."

"'Preciate it, chief."

Pellam sipped his beer. He waited a moment, then said, "I guess I wanted to say this last time, but, well, you looked pretty upset and I held off."

"Say what?"

"I'm really getting hassled. Your buddies – and the FBI now – they're really on my case. They've been on the set and it's messing up the film. I'm worried about my job. I can't afford that right now."

Buffett shrugged. "If you didn't see anything, you didn't see anything."

"Yeah, but *they* don't feel that way and they're all over the place. The FBI's talking about looking into the company's tax returns and corporate documents." Pellam made a helpless gesture with his hands.

"Oh, the feds're pricks from the git-go," Buffett said as if explaining something as basic as gravity. Then he nodded. "Ron Peterson – he's the U.S. Attorney – he's a maniac." He explained about Gaudia and Crimmins and the *60 Minutes* program. "Peterson's going to get Crimmins and nothing in this world is going to stop him."

Pellam continued, "I want to help. I don't want to be a GFY but—"

This brought a spark to Buffett's eyes. He started to laugh.

"What's so funny?" Pellam was irritated.

"Somebody called you a GFY?"

"Your friends. The detectives."

"Gianno and Hagedorn." Buffett laughed again. "Nobody told you what that means?"

"They told me it meant a reluctant witness."

"Pellam, believe half of what cops tell you. It means, go fuck yourself."

"Very funny. Very goddamn funny."

Buffett continued to laugh.

After a moment, Pellam's mouth curled upward and he laughed loud. "GFY. That's good, I gotta admit."

"Listen, Pellam, I got a deal for you. I want you to do me a favor.

You do it and I'll tell the department to lay off. I can't do anything
with the Bureau but they'll listen to me at Maddox Police."

"You'd do that?"

"You got my word."

"What's this favor?"

"No big deal. There's something in my house I want you to
get for me."

"Me?"

"If you wouldn't mind."

"No, I guess not." Buffett saw Pellam's eyes flick to Buffett's
wedding ring. He asked, "Why not have your wife bring it when
she comes to visit?"

"The thing is," Buffett said, as his determined and cheerful
eyes moved from Pellam's face to the fuzzy TV screen, "it'd
upset her."

It was a small neighborhood of bungalows set on postage-stamp-
size lawns five minutes from downtown Maddox. Both the dark
brick houses and the grass were well tended and trim. Pleasant.
Pellam believed he had cruised along this street on his quest for
the perfect Tony Sloan bungalow. The traffic from a nearby
expressway was an irritating sticky rush that filled the air and
yellow haze from a half dozen brick smokestacks hung thick
over the yards.

Pellam climbed off the Yamaha. He paused in front of the
house and checked the address. There was a white Nissan in
the driveway and behind it a brown Mercury station wagon
with Illinois plates.

The small garden in front held the corpses of flowering plants.
Stalks mostly. Bleak. Pellam knew nothing about gardening but

if this had been his lawn, he would have added some evergreens. He walked up the winding brick path to the small porch. One other thing he noticed: There were no tricycles or other toys here as there were in all of the other yards.

He pressed the bell. There was no answer. He opened the screen door and banged a large brass knocker. A moment later the door opened. He was looking at a thin brunette with a long face, cautious and nondescript. Late twenties. She had flawless skin. Every time he glanced away from her he forgot what she looked like.

"Mrs Buffett?"

"Yes?" She held the door as far open as the thick brass chain would allow. A sickening sweet scent – maybe air freshener, maybe cheap perfume – flooded out.

"I'm John Pellam."

A blink. Then understanding. "Right right right. Donnie said you were coming by." A formal smile. She didn't offer her first name. Buffett had told him it was Penny.

"I have to pick up a few things."

"That's what he said."

The door closed then opened, the chain unhooked. She motioned him inside. He saw two other people. Her parents, he guessed. The woman was what Penny would be in twenty years: thin, white-haired with beautiful skin. And very cautious. Penny's father was in his late fifties, with a businessman's paunch under his pink, short-sleeved shirt. They both stared at Pellam. He introduced himself.

"Stan Brickell," the man said. "I'm Penny's father. This's my wife, Ruth." The woman nodded.

It occurred to him that if he said, "I'm sorry" by way of

general sympathy, they might think Buffett had died. He asked, "You live in the area?"

"Carbondale."

Pellam nodded. "I just saw him an hour ago. Donnie. He looked pretty good."

"You on the force with him?"

"I'm a friend."

Penny said, "Donnie's mentioned you a couple times."

He had?

"What do you have to pick up?"

"Some forms for the office."

Penny said, "I could take them."

"I have to stop by the Criminal Court building. It's pretty grim down there, Donnie said." This was the lie that Buffett had coached him on.

"I would, though. If he wanted me to take them there, I would." She said this with great sincerity.

It was then that Pellam noticed the burning candle. It was a funny thing. Red, thick, about three feet high, with charms stuck onto it. It had been burning for a long time; there was a slick puddle of wax in the black saucer the candle rested on, two burning sticks of incense angled out of the shaft. That's what was stinking up the house. Sandalwood or something. It reminded him of high school – black lights, the Jefferson Airplane, peace symbols that meant peace and tie-dye that was fashionable, not nostalgic.

He looked around the living room. The candle was a hint but it did not prepare him for the collection of paintings, statues, and icons. All religious, mostly crudely done. Pellam wondered if Penny had made them herself. There were pictures of native

Africans, thin black men and women, with intense, euphoric gazes. There were wooden crosses, spattered with dark red paint. Posters of pentagrams and star charts and crystals. A large glass pyramid, inside of which was a shriveled-up brown and flesh-colored object. It looked like a dried apricot. Like many of these objets d'art the pyramid was covered with dust.

"Would you like some coffee?" Ruth asked.

"Oh, sure, coffee?" From Penny.

"No, thanks."

Ruth said, "No trouble."

"No, really. I can't stay long. If you could just show me Donnie's office."

Penny pointed the way.

The office was really a bedroom slowly becoming a den. It was small. On the walls were sheets of thin paneling of light-stained wormwood – with tiny black holes like miniature cigarette burns. Donnie had probably done the work himself. Half of the sheets still showed the nailheads. A six-foot piece of unstained crown molding had been mounted where the panel joined the ceiling. A half dozen other pieces of molding sat in the corner. It was going to be a long time before the work got finished, Pellam thought with sadness.

He opened the bottom drawer of Buffett's desk. He moved aside the box Donnie had told him about and found what he was looking for. He slipped the thick envelope into his pocket.

As he stood he heard a woman's voice eerily droning: "Ommmm . . ."

Pellam returned to the living room, where sat three people whose only bond seemed to be this tragedy. Penny was in front of the candle, her voice solid and strong like a car in low gear. Nothing was going to stop it. Tears were in her eyes. She sat Japanese style, on her haunches. She hummed faster and faster.

"Ommmm . . ."

Ruth was sitting back on the couch, tracing the yellow herringbone pattern of the upholstery with a short, unpolished nail. Stan said to her bluntly, "Get me some coffee. And a sandwich. Watch the mayonnaise. You gave me too much last time."

Penny's eyes were closed and from her lips came the melancholy drone of her prayer.

Pellam said good-bye to no one. He opened the door and let himself out.

He was going to wait until he got to the Yamaha to take the envelope out of his pocket. But he stopped on the walk and lifted it out. He saw what was irritating his leg. The hammer of the Smith & Wesson pistol had worn through the paper. Pellam covered it with Maddox Police Department Aided Report forms and walked to the motorcycle.

A fleck of dust pedaled through the air of Gennaro's Bakery. Philip Lombro's eyes followed it for a long moment then turned back to Ralph Bales.

"You're not eating your cannoli."

"It's good. I like it," Ralph Bales said. For a stocky man, a man who loved steak and pasta and hamburgers, he had a curious dislike for desserts. He wondered why it was he always ended up sitting in restaurants eating sweets and drinking coffee and tea on deals like this. "I'm a slow eater. My wife—"

"You're married?" Lombro asked, surprised.

"Was married. She'd be finished with her veal and I'd still have most of it left. It's healthier to eat slower. You should chew your food, each bite, I mean, fifty times. I don't do that, but you're supposed to."

The bakery was not very authentic, Ralph Bales noted. Not like the ones he grew up near. It was, for one thing, very clean, and the girls wore yellow and brown waitress uniforms, and the miniature pastries in the spotless glass cases were like the rings and necklaces in the Famous Barr jewelry department. He didn't like it. A bakery should be dark and full of wood and the pastries should be behind dirty, cracked glass. The room should be filled with the smell of yeast and they shouldn't charge three seventy-five for a damn piece of cannoli.

Lombro was nodding with little interest. "My brother's wife makes these. They're better than this one. I think they fill these ahead of time here. You're not supposed to do that. You were telling me you found the man who was the witness."

"Yes."

"What's his name?"

Ralph Bales had anticipated this question. "Peter James." There were twenty-seven people named Peter, Pete, or P. James in the St Louis phone book. Also, it was a name that someone might mix up. Was that James Peters? Jim Peters?

Lombro examined his napkin and replaced it on his lap. "And you've talked to him?"

"Okay. We had a long talk," Ralph Bales said in a low voice. He recited his next line. "He was pretty damn scared when he saw me coming. But he's agreed to play ball with us."

"Play ball."

"That means—"

"That means he wants some money and he won't identify me."

"That's what it means, yeah."

Lombro sipped his coffee, sitting back, ankle on knee, looking like a Mafia don. "Do you trust him?"

"Well—"

Lombro said, "I mean, if he takes the money will he keep his word?"

Ralph Bales thought for a minute and said, "You're never sure about these things –" He had not rehearsed this but he liked the lines. "– but I got good vibes from him. He's not a pro. He's scared and I think he'll keep his word."

"What does he do?"

This was a question that Ralph Bales had not anticipated. He spent a long time shrugging and sipping coffee. "Works some kind of job in St Louis. I don't know. Computers or something."

"And what exactly has he got to sell?"

"He described you. To the letter. He said he looked through the window and got a complete description."

Lombro touched the silvery hair at his temple as if this news gave him a headache. "Why didn't he tell the police?"

Another foreseen question. "He was scared like I said."

"Did you threaten him?"

Ralph Bales poked at his pastry.

"Did you?" Lombro repeated sternly.

"Okay. I made it clear that we weren't happy. I told him we were willing to go to extremes if we had to. I was trying to, you know, negotiate it down. But I told you – I didn't hurt him."

"Did it work?"

"What's that?"

"Negotiating."

"Not much, no."

"How much does he want?"

Ralph Bales stopped poking and took a bite of pastry. "Fifty thousand."

"Uhm."

Ralph Bales counted to twelve, as his script called for. Then he said earnestly, "I know you don't want my opinion but there's a way I'd rather handle it." This was to make the 50 thousand more appealing.

"No more killing. I forbid it."

Forbid it. Ralph Bales tried to remember the last time he had heard someone use that word. Not his father. Maybe a priest at school. *Forbid*. It was a word that belonged in an old-time movie.

"I'm just telling you your options."

"That's not an option."

With one square of paper napkin, Philip Lombro wiped the flecks of pastry from his lips and when he was through doing so he took another square and wiped the heel of his shoe. Then he asked another question, one that Ralph Bales had not anticipated, though it was one of those questions that did not really need an answer. "I suppose he wants us to pay him in small bills, doesn't he?"

"Hey."

Donnie Buffett opened his eyes.

John Pellam stood looking at him.

Buffett inhaled slowly. "Hi, chief."

"You okay?" Pellam's eyes flickered with concern.

"Yeah. I was . . . There's this exercise. It's supposed to calm you down. It doesn't work too good."

"Well, some beer'll calm you down. You want another beer?"

"Yeah, I want another beer."

In addition to a damp paper bag Pellam was holding a thick white envelope. Buffett looked at it first and the bag second.

Pellam closed the door. Buffett said, "They got a rule against that."

"Yeah? What're you, a cop?" He opened two pint Foster's.

Buffet looked at the blue and red logo. "Oh, yes! That stuff really gives me a buzz. Is that a kangaroo on there?"

"It's not going to hurt you, is it? I mean, like with medicine you're taking?"

Buffett drank down three good swallows. "Oooo," he said slowly. "Jubilation."

Pellam sat down in the chair. He held the envelope in one hand. Buffett stared at it.

"Donnie . . . Uh, your wife?"

"She say anything about that?" He nodded toward the envelope.

"She didn't see it."

Buffett drank more of the ale. He wasn't looking at Pellam.

"She was kind of chanting when I left."

The cop studied his beer. "Yeah, she does that some. It's like a, you know, hobby."

"We get a lot of that out in California."

"She's real sweet. Good kid. And a cook. You want to talk pasta? Penny's the best. She cooks all kinds. She makes white clam sauce. You know anybody else who's ever made white clam sauce?"

"I met Stan and Ruth."

"Yeah. They're all right." Buffett looked around the room.

"We don't have a whole lot to talk about. Stan's a good guy."

"Seems that way. Your wife okay, Donnie?"

"What do you mean okay?"

"It wasn't just the chanting. She had this candle burning . . ."

Buffett laughed – though he guessed his eyes did not join in. He said, "She's kind of superstitious. Like with Reagan, remember? Nancy had an astrologer. A lot of people are into that kind of stuff now. Crystals." He reached over to the table and lifted up a clear green stone. "Green's supposed to make you well again. Penny got it for me." His voice caught and he swallowed. "I'm supposed to wear it. But I figured my Blue Cross goes out the window if they find out I'm getting treated by spirit guides." He laughed again. The sound turned into a shallow cough. "I'm supposed to keep turning. Otherwise, all this shit settles in my lungs." His face went dark and still. "I'm working out, too." He nodded to the jump rope. "I'll be back in shape in no time."

"Wheelchair basketball."

"I'll whup your ass."

"I don't even play basketball," Pellam said.

Buffett was looking at the envelope. "You found it okay."

Pellam handed it to him. "It's pretty beat-up. That's what Maddox issues you?"

Buffett shook the gun out of the envelope and held it lovingly. He clicked it open and looked at the shells inside. He read the engraved, circular word *Remington* five times. He did not seem to hear Pellam's question but a moment later he said, "It's a cold gun."

"What's that?" Pellam asked.

"A gun with the registration filed off. Untraceable. Sometimes you go into a drug bust, there're a lot of cold guns around. So you pick up one and keep it."

"Like for a backup?"

Buffett spun the cylinder then said, "Well, *I* use them for backup. Lotta cops use them for something else. Like for when there's some asshole coming at you in an alley and you tell him to stop but he doesn't." Buffett stopped speaking as if this were explanation enough.

Pellam shook his head.

Buffett whispered, "You see what I'm saying? You take him out with your service piece then slip a cold gun in his hand. When they have the shooting hearing, you tell them you had to shoot him because he had a piece." He found he was sweating and wiped his face.

"That happens a lot?"

"Some. They know it goes on. The thing is, if you die with something in your hand the muscles tighten up on it right away. So it's a hassle to get the guy's prints on it. The shooting board always suspects but unless it happens to the same cop a lot they'd rather come down on our side." He looked up. "Thanks for doing this."

"You really think there's a chance the killer'll come back? Try to hit you here?"

"I just feel a whole lot better with a piece." He nodded at the gun.

"I hear you." Pellam finished his Foster's. "Should've brought some peanuts."

Buffett set his ale down. "Stomach must've shrunk. Used to be a time when I could drink three of these."

"You'll still be able to—"

Buffett's eyes flashed. "Don't do that. I hate it."

"What?"

"Making it sound like everything's gonna to be fine. Everything's going to be hunky-dory. That's what my mother used to say. Hunky-dory. And peachy."

Pellam shrugged. "You're the one bitching and moaning about your capacity to chug. I'm just telling you it's—"

"Well, *don't* tell me, okay?"

"Sure, you want."

"Yeah, I want."

There was a long moment of silence. Buffett said finally, "Look, Pellam, I'm sorry. You're too easygoing. You ought to tell me to fuck off. You ought to slug me."

"I never hit a man with a gun."

"I'm tired. I think I need some sleep. I'll make some calls like I said. Tell the guys to lay off you."

"Thanks. I gotta go anyway. I got a date."

"Date?"

"That local girl you met. The blonde."

"Pretty damn clever, Pellam. You promise 'em parts in the film and then, wham bang, they get a part they weren't expecting. You Hollywood guys."

"Not quite. This one hates movies."

"Hates movies? What's her name again? Nancy?"

"Nina."

"One good-looking woman."

"She's here," Pellam said, nodding toward the corridor. "Her mother had an operation or something." He looked at the Smith & Wesson. "I've got a Smittie at home. I do some shooting sometimes."

Buffett nodded but he was distracted. He kept looking at the gun, imagining what it would feel like when the bullet entered his brain. How long would he continue to think? What would he see?

He thought: *Fuck you, Terror.*

Buffett looked up. "Sorry?"

Pellam had been talking about his famous ancestor and he now repeated the story.

Buffet's eyes showed momentary amusement. "Wild Bill Hickok? Bullshit."

"Well, that's the story. Even if it's not true, it got me interested in American history. And started me collecting old guns."

"What'd he shoot, a .45?"

"Wild Bill? Nope. Gun of choice was an 1851 Navy Colt. Thirty-six caliber. What's that? Three fifty-seven?" Pellam nodded toward the Smith & Wesson in Buffett's hand.

"This? No. Standard thirty-eight special."

"Could I heft it for a minute?"

Buffett handed it to him butt first and as Pellam studied it the cop said, "Pellam, one thing. When you saw my wife did you tell her anything about me?"

"I don't remember. I guess I told her you seemed to be doing okay."

"Did you? Thanks."

Pellam put the gun in his pocket.

Buffett looked at the outline of the pistol. "What are you doing?"

Pellam said, "I think I'll hold on to it for a while."

"Naw, naw, give it here." Buffett thought Pellam was joking.

"I don't think so."

"What're you, nuts? Give it here!"

Pellam said, "I was thinking about it, you know, and it just doesn't make a lot of sense. There's a twenty-four-hour cop up the hall, hospital security guards at the front door. I don't think the killer'd be stupid enough to try to come back—"

"Well, who the hell are you to risk my life?"

"I think I'm *saving* your life, Donnie."

Another blink.

Pellam said, "What were you really going to do with the gun?"

"Give it here!"

"What were you going to do with it?"

"Give me my fucking gun!" Buffett shouted. Then he spat out viciously, "I could slash my wrists. I could take an overdose."

"Well, do it. I'm just not going to help you."

"It's *my* gun!" Buffett cried. "Please." Tears began. He wiped them away angrily. His arms slumped and his hands fell to his lap.

"It's gotta be tough," Pellam said. "But you don't want to do that." He touched his pocket.

"You don't understand," Buffett whispered. "I'm never going to walk! I'm never going to fuck a woman again in my life. Never. I'll never have any kids. You don't understand!"

"The way you feel now isn't—"

"The way I *feel?*" Buffett shouted. "How do *you* know what I feel? How could you possibly know?"

Pellam exhaled slowly. After a moment of enduring the hopelessness in the cop's face, he said, "I'll be in town for another week. You still want the gun when I leave, I'll give it to you then."

"Yeah, what's going to be different in a week?" Buffett snarled. "I'll still be lying on my ass with bedsores, I'll still be pissing into a rubber, I'll have a wife talking to the stars and friends who're embarrassed to come see me."

"One week."

"Give it to me!"

Pellam opened the door and stepped out. "One week."

13

This was not a place he would have chosen to be buried in. Philip Lombro would have preferred more variety: trees, hills, large rocks rising out of the ground like Stonehenge. But he decided this was a foolish thought. How could you have a cemetery with tree roots, uneven ground, stone? Cemeteries were like any other real estate; death had to be financially practical.

The cemetery outside of Maddox resembled the acreage around a prefab midwestern grade school. Beyond, he could see a development of pastel houses, all similarly styled. In each yard were two small maples, crowned with colored leaves – webby, like the sponge of HO-gauge trees in the scenery sets he bought for his nephews.

Lombro parked on the side of the cinder drive and got out of the Lincoln. He walked slowly through the trim grass. Several of the graves were caved in at the corners. He felt queasy as he looked down into these tiny, dark pits, and he wondered if with a flashlight one could see the coffins themselves. This terrified him. He hated this place and he was angry at his brother for buying plots here, instead of Mount Pleasant, where their parents were buried.

The day was milky-sunny and hot. Indian summer, he supposed, though he never knew exactly what that meant. Could it be a metaphor for the Indians' attempting a final assault after they had been conquered by the settlers? But that seemed too lofty and dark for such an innocent phrase. His feet bristled through lawn stubbly with crabgrass, and he noticed his shoes were dusty from disintegrating yellow leaves. He bent down and stroked the grass. It was unpleasantly tough; the stem of a dandelion was the only softness his fingers touched. He stood and continued toward the gravesite.

Lombro wore a dark suit and he was sweating. He would not take off his jacket. The dead, he believed, deserve all our respect.

The cemetery was not crowded. The hour was early, on a weekday, and only dedicated mourners were present. Two elderly women, locked arm in arm, stood nearby over an old grave, which was not marked by a monument but by a small, dark metal plate. Lombro remembered that every veteran was entitled to a marker like this and he wondered if the women were standing above a father who died in Verdun, a husband at Normandy, or a son at Da Nang.

When he arrived at the grave, he did not have the reaction he believed he would experience. He did not cry. He felt numb, hardly touched at all, the way a shy man freezes in front of a very beautiful woman. He looked down at the turned-over earth. He knew they used bulldozers to dump the dirt into the graves and he was glad he did not see any tread marks on the clayish earth. The gravestone was gray marble and polished so smooth, it reflected the dark, wilted flowers.

A breeze disturbed the green tissue enfolding the flowers that he held. He had forgotten they were in his hand. He set them on the dirt then decided the paper would shred in the rain and look bad. He pulled it off and stuffed it into his pocket.

He turned and walked back to his car. As he did, it occurred to him that all his life he had been a man who was not afraid to act. Being this way had made him very wealthy, a linchpin in his family, respected and – in certain circles – held in awe and fear. Yet now he believed that what he had done – killing Vincent Gaudia – had altered him. Altered him fundamentally. Not because it was violent but because it was an act beyond his world of experience. He had put in motion people and forces that were behaving in ways he could not control, in ways he could not even predict.

The gun that had fallen in the tile bathroom of Orsini's – Ralph Bales's gun – and had put the two men together had been the first link in a long, horrible chain reaction of those forces, which had the effect of making him feel small and powerless.

Lombro leaned against his car. The wind was gentle and filled with crackling, dry heat. Lombro saw Ralph Bales driving up the road now, his squat head through the gray glass of the car. Lombro reached into his pocket and pulled out the yellow envelope that contained fifty thousand dollars. He wanted the meeting to be over with as soon as possible.

He wished there were no witness.

He wished he had never met Ralph Bales.

But most of all Philip Lombro wished that the dead all around him, lying in their still beds of level, root- and rock-free earth, would all at once rise and begin to laugh and talk as if they were not dead at all but had merely been lulled into a light sleep by the glorious peace of an unseasonably warm afternoon.

After hours of cruising up and down the riverbanks of the Wide Missouri and the Big Muddy, Pellam at last found the field that would be the site of Ross and Dehlia's catastrophic last heist.

Driving and stopping, then driving on, he had been close to giving up hope. State parks, private yards, rail-road easements, pastoral grass rolling toward the water, boggy grassland, long stretches of revetments of crushed gray and black rock. Nothing that would work for the film.

Sitting on the camper's dashboard was a note from the key grip, pleading for a location within twenty-four hours, and sitting in the seat beside him was the reclining figure of Nina Sassower. Pellam, forcing himself to ignore both, had turned a bend, driven through a stand of dense oak and maple and braked the camper to a squealing halt.

"I think this is it."

The field was a lush five acres defined by dense rows of trees, just starting to color – some leaves would have to be spray-painted or draped with green netting. (The film was set in June.) A church facade would have to be constructed. (Sloan's wish to have the shoot-out involve schoolchildren had given way to his slightly more tasteful burst of inspiration – the innocent victims would be churchgoers.) But those were the only necessary modifications.

The grass was high. An asphalt road stretched timidly between the field and the riverbank, which was a ten-foot-high stone incline that dipped into the soupy water of the Missouri River.

He stepped outside and took two dozen Polaroids, then returned to the cab. He started the camper's engine and sped back toward town.

"Why," Nina asked with curiosity, "is that field any different than the other ones? Because there's less junk?"

"Uhm," he began and decided he couldn't explain.

"I mean, it *is* a nice field and all," she said quickly, perhaps taking his silence as disappointment at her reaction.

Pellam noticed that Nina's interest in film had grown considerably. Perhaps this was due to her employment. She was by all reports an excellent makeup artist. Perhaps it was also due to her reading Pellam's copy of the final revised shooting script for *Missouri River Blues*. It looked like a student's end-of-term notebook, stuffed with smudged, limp sheets – all different colors, indicating the various drafts of Danny's rewrites. It required diligent shuffling to proceed from start to finish. But the script had held her interest all afternoon.

And, more than that, had even brought her to tears.

Driving in silence, heading back to Maddox, Pellam glanced at her again, noting her damp eyes.

She closed the script. "I'm sorry. It's so sad."

John Pellam had not cried for a long time and he could not remember the last time he had cried watching a movie. Nina looked ahead, unseeing, at the road. "I lost a relative not too long ago."

Pellam muttered condolences. "Who was it?" he asked.

Lost in thought, she had not heard his question and he repeated it.

"An aunt. She was elderly, but . . . A car accident." Her voice faded.

Danny's new ending was a slow-motion angle of Ross's Packard tumbling into the river.

"After she died, I had this urge . . . no, not an urge, this *need* to put what I felt into words."

People tended to share things with Pellam and to confess secrets to him. It happened everywhere he went, it happened at the unlikeliest of times. He supposed this was because he was always just passing through. They could unburden themselves and then he would vanish, their confidences safe.

"I looked through some of my books and I found a poem. *Do Not Go Gentle Into That Good Night*. It's funny about poetry back then, isn't it? I mean, it was all stiff and formal, but I could understand it."

"It's a nice poem." Pellam knew the poet was Dylan Thomas. He couldn't remember a word of the poem.

Pellam let the traffic lights guide him. He was lost, but he figured that the stoplights would be denser closer to downtown Maddox, where he could get his bearings. He steered toward the red and green and yellow.

"Did you read it at her funeral?"

"Yes. I was surprised, it went well. Real well. I thought I'd cry and spoil it. But I didn't. Have you ever done that? Read something at a funeral?"

Pellam thought back to the most recent memorial service he might have been a featured speaker at. It had been seven years ago in Santa Monica. The deceased had been his closest friend the actor Tommy Bernstein. Pellam had not attended the service.

She didn't say anything more and they drove in silence for ten minutes, then cruised into downtown Maddox. He parked, with the engine still running, near Tony Sloan's trailer. Sloan would be at the three-monitor Kem editing machine now, reviewing work prints. He would not tolerate being disturbed. Pellam left the Polaroids and a brief location report with Sloan's poor, jittery, ponytailed assistant director and returned to the camper. They drove along Main Street and parked beside a small grocery store. Wishing to change the relentlessly somber mood, he said suddenly, "Watermelon. Let's get some watermelon."

"In October?"

"Sometimes you just get this craving. Come on."

Inside a small grocery store he bought a plastic container of chunks of watermelon.

"It's not real red," she said.

Pellam asked the salesgirl, "Where do you get watermelon in October?"

"Oh, from up north."

Pellam said to Nina, "It's Eskimo watermelon."

"Farmers' Market," the girl said, pointing in a direction he assumed must be north.

Pellam asked for two forks and napkins.

Outside, they walked up the street spitting seeds into their hands and sticking them into the dirt in the big concrete planters along the street.

"Next year," Nina said, "we'll have to come back and harvest the crop."

Pellam didn't really think about Nina in terms of next year.

A dark car cruised past slowly and Pellam had the vague

impression of eyes staring at him. The fork stopped halfway to his mouth and he watched the car as it sped up and continued on.

They wandered out of downtown.

Nina stopped and stared in the window of a store that sold shoes encrusted with costume jewelry – stones, glitter, fake gold. Why on earth would anyone in Maddox buy a pair of shoes like this?

"Wicked Witch of the North," he said.

Nina said, "It was the West."

Maybe she does like movies after all.

"Oh," Pellam said. "I only like the tornado scene."

"When I was a little girl, I used to think it was 'wicker' witch. We had a wicker patio set. I wouldn't sit in it. I thought it, I don't know, was made out of witches."

Pellam smiled. She took his arm and brushed her cheek against his shoulder.

"I finally outgrew it. I still don't like wicker, though. You get splinters in your butt."

He said, "You look good when you smile."

Which seemed to be just the words to deflate it. But she brought a facsimile back to her mouth and said, "Thank you."

That was when they found the factory.

Pellam noticed a redbrick building set back a long ways from the road. The grounds were filled with overgrown trees, brush, and rampant kudzu so thick you could only see the top of the tall, square building. It had high, gracefully arched windows decorated with iron grillwork. The setting sun was visible through them and lit the interior with broad shafts of ruddy illumination.

Pellam started up the path. Nina followed.

The Maddox Machinery and Die Company had been abandoned for years. The building had an odd regalness about it, something castlelike, complete with parapets and a dip in the surrounding ground that was probably a collapsed septic system but could pass for a moat. The bottom six or seven feet of the outer walls were marked with halfhearted graffiti, and the metal door was thickly posted with several generations of *No Trespassing* signs. Metal Art Deco designs, in the shape of lilies and vines and the company's name were set in concrete around the door.

Nina walked up silently behind him. She looked up at the facade. "What a neat old building."

Pellam tried the front door. The lock was long broken though the double wooden panels were chained. He pushed inward as far as he could, separating them by two feet then he worked his way inside underneath the chain.

"Do you think you should?" Nina asked as his boot vanished into the doorway. She timidly followed.

Inside, Pellam paused on the oak floor, worn wavy by years of workers' boots and hand trucks. To the right were the darkened factory offices. Banisters and windows were done in streamlined aluminum, and in faded murals muscular laborers towered high above them. To the left through an arched doorway was a huge, cavernous space, now lit red by the intense sun glowing on the yellowed, greasy windows. The ceiling was nearly forty feet high.

Nina walked up behind Pellam.

"This is too good to pass up," he said.

"I thought the field was all you needed."

"This'd be for another film I've got in mind. I'll get the Polaroid. Be right back."

After Pellam ducked out of the chained door Nina walked to the back wall, where she had seen in the shadows what she believed was an antique calendar and some other artifacts that might be worth swiping before the movie crews descended.

It was not a calendar, though, just a poster of the Bee Gees, which would have been dated circa 1975. She guessed some kids had used the building as a clubhouse years ago. She found an old, empty tin of cat food. A dozen beer bottles, burnt matches. Nina walked into a large, windowless office in which rested a piece of sleek green machinery like a huge sewing machine. She squinted into the darkness and poked around in drawers and cabinets for ten minutes. She found a beautiful antique orange crate but it was too big to get through the chained door.

Clouds suddenly obscured the sun, leaving Nina in gray shadow. She felt a chill and, with it, a sense of uneasiness. She started walking quickly back to the front of the factory. She stopped. In the dust on the floor in front of her Nina could see her own footsteps, leading back to the poster and the machine room. And there were Pellam's sharp-toed boot prints retreating through the arched front doorway.

She saw another set of prints too.

They disappeared into the back of the building, through the offices. They had been made very recently.

Nina gasped in fear and looked at the arched doorway, beyond which was the chained front door. One hundred feet away. And fifty or sixty of those feet led past darkened doorways.

"John?" she called.

There was no answer.

The panic zipped along her spine and seized the back of her neck. Tears popped into her eyes. Step by step, slowly, to keep the fear at bay, she started toward the door. Her jaw began to quiver.

Ten feet, fifteen. Twenty.

She heard a noise, perhaps a footstep.

"John?" The terrified echo of her own voice came back to her from three directions, and it seemed as if there were a trio of ghosts in the room, mocking her. The tears came more quickly. She forced herself with all her will to walk slowly.

Then Nina was almost at the front door arch. Beyond it she could see the glint of the chain on the door. This reassured her and the terror diminished. Pellam would be returning any minute.

She could—

The hand slipped around her mouth and held her firmly. She tasted tobacco and salt. Another arm curled around her chest and yanked her off her feet. The man threw her to the ground, the air knocked from her lungs. She uttered a painful moan. Her breath came in small gasps. Then he was kneeling beside her, his face very close to hers.

14

S he lay on the floor, on wood as cold as iron. The narrow door admitted only reflected light from the main room and she was in shadow. She smelled garbage and urine and mold and tasted her own metallic tears.

"Please!" she cried.

The man stood and walked to the outer door. Only a part of her rational mind was working and this portion believed that he'd simply taken her purse and was leaving. She saw his dark silhouette at the front door, the chained door, looking out. Then he slowly turned and walked back to her. He crouched down and a band of pale light fell across his face. He was wearing rose-colored sunglasses. She saw his face clearly beneath his trim hair. He was young, he was handsome, he was white. All of these surprised her and lessened her fear slightly. On his cheek was a large, oval birthmark or discoloration. The light startled him. He had not expected to be seen.

Her fear returned. He was going to kill her because she had

seen him . . . Whatever else he did, he was going to kill her afterwards.

He ran his hand along her pale cheek. "Put your hands under you."

She did not understand and he repeated the words calmly. When she still did not comprehend this instruction, he illustrated, lifting up her hips and shoving her hands beneath her buttocks. Maybe he wanted her hands pinned so she could not scratch him.

He bent down, kneeling, and put his mouth next to her ear. Nina twisted her head away, wincing and expecting to be kissed. She felt the heat of his breath.

"Please," she cried, "don't."

"I have a message for your friend."

She did not hear this. "Please."

"Listen! . . . Are you listening?"

She nodded, crying again.

"Mr Crimmins knows that your friend saw him in the car that night. You tell him that if he testifies, I'll come back. You understand what I'm saying?"

"What—?"

"Did you hear me?"

Nina said, "Mr Crimmins . . ."

"And if I come back –" he touched her cheek again "– you're not going to like it."

Nina's body was racked with sobbing.

He said, "Don't move for a half hour. Stay right where you are." He stood up. She heard no footsteps, nor did she hear the rattle of the chain on the front door. Because of this she believed he was still there, watching her, perhaps hidden in the shadows only ten feet away. She stared at the distant square of greasy glass, lit by the sun and the thin auras encircling it, the rings of red light that her tears created.

He found her sitting curled up, outside the factory, staring down at the branch-cracked sidewalk at her feet. "Nina?"

She did not look up. Not for a moment. When she did it was with eyes full of tears. He sensed she had been assembling herself – forcing herself to be placid.

"John . . ." Her voice broke with sobbing. She was shivering.

"What is it?" He crouched next to her.

Her arms hugged him hard and she was shaking hysterically. "There was a man."

Pellam stiffened. He took her by the shoulders. "What happened?"

Sobbing again. He had to wait. He wanted to shake it out of her, force her to tell him. But he waited.

Nina pulled away and roughly wiped her ear – where the attacker's mouth had been – as if scraping the skin clean. "He didn't . . . do anything. He just knocked me down."

"Let's call the cops." Pellam started to stand.

"He said . . . He told me to tell you something."

"Me?"

"He said he worked for the man you saw, the man in the Lincoln. And if you tell the police he'd come back and . . . Crimmins, he said the name was."

His hands began to quiver in rage, then his neck. He couldn't control it. Then his jaw and head, shaking uncontrollably. He blinked. His eyes watered with the fury. His jaw suddenly cramped and he realized his teeth were jammed together.

"John—"

"Let's call the police."

She shook her head. "No."

"What? We have to."

"No, John. Please. He didn't hurt me. Not really. But I'm scared of him. He said he'd come back." She looked at him with frightened, wet, round eyes. "Please. Just take me home."

Pellam looked around the field and brush surrounding the factory. He thought back to the dark car that had cruised past while they were on the street. All his enemies in this town were faceless. Where were they? Pellam thought momentarily of his distant ancestor Wild Bill, who fought it out with gunfighters face-to-face and no more than a dozen feet apart (except, of course, for the last one, the one who shot him in the back).

"This guy, what did he look like?" Pellam asked.

She described him as best she could, the hair, the youthfulness, the pink glasses. She thought for a moment and described his pants and jacket. She could not remember his shoes or shirt.

"There's something else about him . . ."

"What?" Pellam helped her to her feet.

"He had a red mark on his cheek. Like a big birthmark. It looked like that red spot on Jupiter." She touched her own cheek.

"Jupiter."

"The planet," Nina said. "Will you please take me home now?"

"I don't need a goddamn appointment."

Pellam shoved the door open. It swung into a bookshelf. A

precariously balanced volume tumbled to the bare floor with the sound of a gunshot.

He stopped. Four people gazed at him. Three were astonished. U.S. Attorney Ronald Peterson looked calmly at Pellam as he walked farther into the room. The others, two men and a woman, were young. Their eyes danced between the intruder and Peterson. Pellam ignored them and said, "I want to talk to you. Now."

"Ten minutes. You mind?" Peterson asked his coterie.

Even if they had, he was obviously their boss, and the only debate they were presented was whether it was better protocol to take their files or leave them. The papers remained where they were and the youngsters walked silently out of the room.

Pellam put his hands on the cluttered desk, knocking aside a windup set of dentures. He leaned forward. "I want protection for myself, my friends, and for everybody with the film company. A friend of mine was just attacked. I want an agent at her apartment *now!* She lives in Cranston, on—"

"Have a seat, Mr Pellam."

Pellam remained standing, glancing from the windup toy collection into the man's serene olive pits of eyes. The U.S. Attorney motioned to a chair. "Please."

Pellam sat down.

"You say she was attacked, this friend of yours?"

Pellam told him about the factory and the man with the birthmark.

"Crimmins." Peterson's troubled eyes scanned the colorful foliage outside his window. He spat out, "That son of a bitch."

"Your agents told me he'd hired some hit man in Chicago or Detroit or something. This's him. This is the guy. I want protection."

"Protection?"

"Agents," Pellam exploded. "You know, bodyguards."

"U.S. Marshals? That's a lot of taxpayers' money to devote to protecting someone."

"You've got this witness protection . . ."

"Ah, the key word. *Witness*."

Pellam said, "Look, you're playing a game. You know his name. Crimmins. Go arrest him."

Peterson said, "I'm confused. If you didn't see him, why would he threaten you?"

"Well, *he* doesn't know I didn't see anything. Why are you hesitating? You want Crimmins. He's just threatened me and assaulted my friend. Go arrest him."

"The attack that you say—"

Pellam was on his feet. "I *say?* . . . My friend—"

Peterson held up a hand. "Excuse me. My mistake. I apologize. Please – have a seat."

Pellam sat down.

The U.S. Attorney said, "What exactly do you want?"

"I want protection. I keep saying that."

"I suppose we could put one man on it for a while. But what happened to your friend isn't a federal crime. It's an assault. There's no federal jurisdiction—"

"You mean it's not a crime to threaten a federal witness?" His voice faded in reverse proportion to Peterson's smile.

"We come back to that again. See what I'm saying? You're *not* a witness. No jurisdiction. There's nothing we can do."

Pellam's voice was soft. "That's the kind of technicality you people like to use."

Peterson paused a moment, maybe wondering which category the *you people* described. "The point is, even if we got a conviction for this attack, the best we could do is put him away for a year, tops. He'd be out and after you again twice as mad. Or after your friend."

"Bullshit."

Peterson pressed an intercom button. A middle-aged woman in a white blouse and tan skirt appeared in the doorway. "Yessir?"

"Bring me the Crimmins file, please."

"All of it, Mr Peterson?"

"No, sorry. Just the background file. The first Redweld." He looked at Pellam. "You really don't know who Peter Crimmins is? Well, let me tell you. Second-generation Russian. Ukrainian, I mean. I suppose we have to be careful with that nowadays. He made a lot of money in the trucking business and we know that he's built up a huge money-laundering operation. It was some people that work for him got into a battle with a Jamaican street gang in East St Louis."

Pellam pictured the windup toys strolling off the edge of the desk and some young assistant attorney scurrying to retrieve them from the floor. "What exactly—"

"Twelve people were killed." Peterson frowned but did not seem to be particularly shocked or mournful.

"What's that got to do with me?"

"'Massacre.' That's what the *Post-Dispatch* said. Not exactly hyperbole. Seven of them were bystanders."

"Tough luck in an election year."

Peterson was immobile for a moment. He lifted a very white finger to his earlobe and stroked it absently three times. When he spoke his voice was temperate. "The office of U.S. Attorney is an appointed position."

Pellam gazed at him skeptically.

"I have no aspirations to be mayor of this city. Or governor of the state or senator. I have yet to understand why anyone would want to be a representative."

The secretary appeared and set a large, battered red-brown file folder on Peterson's desk. The U.S. Attorney opened the file and pulled out a number of stacks of papers and clippings. He upended one stack on his lap and began flipping through it, squinting.

The pictures spun out, flying like Frisbees. Pellam glanced at them. He was surprised they were in color. For some reason he had assumed police photographers used black-and-white film. He was surprised at how bright the blood was. He had seen bodies before; blood in real life seemed darker.

"Those were ten-year-old boys. Though it's hard to tell after what happened to them."

Pellam picked up the glossy photos and tossed them back to Peterson. One fell on the floor. The U.S. Attorney picked it up and stared at it. "Two years ago, we were very close to indicting Peter Crimmins on several racketeering counts. We had a material witness. A young woman, a secretary, who could implicate Crimmins. There was a freak accident. Somehow a pot of boiling water fell off the stove. Third-degree burns on her groin and thighs. She said she was cooking." Peterson's voice rose into an eerie wail. "Third-degree *burns*. Her skin was like cooked steak!" The eyes glowed. "But you know what was

odd, what was very odd? The accident happened at midnight."
Peterson lifted his palms. "*My* wife doesn't cook at midnight.
Do you know *anybody* who cooks at midnight?"

Pellam was silent. Peterson's head bobbled with rage. Slowly
he calmed. He took a Kleenex and wiped his face. "The woman
recanted her testimony before trial."

"So what you're telling me is that Crimmins is a bad man
who has a track record of scaring witnesses."

"Mr Pellam, there is no doubt in my mind that he was the
person who killed Vince Gaudia. He had the motive. He does
not have a convincing alibi. He has ordered people threatened,
beaten and killed in the past. Look what he did to your girlfriend.
The fact is that the RICO charges I've got against Crimmins
are nothing without Gaudia. He'll get three or four years at the
most." Pellam saw more sweat on the dome of Peterson's head.
He saw the finger and thumb rubbing together compulsively,
trembling.

Pellam's voice was patient and tired. "I can't help you."

Peterson came back to earth. He opened another file folder
and, preoccupied, dug inside.

Pellam asked, "What about protecting Nina?"

"I think she'd be safer if she left town. There isn't much we
can do."

"I know some reporters," Pellam said ominously. "They
might be interested in this story. You refusing to protect people
unless they testify for you."

Peterson slipped an utterly good-natured smile into position
on his egg-shaped face. "Oh, I don't think that'd be a very
good story."

"You never know."

Peterson lifted several pieces of paper out of the file. "The problem with reporters," he said, flipping through the sheets, "is that they like the lowest denominators of any situation. This witness story of yours isn't really a grabber."

Pellam waved an arm in frustration and started toward the door.

"*This* story," the U.S. Attorney said with a smile, "would be much better."

The bulletin left Peterson's hand and floated down to the desk. The California bear seal was in the upper left-hand corner and in the center of the white, wrinkled sheet were two photos and several brief paragraphs.

The photos weren't of Peter Crimmins or of live gangsters or dead bystanders but were of John Pellam himself.

He looked exhausted, puffy-eyed, unshaven. They showed him from two angles – straight on and in profile. Beneath them were words in slightly uneven lines, suggesting that they were typed by a cheap typewriter. Among these words were Pellam's name, vital statistics, the date the photo was taken and the names of several Los Angeles County Sheriff's Department deputies. At the bottom of the bulletin was this information: *Charged with: murder, manslaughter, sale/possession of controlled substances.*

15

"**D**oes your boss know you did time?"

Pellam lowered his hand from the doorknob. He returned to Peterson's desk and sat down. He stared at the picture.

Turn your head . . . We want a profile. *Turn your head . . . Him? Yeah, he's the one killed that actor. Yep, sure is."*

Peterson said cheerfully, "You know, I seem to remember something of surety law. Wouldn't your film company's bond get lifted if an ex-felon was on the payroll? Especially with a drug charge?"

"I was acquitted on the drug and murder charges."

"Don't quibble, Mr Pellam. The victim died because you delivered two ounces of cocaine to him, didn't you? This Tommy Bernstein, the young man in question."

The best friend in question.

Pellam reached forward and touched the photo of himself.

"Put this here jumpsuit on, then we cuff you and take you

downstairs. You hassle us, we hassle you and we got batons and you don't, you know what I'm saying? Now, move."

The reason that he had not been able to attend Tommy's memorial service was that he was in a Los Angeles County Sheriff's Department holding cell, pending arraignment.

Pellam, staring at his own gaunt image, was long past feeling the need to explain, to shake his head with a grim, tight mouth and tell how Tommy had begged him for the stuff, crying. *Please, just this once, John, help me, help me, help me. I can't work without it. I see the cameras, man, and I freeze. I mean, I fucking freeze. You gotta help me . . .* Tommy Bernstein, lovable madman and brilliant actor, leaning on Pellam's shoulder, tears in thick streaks shooting down his doughy face, pathetic and looking just like the child that, in the core of his soul, he was and would always be – the child that Pellam should have recognized.

No, he wouldn't explain this to the sour, cold man he now sat in front of. He said only, "It was a long time ago."

Peterson regarded him coolly. "An ex-felon is an ex-felon. You can't ever take that away."

"No, you can't."

Peterson repeated. "Does your boss know?"

"No."

"It's purely a civil matter. I don't have any legal duty to tell him. But I do feel a certain sense of moral obligation. He would fire you in an instant, I imagine."

"I imagine he would. And if I say that I saw Crimmins in the car you'll forget to mention it."

"You've had some conversations with a Marty Weller in the past week."

"Marty? How do you know about Marty?"

"Some conversations about a movie project you're putting together?" Pellam was silent, and Peterson continued, "Following those conversations, you started looking for some money. Your bank in Sherman Oaks, some car dealer who wasn't interested in an apparently less-than-perfect Porsche you happen to own . . ."

"You tapped my phone illegally."

"Not at all. We talk to people. That's all. We introduce ourselves and we ask questions. Most people usually cooperate."

"What's your point?"

"You apparently need some money, some big money. And you need it rather desperately."

"And you think Crimmins is paying me not to testify."

"Yes. That's exactly what I think."

Anger sputtered into Pellam's face. He stood up and leaned forward, his eyes wild and uncontrolled, his right fist balled. Papers and toys cascaded to the floor.

They remained locked in a gaze for a long moment, while Peterson mastered his fear, and Pellam, his anger. Pellam was close to hitting the man.

Peterson whispered, "Please. I say this for your sake. I don't think you want to add to your list of woes at the moment, do you really?"

Pellam finally stood upright and walked not to the door but to the window. For a long moment, as if he were debating something furiously, he looked out over an expanse of green. St Louis was a very verdant place, even in October. The important aspects of his life in jeopardy, Pellam noticed small details. Like the colors of foliage and the shape of trees. He nodded suddenly, but whatever decision he came to, he kept to himself, and walked out of Peterson's office without saying a word.

The ribbed ball rolled along the small grass rectangle.

"You lose," the old man told Peter Crimmins, who smiled and nodded to the other players and then stepped over the black-painted railing. He stood in a small park in a suburb of St Louis, squinting toward a huge complex of redbrick apartments. He wondered how much money it cost to build the place. He had never been in real estate. He considered it too Jewish. But he had lately been thinking about building something. He wanted some legacy and he thought he would like to sink some of his vast funds into something that might be named after him.

Joshua stood nearby, leaning against a lamp pole with the tough serenity of middle-aged bouncers and Secret Service agents. A broad-featured woman in a blue denim cowboy suit talked into a public phone and gestured wildly. Her fat fingers mauled a cigarette.

Crimmins, wearing dark slacks and sandals and a white dress shirt had been playing boccie for an hour. At one time the largely Italian park would probably have been crowded on a pleasant afternoon like this, though even Crimmins, who had lived all his life near here, could not recall when. Perhaps the year of the St Louis Exposition. An era when the town still retained some of its Confederateness. Why, there were even homeless people camped out near swing sets! Crimmins did not approve of homelessness. He thought such people should pick themselves up and get a job as those in earlier eras would have done.

"Bootstraps" was a word Peter Crimmins used often.

He surveyed the park now. Lots of Negroes, prowling slowly

on their bicycles or walking in that fast lope of theirs. Puerto Ricans. White teenagers in leather and greasy denim, with their Frisbees and skateboards and guitars. A few professional people. Women jogging while they pushed babies in strollers that had three huge, cushioned wheels.

And then there were the Chinese.

While Crimmins disliked Jews and feared Negroes and Puerto Ricans he loathed the Chinese.

Crimmins was now looking at four or five Asian families as they picnicked. Crimmins was aware of the tide. Real estate and electronics. Shipping soon.

And money laundering not long after that.

A boy on a skateboard snapped past him in a surfer's crouch. As if drawn by the youngster's wake, a dark-complected man suddenly stepped up to Crimmins. "Hold up there."

Just as suddenly, Joshua was between them, appearing from nowhere, hand inside his jacket.

"Police, big fellow," the man said. "Unless you're feeling yourself up, get your fucking hand out where I can see it."

Shields and ID cards appeared.

"I'm Gianno, Maddox Police. That's Detective Hagedorn over there."

"Maddox," Crimmins spat out.

Hagedorn stood nearby. His jacket was unbuttoned. Gianno said, "We'd like to ask you a few questions."

Crimmins nodded to Joshua, who retreated. He stopped fifteen feet away and stood watching the three men.

"A woman was attacked not long ago."

"Someone I know?" Crimmins was concerned.

"Well, not a friend of yours, that's for sure. She was apparently reluctant to file a report. We got a notice of the assault from the FBI."

Why would an assault be a federal issue? thought Crimmins, reciter of indictments and an expert in federal law. Then he understood. "I see," he said wearily. "And you think I was behind this attack."

"She gave us a statement that the attacker said he worked for you."

Crimmins blinked. "Me?"

Gianno gave him a description of a young man with the birthmark.

"I don't know anyone who looks like that. Besides, I wouldn't threaten anyone."

"No." Gianno laughed. "Of course not."

"Where have you been today?" Hagedorn piped up.

"Home, then I came here."

"Had to make some phone calls that nobody could hear, did you?" Gianno nodded toward the public phone.

Crimmins rubbed his finger and thumb together in irritation; the thumbnail turned white under the pressure. "Are you arresting me?"

Hagedorn said, "Will you give us a list of all your employees?"

"I don't think I have to do that."

"We hoped you'd be cooperative," Gianno said.

"It would look better," his partner offered.

"I don't really care what anything looks like. I—"

Gianno said to Hagedorn, "Let's get out of here. This guy's no help. We'll follow up with Pellam—"

The blond detective wagged a subtle finger and his partner

stopped speaking as if he had caught himself at a social blunder. They looked for a moment at Crimmins, who kept his face blank. The two policemen then walked away.

When the detectives had turned the corner, Crimmins walked along the street, away from the phone booth, motioning Joshua after him. When the bodyguard caught up with him, there was a crown of sweat on Crimmins's forehead and his face was white. These were not the symptoms of physical exertion.

"Find me Stettle," Crimmins growled in a furious whisper. "I don't care where he is, what he's doing. I want him now."

The river was muddy today.

The water seemed no more turbulent than on any other day – the wind was brisk but it still hadn't broken the surface into whitecaps. But some disturbance was churning up clayish mud and staining the wide water from shore to shore.

John Pellam stretched out in the driver's seat of the camper and tried Nina's number once more. Her machine answered and he hung up without leaving a message. They had had a brief conversation earlier during which she assured him she was fine. She simply wanted rest. Could he call the head of Makeup and explain? . . . Of course he would. Was there anything else he could do? Did she want company? No, she'd visited her mother at the hospital and asked the woman's doctor for a couple of Valium for herself. Pellam could hear the slurred words and he hung up to let her get some sleep.

He had just now replaced the phone when a very distraught Tony Sloan called and said the final shoot was about to go down. Pellam knew this and had planned on attending. What was ominous was that Sloan had summoned him so adamantly.

He couldn't possibly be thinking of new locations, could he? The key grip had let slip the information that Sloan had fifteen straight days of film – that was *twenty-four-hour* days of celluloid – to boil down into a 125-minute movie. Pellam, thanking the Lord he was not Sloan's film editor, promised he would be there before the last blank gun shot was fired. He stood up and adjusted his Abel Gance *Napoleon* poster, the only decoration in the camper. He slipped the Colt into the inside pocket of his bomber jacket and was about to leave when his phone buzzed again.

"Nina?" he asked.

"Are you sitting down?" The voice was a man's.

"Hello?"

"Sitting down?"

"I can hardly hear you, Marty. Where are you?"

"I'm in Berlin."

Pellam pressed the cellular phone hard into his ear, as if that might improve the connection from the state of Missouri, in which Winston Churchill coined the term *Iron Curtain*, to the place that had once·been behind it.

"I tried to get you in London and Paris," Pellam shouted. "Look, I'm sorry about the other night."

"You don't have to shout. You break up when you shout. I can hear you fine. What?"

"I'm sorry I missed you. I had an accident."

"Well, it was a damn expensive accident. Telorian *was* interested but he got pissed because you blew him off a second time. What's the trouble, John, some Freudian thing against Iranians? Excuse me, Persians. You should've called. Are you sitting down?"

"What do you mean?"

"I've got some Hungarian money lined up."

"What?"

"I know. It's weird. Paramount balked at the last minute on the terrorist script. It's *totally* cratered. So it's a green light for *Central Standard Time*. This guy in London put me in touch with these investors in Budapest. They're a real East Village duo. Young guys. I pitched you sort of as a Jarmusch."

Hungarians financing a cult film noir flick set in Wisconsin. So this was the New World Order.

"Well, I'm happy about that, Marty. What do we do now?"

"You can get a hundred fifty?"

"If I hustle."

"Well, hustle, boy."

"They understand I'm directing?"

"They're all for it. They know all about you, John . . . It's not a problem." His voice filled with transatlantic sincerity. "You know what I'm saying?"

The death of Tommy Bernstein was what he was saying.

"They like your work. They like you. Or who they *think* you are. Don't disappoint them."

"Who are these guys?"

"Their names, you mean? Unpronounceable. Funny marks over the letters. Who cares? Get your money. I'm having my shyster in New York put together the partnership agreement. Let's try to sign it up by the first of the month. Is it doable?"

"It's doable. It's very doable . . . Listen, Marty . . . thanks. You know what this means to me."

The broken connection mercifully cut short the gratitude and Pellam found the conversation was over.

Outside he kicked a piece of dried mud off his Nokonas and walked to the Yamaha.

16

"We saw your advisory about the assault on that Sassower woman."

Ronald Peterson cocked an eyebrow at Bob Gianno. *And?*

"We talked to Crimmins."

Neither of the Maddox cops noticed Peterson's eyes flick with minute satisfaction toward Nelson, who could not restrain the less subtle smile.

Hagedorn continued, "He denied having anything to do with the assault, of course. What did you expect?"

What indeed?

"But naturally we didn't care about that. We just wanted to flush him. We mentioned Pellam's name. We pretended it was a slip. You should have seen his eyes."

Peterson said, "That was a clever move."

"We thought so. He'll do something now. Either try to hit Pellam directly or just spook him. Either way, we'll move on him."

They sat in Peterson's office. The cops had noticed the toy collection and each seemed to be trying to think of something witty to say about it and came up blank. Peterson was oh so happy with their immense discomfort.

"Keeping the pressure on Pellam. That's good." Peterson took a long moment to read a low-priority report that had nothing to do with this meeting. He dashed a note in the margin and dropped it on the desk. "You know Pellam did time."

"What?" Hagedorn laughed.

"Manslaughter. San Quentin."

"Damn. San Quentin," Gianno said. "Hard time. How 'bout that."

Peterson watched the local detectives stew a bit as they were poked by guilt that they themselves hadn't unearthed this information. He asked, "Can you use that?" He himself had considered Pellam's criminal record and concluded that local police couldn't do much with it.

Hagedorn and Gianno looked at each other. The blond, good-looking cop – more handsome than most of the FBI agents who worked for Peterson – lifted his hands and scrunched his lips together in reflection. Finally he said, "I don't see how. Film permits are already issued. I mean, I don't think a prior conviction has any bearing on that. But what about parole?"

"Parole?"

Hagedorn continued, "Did he break parole by leaving the state?"

This was something Peterson had not thought of. A microscopic frown crossed his brow. Being outthought by this smarmy shit-town cop. Peterson decided that Nelson would twist in the wind a few revolutions for missing this. "Given the dates of the crime and his traveling-man career, I doubt that's an issue but I'll have my associate check into it. Now, I think we've agreed that Crimmins knows Pellam reported him for the assault on the girl, and – thanks to the clever thinking of our friends from Maddox here – he may make some overt move against Pellam. We'll monitor that. But I think we need to step up the pressure too."

"Any ideas?" Gianno asked glumly, suspecting sarcasm but unable to identify it.

Peterson responded, "I have one, yes. Two of my agents were on the movie set the other day and they found something interesting. I'd like to ask them to stop by and tell us about it."

*

MISSOURI RIVER BLUES
SCENE 179E – EXTERIOR DAY – ROAD BETWEEN FIELD AND RIVER
This is a narrow road between the field and the river. There is a small, one-story CHURCH on the river side road, surrounded by bushes and trees. Past the BUSHES the road continues through the field, open space on either side.
MEDIUM ANGLES OF ROSS'S PACKARD parked fifty feet past the church. Dehlia dabs FAKE BLOOD on her forehead and stretches out in the front seat of the car with the door open. Ross and the three GANG MEMBERS take their MACHINE GUNS and hide in the bushes, waiting for the armored truck. Ross stops and runs back to Dehlia. He gives her his FAVORITE PISTOL.

ROSS

In a half hour, little love, we're gonna be across that
river and we're gonna be free.

DEHLIA

If anything happens . . .

TWO SHOT of Ross touching his finger to her lips to
shush her. They KISS long and then he stands up, cocks
the MACHINE GUN, and runs to the bushes.

"Finale time, everybody! Let's try to bring it in under a
hundred takes." Tony Sloan took his position, standing in the
shadow of a big thirteen-ton Chapman Titan motorized crane.
He surveyed the battlefield to be.

Sloan, the second-unit director, the DP, the ever-nervous
ponytailed assistant director and the stunt coordinator had just
finished trooping through the weeds and grass and scrabbling
over the revetment of stone down to the yellowish water,
blocking out the climax of the movie. This was the armored
truck attack. The owners of the transport company, tipped
that the truck would be hit by Ross's gang, had replaced
the shipment of cash with bags of cut-up newspaper and
substituted Pinkerton agents for the regular guards. Dehlia
would be reclining, supposedly injured, helpless and beautiful
at the scene of the fake car accident, bringing the armored car
to a stop.

But before Ross could slip a smoke grenade into one of the
truck's gunports, the guards were to come out blazing. Pious
citizens, just leaving a church at the wrong moment, became
pious victims as they walked into the middle of the carnage.
Ross and Dehlia would then escape. But they would drive only
a half mile down the road before a young boy – whose father

Ross had accidentally killed fifty scenes before – darted in front of them. Ross would swerve and the car would sail into the river. (Pellam had suggested they rename the film *The Postman Always Rings Twice for the Wild Bunch*.)

More than one hundred crew members and thirty actors and extras tested lights, oiled dollies, adjusted hydraulic lifts, plugged in cables, mounted film magazines, prefocused cameras, took light readings, positioned microphones and read and reread scripts.

But the man of the moment was none of these. Nor was he the lean, wild-haired director of photography or even Tony Sloan himself.

The center of this afternoon's particular universe was a thin, balding fifty-one-year-old man of quiet demeanor, wearing neither period costume nor Hollywood chic but dark polyester slacks, a neatly pressed blue dress shirt and penny loafers.

There was a delicacy about Henry Stacey, known both here and in Hollywood only by his nickname, Stace. His careful eyes scanned the set in front of him with the attention of a seasoned cinematographer. His job was in fact considerably less artistic although it was – in the mind of directors like Tony Sloan (and most of Sloan's fans) – far more important than the director of photography's.

Stace was the company's arms master.

The actors and actresses in *Missouri River Blues* had so far fired close to seventy thousand rounds of blank ammunition at each other, which probably far exceeded the total number of live rounds fired by all the real-life crooks and law enforcers in the Show Me State since it joined the Union.

The arms and prop assistants had been working since four

that morning, supervising the loading of an armory's worth of submachine guns, rifles, and pistols for the final scene. Stace himself oversaw the loading of every weapon to make certain that no live ammunition accidentally got mixed into the magazines.

He also had worked with the unit director and his assistants to oversee the placing of hundreds of impact squibs – tiny electrically detonated firecrackers – whose explosions would resemble striking bullets. He did the same with wardrobe and makeup to rig the blood bladders on the bodies of actors destined to be wounded or killed in the shoot (and who stood with great discomfort as they, unprotected, were wired up by assistants who wore thick gloves and safety goggles). The squibs were connected to a computerized control panel and could be triggered either by an operator or, with additional rigging, by the trigger action of the gun that was supposedly firing the bullets whose impact the squibs represented.

Stace and his crew also rigged debris mortars and vaporized gasoline bombs for the shots in which the mock-ups of the antique cars exploded. Reminding actors and actresses to stuff their ears with cotton before the filming was another part of the job as was instructing them how to work the guns, how to stand when they fired and reminding them to provide the gun-bucking recoil that occurs only with live ammunition. He had running battles with Sloan (as he did with all directors) because he urged the actors to point the muzzles slightly away from their victims for safety, while the directors, for the sake of authenticity, wanted guns aimed directly at their targets.

A competitive and award-winning pistol marksman, Stace

was also the set rifleman – occasionally manning his own bolt-action .380, or M-16 automatic, to fire wax bullets for impact effects on surfaces that couldn't be rigged with squibs – windows, water, or even, if they volunteered, a stuntman's bare flesh.

The final scene in *Missouri River* would involve the firing of five thousand rounds in several setups. Once the medium- and long-angle shooting was finished, the rigging would be done once more for the close-up and two-shot angles. This was going to be a long day. The exhausted key grip looked over the prep work, then at his watch. "Man, we'll be fighting the light on this one." Meaning working until dusk.

"Are we ready?" Sloan shouted through his megaphone.

Various crew members, not knowing whether or not they were the subject of this inquiry, assured him that they were.

Stace checked the location of every weapon, noting it on a clipboard, and walked back to the fiberboard table on which was the squib control board. Three of his assistants sat like puppeteers, both hands above rows of buttons. Because the scene was newly added to the script and was so elaborate, there had been no time to rig the guns themselves to fire the squibs. The young assistants – two men and a woman – would use their judgment in deciding where the machine-gun bullets would land and push the corresponding buttons.

Stace said, "Ready."

"Okay," the unit director shouted. "Everybody in position."

Dehlia sprawled out of the open door of a muddy Packard.

The Pinkerton agents piled into the armored truck and it backed down the road.

The parishioners walked into the church.

Ross's soon-to-be-dead fellow gangsters checked the harnesses and cables that would jerk them backward as they were shot by the agents.

The director of photography and the camera operator climbed into the Chapman crane's twin seats and rose twenty feet into the air. Sloan released his own death grip on the boom and wandered over to the unit director.

"Pep talk," Stace wryly whispered to his assistants.

Sloan lifted his megaphone. His voice crackled, "Could I have everybody's attention please? Quiet please! I'd just like to say one thing. This next eight minutes is costing me a quarter of a million dollars. Don't fuck up."

Pep talk . . .

He returned to his place beside the crane.

The unit director nodded to the senior gaffer. The lights clicked on, replacing the mute aura of overcast sunlight with a wash of light that seemed to bleach the colors out of the scene but that would translate into natural sunlight by the time Technicolor was through with the film. The temperature on the set immediately rose five degrees and kept going.

"Cameras rolling."

Assistants stepped in front of each camera and snapped clappers.

"Action!" the unit director shouted.

The bulky gray armored truck eased along the dirt road, passing the church, then slowing as it neared the Packard. It stopped. Dehlia lifted her head, stained with the phony blood, and motioned for help. The driver and the front-seat guard hesitated. They mouthed words to themselves, they spoke into the back of the truck. The front doors slowly opened. The guards stepped out onto the road. Ross lit a smoke bomb and ran, crouching, toward the back of the truck.

"Now!" the driver shouted, pulling a machine gun from the front seat.

The back doors of the armored truck burst open.

Parishioners stepped from the church, smiling and nodding. The two guards began firing at Ross and the other gangsters, who were approaching from a stand of trees. Tree branches snapped, dirt puffed up, signs were riddled, the side of the truck was dotted with bullet holes, bodies of gangsters flew backwards. Churchgoers littered the ground.

"Go, go, go!" Tony Sloan was mouthing. "Beautiful."

Dehlia was trying to start the Packard. Ross was covering her and retreating. The other gangsters fell back. The preacher came out onto the steps. He was brandishing a Bible; a guard accidentally gunned him down . . .

"Stone cold beautiful," Sloan whispered.

It was into the middle of this battle – directly between the warring factions – that two modern navy blue sedans and a white Ford Econoline van skidded to a halt. Men in suits climbed out leisurely, examining the set with some amusement.

Sloan's mouth opened in astonishment. Everyone began talking at once – many of them shouting because of their earplugs.

"Jesus Christ," Sloan shouted. No one had any trouble hearing this. "Who the hell are you?"

The unit director was too shocked to order the cameras shut off. Finally the assistant director, holding her ponytail in a death grip, woke out of her stunned silence and shouted, "Cut. Cut! Save the lights."

The huge lights clicked off.

The assistant whose job it was to keep the road closed ran onto the set. Sloan pierced her with a glance of hatred. "They came right at me," she sobbed. "They wouldn't stop."

A tall, gray-haired man climbed from the first sedan, looking around. When he saw the director he stepped toward him.

"What," Sloan said, "in God's name are you doing? Do you have any idea of what you've just done?" His face was crimson.

An ID card appeared. "I'm Agent McIntyre. You in charge?"

"Who are you?"

"We're agents with the Bureau of Alcohol, Tobacco and Firearms, Department of the Treasury. We've been informed by the U.S. Attorney in St Louis that you're in possession of unregistered automatic weapons and we're here to confiscate them."

"You can't do that!"

"Clear the chambers on those weapons," McIntyre shouted to the actors. "Put the safeties on and set them in the van here."

Sloan stormed up to McIntyre, who ignored him.

Another man got out of the car, studying the smoke and destruction around him. Detective Bob Gianno looked at the director. "Are you Anthony Sloan?"

"Damn right I am; do you know what you've just cost me? This scene—"

"You're under arrest for violation of the Missouri state laws governing possession of illegal weapons. Would you hold out your hands, please?"

———◆·■·◆———

17

S tace Stacey smoothed the tufts of graying hair above his ears and said with utter calm, "I'm afraid you've made a mistake."

He sat in the office of Ronald Peterson. Beside him was a fidgeting, furious Tony Sloan, who stared with particular contempt at the collection of windup toys littering Peterson's desk.

"Mistake?" Peterson asked Stace. "Oh, I don't think so . . . But first, I want to make perfectly clear that you are not being charged with any federal crime whatsoever. We have noticed an apparent violation of federal law but are withholding any decision to proceed. Under *Missouri* law possession of automatic weapons not registered by the BATF is a *state* violation. Our colleagues in Maddox have decided there's probable cause for your arrest. *They're* the ones who've acted on that. It was not a federal agency."

"You're a prick," Sloan said.

"You understand what I'm saying to you?" Peterson cocked

an eyebrow enthusiastically.

"I understand that we'll never make a movie again in this state. *That's* what I understand."

Peterson shrugged. "You're not under arrest so you can speak to me without a lawyer present."

"I understand already!" Sloan barked.

"Please continue, Mr Stacey."

"I'm qualified as a class-three federal firearms dealer." Stace set a small piece of paper on the desk, next to a tiny walking football. "That's my license. I think you know perfectly well almost all property and arms masters in Hollywood are class-three dealers."

Peterson glanced at the license momentarily. "I don't doubt you, sir. It's the weapons I'm concerned about."

"Every one of those guns is registered, tax stamps have been duly bought and I have a right to transport them over state lines. The—"

"Actually, that's not quite accurate. BATF notice is required . . ."

"No, sir, it is accurate." Diminutive Stace Stacey clearly dominated the conversation despite his calm, unfazed voice. "The notice is generated by the firearms rental company. I rented those weapons from Culver City Arms and Props. They're on the Motion Picture Association computer link to BATF's Washington office. I'm surprised I have to be telling this to a U.S. Attorney."

Peterson took scrupulous notes. He looked up, frowning. "Unfortunately we can find no record of the notice."

"I'm a good friend of Steve Marring in the BATF district office on the Coast. I suggest you give him a call immediately."

"It wasn't a BATF-initiated operation. Several FBI agents were on the set looking for one of your employees—"

"Pellam," Sloan spat out.

Peterson hesitated and then said coquettishly, "Yes, as a matter of fact, it was Mr Pellam. How did you know that?"

Sloan, sloe-eyed with fatigue, rubbed the bridge of his nose. When he did not respond Peterson continued, "My agents noticed the machine guns and reported their presence to me. Naturally, we're concerned about such weapons falling into irresponsible hands—"

Stace said pleasantly, "I heard not too long ago about a man in San Francisco selling fully automatic Uzis to high school students. I'd *think* you might be more concerned about situations like that."

"A tragedy, I'm sure. But my bailiwick is Missouri."

"I've had about enough of this," Sloan shouted. "You've cost me hundreds of thousands of dollars. I'm calling my lawyer—"

Peterson shook his head. "Mr Sloan . . . Oh, by the way, I really enjoyed *Helicop*. I figure it cost me about two hundred bucks after buying the kids all those toys for Christmas. But I did enjoy that movie."

"Why are you doing this to me?"

"Are we reaching an understanding?" Peterson asked heartily.

"Understanding?"

"Have I explained to you how I learned about those weapons? I have, haven't I?"

Sloan had calmed down. There was a cryptic tone in the conversation reminiscent of what one heard in offices and restaurants throughout Beverly Hills and West Hollywood. It was very Zen – to speak while not speaking. "Pellam?"

"Why don't you talk to him, Mr Sloan. Just talk to him. See if he can remember anything about what happened that night of the Gaudia murder." He looked at Stace. "You talk about Uzis in San Francisco. Well, Mr Pellam can help us put away a man who's been doing a lot worse than that. But without his help that man's going to go free and a lot more people are going to get hurt."

Sloan said, "I understand Pellam claims he didn't see anything."

"'Claims.' Well, I know he *claims* he didn't see anything."

"Why is he holding out?" the director wondered.

"Maybe he's afraid – although I've assured him we can protect him. My personal feeling is he's being paid off . . . No, don't protest too fast. You'd be surprised what people will do for money. He is, after all, an ex-convict."

"What?" Sloan whispered.

"San Quentin. Served almost a year. I assumed you knew."

Stace folded his hands in his lap. He stared directly into Peterson's eyes. "John Pellam is a good man. He had some trouble. We've all had trouble at times."

"You *knew* about it," Sloan shouted to the arms master, "and you didn't goddamn tell me?"

Stace Stacey was not an employee of Missouri River Partnership and Tony Sloan was only one of nearly thirty directors who regularly hired him. Sloan was also, among these clients, the largest pain in the ass. Stacey now easily won a staredown with the director and smiled sadly, as if embarrassed at the man's childishness.

"Manslaughter," Peterson said, pleased that Sloan had lost yet another round at this meeting.

Stace said, "He did his time. He got out. He was a good director then, he's a good location scout now."

"Pellam *directed?* Why didn't I know this?"

"You were probably making running-shoe commercials in New York at the time," Stace offered, without a hint of discernible irony.

Peterson jotted a note. "I'll check out what you've told me about your guns, Mr Stacey, and if you're correct you can pick them up first thing on Tuesday morning and the state charges will be dropped."

Stace said, "I am correct, sir, and I'd advise you to release them to me right now."

"Tuesday?" Sloan blurted. "I can't wait three days. We're already overbudget. We're—"

"But unfortunately," Peterson explained, "it's Saturday. There's no one in the Washington office, of course. Tomorrow's Sunday. And Monday—"

"Columbus Day." Sloan closed his eyes. "Christ. Why did you wait until this morning? You've known we had the guns for two, three days."

His eyes were on Sloan. "Do you think we're reaching an understanding? Do you?"

Sloan's anger was diminishing. "Maybe. Possibly."

Stace began to speak. "What you seem to be suggesting is—"

It was Sloan who silenced him with a wave of the hand.

Peterson said, "Then if there's nothing else, gentlemen . . . Oh, as a show of good faith, I'll talk to those city detectives. I'll recommend you're released on your own recognizance."

"I appreciate that. You seem like a reasonable man."

"One more thing, Mr Sloan." Peterson slid a piece of paper

toward the director. "Any chance of an autograph? You know, for the boys?"

The FBI again?

The severe rapping on the camper door sounded just like that of federal agents. But Pellam was running up a long list of potentially hostile visitors, so who could tell? When he opened the door he held the Colt Peacemaker hidden beneath his black Comme des Garcons sports jacket.

Tony Sloan nodded a greeting as he walked inside without waiting for an invitation. Pellam thought about making a wisecrack like "Waking the dead?" referring both to the pounding and to the deceased Ross and Dehlia. But Tony Sloan's expression was far too grim for jokes and all Pellam said was "Come on in" after Sloan already was.

Sloan walked directly to the counter, where sat a bottle of bourbon. He poured two glasses. "You were at the shoot?"

"Got there late. But I heard. Some problem with the guns?"

Sloan gave him a brief account of the events that culminated in his handcuffing.

"My God," Pellam whispered. "Stace is a very buttoned-up guy. I can't imagine he made a mistake like that." Sloan was strangely pensive. His eyes did not flit around the camper. They were sedate. They were almost sad.

The director inhaled the whiskey fumes and drank down half the glass. "Okay, John, no bullshit. Just tell me. Did you see that guy?"

Pellam thought he meant the cop who arrested him. "I told you, I got there late. I—"

"The man in the *Lincoln* is what I'm talking about."

"Is that why you're here?" Pellam laughed. "You've been talking to . . . who? The detectives in Maddox." *No, of course not*, he thought. "Peterson. You've been talking to Peterson."

"John, they can close down production for three days. If that happens the studio or Completion Bond's going to take over. This movie might not get done."

"If I'd seen him I would've told somebody. I would've told *everybody*. Look, Tony, this's extortion. On Tuesday Peterson'll say, sorry, we made a mistake. Call the studio's legal department. Call Hank."

"John, what's this about the money?"

"Money?"

"I hear you're trying to put something together with Marty Weller, you're looking for some bucks."

"I am. That has nothing to do with you or anybody else here."

"Somebody paying you so you won't testify, John?"

Pellam lowered his head slightly and eased a long breath of whiskey-scented air into his lungs. "I think maybe you and I don't have much more to talk about."

"No," Sloan leaned forward, pointing a nubby finger at Pellam. "We got *one* thing more to talk about. You tell Peterson that it was this Peter Crimmins in the Lincoln. I don't care whether you saw him or not. *I* know he was in the car and I don't even know who the fuck he is!"

"Sorry, Tony."

"How much is he paying you?"

"I'll ask you to leave now."

"You want to stay on this job and get your fee, you'll tell Peterson what he wants to know."

"That's money you owe me."

"If I can't wrap this picture in three days there won't be any money for anybody."

"That's not my fault. I did my job. Sell one of your Ferraris and pay me."

Sloan set the glass down on the camper's tiny counter. He seemed calm but the tendons in his neck were bulging and pronounced just beneath his dark beard. His teeth were set. "Oh, I got your number, Pellam," he said viciously. "I asked around about you. You and your artsy films, you and your *Cahier du Cinéma*, you and your buddies sitting around and talking about Cannes and *auteur* theory. You make your jokes, you make the crew giggle. *Bonnie and Clyde, The Wild Bunch.* But just tell me, Pellam, how many of those crew people are *you* paying? How many of their kids are *you* putting through college? How many people came to see *your* films, and how many come to see *mine?*"

Pellam's last film as director, *Central Standard Time*, was never finished. It would have starred Tommy Bernstein, who died of a massive, cocaine-induced heart attack on the set during the second week of principal photography. The film Pellam had directed just prior to that had won a *Palme d'Or* at Cannes but was seen by North Americans only in New York, Montreal, Toronto, Los Angeles, and in those cities with video stores that indulged in cult films. What Tony Sloan was saying now was absolutely correct.

Pellam said evenly, "I won't tell Peterson I saw who was in the car."

"Then you're fired. Clear out. Get the paperwork and any equipment of the company's to Stile. He's taking over as location manager."

"I'll sue you, Tony. I don't want to but I will."

"If this film doesn't wrap, Pellam, I'm coming after you for *my* fee. That's a million seven. And even if I lose you'll piss away a half million in lawyers' fees alone. You don't respect who I am, Pellam, okay, but you got no right to cut my legs out from underneath me."

"Did you know this?" Ralph Bales asked.

Stevie Flom looked at the offered page of the Maddox *Reporter* and could not figure out what he was supposed to know. "I read the *Post-Dispatch* mostly."

"Okay, it was in the *Post-Dispatch*, too, I'll bet. See, it's the Associated Press. That means a lot of papers get it."

They were on the riverfront in St Louis, the silvery arch towering over them and looking lofty and weird at the same time, like a huge toy. In front of them, unhealthy-looking water, bilish and milky, splashed at pilings. From the speakers of a candy red excursion boat, a paddle-wheeler, came brassy jazz. Ralph Bales had been reading when Stevie Flom walked up to him. Reading and leaning up against the scabby railing, really lost in the paper.

Stevie Flom was cold and he was not interested in what was in the paper. He hadn't slept well the night before, turning over and over, listening to the wind rock the single tree outside his bedroom window. He'd stared at the tree for a long time. When he had gone to bed there were seventeen leaves on it. When he had wakened there were eight. His wife had slept with a smile on her face and that pissed him off.

Then she woke up cheerful and happy and that pissed him off too.

What it was he was supposed to know about was this airplane that took off vertically, then the wings twisted forward and it flew like a normal plane. "That is a *great* idea." Ralph Bales pointed at an abandoned dock beside the river. "See, it could land there. You wouldn't have to go out to Lambert. That's the biggest pain in traveling, getting to the airports, you ask me."

Stevie Flom didn't travel much. Reno, of course. Then he and some of the guys had gone to a casino in Puerto Rico once. He'd taken the wife to Aruba, which was nothing but sand and wind and as hot as an engine block. He wondered why Ralph Bales traveled so much he had to worry about getting to the airport.

"I wish I had a piece of that."

"Yeah," Stevie Flom said, and he looked at the picture of the airplane, which, after a moment of reflection, he decided *was* a pretty good idea. He thought that with the money he was going to make from Lombro, he would take the wife on another vacation. Or maybe one of the girlfriends. He'd have to decide which one.

"I've got the go-ahead," Ralph Bales said. He turned the paper to the front page, where there were no airplanes or other clever ideas at all.

"You got . . . Oh, to take care of the guy in the camper. The beer guy! Why'd it take so long?"

"Lombro was nervous. I don't know, he's a—"

"Weird dude is what he is."

"Yeah. Weird. He's upped your share to ten."

"Ten *thousand?*"

"Of course, thousand. What do you think?"

"Well, why?" Stevie grinned deep creases into his baby-skin cheeks.

"Why? Excuse me, you want me to call him up and give it back?"

"I'm just curious."

"Curious. He's curious," Ralph Bales whispered. "You've got to make it look like an accident."

"Accident? Why?"

"Because it's got to. That's why the extra money. I was thinking, maybe something with that motorcycle of his."

"He's got a cycle?"

"That yellow Yamaha. He keeps it on the back of his camper."

"Sure," Stevie said. "A cycle accident. That's easy."

Like he did it every day.

Stevie Flom thought: Maddox is an easy place to steal a car but a tough place to drive one around once you'd boosted it.

The cops didn't have much else to do but check out hot cars and the place was hardly big enough to get lost in the camouflage of heavy traffic. He was eyeballed by two cops as he made his law-abiding way out of town. Stevie was also unhappy that this particular Dodge's former owner was a rent-a-car company, which meant that the forty-eight thousand miles on it were hard miles, careless, heavy-foot miles. The damn thing rattled and clanked and there was a hiss coming from the AC even though it was off.

But it moved pretty fast and he was able to keep up with the cycle though the beer guy drove like a son of a bitch. Stevie worried that if the Yamaha started lane-hopping he could kiss the man's ass good-bye. He goosed the accelerator and closed on the cycle.

He may have had a lemon car but Stevie was lucky in one respect. He had arrived at the Bide-A-Wee trailer park just as the guy walked out of the camper and jumped on the Yamaha. He'd even glanced at Stevie's car but just briefly, not even looking in the driver's seat. Stevie drove past. In the rearview mirror he watched the man kick-start the Yamaha. Stevie made a slow U-turn and followed.

Now, on the expressway, the beer man changed lanes, shot forward, braked hard, then settled into the express lane, about twenty miles over the limit. Stevie, hands sweating, managed to keep with him and soon they were cruising smoothly toward St Louis.

As he tapped his gold pinkie ring on the steering wheel, Stevie was thinking about his father. He had a limited, but severe, repertoire of images of the old man and he realized now that some of them matched this fellow on the bike. Lean, mid-thirties, leather jacket, cycle. This thought put him in another bad mood, and, agitated, Stevie leaned forward to turn on the radio. It was a digital model and he couldn't figure out how to set the station for the boss sound, We Rock St Louis all the hits all the time. The old radios, you just twisted the dial to where you wanted it, then pulled the button out and shoved it back in. All this electronic stuff. Crap!

He kicked it hard with his boot heel and cracked the housing. It kept playing something classical. He kicked it again and plastic snapped and the speaker went silent except for a hiss.

Stevie Flom stopped worrying about music and concentrated on the motorcycle.

Donnie Buffett did not see her right away. He opened his eyes and was afraid to move his head. He thought it might make him vomit, the motion. He had been on pills for a flare-up of pain in his shoulder – the gunshot wound – and they made him nauseated.

"I'm so sorry," she said.

"Penny, honey . . ." He lifted his hand out toward her, and – this was the weird thing – she grabbed it in both hands and kissed his fingers, then rubbed them against her cheek.

He looked at her as though he had not seen her for months, as though he had never before seen her. Dark, thick hair, a narrow face, pretty. Good figure, bad posture, shoulders forward, to conceal large breasts of which she was self-conscious. She wore clothes he knew she owned and had worn before but which weren't familiar to him: a gray suit, an orange blouse, light-colored nylons.

Buffett wished they had a child, someone for Penny to be with. Someone whom Penny would have to be strong for. She had strength somewhere in her, he believed, but she needed someone, or something, to bring it out.

She handed him a shopping bag. She had baked him some cookies (what he had told Pellam was true; she was a hell of a cook) and brought another bag of Ruffles potato chips and a container of Sour King French onion dip. A *Reader's Digest*, some crossword puzzle books.

Donnie Buffett had never done a crossword puzzle in his life.

She bent down and kissed him, brother-sister, on the cheek. He smelled her perfume. Buffett wondered, If you got shot in the neck do you lose your sense of smell?

But, of course, he hadn't been shot in the neck. He had

just been shot in the back. Luckily. He could still smell like a sonofabitch.

He looked at the crossword book. "Thanks, hon."

"I've marked these for you." She opened the *Reader's Digest* for him. "My Battle with Leukemia." There was another. "Live Your Life 365 Days a Year."

Another article was from *Higher Self* magazine, entitled "Joy: Go for It."

Buffett looked at the food, and Penny said, "I don't know if you can eat those things."

"Sure. It's not like I had my appendix out or anything."

She nodded earnestly.

Buffett's hair was a mess. It fell across his forehead. He was always pushing the dark strands off his face. He did this now and his arm went out of control. It crashed into the metal headboard of the bed.

"Shit," he whispered.

Penny's pretty face was shocked. "The nurse," she said, alarmed, standing up abruptly, looking for the call button.

"I'm okay. It's nothing. The pills I'm taking."

"The nurse!"

"Penny."

Neither moved for a moment. "I'm so sorry."

"Stop saying that. Why are you saying that?"

He opened the potato chips and ate a couple, to show her that he liked them. He could not bring himself to eat the dip. Then he ate a cookie. They were good. He ate another one. The sweetness reminded him of his Last Supper, the doughnut and coffee Pellam had brought him. He picked up the bag she had brought, intending to set it on the floor beside the bed. He felt the candle inside the bag. He took it out. "Penny . . ."

"I know what you think but it can't hurt. And you've got oil, too."

"Oil."

She stood and took the bag from him. "It's wish oil."

"Wish oil."

"What it is, you pour some in the bathtub—"

"Well, I can't *take* a bath." He was exasperated. "How can I take a bath?"

She stared at him, tears welling. "I don't think you have to put it in a bath. I mean, if it works in the bath it'd work just as well dabbing it on you, wouldn't it?" She added, "I know it works. You keep wishing that you'll get well. Put the oil on you, then wish and wish and wish. I meditated for an hour and seven minutes last night . . ."

The Terror hears this and rolls upright. It starts to prowl through Donnie Buffett's guts.

Sweat pops onto his forehead.

Bleeding Christ, is it restless! Dodging around inside him, playing with the pain in his legs, slipping up to his heart, dancing over his crotch. (Can't get south of there, can you, you shit?)

The Terror . . .

He fights it down. He presses his nails into the palm of his left hand. He concentrates on the pain, willing it to become a wave of agony. This numbs the Terror. Its prowling slows and it grows tired. Buffett begins to calm. Penny does not seem to notice her husband's absence and continues to talk about shopping and her parents and a consciousness-raising group she's been attending.

The Terror finally falls asleep.

Buffett took a deep breath and calmed down, then interrupted her to say, "I'd like you to meet my doctor."

Penny blinked.

Buffett continued, "Dr Weiser. She's the best in the city."

"You know how I feel about doctors. You need more than—"

"But I *do* need a doctor, honey," he said. "Come on, please. Just meet her."

"Okay," she said cheerfully, eyes sparkling, "I'd like that. I promise I won't lecture her on . . ."

What was she going to say? On the *right* way to practice medicine? *Holism? Spiritualism?*

Penny did not continue her thought but instead crossed her heart like a coy schoolgirl. "Promise." She nodded broadly, acknowledging, though she probably didn't know it, her excessive sincerity.

There were some moments when Penny appeared completely normal. Her hair would be shiny clean and curled nicely, her face – from the right angle – was soft, her collar turned up, covering the dark bones of her shoulders. Her hands would be folded; the torn cuticles and ragged ripped nails were out of view. A dancing light would be in her eyes – a little mystified, a little shy. It was charming.

At those times, Donnie Buffett remembered the woman he had fallen in love with.

He listened to her tell him about how she and her friends were going to be chanting for him.

"Chanting," Donnie Buffett said, and was suddenly tired. Exhausted. He closed his eyes and suddenly all he wanted was to fall back to sleep. The sleep in which he dreamed of pain flowing through muscles that now felt no pain. Fatigue wrapped around him sensuously and squeezed tight like a college girl making desperate love.

"I'm beat, honey," he muttered, pretending to doze.

"You should sleep," Penny said. She touched his hand.

"Uh-huh." Buffett almost opened his eyes and looked at her. But he chose not to. He felt momentarily guilty about this deception.

I'm a lucky man. Lucky lucky lucky. I didn't get shot in the brain. I didn't get shot in the heart. I didn't get shot in the neck. I can still smell.

And he could hear her voice in a detached little whisper, "You sleep now, honey. I'm going home." He heard paper crinkle. "These are the instructions for the candle."

Donnie Buffett breathed deeply like a man asleep. And in less than a minute this lie became the truth and he was dreaming that he was skiing down a panoramic mountain of huge white cliffs rising into an infinitely blue sky.

Halfway to St Louis, Stevie saw his chance. He gunned the engine and the car sluggishly responded, moving ahead of a lumbering truck.

He eased up right behind the Yamaha. A dirt bike, it looked like, with the high fenders that doubled as mudguards and the long shocks that would take the potholes and shitty city streets easily. The rack was cockeyed. Stevie studied the yellow fenders and the silver bars and the red helmet and the leather jacket of the driver and then started looking for an exit ramp.

He saw one a half mile ahead and glanced in the rearview mirror, at what loomed behind him. It was a White semi. Not the trailer, just the tractor, the sort with the ten forward gears and a steering wheel wide as a tire. The truck would have air brakes and little weight, but at sixty it'd skid for a hundred fifty feet.

A quarter mile away.

Stevie Flom started signaling.

He accelerated until he was three feet from the beer man, who was hunched forward, sunlight flaring off his helmet. The truck driver was holding back, seeing Stevie's turn signal but maybe a little confused because the Dodge was not slowing.

A hundred yards.

Stevie eased into the left side of the lane.

The truck driver must have figured the signal was a mistake and had accelerated again, driving up to within two car lengths of Stevie. On the right, the exit ramp blossomed outward.

Stevie floored the pedal and looked to his right, then cut the wheel hard.

His left front bumper goosed the rear wheel of the Yamaha right out from underneath him.

A mad flurry of motion from the bike – a panicked glance over his shoulder as the Yamaha began to lie down. The horn and the gutsy squeal of the truck's brakes filling the air. The man's left boot slamming down onto the highway in an automatic way, hopeless. Reaching up, pitching forward, flying over the twisted handlebars.

Sparks sailing off the gas tank of the cycle. The beer man, his mouth open in a shout that Stevie could not hear, hands outward, began to tumble on the concrete at fifty miles an hour, the fiberglass of the helmet shredding.

Stevie skidded the Dodge into the off ramp, just missing a yellow plastic collision barrel as he braked to twenty-five. He was too busy controlling the skid to see exactly what happened on the expressway. Then he was at the bottom of the ramp. He heard the squealing of tires and horns. Then he caught the end of a yellow light and made a leisurely turn onto a grimy, cobble-stoned street of body shops and empty warehouses and shabby bungalows, not far from the Mississippi River.

18

The service was in a boxy building in downtown Maddox. Beth Israel Memorial Chapel.

Pellam hadn't known that Stile was Jewish. They had talked about many things, from women to whiskey to real estate, but religion was in that category of topics where their conversation did not go – for instance, why Stile remained in his profession and never sought to do second-unit directing, as so many stuntmen do. Or why Pellam stopped directing after Tommy Bernstein died.

Pellam had spoken to Stile's cousin in San Diego – his closest living relative – and he had learned that Stile had been raised Reform Jewish. Calls were made, and a service arranged.

The body was en route to southern California and 168 people now stood in a dark building in a shabby part of a dark Missouri town that had long ago lost whatever allure, or novelty, it might have had for them. From the outfits, this seemed more like a fashion show than a service: No one had brought funeral clothing, of course, but this was a Hollywood crew so there was plenty of black, albeit in the form of minidresses and spandex and baggy suits. Adding to the surrealness were the yarmulkes perching on the men's heads.

The stunt coordinator, Stile's boss, was a tough sixty-five-year-old with blurred tattoos on his forearms, now covered by the sleeves of a wrinkled gray suit. He had fallen off horses at John Ford's direction and crashed through windows at Sam Peckinpah's and he was now crying like an infant. A lot of other people cried too. Nobody had disliked Stile, the man who fell from 130-foot cliffs and who walked through fire.

Pellam had no idea what to say, not to anyone. Stile had died because of him. The Yamaha had been the property of the Missouri River Blues Partnership and when Pellam had turned over the location forms and files to Stile, according to Sloan's orders, Pellam had added, "Take the Yamaha, too, if you want it. Tony's gonna make me give it back sooner or later." Stile thanked him, left the rental car at the campground for Pellam's use, and burned rubber away to the interstate. He had a date in St Louis with Hank the lawyer about location releases for the infamous final shoot-out scene in *Missouri River Blues*.

What could Pellam say?

He put his arm around the shoulders of one of the young actresses and let her cry. Pellam smelled bitter hair spray and cigarette smoke. She wasn't hysterical. She trembled. Pellam didn't cry. He went to a pew and sat next to several other crew members, older men, gaffers. A rabbi – or maybe just the funeral director – walked to the front of the room. He began talking. Pellam did not pay attention to the words; they were not, for him at least, important. The purpose of the ritual had nothing to do with Stile, not now. It was not the sermon but the interval it occupied – this hour in a woody, mute room with a respectful velvet hat on your head – that was the point: a block of time reserved solely for death.

Pellam heard the drone of the speaker's words, a soft baritone.

He wished he knew how to pray.

He decided he would suggest that Sloan dedicate *Missouri River Blues* to Stile, a film that had turned out to be not the product of artistic vision at all but simply one hell of a stuntman's movie.

No, not suggest. Whatever else there was between Sloan and him, Pellam would *insist* on the dedication. It was something he could do.

But it wasn't enough.

What Stevie Flom was going to say: First, you didn't describe the guy very well. Second, the guy walked out of the camper and got on the cycle. Third, you should've done it yourself . . .

He got as far as "First—" before Ralph Bales grabbed his Members Only black jacket by the lapels and slammed the terrified Stevie into the wall of Harry's Bar.

"Gentlemen." The bartender wagged a finger but in a lethargic way. This was a dingy, Lysol-scented place overlooking one of the less picturesque refineries in Wood River, Illinois. It was that sort of bar, where the management would let two men – two *white* men, not too drunk or strung-out – go at it. Up to a point.

Ralph Bales looked from the frightened eyes of Stevie Flom to the cool eyes of the bartender and let go. He had been right on the borderline but now decided not to break his partner's nose. Stevie slumped and ran his fingers through his razor-cut hair. "Aw, Ralph, come on."

Ralph Bales turned and walked through the bar into the restaurant behind. He slid into one of the booths. Stevie followed him like a butt-swatted puppy and sat opposite.

Ralph Bales said, "You're an asshole."

"First, what it was, he walked out of the camper and got on the Yamaha. How was *I* supposed to know there'd be somebody else inside? You said he'd be riding a bike. And like, anyway, you didn't describe him."

"Shut up and listen to me. Lombro is *really* pissed now."

"It wasn't my fault."

"Excuse me, I mean, excuse me? When're you gonna learn that guys like this don't *think* about fault. What're you going to say? 'Gee, Mr Lombro, first I shot a cop and now I killed the wrong man but I've got an excuse'?"

"Did you tell him I did it?" Stevie whispered.

To Ralph Bales's glee the kid was seriously nervous now. He let Stevie hang in the wind for some very lengthy seconds. "I didn't tell him your name."

"Thanks, Ralph. That was all right of you."

"I just told him a guy we hired made a mistake."

"'*We* hired.' Like you and me, we hired somebody else. So he won't think it was me." Stevie nodded. "That was good."

"He was pissed but he's not going to do anything about it. He's not going the whole nine yards with the bonus, because of the screwup but he'll give us something. If you do it right this time."

"Maybe what you could do is describe him better to me."

"Maybe what I could do is hold your hand and take you up and introduce you . . ."

"Aw, Ralph, come on . . ."

"Look, this thing is running away from us."

"Maybe we should just vanish."

"Without a penny? I wish you'd done the cop right."

"You could've, too," Stevie said cautiously.

Ralph Bales opened his mouth to protest then remembered his gun muzzle nestling in the cop's hair. "I could have, too. Yeah."

The waitress came by and they ordered boilermakers and hamburgers. When she left, Ralph Bales said, "Okay, well, do the witness this time and do it right."

Stevie said, "All right, sure. You still want it to be an accident? I mean, if that's what you want . . ."

Ralph Bales considered this. "Do it however you want. I don't care."

This relieved Stevie immensely and he said, "I just want to say one thing. First, you didn't describe him very well—"

Ralph Bales turned on him.

Stevie lifted two palms and grinned. "Joke, Ralphy. Joke. You got to keep a sense of humor about these things."

"He killed my friend," Pellam said, "and I'm going to get him."

Donnie Buffett was not interested in what Pellam was going to do. Penny had called and chanted over the phone to him for five minutes while he stared at the receiver, first in disbelief, then in disgust. He had finally hung up and left the phone off the hook. Then he had been taken downstairs and poked and probed all morning. He had been told to contract his sphincter. He had said peevishly, "My *what?*" And the young intern had said, "Your rectum, contract it." And Buffett had said loudly, so that patients up and down the hall could hear, "Oh, you mean my *asshole?*"

The rest of the exam had gone like that.

Now here was Pellam, sweating and wild-eyed and talking about getting people.

"Look, you steal my gun, you give me a lecture about things you don't know from, then you come in and you start rambling about some killing or another. What," Buffett said evenly, "do you want from me?"

Pellam leaned close. Buffett blinked at the nearness of his face, the pores he could see clearly, the way the dark hairs on the top of the man's forehead disappeared smoothly into the skin.

The look in Pellam's eyes reminded him of young cops after their first firefight. Eager and energized but also quiet – ironically calmed by death. And because of that, scary. Extremely scary.

Pellam said, "The man in the Lincoln killed my friend."

Buffett did not respond and Pellam told him about Stile's death. "They got us mixed up. They saw him leave the camper on the bike and they killed him. They thought it was me."

"Look, Pellam, it's crazy to drive a cycle in the city. Accidents happen. I could tell you the statistics."

"Hell with statistics. I want you to tell me how to do it."

"Do what?"

"Arrest him. Can I shoot him if I have to?"

The chanting and the poking and probing faded from the

cop's mind. Pellam and his calm, scary eyes had Buffett's full attention. "Let me make a call." He was on the phone for ten minutes as Pellam stared out the window. Pellam's lips moved silently from time to time. Into the phone, the cop asked, "Any chance it's related to the Pellam thing? . . . Uh-huh. Yeah, well, I know how you guys feel but I'm starting to think he's okay . . . Yeah, Pellam, I mean. I'm not so sure he *did* see the guy in the Lincoln."

Pellam's head turned.

Buffett said, "Well, do what you gotta, I understand. But take it easy on him. It was his buddy got killed."

When he hung up the cop said, "They're calling it an accident. Hit-and-run. The truck driver said the car clipped the cycle. The tag number's from a stolen Dodge."

"There. Stolen."

"Most hit-and-runs involve stolen cars. That's why they're hit-and-runs."

Pellam leaned forward again. "Look, I know it was the guy with the mark on his face. He must've seen me go to Peterson's office after Nina was attacked."

"I'll have Gianno and Hagedorn look into it. They—"

Pellam exploded, "Look into it? Look *into* it? All they do is hassle *me*. You don't understand. I'm going out that door in five minutes and I'm going to find the guy who killed my friend and I'm going to get him. If you won't help then the hell with you!"

"Look, Pellam, if he did it then the guy's a pro. He's not going to let you just arrest him. You, by yourself, no backup? Are you crazy? Are you ready to waste him if you have to? You ever shot anybody before?" Buffett shook his head with a condescending smile.

Pellam unzipped his jacket and pulled the Colt Peacemaker from his belt. The grin left the patrolman's mouth and his uneasy eyes followed the gun as it went back into the waist-band.

"One thing you might want to remember," Pellam said quietly. "The guy with the mark on his face? He's probably the partner of the man I saw get out of the Lincoln and that makes him the one who shot *you*."

No, Buffett hadn't thought about that. But he did now for a long moment. He said slowly, "I'm a cop. I can't help you kill someone. I don't care who it is."

"I'm not going to kill him. I'm going to arrest him."

Buffett's tongue gingerly touched the corner of his lips. "I don't know what to tell you."

"How do I make a citizen's arrest? Do I have to get him to confess? Can I just arrest him, like in the movies? Do I have to read him his rights?"

Buffett the cop considered. "Well, you don't have probable cause. The truck driver didn't get a look at the guy driving the Dodge. The procedure our guys'd use is to find a suspect, then bring him in and interview him. Not arrest him. Just talk to him. He doesn't get a lawyer for that but he can get up and walk out any time he wants."

"Just talk to him?"

"Try to find inconsistencies. Maybe he'll mention people who're supposed to be alibis, but we can squeeze them and get them to turn. It's a hell of a lot of work, Pellam. You don't just arrest somebody."

"What if I had a tape recorder with me and got him to say something in it?"

"You can tape yourself talking to somebody without a court order. That's okay. But it's a little risky, isn't it?"

"It'll be admissible and everything?"

"Probably."

Pellam shrugged. He walked to the door and stopped. "What you told them. I appreciate it."

"How do you mean?"

"What you told the detectives, about believing me."

Buffett shrugged. Pellam noticed him rub his eyes in a resigned way. He seemed as tired as the wilting flowers that littered the radiator cover of the room. "You okay?"

"Yeah. I guess. My wife came for a visit." He opened his mouth and was suddenly overwhelmed by the volume of things he wanted to say; they rushed forward. But just before he spoke, the torrent dried up instantly, and he asked, "Hand me the *TV Guide*, would you?" Buffett motioned across the room. "Son of a bitch orderly left it on the dresser. What good's it doing me over there? I mean, some people, they just don't think."

19

A knock on the half-open door woke Donnie Buffett. He was dozing and he awoke from a dream he could not remember but that left a residue of longing. "Yeah?" he muttered. "Hello?"

The door pushed wider open and a blond woman's face appeared, her head tilted sideways. The face, which he did not recognize immediately, was delicate and pretty. She stepped into the doorway. The lope of her walk, combined with the delicacy and prettiness, made her sexy. This in turn depressed Buffett even more than Pellam's visit.

"Hi. You're not asleep?"

Hearing her voice, he remembered her name. "Nina, right? Pellam's friend?"

As if she now had permission she entered the room. She wore a tight-fitting brown silk dress. A beige raincoat was over her arm. Donnie Buffett commanded himself to look at neither her abundant breasts nor her sleek, pale legs but only at her face.

"You're Donnie."

"You just missed him." He smoothed his hair and stroked his two days' growth of beard with forked fingers.

"Did I?" She grimaced and Buffett wondered why he had thought even momentarily that she had come to visit him. She asked, "When did he leave?"

Buffett looked at his watch, surprised. He thought he had slept for hours. "Thirty, forty minutes ago."

"That's John. Hard to pin him down. Oh hey! Nice roses. The ones I get never open up."

"There's this stuff in a packet that comes with them. You put it in the water."

"They smell nice, too. You don't know where he's gone off to?"

If you only knew, lady.

"Sure don't, no. Look, take some flowers. You want the roses, take them." But she shook her head. He remembered that he'd tried this once before. Nobody liked hospital flowers. He figured people thought they were bad luck.

"Pellam told me about what happened to you in that factory downtown. That's a tough neighborhood. You okay?"

She nodded but said nothing, as if the memory were too troubling; Buffett was sorry he'd brought up the attack. But he felt compelled to add, "Maybe you should, I don't know, leave town or something, until they find who did it."

"I could do that. I was thinking I would."

What she did at the moment, though, was straighten a disordered pile of magazines on the bedside table until the corners were perfectly aligned.

Buffett's eyes returned to the TV. Watching sports increased his depression but he had developed a taste for bad afternoon movies, provided the sound was off. Hearing the dialogue spoiled the experience. He had fallen asleep watching a silent, bad movie about the hijacking of a ship. He wanted either to go back to sleep or to watch his movie. He was becoming irritated with her. "I thought visiting hours are over."

"I smiled at the cop outside and he told the nurses to let me in."

Buffett grunted but he tried to make it a pleasant grunt.

She walked further into the room. He did not like her putting her raincoat over the back of the chair. This meant she intended to stay. She kept looking at him. He felt like a freak. Why wouldn't she leave?

"How are *you* feeling?" she asked.

"Great. I'm great." On the screen the ship hijackers were chasing the good guys around the decks. Or maybe it was the good guys who were doing the chasing.

"You don't sound real great."

He looked back at her. "I get kind of groggy sometimes. Just sitting here."

Her eyes flicked to his hand. "You're married, right?"

"Yep."

"Your wife visits you every day?"

"Sure." *She's a great little trouper.* "Brings me cookies. You want a cookie?"

"No, thank you. Any kids?"

"Nope. Sour cream dip? I think it's onion. I don't remember."

Nina was not going away. Why was she forcing him to have a conversation with her? Why was her mouth curled into a tiny little smile when there was nothing to smile about?

Buffett said, "You've got a relative here, right?"

She nodded. "My mother. I was just visiting her. I got bored and left. Is that bad of me?" She asked this in a pouty way – the schoolgirl routine that she seemed to have perfected – and he understood he was supposed to tell her that it was not bad of her, which he did, though not very sincerely. Buffett watched the silent machine guns firing at fleeing sailors, who called silently for help. A number of them got gunned down. Several were shot in the back.

"Well," she said, no longer smiling. "You're sure Mister Quiet."

Commandos were coming to save the ship.

"I guess I'm watching TV."

"With the sound off?"

He clicked the off switch. He'd denied himself the treat of the commandos' rescue and now she would sense his resentment and leave.

But, no, she was walking around the room in a very leisurely way, straightening his magazines. Then she started on the vases.

"I think I'm becoming a curmudgeon," he said by way of apology. "What is that exactly?"

"Got me. An old fart, I guess." She began to throw out the dead flowers. "I'd think the nurses'd take better care of them."

"They're pretty busy. Everybody's busy."

Except me. I sit on my ass all day long. I can tell you all about fabric softener, breakfast cereal, and tampons. I could learn how to hijack ships if you'd leave me the hell alone.

She washed the vases in the bathroom and left them upside

down to dry on the top of the toilet. Buffett took grudging pleasure in watching her. The glass was immaculate. Some women are good at this, he thought. Give them a dirty bar of Ivory and a cheap paper towel and they'd make anything spotless. Penny had been this way.

Penny *is* this way, he corrected.

Nina walked to a low dresser across the room. Nothing more to wash. No more silent hijackers or Monistat commercials. No more crazy location scouts.

No more nothin'.

"Well, I'm pretty tired," Buffett said, and yawned a fake but large yawn. "I think I'd like to get some sleep."

"Naw," Nina said, picking up a deck of cards from the dresser. "Don't you think you'd really like to play gin rummy?"

John Pellam, his bomber jacket covering Samuel Colt's deadly brainchild, walked with the oblivion of landed gentry through the streets of Maddox, Missouri.

He kicked at a tuft of tall grass springing from a perfect hole in the middle of a cracked sidewalk slab. He continued on. There was no traffic here, foot or auto, along this row of buildings. The tallest structure on the block – a three-story factory – may have bustled in its heyday but the building now mocked its past; the roof had collapsed long ago and the old green sign on the facade read *FINERY*, the *RE* ironically worn down by some trick of erosion.

Looking behind him, looking down alleys, looking more often in the reflections of windows than at the sidewalk where he planted his brown Nokonas, Pellam saw no one following.

He turned from this part of town and ambled down Third –

past the spot where Donnie Buffett had been shot. Here, too, he lingered. The rains had washed away the blood he'd seen, if it had been blood, and the cobblestones were everywhere clean. This is one advantage of ghost towns – fewer residents to toss litter on the streets. Pellam, unzipping his jacket slightly, paced back and forth. He wandered several blocks to the alley through which he had eluded the sedan several days before. All deserted.

Tony Sloan and the film company – still without their precious machine guns – were filming the few remaining scenes. Sloan was also, Pellam guessed, spending many hours on the phone arranging for extensions of the financing. Pellam himself avoided the set. Sloan wouldn't speak to him. Besides, he had friends there and he wanted to keep what was about to happen as far removed from them as he could.

He lingered outside the camper at the Bide-A-Wee. He walked slowly around, then through, the old factory where Nina had been attacked. He wandered among the gray, corrugated metal Quonset huts, uninhabited, it seemed, since World War II. He walked along side-walks of stores selling dusty office supplies and medical supplies. He found himself scanning the street in a window's reflection for a long moment and realized he had been staring intently at thick mannequins wearing heavy girdles, chastely muted by an amber plastic sunscreen and the store clerk had been studying *him* with amused curiosity.

Where is he? Where is Stile's killer?

Pellam walked to the river and watched the sunset from a disintegrating bench in the scrubby remains of Maddox Municipal Park. The ambitions of the entire town were expressed in a small store behind him. The wood sign that proclaimed the owner's name was illegibly faded, but on the facade itself was a larger message, sloppily hand-painted: *Scrap Metal Bought. All Kinds. All Grades. Cash NOW!*

After a dinner of a hamburger and a beer, Pellam wandered the streets again, streets he shared only with the few people meandering between the Jolly Rogue and Callaghan's, and with packs of scrawny dogs with wild eyes but hopeful prances that sadly suggested domesticated puppyhoods.

At midnight he sat again in the park, with a beer he did not drink, watching the moon's stippled reflection in the water, smelling the cold, marshy air and an oily smell from some distant factory or refinery.

When is he going to find me?

Yet nothing found him that night but sleep, and Pellam woke on the bench at 4:00 A.M., astonished at first at the extent of his exhaustion, then at his carelessness, and finally at his extraordinary good luck at escaping unharmed. He returned to the camper, sore and chilled, his hands shivering and the only warm aspect about him the wood grip of the Colt pressing hard against his belly.

Dr Wendy looked good.

Breezy. That was the way she walked. Breezy. What did they say in high school? There was a word. What was it?

Bopping.

Right. And you had to snap your fingers when you said it. Bopping. *Yeah, you see that girl? You see the way she bopped into the lunchroom?*

"Yo, Dr Wendy."

"Morning, Donnie."

He wondered if she sailed. He pictured her in a white bikini, with thin straps. She would have a small mound of a belly – he remembered the leather near-miniskirt – but that was okay. He wondered if she owned a boat. No, probably not; she spent all her money on clothes and weird earrings. But her boyfriend might have one.

He wondered if she spent every Sunday on his boat. He wondered what it would be like to be married to her.

He wondered if she ever went out with patients. Donnie Buffett decided he was going to ask her on a date.

She swung the door shut and did her cigarette routine. "I wanted to come right by. We've got the results, Donnie. The sexual response tests."

"Okay, I'm sitting down – as if I had an option." His smile faded and his brow creased with concern. "What's the verdict?"

"You're reflex incomplete."

He had forgotten what this meant, but the way she said it, the significant tone and smile of minor triumph, he guessed it was good news.

". . . nearly one hundred percent of these patients can have erections, either reflexogenic or psychogenic. Not all of them, but a good percentage, can ejaculate. There will be a lowered sperm count but all that means is if you want to have children, you'll have to try harder."

Weiser shook his hand as if they'd just completed a business deal.

"Well, there you go," Buffett said happily, and began to sob.

The cop's eyes flooded with tears and his breath shook

out of his body in spasms. His face swelled with a huge pressure.

He tried to speak but was unable to.

What's happening to me?

Weiser said nothing.

Buffett was choking on tears, he was drowning in them. They were going to kill him, drain away his life like spurting blood. Was he going crazy? Had it finally happened? *What stage of recovery is hysteria, sweetheart?* Crying harder than when he was a kid, harder than when he broke his nose, harder than when his mother died . . . He could . . . not . . . breathe . . . He struggled to control the jag. Finally he did. The air sucked in deeply and he relaxed. "I . . ." Another attack struck. He buried his face in wads of Kleenex. "I . . ." He substituted a pillow for the tissue and cried some more. Gradually the tears ceased.

"Can I get you anything?" Weiser asked.

He shook his head, gasping.

He didn't want her to see him this way. The beautiful, breezy doctor with the spaghetti-strap bikini and the twenty-foot sailboat. The doctor with the boyfriend and her twelve-year-old daughter. But he was out of control, gasping for breath and crying like a swatted newborn.

She asked if he wanted to be by himself and he shook his head and threw his arm over his face. After a few minutes he began laughing softly. "I'm a nut case," he wheezed.

"You don't have any idea the kind of stress you're going through."

Buffett felt no Terror and no Depression but instead a roaring mania. "I don't know why I'm crying, I don't know why," he whispered as the sobbing began again. "I don't know why . . ."

Weiser did not offer any explanation. She sat for a moment, watching him, then stood, opened the window, and lit another cigarette.

Afternoon in Maddox, Missouri.

Pellam had spent hours wandering around again, playing bait. He walked through antique stores, up and down the streets, had a beer at each of three interchangeable taverns, walked some more, looking from behind his Ray-Bans for the man who was looking for *him*.

As he walked, he stayed apart from the crowd, he wandered slowly, he put his back toward several alleys and many cruising cars.

Pellam decided he had gotten very good at making himself a target.

At 5:00, after eight hours on his feet, he found himself in the crowded farmers' market off River Road. The dusty parking lot was filled with stalls where farmers – traditional ones as well as past and present hippies – from Missouri and southern Illinois sold cheese and veggies and muffins and apples and – sure enough – northern watermelon. Pellam looked at the bleak gaiety of the place with its faded banners and a doleful clown tying balloon animals for a small crowd of children with soiled hands and cheeks. He heard twangy country western music vibrating out of cheap speakers.

A half hour later, Pellam decided it was time to return to the camper. He bought a bottle of wine, some cheese, crunchy Dutch pretzels, and two plums.

He clumsily discarded his boots and jacket when he entered the Winnebago. He washed his face and sat in the back bunk, eating the cold supper. Pellam did not care for apples but the only liquor for sale at the market had been apple wine. He bought it reluctantly, hoping that alcohol would be more prominent than the apple taste. This was somewhat true though it was overwhelmingly sweet. He drank half of it down, three straight glasses, and shivered hard at the sugar hitting his bloodstream.

He had an urge to see Nina but he dared not, for fear of imperiling her again. This happened so often in his life – wanting, then pursuing, regardless of the danger. Oh, John Pellam did not like this aspect of himself – how he welcomed risks. This nature had led him to be a stuntman for a time, had prodded him to make movies that critics may have loved but that lost big money for many people. He easily forgot that others might get hurt because of him. John Pellam believed in his darker moments that he carried in his heart more of his gun-fighting ancestor than was good for him. And for those around him.

He rose, poured another glass of wine and, carrying the bottle, returned to the bunk. Apple wine. Disgusting. He looked at the label, a picture of attractive, thirtyish farmers, a husband and wife couple, hefting a bushel of apples onto a flatbed. He decided he detested these particular farmers and their natural, no-preservative, rosy cheeks.

He put on a Patsy Cline tape.

No. Too sappy.

He put on a Michael Nyman. Better. He noticed a magazine on the floor. It had fallen open to the horoscope page. He tried to read his and lost interest. He lay back onto the bunk.

Taurus. April 22-May 21. A bad time for investments. Career plans may go awry. Control your temper and don't wander the streets of small cities with a loaded pistol.

When Pellam woke an hour later he couldn't find the wine bottle. Because of the intense throbbing in his temples, he assumed with some remorse that he had finished it.

But he was wrong.

The man who stood in the middle of the camper was holding the bottle to his lips, taking a long drink. His head tilted back as he gulped, but his calm eyes studied Pellam curiously.

The man winced – maybe at the sweetness of the wine – and set the bottle down on the table. He wiped his mouth with his fingers, the same fingers that picked up the Colt Peacemaker from the dining table and slipped it into his pocket. He walked forward toward where Pellam lay. He was handsome and young and he was wearing a suit.

Pellam was surprised at only one thing. At how much the birthmark on his cheek *did* look exactly like the spot on Jupiter.

He thought of many things to say. They came to him quickly. Some funny, some ominous. But he was drowsy and he had a serious headache; he didn't feel like talking. Pellam opened his slurred eyes wide to help him focus and continued to stare.

The visitor touched the rim of the wine bottle and moved his finger in a slow circle around its perimeter. Outside, water lapped on the revetment, a truck diesel chugged in the distance.

Neither man said a word.

Pellam swung his feet around to the floor. The intruder's hand left the bottle and strayed toward his hip, where presumably a pistol rested. Pellam moved slowly – not in fear that he might startle the man but because of the pain in his temples.

He yawned again.

The man said, "You went to Peterson."

When he had yawned, Pellam's eyes watered. He wiped the tears away.

The man said, "Didn't the girl give you the message?"

"She told me."

"Mr Crimmins isn't real happy you went to the prosecutor. He hasn't been arrested so he can only assume you kept your mouth shut."

"I don't have anything to say about Crimmins."

"He knows you saw him in the Lincoln that night."

"What do you want?"

The man was big – six two or three. The clothes fit tight, as if he had very good muscles. Pellam wondered if he had had an erection when he touched Nina.

"I want to be sure you forget you saw him."

Oh. Was that it? Was he going to leave now? Just like that? *Make sure you keep telling people you didn't see Peter Crimmins? Have a nice night.*

The birthmark man buttoned his jacket and pulled on gloves. He's leaving.

But why the gloves? It isn't that cold outside.

The man stepped forward quickly. Before Pellam could lift his arm to deflect the blow, the fist caught him in the side of the head. Pellam fell backwards and landed heavily in the bunk. It had been a glancing strike but on top of an applewine hangover, the pain howled through his head. He moaned and shook more tears from his eyes.

"Damn," Pellam gasped. "Why'd you do that?"

He struggled to his feet, grasping toward a cabinet to steady himself. Then his wrist was snared, painfully, by the man's powerful hand and he was yanked forward into the man's right fist once again. It connected with jaw. Pellam sank down again, stunned.

"That girlfriend of yours, her face is real pretty. The rest of her's probably pretty nice, too."

Pellam stood slowly and touched blood away from his cheek. He nearly fainted from the pain. When the black dots in his eyes settled and his vision returned, he leaned against the camper wall for a moment. Then he made his way unsteadily toward the bathroom.

He mumbled, "Excuse me," as he walked past the man. He sounded polite.

"Watch it." A pistol appeared, a dark blue revolver. He showed it to Pellam in profile, opening his hand quickly and then closing the large, still-gloved fingers. He replaced it.

Pellam leaned against the door to the bathroom. He clicked the light on, but he did not enter. He closed his eyes for a moment, leaning against the doorjamb. He heard the feet come toward him. The familiar Morse code of the camper floor creaking under the man's weight. He smelled sweet aftershave. (Was this what Nina had smelled? Stile had smelled nothing at all, except oil and gas and asphalt and then blood, blood, blood . . .)

"What're you doing there?" the man asked.

Pellam reached into the pocket of the bomber jacket, which was hanging next to the bathroom, and took from it Buffett's pistol, the cold gun. As he turned, Pellam said, "I want you to lie down on the floor."

Instantly the man dropped into a crouch and yanked the pistol off his hip.

The explosion of the gunshot was huge.

It rattled the glass windows and spattered the walls with bits of gunpowder. Cabinet doors shook, and from behind a glass-faced poster frame, a somber Napoleon rocked under the muzzle blast.

Donnie Buffett heard the footsteps and opened his eyes. A shuffling along the corridor outside his room.

He had seen doctors – looking somewhat funny – in plastic booties. They made the same sort of sound. But he doubted what he now heard was made by a doctor. He looked groggily at his watch. Ten o'clock. Did doctors operate at this time of night?

Perhaps it was a nurse. The nurses sometimes brought around snacks and although the lights in his room were out and Buffett had been dozing, if snacks were on the agenda Buffett was going to get a snack. If this was the case he hoped it was the blond nurse. He like her. She was gentle and chattered while she did the things she had to do. The redhead was silent and seemed to resent her complicated duties with the tubes and bottles and bags.

But he didn't think it was either of these women. Donnie Buffett, husband of a self-proclaimed psychic, suddenly had a bad premonition about this visitor.

He groped for the telephone. But before he could grab it the door began to open.

He couldn't run, he couldn't hide.

But he could fight.

Buffett closed his eyes, forced his breath to slip in and out of his lungs leisurely, like a man in contented sleep. His right hand curled into a fist, a fraction of an inch at a time. The footsteps came closer. Buffett tensed the muscles in his arm. Whoever it was came up slowly on the left side of the bed. Buffett decided he would grab the guy's crotch with his left and when he howled and doubled up go straight for the nose with his right fist . . .

He wondered if it was the man who shot him, coming back to finish the job. If the MO was the same as the Gaudia hit he'd have a small-caliber gun. A .22 or .25, which doesn't hurt very much and doesn't have any stopping power at all. Buffett would not die immediately and before he did he could do a lot of damage.

Basketball player, softball pitcher, jump-rope tugger, Donnie Buffett had very strong hands.

He was suddenly hungry with lust – the same feeling that seized his body just before the kill when he was hunting. His shoulders started to tremble. His arm muscles tensed.

The footsteps stopped two feet from the bedside.

"Donnie," the voice whispered.

He opened his eyes and looked at the shadowy silhouette above him. A hand disappeared under the lampshade and the room was suddenly filled with jarring light.

A white-faced John Pellam sat down in the chair beside the bed.

"Hey, chief," Buffett said in an unsteady voice, "how'd you get in here? Visiting hours are over."

"The back stairs."

"Some security. You scared the crap out of me."

"I've got to talk to you, Donnie." He stared at Buffett. No, *past* him. His face was pasty. The cop wondered if he was sick or if he'd fainted. Pellam held something in his hand, something small and dark.

Buffett felt his own hand start to cramp and realized it was still jammed into a large fist. He relaxed it and felt the pain subside. His heart pounded and he felt a surge of weakness melt through his chest and his abdomen. "What the hell are you doing here at this hour?" He too was whispering.

What's he holding?

Pellam glanced down at his own hand, at the object he held. He looked back up at Buffett and said, "He broke into the camper. The man who attacked Nina, the one who killed my friend. I don't know how, he just got in. He hit me a couple times." He looked at Buffett for a long moment. "I took out your gun—"

"The cold gun?"

"Right."

"Jesus."

"I took it out. I shot him with it."

"Jesus, Pellam, you shot him?"

"I wasn't going to. I was just going to arrest him. He pulled his gun out and . . ."

"He's dead? Well, let's think. Any witnesses? Anybody hear anything, you think?"

"There's more," Pellam whispered.

"Don't panic yet. Let's think. It was a break-in. That's burglary, and you've got a right to use deadly force, even if it's a mistake. An absolute right. Okay, let me call . . ."

Pellam held up his hand. The object was a wallet.

"Where were you parked when it happened?" Buffett took the

wallet which Pellam had thrust toward him. Absently he turned it over and over.

"There's *more*," Pellam blurted once again.

The cop was still talking about what Pellam could do, lawyers he knew, what sections of the state penal code covered justifiable homicide. He opened the wallet. He stopped talking. After a moment he blinked. "Oh, my God."

Pellam asked him, "I just killed an FBI agent, didn't I?"

Pellam kept staring at the ID.

Buffett said, "It's over the line. Peterson wouldn't do that."

"It's true."

"Peterson wouldn't *do* it. He wouldn't dare."

"He was making it look like Crimmins was threatening Nina and me so I'd testify against him. How else can you explain it?"

Buffett shook his head. "He's the U.S. Attorney."

"This was the guy that threatened Nina. There's no doubt about it."

"Impossible."

"She described him perfectly."

"A U.S. Attorney is not going to send an agent to assault somebody. Maybe the guy *is* working for Crimmins. Or was. A rogue agent. On the take, you know."

"No, it's Peterson."

"He'd be crazy. Peterson, I mean. Too much risk."

Pellam lifted his palm. "He *is* crazy. You know he tried blackmailing me to get me to testify?"

"Blackmail?"

Pellam took a long moment to hook a thumb through a belt loop. "I did some time."

"Time?" Buffett did not understand.

"San Quentin," Pellam said, volunteering nothing more. Buffett stared for a moment, and said nothing. Pellam continued, "He was threatening to tell the film company."

Buffett took a breath to speak, then he paused. Finally he said that he just didn't know.

"My friend. This guy killed my friend."

"No," Buffett said emphatically. "If he's a rogue agent on a private job for Peterson, murder's *too* over the line. Peterson's on some kind of moral crusade to put Crimmins away, okay. But murder, no way."

"Maybe it was an accident. Maybe he was following the bike to scare me. He misjudged or something."

Buffett conceded that was possible. "What did you do with the body?"

Pellam thought for a minute, as if he'd locked away the memory in a hidden part of his mind. "His car was outside, in the alley across the street. What did I do? I wrapped him up in some garbage bags and put him in the trunk. I drove it to the parking lot by the bus station. There were a lot of cars there. I don't think anybody'll notice it for a while. Oh, I wore gloves."

"You had to do it. You didn't have any choice."

"Jesus," Pellam whispered, shaking his head, numb.

"Where's the gun?"

"I put it next to him. If anybody found him they might think he'd killed himself."

"Pellam, that's not the way people kill themselves."

"I wasn't thinking too clearly."

"Did you wipe off the gun?"

"Yeah. For fingerprints, you mean? Yeah."

"It was a revolver, so you'll have traces of powder on your hands, but you aren't going to be picked up in the next twenty-four hours on this. When the guy doesn't check in, Peterson'll know something's wrong, assuming he does – *did* – work for Peterson. But what's he going to say? He'll have to deny everything. I think you're pretty safe."

"I—"

A nurse entered the room. She smiled at Donnie. She had a tray with a small container of ice cream and two cookies. She gave him two pills in a cup.

"Snack time," she said.

Buffett smiled back. "What are these?" he asked. "The pills."

"Sedatives. Usual."

He took the pills. "Ativan? Half a milligram?"

She called him "Doctor" as she said goodnight.

"I always ask. They make mistakes sometimes. About the pills, I mean. You ever in the hospital, always ask."

Pellam took a Kleenex from Buffett's dresser and was carefully wiping the agent's ID case.

He said to Pellam, "You want some ice cream?"

"Uh-uh. I don't like ice cream."

"You sure?" Buffett opened the ice cream and began to eat

it. He stopped and set down the spoon. "Pellam, you did what I would've done."

"Yeah."

Buffett picked up the spoon again. "You know, there's something else." Pellam took a cookie from the tray and ate it. The cop continued, "Let's assume you're right and this guy, the one you shot, was working for Peterson."

"Uh-huh."

"Then the one who's looking for you, the one who killed your friend, he's still out there."

"I guess he is." Pellam had not thought about this. "But what can I do about it?"

"Dusting off your passport might be a good idea."

Nina, on the other end of the phone, said, "I'd like to see you tonight."

She sounded seductive. Pellam was not in the mood to seduce or be seduced. He was sitting on a banquette three feet from where the carpet had been stained with an FBI agent's blood. He had used Clorox to scrub it. This had worked pretty well but the camper smelled fiercely of bleach.

"I called three times and you never answered."

"I don't have a machine in the camper," he said, although he did. He often did not turn it on.

"There's all kinds of talk around the set about you. Mr Sloan's been saying some things that aren't real nice. He's talking about suing you. I'm real sorry about your friend, John. I don't remember him, but I think I met him once. He seemed real nice."

"He was."

"So you want to be alone tonight?"

"Something like that."

"I don't think it's good for you."

"What's not good?"

"To be alone. Come over. Cranston's only twenty minutes away." Her voice was a breathy singsong.

"It's just not a good time."

"Okay, if that's what you want." Melodious became brittle. *Oh not now please.*

"Are you trying to tell me something?" she asked.

Brother.

"No, no, it's just, this thing with me being the witness and all."

"What about it?" she asked testily, and obviously wanted an answer. It seemed patently unfair to have to argue like this with someone you were not sleeping with.

"It's taking up a lot of my time."

"It's probably not taking up time tonight."

"Well, it is. There've been some complications."

"Complications? I thought you were a simple kind of guy." She was being playful now.

Perhaps their fight was over.

"I don't know . . ." He kept picturing the way the FBI agent fell, surprised, spiraling down. That was it. Just a fall. Then he was dead. Just like that.

Please, he heard Nina saying. She had to see him. "Please, John."

The man had just lain there, and Pellam had walked into the kitchen and dug under the sink for garbage bags in which to wrap up the body.

"It's only twenty minutes?" he heard himself asking.

Because his brother was a union carpenter and had taken him on dozens of jobs, Stevie Flom appreciated good wood-work. He took pleasure in the way joists and studs met and how crown molding fit perfectly in the corners of ceilings. Tonight he wandered through the dark basement of a ram-shackle Victorian house by the riverfront and checked out the handiwork.

Not bad, not bad at all.

Though he wondered why anybody would renovate a house here, where the only views were of a cement plant, a trailer camp on its last legs, and Pelican Island.

Stevie looked at the structural work again. He approved of the wooden studs, instead of the metal ones most builders used. That meant the wall was going to be nice and solid. He looked at the wiring. Electricity was one thing he wanted to learn about. He was good with hydraulics and mechanics but the idea of electricity was kind of weird.

The concrete floor, he observed, was not in good shape. A lot of cracks and places where it had crumbled. He saw evidence of standing water. That was one thing his brother had told him to look for in basements.

Evidence of standing water.

Stevie wished he had something to read. He thought of his old man, who kept newspapers and *Time* magazines piled up in the basement at home – stacks and stacks – with a few *Playboys* hidden between them, their places marked with twigs. But here – nothing but the boiler instructions encased in plastic. His brother had once returned with three hundred bucks he had found in an old book while doing some work in Alton. This place was nothing but old basement.

With evidence of water damage.

He was dying for a cigarette but he knew he shouldn't smoke. The ash would be evidence. He had seen that on *Magnum PI* one time. Evidence of a killer. Or was it a *Matlock* rerun?

So he just walked to a half window and gazed outside, across the street to the empty trailer court.

Wondering when the hell was the beer guy's Winnebago going to return.

He put his head against Nina's hair and inhaled.

He liked the smell. Animal-musky and sweaty and perfumed. He breathed in again and woke her up.

"Hm?" she asked.

"Go to sleep," Pellam whispered.

"I was asleep."

"Go back to sleep."

"Hm."

Regardless of Pellam's mood and inclination several hours ago, a seduction it had been.

Cranston, just off the expressway, was a town much smaller than Maddox and more affluent and ginger-bready. A riverfront tourist trap, the town was filled with shops selling antiques and gadgets and Cute Things. Nina apparently did much shopping there; her apartment was filled with gingham pillows, needle-points of children holding hands, plaques of geese dressed in colonial garb, wooden hearts and stuffed animals and silk flowers.

Pellam hated it all. He had hoped the bedroom might be less

cute, but of course, it was just the same. Worse, in fact, because Nina's hobby was photography. No, not even. Snapshooting. The bedroom contained her collection of photos – fifty, sixty, a hundred of them, all in precious little Lucite and pewter and china frames, lining the radiator cover and windowsill and bedside table. Pellam was afraid to turn around abruptly. They made love under the eyes of Nina's extended family, and during one particularly energetic moment, a round frame fell to the floor, bounced several times, and rolled for a long time in an exorbitantly distracting way.

Oh, yes, a seduction.

But an odd one.

She had greeted him at the door wearing a white T-shirt and short, tight, dark gray skirt sans stockings. Barefoot. She reminded him of Lynn Redgrave in *Georgy Girl*. They had ordered out Hunan beef and cold noodles in sesame paste and eaten while they watched a bad TV show. Nina had loved it. A murder mystery. Pellam watched her lips moving as she whispered to herself, reciting the clues and trying to figure out who the killer was. He sat closer and put his arm around her. She rubbed her head against his as she announced that the victim's brother-in-law had done it.

She had been wrong. Then, instantly, she was tired of mass media. Just as the Midnight Movie came on, Nina turned off the TV, hiked her skirt up, and sat on his lap. He got an unabashed view of sensible white panties and she began kissing him. Her arms lashed around his shoulders and in a frenzy she pressed her mouth to his, shoving her tongue into him, rocking her hips desperately.

He tasted Chinese food as much as he tasted Nina and because he was so startled by the assault it took a minute or two to pick up the pace.

"The thing is," she whispered, "I have something to say."

He responded by taking off her T-shirt. Her bra was shimmery and silver and very transparent and it half-heartedly supported large breasts that she kept playing against his chest.

"What?" he whispered.

She kissed him. "It's important." Her breasts battered him again, and he bent toward one. "Listen to me," she whispered insistently. But it was a breathless insistence, and he did not. Instead he kissed her for a full minute.

"*No*, I mean it." She slapped the back of his hand as it probed.

Pellam lifted his head, startled. They lay half-reclining, half-naked, pressed against each other. He gave her his attention but she did not speak immediately. He reflected that there is nothing more ridiculous than two people in the posture of lovemaking when they are not making love.

"I don't want you to stay over," she said.

Pellam was looking for hooks and eyelets.

This's what you want to tell me? Just explain it to me as you go along.

"I'm ovulating," she said as if it were a trade secret.

"I'll be careful."

She blinked and pressed her mouth to his for a long moment. When they could both breathe again she said, "Well, of *course* you have to use a condom. But what I'm saying is don't make too much out of this. I'm not really in control. It's just hormones."

"I don't care what it is." He meant this sincerely. His hand danced along sparkles of the mesh bra.

She leaned away and pressed a finger to his lips. "You have to promise me you won't stay tonight."

He whispered, "You're beautiful."

"Shhhh." She frowned. "Just promise."

What was the question? "Okay, sure. But you're still beautiful."

"No, I'm not."

"Can I stay for a few minutes, at least?"

She kissed him again. "Just not all night." She rubbed against him. She smiled girlishly and he believed whatever had so enigmatically interrupted the moment was past.

Now, an hour later, lying in the huge bed (huge to him; he was used to Winnebago bunks), smelling the animal scent of her scalp, Pellam felt better. There were times when there ought to be nothing but this, being as close as you can to another human being, overlapping skin, mixed sweat, lying in silence and scents.

He found himself aroused again. His hand slid down her belly and touched the curled pale hair that reminded him of the fine hairs at her temple.

She swatted his hand again – this time with more energy than he thought necessary.

"Are you all right?" Pellam had whispered this same question at other moments like this. The query did not have its literal meaning, of course, but was intended as an emergency exit that allowed other words – whatever she wanted or needed to say – to escape.

Nina whispered, "I have to tell you something."

"Hormones," Pellam said, to be light about it. "It's all right. I understand." He kissed her hair. She moved away from him. "You want me to leave?" he asked, already offended.

"Well, yes, I do. Not this minute, though."

"You're beautiful," he said, trying to recapture some romance.

"Stop saying that." The curtness in her voice seemed not so much irritation as distraction as if she was considering how to express a complicated thought and was running through variations before she spoke. When she did speak, finally, sitting up and pulling the sheet around her, the message was not as tricky as he had anticipated. She said, "Your friend, Donnie. The cop? I just wanted you to know that I slept with him the other night."

When Stevie Flom heard the sticky sound of the camper's slowing tires on damp asphalt he stood up fast and notched the back of his hand on a bolt.

"Damn," he whispered, and sucked the small wound. He tasted blood and rust and he wondered if he ought to get a tetanus shot. But then he figured that if the cops looked around this building after they found the body, they might see some blood on the bolt and search all the hospitals for people who'd gotten shots. He was proud that he'd thought of this.

For the third time that night he checked the Beretta. He pulled the slide back slightly; there was one round in the chamber and the clip was full. They were small bullets. Just .22 longs, not even the full-size long rifles. But they had advantages. For one thing, you needed no silencer. Another advantage – the gun was so small and the recoil so slight that you could group rapid-fire shots real close.

Tricks of the trade.

Stevie watched the Winnebago rock to a stop in the trailer park. The man stepped outside and hooked up the hose and plugged in a large electrical cord into a junction box. He returned to the camper.

Stevie then made his way out of the structurally sound basement that contained evidence of water damage. He cocked the gun and slipped the safety off. He started across River Road.

21

H e was thinking he had done it wrong.

Forget what she had said and what she had not. Pellam should have stayed.

This was one of those rules about relationships that no one ever teaches you. Sometimes you were supposed to leave and sometimes you were supposed to stay and you had to read a lot of data fast to figure out which.

Now, locking the camper door, Pellam debated the matter with himself. It was complicated because he doubted he, or any man, would have done what she did. A confession like that? At some time, sure. (Well, maybe.) But lying in a bed with three scratch marks from her pink nails on his biceps?

Never.

"We played cards for a couple of hours," she had explained. "I wasn't supposed to be there. It was after visiting hours. I sat on his bed. He's very sensitive. You wouldn't think he would be, being a cop. But he is. His hands were the giveaway. They're very soft."

Spare me no details.

"His wife's a fruitcake and he's been very depressed. He said people are afraid to come see him because he can't walk. They're afraid of him. I think he's a very funny man."

"Is," Pellam had agreed.

"One thing led to another. Finally he started to cry. I'm a sucker for men who cry. He said he didn't think he'd be able to, you know, perform anymore. It's the one thing that's eating him up. Even more than not walking. I asked him if I could hold him. And I sat on the bed. And, I guess . . ." She had shrugged her shoulders, and the beautiful breasts that had been pulled and prodded by two men in as many days slipped out from under the sheet. She covered herself again.

"And he was able to, uhn, perform?" Pellam had asked. He shouldn't have. He had forgotten he was talking to the Queen of Detail.

"Oh, yeah," she had said enthusiastically. "Twice. We were both pretty surprised."

"Twice?"

Pellam thought, But you slapped my hand when *I* wanted to do it twice. This, however, would have sounded very juvenile, and he had contented himself with picking up his clothes with dramatic swipes. "I better be going."

"Don't hate me, John. I'm sorry."

She had started to cry.

"I don't hate you."

"I just saw him lying there so sad . . ."

"You did a good thing for him. I know how depressed he's

been . . ." Pellam had spoken with reassurance and in a kind voice; on the other hand, he was dressed in three minutes and out the door in five.

Naw, he now reflected, *should've left. Glad I did*.

Pulling his shirt off as he walked into the Winnebago's tiny bathroom, smelling her perfume on the cloth. He turned the shower water on. The hookup was not very good, the pressure was low and the water was full of minerals, which meant that the soap would not lather; it scummed.

He stepped into the bedroom area, dropped his change and bills and wallet and keys on the bed in one big, messy pile. He thought how much he liked living alone. He pulled off his pants and stepped into the shower.

Stevie Flom decided he couldn't shoot a man who was naked. So he sat sideways in the driver's seat of the camper and looked at the worn controls. He listened to the electric-motor sound of the water. He licked his gouged hand. He was suddenly very tired and decided he needed a vacation. From Ralph Bales. From Lombro. From this piss-ant river town. What Stevie was going to do was take his money from this job and spend two months in Las Vegas. Maybe while he was there he would check around for local work. He liked the idea of perpetual sun. He liked the idea of glossy casinos open twenty-four hours a day. Free drinks and soft flesh. And many hours away from the wife.

He thought it was funny, killing someone whose name you didn't know. He looked around the dash and found an ID card for a movie set. He learned that the beer man's name was John Pellam.

Pellam, Pellam, he repeated to himself.

The water stopped hissing.

Footsteps. The camper creaked. The door opened. He smelled shampoo.

Stevie lifted the gun.

Pellam, wearing a thick brown bathrobe and socks, stepped into the hall. He blinked. "How'd you get in here? Who are you?"

Stevie Flom smiled coldly.

And he felt a sudden jolt of nausea, a burn spreading through his gut. His hands started to shake. His teeth, bared by the mad smile, were rattling. He pushed the gun closer toward Pellam, who was speaking, though Stevie couldn't hear the words. He didn't know whether the guy was yelling in anger or begging not to be killed. Stevie simply checked out to anxiety and his whole body started sweating. He pulled his right elbow in close to his body to stop the trembling. No effect. His head shook, his neck. He tilted his head sideways, as if that would let the nervousness run off him onto the floor. But he kept shaking.

Trying to calm himself, he ordered Pellam to sit. But the man just stood there, looking at him angrily, ignoring.

"Sit *down*," Stevie growled. The words were lost in a nervous swallow.

Pellam remained standing. His eyes began to scan the room. Stevie heard some words. ". . . my friend? . . . *You* were the one? . . . The motorcycle? . . ."

Stevie took the gun in his left hand and wiped the palm of his right on his pants, then gripped the pistol again. Pellam took two steps sideways and picked up an empty wine bottle like a club. "Okay," Pellam said.

Okay? What does he mean by Okay? He's got a bottle, I've

got a gun. What the hell does he mean by Okay? Stevie told himself to hold the gun out, then he realized he was already doing so. He stepped closer to Pellam. *What the hell does he mean by Okay?* Stevie stepped back again.

Squeeze.

Nothing happened. His finger would not respond. He looked at his hand. This did not help.

Squeeze the fucking trigger. He realized he had mouthed the words. Maybe he had actually said them.

Pellam was saying, "Put it down."

Stevie's mind suddenly went blank. He stuck the gun out in a single furious motion, pointed it right at Pellam's chest, closed his eyes, and began to pull the trigger.

The cloud of glass surrounded Stevie Flom. Bluish smoke and a thousand splinters from what had been the window of the camper enveloped him. The explosion seemed to occur a moment later, as the dust of shattered glass settled on the floor.

Stevie Flom turned toward the window, his muscles now relaxed, the trembling gone. He turned toward the window and said, "It's all right. It'll be fine. Really."

Then he dropped to the floor.

The door of the camper swung open and a man stepped inside, filling the room with his huge bulk, wearing a sport coat and jeans. Moving fast on small feet, he ignored Pellam, who stepped back out of his way.

What the hell was going on?

Shutting out lights.

"Who are—?"

"Quiet," the man barked.

"Sure," Pellam said. Bright light angled in from the kitchen and gave the room a tilted appearance, like a fun house. The man shut this light out, too. He went to the window and looked out. In the darkness Pellam said, "Are you a cop?"

"Shhh." He walked to Stevie Flom and felt his neck, pocketed his little gun, then walked to the opposite window of the camper and looked out once more for a long moment. He turned and looked at Pellam's hand, which held the apple wine bottle by the neck. "You got that for any reason?" His voice was thick but accentless.

"No. Uh-uh." Pellam put the bottle down.

"You Pellam?"

He nodded and asked, "Who are you?"

"Tom Stettle. I work for a Mr Crimmins. He—"

"Crimmins?"

"Peter Crimmins."

Pellam looked at Stevie. "*He* works for Crimmins . . ."

"Uhn, no, sir. That he doesn't," Stettle said matter-of-factly. "Mr Crimmins hired me to keep an eye on you."

"Oh." Pellam stared at the body. "Who's he?"

Stettle did not answer but bent down and started emptying Stevie's pockets. "He was going to kill you."

"What's exactly going on?"

Without looking up from his task, Stettle said, "Mr Crimmins knows that you didn't see him in that car the night Vince Gaudia got killed. He didn't have nothing to do with the hit. He wants to make sure you stay alive to tell everybody that. So he's had me looking out for you. You're a tough man to stay on top of, let me say."

Stevie Flom didn't seem to be bleeding. Was he really dead?

This he asked Stettle, who seemed surprised at the question. "Well, sure he is. Help me, huh? Let's get the body into my car. I just happened to check by tonight. It was, like, lucky. I didn't figure he was here already. I figured they'd do you on the street like they did Gaudia."

"He's the one who shot the cop?"

"I dunno. Probably," Stettle said. "You have any garbage bags?"

"Beg your pardon?"

"Garbage bags? Thick ones, if you've got them."

"I've got some, sure."

Pellam went into the kitchen and drank a full glass of water. He found Stettle standing in the doorway, looking at him. "You want some?"

"Sure."

Pellam poured another glass and held it out. Stettle took it in a huge hand. Pellam asked him, "Did you see the other guy out there?"

"What other guy?"

"There are two of them." Pellam motioned to Stevie Flom. "He's not the one I saw get out of the Lincoln."

"He isn't?" Stettle drank the water. "You mean there's somebody else?"

"Yeah. Heavy guy. Balding."

Stettle grimaced. "I'll do what I can to keep an eye out for you. But I can't be your roommate. After this –" he nodded at Stevie's body "– whoever was in the car is going to be after you in a big way. You should take a vacation. Take a year off or so."

"That's what people keep telling me."

Stettle was eager to leave. He finished the water and took a paper towel then wiped the glass off. With this same towel he wiped everything else in the camper he had touched.

"You got to get a new window," he said, and broke out the rest of it with his elbow. Pellam assumed he didn't want to leave an obvious bullet hole.

Pellam stared as the bits of glass flew outward. "I guess I should say thanks. I mean—"

Stettle was uninterested in gratitude. He soaked the paper towel that held a dozen of his fingerprints and wadded it up, slipped it into his pocket. "Garbage bags?" he asked.

"Sure." Pellam handed him some.

"Rubber gloves?"

"Gloves?"

"Playtex, you know."

Pellam found two old pairs. Stettle and he put them on. "The blood. Nowadays you can't be too careful, you know."

And for the second time in two days John Pellam was wrapping a body in green Glad bags. Three mils thick.

She pulls off the brown dress.

This scares him, seeing the arc of the dress falling onto the chair. He smells fruity perfume.

She is undoing pins from her wispy hair, which tumbles down her neck. The hair is like white light. It ends just above her substantial bra. She smooths her hands along it, from her neck over her breasts down to her waist. She tosses her head. Her hair terrifies Donnie Buffett.

Not saying a word, she leans forward and lets the hair stream over his arm and face. His eyes are locked on to her hair.

Terrified but unable to look away. His hand closes on it, he rubs it between his fingers, he weighs a huge handful.

No. Don't do this to me. Please. Don't . . .

She looks down at him, at the terror on his face.

I want to go to sleep. I want to—

But she is bending forward, a slight smile on her face. He is enveloped in her perfume, strawberry and spice, and she is kissing him, her mouth firm against his. He feels her tongue, just its tip against his lips, then through them. She is kissing him hungrily.

He is trembling.

She backs away.

She is wearing a large silver sparkly bra, garter belt and stockings, and white panties. All white, all lacy and glistening in the low light.

"Look," Donnie Buffett says and he is sweating. "Don't—"

"Shhhh." *She bends forward and kisses him again. He feels the pressure of her breasts under the silky cloth. She knows he feels it and rubs against him as she kisses him. Her tongue slips farther into his mouth. He doesn't know what to do. He kisses her back.*

Wondering if he'll feel anything, if he'll feel that twisty-warm sense, but then no, he doesn't. And then he wants her to go away, wanting that more than he's ever wanted anything in his life . . .

She backs off again, still smiling. He is terrified and begs her to leave. "The thing is, with this accident . . . Like I was saying. You . . ."

She turns her back to him, ignoring him. He hears her whisper, "Help me."

His arms slump. "I'm sorry . . ."

"Please," she whispers. "For me? I want it for me."

Somehow this changes everything. He lifts his hands and undoes the hook of her bra and she is backing into him, forcing his hands to encircle her breasts and grip them. Her neck is inches from his mouth. He lowers his mouth to it and is caught in an avalanche of her hair. He tastes it. He smells strawberry. When she rubs against him it is as though they are underwater and their bodies are sliding past each other on the current. He turns her around in his arms and kisses her hard.

She slides off the bed and stands in front of him as she slips her panties down. He sees the blond fuzz. This hair, too, fascinates him; it is so fine you can't really see the hair, it's more a blur of focus where her legs come together. She begins to touch herself, running her hands over her body, taking handfuls of her head hair and spreading them around her flesh.

Then she hops up on the bed again, puts one leg on either side of his head, and bends forward, kissing his chest and stomach as she pushes the blankets aside. He is muttering no no no, but the way it is working out, his mouth being where it is, she can't hear his words anyway and he gives up talking and all he can do is think, hell, let's do it do it do it . . .

This – a memory, not a fantasy – was prominently in Donnie Buffett's mind when he opened his eyes and saw John Pellam standing in the doorway of his hospital room.

Buffett blinked then he cleared his throat. "Hey, chief. I wasn't expecting you."

"Hello, Donnie." Pellam walked into the room. His boots made a particularly loud noise.

Oh, Christ. He knows.

"Listen, John . . ." Buffett looked up at the blank TV screen, then at the row of flowers. His face felt suddenly thick and hot, as if filled with steam. *Oh, man, here's the guy bought me beer and has treated me like a real person, he's the first one in the whole world after the accident to tell me to go to hell, no kid gloves, no bullshit, and what do I do? I fuck his woman. Oh, man. Oh, man . . .*

"John, listen, I was going to tell you."

Pellam was grinning. This made Buffett feel a thousand times worse.

"It wasn't like I planned it. I know I was ragging you about the casting couch thing but it's not like I said to her, 'Oh, poor me, I can't get it up.' It wasn't a trick or anything."

That did *work, though, come to think of it.*

"It's all right, Donnie."

"I'm not saying she came on to me. I'd never say that to avoid taking my own lumps, you know? But she was easy to talk to and I was feeling really bad. She hugged me and . . . It just sort of happened. I really *was* going to tell you. Really, man. But last time you were in, you were so, you know, upset about your friend . . ."

"She isn't for me," Pellam told him.

"No, no, she likes you. I know she does." *Wait. Would this make him feel better or worse?* "What happened . . ."

"Donnie, I've got no claim on her."

"I talked you up afterwards." He said this cautiously.

Pellam was sitting down in the chair. "I wouldn't've come by today if I was mad."

Buffett could think of nothing to do but extend his hand. They shook solemnly, and Pellam seemed amused by this formal gesture of apology. "I need some help, Donnie."

"Anything. You name it. My buddies still hassling you? I'll get them off your case, John. Don't worry. I'll call the mayor if I have to."

Pellam looked over the untouched dinner tray. Donnie followed his eyes. He asked, "Break bread?"

"Haven't eaten in a day."

"Help yourself."

It wasn't bread, it was soup, rice, and red Jell-O. Pellam ate the soup, Buffett, the rice. They split the saltines and divided the Jell-O into two bowls.

"You know, don't you," Buffett said, "Jell-O really sucks?"

"Uh-huh." But Pellam seemed hungry. And with milk poured over it the Jell-O was not bad, though Pellam didn't get much milk; he had the fork and Buffett had the spoon.

One cube slipped away from Buffett and he chased it off the tray and onto the sheet and blanket. "Shit." He cocked his middle finger against his thumb and flicked the cube into the wall. It left a pink wound on the wall and splatted on the floor. The men laughed.

Pellam told Buffett about an old record of his uncle's, a comedy record from the fifties. Who was the guy? Del Close, he thought. It was called *How to Speak Hip*. There was this routine, he explained, about a man who gets hung up on Jell-O. He keeps eating these bowls of Jell-O and ordering more. Going from restaurant to restaurant. Everybody's staring at him. What flavor was it? Strawberry, he thought. Or raspberry. "It's to teach you the expression 'hung up on.' You know, like beat talk was a foreign language." Pellam said that he had listened to the record a hundred times when he was a kid. He loved the Jell-O routine.

Buffett smiled politely, waiting for the punch line, but apparently there was none.

"You have to sort of hear it," Pellam said. "And be in the mood."

"No, it was funny," Buffett said quickly. Today, at least, he was Pellam's toady.

But Pellam seemed to have lost his taste for humor – as well as for Jell-O and for conversation. He wiped his face. He nodded to the bedside table and said, "I guess I better do it. Let me see that phone for a minute, would you?"

The U.S. Attorney was in court when the call came in.

The secretary buzzed Nelson's office and asked, "There's a man on three. He says it's important. When will Mr Peterson be back?"

"Take a message, darling," Nelson snapped. He returned to a lengthy set of interrogatories.

"It's a Mr Pellam and he says—"

Click.

"Mr Pellam, Mr *Pellam*. How are you? This is Mr Peterson's assistant, Nelson Stroud. Is there something I can do for you?"

"I want to talk to Peterson."

"Is this about the Crimmins situation?"

Pellam said that it was.

"Well, is there anything *I* can help you with?"

"Where is he?"

"Mr Peterson? He's in court. He won't be back for several hours."

"Oh." There was a long silence. Nelson gripped the phone hard and believed that if he breathed too loud, he would blow away the fragile phone connection.

"You're a lawyer?"

"Assistant U.S. Attorney for the—"

"Okay. I want a meeting."

Bingo!

"Fine, absolutely fine. You name a time, you name a place. Whatever."

"Your office, I'd like it to be in your office."

"Sure, that's fine. Tomorrow? Tomorrow morning?"

"Sure, tomorrow morning. Only . . ."

"What is it?"

"Only there's a problem. I need some assurance from you."

"Assurance, assurance, of course." Nelson's hands were vibrating. This was the big time, this was negotiating with vital witnesses, and he was terrified. "What exactly do you have in mind?"

"I want some guarantee that I won't be prosecuted," Pellam said.

"Why would you be prosecuted?"

There was a pause. "Because I lied when I told you I hadn't seen Peter Crimmins in the Lincoln."

22

The press conference that evening was short.

The reporters had hoped for something hot – perhaps Peterson's announcement that he was resigning to run for the Senate or that he was handling some big corporate whistle-blower case or that the Justice Department would dish up something photogenic for the newshounds – like a good drug bust, the sort where the FBI and DEA lay out all the Uzis and Brownings in the front of the table and all the plastic bags of smack or coke in the back and declaim about the progress in the war on organized crime.

But all they got was Peterson standing at a chipped podium emblazoned with a U.S. Department of Justice seal, droning on and on and on . . .

He spoke to them in the vast monotone that marked his delivery at all of his press conferences. "I'm pleased to announce that a witness in the Vincent Gaudia killing has come forward and agreed to testify before the grand jury. This is an individual whom my office identified immediately after the killing and who had serious, and understandable, concerns about his safety, and who expressed those concerns, but who has now come forward in exchange for my agreeing not to prosecute for obstruction of justice."

Which was a jaw-cracker of a sentence and left the reporters thinking up fast paraphrases.

When asked if this was a reliable witness, Peterson said, "He looked into the front seat of the car driven by the man we are certain is responsible for the killing. He was no more than three feet away. He assures me he can make a positive ID."

A reporter shouted, "Has Peter Crimmins been identified as the man in that car?"

But Peterson knew the game of reporter dodge; he was not going to give the defense lawyers a chance to claim prejudice. He said, "All I can say at this time is that the witness will be giving us a formal statement at nine-thirty tomorrow morning. We anticipate an arrest within twenty-four hours of that."

Peterson then deflected a number of questions about the killing and talked about several drug busts and other recent prosecution victories of the U.S. Attorney's office recently.

"I heard rumors," a woman reporter called in an abrasive voice, "that you arrested Tony Sloan, the movie director who's currently shooting a film in Maddox."

Peterson glared into the video camera lights. "That is *absolutely* untrue. The movie company brought a large number of automatic weapons into the district. Both FBI and BATF agents from the Treasury Department observed what appeared to be an irregularity in the firearm permits and we just wanted to keep an eye on them to make sure they didn't fall into the wrong hands.

We did not at any time contemplate criminal action against Mr Sloan and the film company. The local police in Maddox, I understand, took it upon themselves, for some reason, to make an arrest. Our findings are that the permits are in order and I'm releasing the weapons presently."

"Are you saying that the Maddox police arrested Mr Sloan improperly?"

"I won't comment on the judgment of fellow law enforcement agencies. The arrest was a Maddox Police Department decision. Ask them about it."

There were several other *no comments*. Finally a very preoccupied Ronald Peterson wandered off the stage, leaving the press corps to call their desks or tape their intros. Most of the TV reporters were far more interested in the Tony Sloan angle than the Gaudia killing and decided to run some clips from *Circuit Man* in the segment about Sloan's arrest.

But hard news is hard news and everybody wrote up at least a news bite about the witness for ten o'clock. Vince Gaudia was, after all, Maddox's only honest-to-God hit for as long as anyone could remember.

As it turned out, Ralph Bales was playing darts and did not happen to hear the story. Philip Lombro, however, did. And by nine that evening was on the phone. "He cheated us," Lombro said. "He took the money and he cheated us! He's going to testify!" His voice was high. Some of this was indignation and some of it was anger. But most of his agitation came from disgust with himself that this whole thing had gotten wildly out of hand.

"Looks that way," Ralph Bales said. "He's meeting Peterson tomorrow?"

"At nine-thirty."

After a lengthy silence, in which he heard the sound of male laughter in the background, Lombro said, "What exactly are you going to do?"

"Okay, I think you've gotta agree we don't have much choice."

Lombro sighed deeply. He did not agree with anything that Ralph Bales said or thought. But the whole matter had moved beyond him now. He realized he was being asked a question and said, "What?"

"I said, you haven't by any chance heard from a guy named Stevie Flom, have you?"

"Who?"

"A guy working with me."

"No. I don't even know him. Why would I?"

"No reason. I haven't heard from him."

"Why would he call *me*?"

"I mentioned I worked for you once. It's not important. Anyway, about our situation—"

"Just finish this thing," Lombro said desperately. "Finish it."

"You want me to . . ."

"Do what you have to" were Lombro's closing words but they had hardly the energy to carry forty miles to the other end of the phone line.

The hour was not late; it was not his normal bedtime, but Philip Lombro, hoping that tomorrow would appear and then vanish with invisible speed, took two sleeping pills and, in his silk pajamas, slipped into his bed.

He lay awake for a long time, tormented by thoughts of what he had done, thoughts about the witness's betrayal, thoughts about how he was soon going to have another man's blood on his hands. But under the sedation of the Valium, he calmed, and eventually the man who was going to die tomorrow did not occupy his thoughts. Nor did Vincent Gaudia nor Ralph Bales. Philip Lombro was in that netherworld between sleep and waking. Bits of dreams floated past like the papers caught in the fickle currents around the Maddox Omnibus Building. He saw faces, most of them grotesque. Melting into other shapes. They were real to him, intense, three-dimensional. They reminded him of the images seen through those plastic three-dimensional viewers he used to buy his nieces and nephews thirty years ago, the ones that held cardboard disks of fairy tales and cartoons.

One of these faces, though, was not grotesque. It was a girl's face, a young girl's. She was beautiful. Her features did not melt. Her eyes simply looked toward him. Lombro was powerless to touch her or speak. He was merely observing; you don't participate in dreams like this.

Then the girl's face suddenly grew so terribly sad that Lombro became completely awake, pierced by an urge to cry, and he sat up abruptly.

This was the hardest part of living alone, Philip Lombro knew. Waking from dreams by yourself.

Pellam was up at seven-thirty. He had slept in a location van – one of the big Winnebagos used for makeup. He rose silently and walked into the bathroom, where he took a tepid-water shower. Then he brushed his teeth with his fingers and a spoonful of Arm & Hammer. He felt groggy and hoped he would find something energizing in the medicine cabinet – diet pills, NoDoz. But there was nothing other than a prescription drug he had never heard of. The label warned against operating machinery or driving a car while taking the medicine.

It would be coffee or nothing.

Pellam dressed in the bathroom, the cloth of his shirt and jeans darkened by the water he had failed to towel off. He brushed his damp hair and forwent the noisy blow dryer. He was here as a spy or, at best, refugee, and wanted his presence kept secret. Slipping outside, he hurried down the front steps and shivered in the cool fall air. There was a rich, loamy scent of water, which he knew would be the river though he could not see it from here.

At the curb he paused to let pass a powder blue car, slowing as it passed the trailer. On the side was a sign. *Out of Work 117 days.* The number 17 was on a separate piece of cardboard, freshly taped over the previous day's record. "I do odd jobs," the man called but he drove on before Pellam could say a word.

Ralph Bales found his heart was beating like the wings of a panicked sparrow.

He looked at his wrists, focusing on the veins, surprised that they were not vibrating with blood. His hands returned to the steering wheel. Ralph Bales was waiting downtown – in a stolen Chevy – outside the Federal Building on Mission, waiting for John Pellam to arrive. And the reason his heart was beating so fast was that this was a terrible site for a hit.

On the way here, he had passed a car wash whose name was World O' Wash. The phrase kept going through his mind, and all he could think of was World O' Cops. FBI, Treasury agents, federal marshals and city cops and probably Missouri Bureau of Investigation agents all over the place – them, plus court security guards who had never fired a piece except to get their tickets and had been waiting for years to draw first blood in the line of duty.

World O' Cops.

Inside the entryway of the building were two white-shirted guards, big men, with large, square heads crowned with fade cuts. Secretaries and clerks and lawyers in running shoes over their dress socks or stockings were streaming into the office. Everyone looked young and eager.

There were several entrances to the Federal Building but Ralph Bales was parked in front of what seemed to be the main one. He supposed there would be a service door or two. He could see a driveway that seemed reserved for garbage pickups. That would be a good place to sneak a witness in. But he had no partner – Stevie still had not shown – and all he could do was cover the main entrance.

He had arrived early, thinking the beer man would get here well before nine-thirty for security reasons. For an hour Ralph Bales sat in the car, the engine running. He moved it only once, when a meter maid waddled by. She held her citation book out like a gun, threateningly. He did not let her get close enough to see his face. He pulled away slowly, did an around-the-block and by the time he got back – maybe three minutes later – she was gone. He parked again in front of the building.

It was now nine-fifty.

He watched the mist in the air, the sunlight flashing off the tall arch; he smelled the burnt metallic air laced with exhaust. The factories on the east side of the Mississippi were busy this morning. His heart fluttering . . . Maybe it was the caffeine in the coffee. He glanced down. He had left the cup in the car, the cardboard carton, blue and white, with pictures of Greek gods or Olympic athletes or something. A cup with his fingerprints all over it. Careless.

He reached down and picked it up, crumpling the cardboard and slipping it into his pocket.

It was then that the trash basket – one of those big, filthy orange things – went through his back window.

Jesus Mother Holy . . .

Not exactly *through* the window. Even cheap American cars had strong glass. The bottom rim of the basket pushed the window in a couple inches, and the glass turned opaque with frost from the fractures. The basket rolled off the car and onto the street.

"Son of a—"

When he turned back to pull the door handle up, there was a gun muzzle in his face, and the man's other hand was shutting the engine off.

He understood. Ralph Bales knew exactly what had happened.

"Put your gun in the back," the beer man said. "On the floor."

Ralph Bales said, "I don't have a—"

The man's voice terrified him with its serenity. "Put your gun on the back floor of the car."

"Okay, whatever you want."

"Put your—"

"I heard you," Ralph Bales said, "I'm going to do it."

"Now."

"Okay."

This reminded Ralph Bales of when the cop caught him just after the Gaudia hit. Only today there'd be no Stevie Flom acting like a madman and stepping out of an alleyway to save him. With a sudden sickening feeling, he had a good idea about what had happened to Stevie Flom.

He dropped the Colt in the back. The man opened the back door and scooped it up. He sat in the backseat and pressed the muzzle of his gun, an old one, against his ear. "Turn all your pockets inside out."

What if the meter maid shows up now? Christ, this guy could panic and shoot them both.

"I don't have anything, I mean, like a weapon or—"

"All your pockets."

Ralph Bales did, dropping the contents on the seat. The beer man prodded the money and the wallet and the crumpled cup and the Swiss Army knife. "Okay, put it back in your pockets. Except the knife. Leave the knife."

Ralph Bales laughed. "The knife? You're kidding."

He was not kidding. Ralph Bales did what he was told.

The man put his seat belt on. "Drive to Maddox. Now."

"But—"

"Drive."

Bales reached for the shoulder strap.

"No belt." He rested the gun against the back of Ralph Bales's neck. "This is a single-action gun. You know what that means?"

"You have to cock it before you can pull the trigger," Ralph Bales said like a student answering a teacher's question.

"I have it cocked. It goes off real easy."

"Okay, listen. If we hit a bump . . ."

"Then I'd drive real slow if I were you."

The dream was wonderful.

She was beautiful.

Nina Sassower believed that although men came on to her – and did so quite frequently – they did so only because of the size of her breasts and her thin legs. She believed they tolerated her face, which she saw as pointed and narrow and pinched.

But in the dream, something had happened. Perhaps she had had an operation, maybe she had just been mistaken all her life. She did not know what had changed. But the person she was in the dream was tall and willowy and had sharp, intelligent, beautiful eyes.

The image didn't last long. It shifted into something else, a street she couldn't identify. Then other people began milling around and the dream ended.

She woke up.

For perhaps two seconds she felt the afterglow of the dream.

She sat up straight, looked at the clock, and spat out, "Oh, no! Son of a bitch!"

It was nine o'clock.

She pulled off her nightgown and yanked open the drawer to her dresser. Panties, bra – no bra. She couldn't find one. She kept looking. *Forget it!* She slipped a sweater on, thinking that it was the first time since the age of thirteen that she had left the house without a bra. Slacks, anklet stockings . . . *They don't match, where's the mate, where? Hell with it! Go!* Beige pumps.

Go, go, go! . . .

Nina pulled on her blue jean jacket. She hadn't washed her

face and she felt a rim of sweat on her forehead. She paused in the mirror to brush her hair and she did that only because she didn't want to look conspicuous.

For what she was about to do, conspicuous would not be good.

She left the house and hurried to her car. After she started the engine, she looked into her purse to make certain that it contained what she had put there the night before.

A military-issue .45 semiautomatic pistol, the classic 1911 Colt, sat heavily between an Estée Lauder compact and a pink plastic Tampax container.

Nina knew the gun about as well as she knew her Singer sewing machine. Although she could not field-strip it blindfolded she could dismantle it sufficiently to clean and oil the bore and the parts and did so every time she fired it. This gun happened to be identical to the ones Ross's gangsters carried in *Missouri River Blues*, although Nina's was loaded with ten rounds of live ammunition and was not registered with the federal government or with anybody else.

Nina now started the car's engine and, not even slowing at a single stop sign or red light, sped through the quaint, quiet burg of Cranston, Missouri, then skidded onto the expressway, hurrying south toward where she believed John Pellam would be.

———•◦•———

23

B eing a lawyer, he was used to rewriting.
      Ronald Peterson never signed off on a letter, interroga-
tory, complaint, motion, or brief without hours of revision.
But the two-page press release describing Peter Crimmins's
indictment for the murder of Vince Gaudia had taken more time,
per word, than anything that Peterson had written in years.

He had just learned, however, that this was one press release
that was not going to be released to anyone.

"He changed his mind?" Peterson whispered, barely controlling his fury.

"That's what the message said," Nelson explained cautiously,
looking away from his boss's enraged eyes. "And there's no
answer at his phone, the phone in his camper. I sent an agent
to Maddox. The camper's not in the trailer park. Somebody in
one of the vans said Pellam'd been fired and they don't know
where he is."

"Think Crimmins got him?"

"Well, according to the receptionist, he didn't sound coerced."

"Why the fuck didn't she put through the call? She's fired. She's out of here."

Nelson said delicately, "He didn't *want* to speak to you. He wanted to just leave a message."

"What exactly did it say again?"

"Just that he'd changed his mind. That was it."

Peterson clicked a fingernail and thumbnail together seven times. "Any hint from the taps on Crimmins?"

"Nothing useful. Business as usual. We can take that one of two ways. Either he's using a safe phone to talk to his muscle. Or he heard the press conference and for some reason he's not concerned about the guy testifying."

Why wouldn't he be concerned?

One reason: He wasn't the man in the Lincoln after all.

"Why," Nelson pondered, "would Pellam be jerking our leash like this?"

Peterson had told no one about the free-lance FBI agent who had gone after Pellam's girlfriend and then Pellam himself to "help" Pellam remember about Crimmins and vanished shortly afterward. Nor did Nelson know that there was nothing whatsoever wrong with Tony Sloan's federal firearm notices. Nelson therefore didn't know that Pellam had some very good motives for jerking leashes. "Cold feet, I suspect," the U.S. Attorney suggested.

"What about the first option? That Crimmins got to him?"

Peterson shook his head. "Even Crimmins wouldn't be that stupid. Hell. The press'll play it like we've got hairy palms."

"What do you want to do?" Nelson gazed down at the press release.

"What's your assessment of the case against Crimmins without Pellam's testimony? I'm speaking of the Gaudia hit."

Nelson thought for a minute. Peterson made a cat's cradle with a rubber band and studied his protégé, whose squinting eyes and pursed lips only partially revealed the lavish anxiety he felt. "I'd say probable cause if we want to arrest him. But we won't get an indictment." Nelson cleared his throat.

"And the original indictment, the RICO charges, without Gaudia's testimony?"

He said, "Acquittal. Sixty-forty." Nelson's grimace was the equivalent of hunkering down in a bunker before a bomb detonated.

But Peterson's sole reaction was to press his teeth together. His breath hissed out from between them and then he chewed on his tongue in rapt contemplation. He slowly concluded that there was as much danger for him in the Crimmins case as there was potential to score one for the good guys.

It was time for the whole thing to go away.

He told this to Nelson and added, "Call Crimmins's lawyer. See if we can plead him away for a few years."

Nelson quickly responded, "Will do," and noted coolly that this order was tantamount to scuttling two years of work. "What about Pellam? There's still somebody out there looking to hurt him. Should we get Bracken or Monroe on it? I mean, the guy could be in trouble."

Peterson wound up a toy Donald Duck, which walked for ten inches, hit an indictment, then marched in place until the spring wound down. "It's Pellam's problem now. He's on his own."

She drove quickly, racing along Main Street in Maddox, past

the empty storefronts, the darkened real estate brokerages, the Goodwill Store. The car spun up a wake of bleached, dull leaves.

Nina had driven from Cranston to the Federal Building in St Louis. She hadn't been able to find Pellam though his camper had been parked in a lot across the street. It had been empty. Where, she wondered, had he gone? She paced in panic up and down the sidewalk. She suddenly believed she knew. She had leapt into the car and sped back to Maddox.

Now, driving along deserted Main Street, she was not so sure she had guessed correctly. The emptiness seemed to laugh at her. Where the hell is he?

As she skidded around a curve beside abandoned grain elevators, images jumbled in her mind. Pellam standing in the field beside the brown Missouri, aiming his Polaroid. Nina herself applying makeup to a petite blond actress wearing a yellow sundress riddled with bullet holes. Pellam lying in bed next to Nina herself. The huge kick of the Colt automatic that jarred her arm from wrist to shoulder every time she fired it.

"You know something?" Ralph Bales asked the question in a normal volume, though it echoed loudly through the empty factory. He looked around quickly, startled by the sound of his own words returning.

The beer man did not apparently want to know anything. Ralph Bales continued, "I don't even know your name."

Introductions were not, however, made. The man prodded him farther inside with the barrel of the cowboy gun.

Despite the muzzle at his back, though, Ralph Bales did not feel in danger. Maybe it was how the man was holding the gun – without desperation, more like a bottle of beer than a weapon. Maybe it was his eyes, which were no longer as eerily serene as they had been. They seemed more purposeful, as if the man just wanted to talk.

In the rear of the warehouse was a small cul-de-sac beneath a balcony. It was very dark here, lit only by indirect light filtering in from the huge arched windows, covered with grime and dust. The floor was dusty, too, but much of that had been disturbed by footprints. Directly in front of a Bee Gees poster was a wood-and-canvas director's chair.

Ralph Bales stopped. The beer man motioned him forward to the chair. "Sit down."

He sat. "This place is pretty nifty. You shooting your film here?"

"Put these on each wrist." The man handed him two pairs of handcuffs. "Right first, then hook it to the arm."

"Kinky." Ralph Bales looked at them closely. *Property of Maddox Pol. Dept.* was stamped on the side. "Where'd you get these?"

"Put them on."

Ralph Bales relaxed further. A guy like this, an amateur, was *definitely* not going to hurt a man handcuffed to a chair. He clicked one pair of cuffs on his right wrist then to the chair. Then he locked the other cuff to his left wrist. The beer man stepped forward slowly and, with a ratcheting sound, hooked the remaining cuff to the other arm of the chair.

He stepped back like a carpenter surveying a good flooring

job. He pulled the Colt out of his belt. "Now. Who was in the Lincoln?"

So he had a tape recorder hidden somewhere, trying to get a confession. "What Lincoln would that be?"

"Who was it?"

"Okay," Ralph Bales said with amused frustration. "This is some kind of bullshit."

"The man in the Lincoln. Who?"

"I don't know what you're—"

"What did you come down to the Federal Building for?"

Ralph Bales lifted his hands as far as he could. The tiny chains clinked. "I wanted to talk to you is all."

"What did you want to say to me?"

"Okay, I was going to pay you to keep quiet about what you saw."

"But you had a gun in your pocket, and only –" He squinted, trying to remember. "– forty bucks on you."

"I was going to pay you a lot of money – more than I'd want to carry around—"

"Who was in the Lincoln?" the beer man recited persistently.

"I don't know, I really don't. Sorry."

"I wish you'd be more cooperative," the beer man said with disappointment, and shot Ralph Bales squarely in the center of his stomach.

John Pellam walked through the cloud of sulfury smoke and looked down. "Not bleeding badly," he announced.

Ralph Bales stared in terror at the wound. His mouth was open. "Why . . . ?" he whispered. "You shot me . . . God, that hurts."

"Who was in the car?"

"Why'd you do that for, why'd you *do* that?"

"Who," Pellam asked evenly, "was in the Lincoln?"

"My God," Ralph Bales whispered, gazing with shocked bewilderment at Pellam. "I'm going to die."

"If you don't tell me I'm going to shoot you again."

"I don't—"

Pellam shot him again.

A huge explosion. The bullet hit a few inches to the left of the first wound.

"No, no, man . . . Stop! I'll tell you." Ralph Bales jerked his head to flick sweat out of his eyes. "Okay! Philip Lombro! Now call a doctor!"

"Who's he?"

Ralph Bales did not hear. "Please! I'm going to bleed to death. Please . . ."

"Philip?"

"Lombro! Lombro!"

"Who's he?"

"Oh, man, I'm going to faint."

Pellam cocked the gun. *"Who is he?"*

"No, no, don't, man, not again! He's some real estate guy. Don't do it again."

"Spell it."

"Spell what? Oh, man . . ."

"His name."

"L-O-M-B-R-O."

"Why did he want Gaudia dead?"

"I don't know. I didn't ask. I'm going to faint. Oh, shit. Some personal thing. I swear to God. He hired me to do it. I'm bleeding to death."

"Where does he live?"

"I don't know. Man, believe me. I don't know. In Maddox somewhere. His office is on Main, that's all I know. He's in the phone book. What do you want from me? For Christsake, call a doctor." With tearful sincerity he said, "I'm a good Catholic."

Pellam did not move for a minute. He smiled.

"No, man, no. Don't do it. You're just going to leave me, aren't you? Don't let me die! I told you what you wanted. Call the cops. Turn me in. But for God's sake, get me to a doctor!"

"Would you testify against this Lombro?"

"Absolutely. Oh, man, you want it, you got it."

Pellam repeated the word softly. "Absolutely." He rubbed the gun with his left hand. Ralph Bales was crying. This seemed to irritate Pellam. He said, "They're wax bullets."

Ralph Bales kept sobbing.

Pellam said again petulantly, "Would you stop crying? They're not real bullets."

"What?"

"I wish you'd stop that," Pellam said, referring to the crying.

Ralph Bales slowly caught his breath. He frowned. He looked down at his gut – at the two large splats of bright red blood. As far as the handcuffs allowed, he pulled his shirt apart. There were huge reddish welts where the bullets had struck him but the skin was not broken. Fragments of white wax were bonded to the cloth which was stained with dark blood.

Ralph Bales began to cry again, but they were tears from hysterical laughter. "You son of a bitch, you god-damn . . ."

That was when a shadow appeared on the floor beside the men.

The heads of both the men snapped sideways. They saw sensible pumps, a woman's pants, a denim jacket. Nina Sassower's pale, pretty face.

And the gun in her hand.

"Nina!" Pellam called.

Ralph Bales began to relax.

Pellam said, "What are you doing here?"

Her voice was distant, as if she were speaking through layers of silk or gauze. "I thought you'd come here."

"You should leave. What's that gun for? This's got nothing to do with you."

She stepped closer, looking gaunt and pale. Her skin was matte and her eyes were two dark dots. She looked at them both and her eyes quickly settled on Ralph Bales's wounds.

"Oh, God, Pellam . . ."

He told her they were fake bullets, then squinted as he noticed her concerned eyes gazing at the man in the chair. "Do you know him?" he asked.

She turned to him. "I'm sorry, Pellam."

"What do you—?" He started toward her.

She quickly lifted the big Colt toward his chest. "No. Stay where you are."

"Nina!"

"Put it on the floor. Your gun, put it down."

Pellam did. Then he laughed bitterly. "It was all planned, wasn't it?"

"It was all planned," she whispered.

"You picked me up at the hospital, you had me get you a job

so you'd be close by . . . Who are you working for? Lombro? Or Crimmins? Peterson? Who?"

"I'm sorry, Pellam. I'm so sorry."

Ralph Bales said, "Did Phil send you? Oh, man . . ." He moaned in relief. "Come on, honey. Get me out of here."

Nina squinted, almost closing her eyes. Pellam knew what this meant. He leapt to the floor as the three jarring explosions from Nina's automatic filled the room. Windows rattled, and dust from the tin ceiling floated down around the three of them like gray snow. The shadows of startled pigeons zipped across the windows.

———•◆•———

24

Pellam slowly stood, dizzy from both the fall and the pounding to his ears from the gunshots.

Reluctantly he looked across the room.

Ralph Bales had taken all three rounds in the chest. The chair had not toppled backwards but had turned forty-five degrees sideways under the impact. The man sat motionless, head down, facing the windows as if he were dozing in the weak sunlight.

Nina carefully unchambered the next round and extracted the clip. The empty gun, the slide locked back, went into her purse. She then stooped and began to collect the spent cartridges from the floor with impatient but fastidious care as if she were picking up socks from her bedroom carpet before vacuuming.

Pellam quickly uncuffed Ralph Bales's wrists, pocketed the cuffs, and wiped the chair free from fingerprints. He then hurried Nina outside and into the car. His fear of impending police was unwarranted, however; the gunshots had not been heard or, if so, had perhaps been attributed to the final scenes of *Missouri River Blues*. They drove to a nearby park on the river bank.

"You know where I got the gun?" Nina whispered. "My father kept it in his upstairs desk drawer of our house." She wiped her tearful eyes.

"Oh, you should have seen that desk," Nina continued. "It was a rolltop. Oak, I guess. Dark, with those thin yellow streaks in it. You unlocked it with a brass key that always needed polishing. There was such a wonderful sound when the lock turned. Then you'd lift up the top and there were dozens of these little compartments, lined with green felt. Some of the compartments had . . . Some of them had . . ."

She cried for a moment. Pellam made no gesture of comforting her.

"Some of the pigeonholes had little doors with knobs on them. We would go searching for secret compartments. We looked up under drawers, we tapped the back with hammers, listening for hollow spots. We found the gun when we were children, but we didn't think much of it. It had been years since I thought of the desk. Then last week I remembered it. I remembered the gun and I went over to my mother's and got it. I've been practicing since then. That brought back so many memories. The two of us looking through the desk. As little girls. Looking for toys, for paper clips, for—" The tears were strong now. "My sister and me . . ."

"Your sister," Pellam said, and finally he understood. "She was the woman with Vincent Gaudia, the one who was killed that night."

Nina said, "All the papers talked about was the cop who was shot and about Gaudia. Nobody said anything about Sally Ann.

Nobody cared about her. The day after she was killed I stayed up all night trying to figure out how to find the man who'd done it. I thought I'd wait until the police caught him and then at the trial I'd shoot him. But that might take months and maybe by then I wouldn't have the courage to do it. So I decided to meet Donnie. I saw his wedding picture in the paper and it said he was in Maddox General. I planned to get to know him and see if he could tell me the killer's name."

"And you met me instead. Your mother wasn't really in the hospital?"

"No. My sister was my only family. She was the relative who died I told you about in the camper, the funeral – when we were looking for that field. Not my aunt. That's why I started to cry."

"You overheard Donnie arguing with me. You heard him say I knew who the killer was."

She nodded. "I'm sorry, Pellam." There was sadness in her voice. But contrition? None at all.

"Why the job with the film company?"

"I knew he'd be looking for you. I thought sooner or later he'd find you."

"You had that gun with you all the while?"

"Some of the time."

That was why she had been so upset when she was attacked at the factory, she explained. She hadn't had the gun with her then; she regretted missing the chance.

The chance to shoot an FBI agent. Pellam didn't tell her this. "But her name wasn't the same as yours. Your sister's, I mean."

"No. Sally Ann's name was Moore. It's her married name.

She was divorced a few years ago. Pellam, was I wrong? I mean, think about it – the policeman was doing his job and he got hurt. And Gaudia was a terrible man and he got killed but all my sister did was go to dinner with him. She was innocent."

Pellam doubted whether going out with Vince Gaudia qualified you as a totally innocent human being. But he didn't think Nina was wrong at all to do what she'd done. Why, he himself had been wandering the barren streets of Maddox with a gun for exactly the same reason – to get revenge for Stile's death.

"*I* wanted to kill him," she said. "I didn't want him to just go to jail. I had to do it myself."

Pellam said nothing.

He leaned forward and put his arm around her. He smelled the sour cordite in her hair from the gunsmoke. He rocked his head against hers. But this gesture was halfhearted. Pellam's thoughts were elsewhere.

They drove up the street for a short ways until they found a pay phone. Pellam stopped, climbed out of the car.

"Are you going to tell the police about me?"

He looked at her for a long moment but said nothing. Her reaction was to pull down the car's visor, flip it open, and begin to brush her wispy blond hair.

Pellam consulted a card in his wallet then dialed a number.

In a slightly accented voice a man said, "Hello?"

"Mr Crimmins, this is the friend that spoke to you last night." Pellam had called the man to tell him not to panic when he heard Peterson announce an impending arrest.

"Ah, well, yes. How are you?"

"Fine. You?"

Crimmins chuckled at the etiquette. "I'm great. I assume things've worked out."

"There's been a slight complication."

"Serious?"

"No, not really."

"That's good."

"But I wonder if your associate, Mr Stettle's free to help me for about an hour."

"I think that could be arranged."

"Tell him to meet me at the corner of Main and Fifteenth in downtown Maddox in half an hour."

"Is this a possibly risky situation?"

"I don't think so. But could you ask him if he'd bring some garbage bags?"

"Garbage bags?"

"He'll understand."

They went to the lounge and meeting her there, rather than in his room, replaced the evening with Nina as the best thing that had happened to Donnie Buffett for a year.

"You shouldn't smoke," he told Wendy Weiser as she lit her cigarette.

"I know." She inhaled three times and stubbed it out. "That's all I smoke anyway. And just twice a day. Well, three times."

He nodded at the lie and looked her over. She was off duty today and had come in solely to meet with him. She wore tight, faded blue jeans and a leather jacket over a T-shirt imprinted with a slogan. He made her pull the jacket aside to reveal the words: "Once I thought I was mistaken. But I was wrong." He liked her earrings: A tiny gold fork hung from one lobe and a matching dinner knife from the other.

What was so good about the meeting was that he was no longer a prisoner. Or rather, he was not the same *degree* of prisoner. He had been in maximum security and now he had been upgraded to minimum. It wasn't yet straight time but that was okay. For the first time in almost two weeks he had a sense of motion – Buffett moved past things rather than being the stationary object. The breeze was stale and it smelled of antiseptic and steam-table food but it *moved* nonetheless and that was wonderful.

His maiden voyage in the wheelchair. He had insisted on piloting himself and Weiser hadn't objected though she said it was against the rules. He had a feeling that Weiser knew what the hospital could do with their rules and probably told them so frequently. Buffett shoved off hard from the doorway of his room. But his arms were stronger than expected and he had lost control, caroming off a water cooler and a candy striper's backside before he got the feel of the chair.

They had wheeled, and walked, down the corridor, Buffett considering whether to tell Weiser about the night with Nina Sassower. It was the sort of thing that she probably ought to know; it might help with his therapy. But he kept mum. He hardly wanted Nina to get into trouble. Anyway, if he didn't blow the whistle there was always the chance she might come back again.

He wondered if he could do it three times in one night.

The lounge consisted of a dozen Formica tables, bright blue and chipped. Against one orange-painted wall were old, battered vending machines, for coffee and hot chocolate, for candy, for soda. Some bulbs in the soda machine were burned out. The front said, *OCA OLA*.

She asked what he wanted.

Buffett said he'd have an 'oke.

Laughing hard, she said, "I'll have an 'iet 'oke."

"How come? You got a great 'igure."

They laughed some more and she walked over to the snack machine. She bought a pack of peanut butter crackers. "Dinner," she said. And he almost asked her out then – casually, thinking he would just wonder out loud if sometime she'd like to grab a bite with him. But the Terror nuzzled him viciously and the opportunity to ask the question suddenly closed. Then she was at the table, lighting, inhaling on, and stubbing out the cigarette.

He was slightly disappointed when she took a manila folder out of her attaché case. This made the meeting more professional, less social. She set it in front of her but did not open the file.

"Donnie, you're out of spinal shock now. There has been good restoration of sensation and control to many of your functions. I think bladder and rectal control will be almost normal. And, as I told you, there's no reason that I can see that sexual functioning won't ultimately be fine . . ."

Buffett was clamping down on the inside of his cheek to keep from smiling. "Ultimately."

"It's clear now that the most serious and permanent damage will be to your legs. There may be some improvement but most likely it'll be along the line of faint response to external stimuli. As far as walking again, on your own, well, it's the way I told you before, Donnie."

She offered him a cracker. He shook his head. She ate it then sipped the soft drink.

"There's a lot of research going on now in this area; most of it's trying to isolate substances – some are like hormones and some are structural proteins . . ."

He smiled to himself as he felt himself sinking into the brilliant quagmire of her brain.

". . . that affect how the neurons reach and talk to their receptor cells—"

Donnie nodded and appeared, he believed, to be interested.

". . . something called FNS."

"Feminine . . . ?" He wanted to make a joke, but his mind went blank.

"Functional neuromuscular stimulation." Her eyes sparkled as they always did when she spoke about science and she explained about some contraption that you hooked up to your leg muscles to send in jolts of electricity to stimulate them in a certain order. Eventually, using this device, you could propel yourself in a jerky fashion by using canes or a walker.

She kept talking but Donnie Buffett stopped listening. He was deciding that whatever FNS was exactly he'd never get hooked up to anything like that. Buffett knew he could sit in a wheelchair for the rest of his life and maybe cry sometimes and maybe scream and he could see himself pitching a lamp through the TV set after watching *Jeopardy!* or *Wheel of Fortune* one too many times. And he could picture himself wheeling out of the house and getting a job. Learning to do wheelies, learning to go over curbs by himself, developing huge, ball-buster arms and a fifty-inch chest. But no machines. Just like, if he were blind, he would use a cane but never rely on a dog. He couldn't explain what this distinction was exactly but to him it was real and it was the difference between his heart being alive and being cold dead.

He noticed that Weiser had stopped talking and it seemed as if she had asked him a question. He didn't feel like asking her to repeat it. He said, "Would you go out with me?" He added, "I mean, have dinner."

When she declined, as he had somehow known she would, it wasn't with a shocked or, what would have been worse, maternal smile. She looked at him with the intrigued gaze of a married woman at a party, propositioned discreetly by a man she finds attractive.

A pleasant regret, not an astonished surprise.

She added, "We should stay friends, you know."

And when she said that, the Terror nudged Donnie Buffett once, hard, bringing sweat to his forehead, but then it curled up somewhere inside him and, for the time being, fell into a deep, deep sleep.

25

∎◆∎

"There's a man to see you, sir. He says his name is Pellam."

"Pellam? Do I know him?" Philip Lombro said, running a chamois over his Bally shoes.

"He knows you, sir."

"I'm busy. Take his card."

Lombro sat back in his leather chair and stared at the floor. Dense clouds passing by outside would cast diffuse shadows on the green carpeting, then a moment later the harsh sunlight would return.

The intercom clicked again and startled him. The electric voice said, "He says it has to do with the late Mr Bales."

Lombro cleared his throat. "Send him in."

Pellam walked into the office. He looked around at the somber burgundy and navy books – business books, lawyer books. The desk. The pattern of cloud shadows on the verdant carpet. The view out the window, the smooth deco designs on the old brick building across the street.

Pellam sat down, uninvited, in the chair directly opposite Lombro's. "Your hit man is dead."

Lombro swallowed and folded the square of chamois carefully. Yes. It was him. The one with the case of beer, the man who'd seen him. "You're the witness."

"The witness." Pellam said the word slowly, tasting it, letting the sibilant draw out over his teeth.

"Mr James?"

"No, it's Pellam."

Lombro shook his head at this, confused. Then he said cautiously, "You cheated me."

Pellam frowned. "I'm sorry?"

"You took my money and you still went to the U.S. Attorney. I heard the news conference."

"What money?"

"The fifty thousand? The money Ralph gave you . . ."

The voice faded and Pellam obviously came to the conclusion that was setting prominently into Lombro's mind. They shared rueful smiles.

Lombro said, "I see."

"The quality of your hired help leaves a little bit to be desired."

"So it seems. He's dead, you say?"

"An accident."

"I see. Are you here to kill me?" This he asked in a matter-of-fact voice.

"No," Pellam said.

"I swear I forbade Ralph to hurt you. All he was going to do was pay you to—"

"But, he came to the Federal Building yesterday with a gun. You knew that."

Lombro's mouth closed and he touched some strands of silver hair at his temple.

"I want to know why you had Gaudia killed."

"Are you a policeman?"

"No."

"But you have a microphone on you."

Pellam took off his jacket and turned out the pockets of his shirt and jeans. Lombro, eyes fixed on the grip of the Colt in Pellam's waistband, took the bomber jacket and felt through the pockets.

"I just want to know," Pellam said sincerely.

Lombro crossed his legs and gripped his ankle with his right hand, rubbing his fingers along it. He did not sort through his thoughts. This was a story he had planned to tell for some time. Perhaps to his prosecutor. "I love my nieces like daughters. I've never been married. Never had children. Have you?"

Pellam didn't answer.

"One niece of mine was eighteen. She was a sweet, sweet girl. But she was somewhat heavy, unsure of herself. She was going to school and working part-time as a waitress in a restaurant that Vincent Gaudia would sometimes eat in. Gaudia was a generous man with money. He would give her twenty-dollar tips. Then it was a fifty-dollar tip. And after that it was the promise of a hundred-dollar tip. I suppose you can guess what happened.

"They spent a few nights together, and then Gaudia simply forgot that she existed. But the poor child believed she'd fallen in love with him. I tried to convince her otherwise but she was inconsolable. He refused to take her calls and answer her letters. Finally she went to his home. It was late at night, after she got off work at the restaurant. She left his house at two in the morning, and on the way home, drove through a red light. Her car was hit by a truck and she was killed. She had been drinking and had had sex just an hour before. The evidence indicated the sex was of a sort I choose not to describe."

"One of the two thousand," Pellam mused.

"I'm sorry?"

"I've heard Gaudia had his share of women. She was a conquest."

"Just so."

"The police said the accident was her fault but, of course, it wasn't. It was Vincent Gaudia's. He seduced my niece. It's as if he murdered her. This is what Gaudia did to my family and when my brother refused to do anything about his daughter's death, I decided to."

"Old World revenge."

"If you will."

"You knew that Bales or his partner killed the woman who was with Gaudia too. Then shot that cop. And a friend of mine."

Lombro shook his head. There was alarm and sorrow in his face. "This has all gone so wrong. So wrong! I should have done the manly thing. I should have killed him myself and taken the consequences. I'm not a coward. I just didn't understand how these things worked. Have you called the police?"

"Not yet, no," Pellam said. He looked around the office, at the paneling, the prints on the walls. He asked, "What're you worth?"

"Pardon?"

"Money, you know. How much do you have?"

"I don't really know."

"A million?" Pellam suggested.

Lombro smiled. "More than that. Why are you asking?"

Pellam said, "What does that mean? 'More than that.'"

"I don't exactly *know*," Lombro said stridently.

"You're in the real estate business?"

Lombro reached toward his knee and picked a piece of lint from his slacks. "And I've been in that line long enough to understand when an offer is about to be made."

"You know," Pellam said, "they have this service in some states. It's called the crime victims' reparation fund or something like that. You ever hear about it?"

"No."

"When someone's mugged or raped they get some money. Somebody gets killed, the family gets it."

"And you're suggesting I pay you something."

Pellam hesitated, then he laughed. "Yep. Exactly."

"How much?" Lombro opened his drawer. Then, perhaps deciding a check might not be the way to handle something like this, closed it again.

"I'm thinking mostly of the policeman that got shot."

"Whatever. How much did you have in mind?"

"He's paralyzed, the cop. He'll never walk again. Life's going to be pretty expensive for him. Housekeepers, special cars. And by the way, I got fired thanks to you."

Lombro looked up from his shoes, which he now planted on the carpeting. "I am being very honest when I tell you that I didn't want you hurt and that I didn't want anyone to die except Gaudia. I hope you agree I had a . . . well, an honorable motive for doing what I did. I don't think you'll hurt me."

"No," Pellam said, "I don't have any intention of hurting you."

"You can, of course, go to the police and tell them what happened. But what it really comes down to is my word against your word. I've been involved in plenty of litigation. Lawyers call cases like this a liar's match. Who believes whom? I think I stand as good a chance of being believed as you do. I'm influential in this town. I'm one of the few businessmen still able to pay taxes, which I do in great abundance. I'm well known in the assessor's office and in city hall, too. So, although I sympathize with you and your friend, you don't really have much leverage. I'd consider ten thousand for each of you."

"Nope, that's not enough." Pellam took a small cloth square from his pocket and dropped it on the desk. "Take a look." Lombro unfolded the handkerchief and looked at the business-card case inside. He opened it up, shrugged, and dropped it back on the handkerchief. Pellam scooped the case up and put it in his pocket.

"And who," Lombro asked, "is Special Agent Gilbert?"

"He's the man buried in the foundation of one of the buildings you're putting up. A project outside of St Louis. Foxwood. I get a kick out of those names for condominiums. Stonehenge. Windcrest. Do people really—"

"*What?* There's no one buried in—"

"And sad to say, he'd been shot with a gun that's buried in your yard at home."

"Impossible. I don't own a gun."

"I didn't say you own a gun. I just said the gun was buried on your property."

"This is nonsense."

Lombro's silver face flushed and his eyes darted. A distinguished man made common. A powerful man, impotent. "Your policeman friend. Is he helping—" Lombro stared at Pellam's jacket pocket. He whispered, "And I just put my fingerprints on his ID card, didn't I?"

"Not to say they'd convict you. But Agent Gilbert *was* involved in the Gaudia murder. He threatened me and my friend." Pellam added, "And I'd feel obligated to cooperate, being a personal acquaintance of the U.S. Attorney. I'd feel it was my duty."

Philip Lombro looked out the window at the brick of the building across the way. He glanced down, licked his finger, and lifted a fleck of paper or dust off the heel of one of his shoes, black cherry, tasseled Ballys, polished like dark mirrors. Pellam started to speak but didn't. He paused, staring at the shoes, frowning, as if he'd seen them somewhere before but was unable to remember exactly where.

Tony Sloan was still not, in general, speaking to Pellam but he made an exception to explain that because the machine guns had been released and the ending of the film was successfully in the can, half of Pellam's fee would be released. The rest Sloan was retaining to help defray the cost of the delay.

"You want to play it that way, Tony, then I'll see you in court."

Sloan had shrugged and taken up the vow of silence again, returning to the editing van, where close to five hundred thousand feet of film, and an extremely discouraged editor, awaited the arrival of the director's artistic vision.

Pellam had gone directly downstairs to the Marriott's Huck Finn Room to crash the wrap party.

There he drank Sloan's champagne and ate the cat-fish tidbits and hush puppies, while he chatted with the cast and crew, all of them so exhausted from the trials of the final days of shooting that they did not know, or care, if he was still an untouchable.

He looked over the crowd. He saw the makeup artists in the corner; Nina Sassower was not among them.

Pellam wandered over to Stace Stacey, as exhausted as anyone but still retaining his unflappable good spirits. Pellam handed over the unused wax bullets and the empty .45 casings Stace had loaned him. Pellam nodded at them. "Wouldn't mention this."

Stace pocketed the munitions and touched his lips with a forefinger.

Pellam told him about Sloan's holding back his fee. Now on his third or fourth cuba libre Stace was pretty loose. "Trying to squeeze you, is he? That man is a hundred percent son of a bitch," the arms master said, using the strongest language Pellam had ever heard him utter.

"But you'll work with him again."

"Oh, you betcha. And you'll be in line right behind me."

"Probably," Pellam said.

A woman appeared in the doorway of the banquet room. Pellam recognized her as one of Sloan's secretaries. She urgently waved a slip of paper at him. He wondered if Sloan had changed his mind and was reluctantly releasing the rest of the money. Not that it truly mattered. Fifty thousand dollars had just been transferred from Philip Lombro's investment company into Pellam's account at a bank in Sherman Oaks.

"You got this fax, John. It's from Marty Weller Budapest."

And was apparently just about to be transferred out again, to finance *Central Standard Time*.

She handed it to him and headed back toward a cluster of actors but got no farther than Stace Stacey, who encircled her waist and rose on tiptoe to whisper something in her ear. She giggled.

Pellam unfolded the fax. It took a whole page of producer-babble for Marty Weller to break the news to him that Tri-Star was going to be picking up Paramount's fallen standard and financing the terrorist script, which Weller would be producing in lieu of *Central Standard Time*. The Hungarians were going to Tri-Star with him. They asked Weller to say hello to Pellam, whom they felt they knew already and whom they had dubbed the American *Auteur*: They hoped that perhaps in the future they all might work together on a "clever-scripted, hey knock-em-dead cult film noir project."

Pellam folded the paper and slipped it into his back pocket. He lifted another champagne off a passing tray. He closed his eyes and rubbed the cold flute over his forehead.

Stace returned a moment later. He was without the secretary but the expression on the arms master's face was not that of a rejected man. He smiled agreeably and said to Pellam, "Tomorrow morning, let's you and me go shooting, what do you say? We'll take the Charter Arms and the Dan Wesson and shoot up some cans. Maybe they even have rattlesnakes around here."

Pellam opened his mouth to make excuses, but then he said, "As long as I don't have to get up too early, Stace."

"Oh, no, sir. Film's over. We're on vacation now."

The basketball court on Leonard Street in Maddox is closed most of the time. It's part of a school playground but because of budget cutbacks, the Department of Education can't afford to keep it open when school's not in session, and the gate is locked at 5:00 P.M. Not that it matters much; the local kids have pried apart enough chain link gate to slip through for pickup games any time they want.

The court is asphalt. There's a lot of graffiti on the brick walls surrounding it – names of kids and gangs and some of those flashy, three-dimensional block letters and drawings that the talented punks do. But the asphalt itself is clean as black marble in a church. Nobody messes with foul lines.

Tonight, a mild, humid night in December, two men are at the fence. The opening in the gate would be big enough for them to pass through if one of the men weren't in a wheelchair. It's a small chair, gunmetal blue and sporty, with wheels tilted; at the top, they're closer together than at the bottom. The man who is standing looks around and takes a geared, carbon-tempered bolt cutter from a large, cylindrical canvas sports bag. He props one long handle on his hip and, using both hands on the other handle, severs one side of a link of chain, then the other.

They enter the court. The man in the chair speeds forward under the thrusts of his powerful arms, which are dark with hair.

Pellam says, "Go easy with an old man, huh?"

It takes a while for Donnie Buffett to get used to dribbling but he's played good offense for years and knows how to keep the ball away from his body while controlling it. He does have a problem, though, because he can only coast in for a shot: If he uses his arm to move forward, he goes in circles. What he does is, he sets the ball on his lap and speeds in for the lay-up.

Pellam whistles loudly through his teeth and cries, "Traveling."

"So what're you back in town for?" Buffett asks him after sinking the shot. "That *Missouri River* movie?"

"Nope. That's in post production now. July release date. I'm suing the director for my fee and credit."

"That's a hassle."

"Goes with the territory. I just came back to do some scouting for another script."

"What's this one called?"

"Central Standard Time."

"Sounds boring. Who's going to be in it? You should cast Geena Davis. I really like her. Or Shelley Long. You ever watch *Cheers?*"

"Nobody's in it. Nobody's even *making* it yet. When I was here I saw some locations that looked pretty good. I wanted to check them out this time of year. That's when the story takes place. Winter."

"That's pretty wild. Two movies in one year. Maybe Maddox'll be the new Hollywood."

"Hollywood started out as a desert," Pellam tells him.

"How long you here for?"

"A week or two. Then I'm heading on to my mother's place, upstate New York, for the holidays."

Buffett usually makes his shots, which Pellam finds extremely frustrating. Pellam has been watching the Lakers all season. He tries to fly up to the basket and stuff the ball in, but he comes nowhere close. He is terrible player. The Nokona cowboy boots don't help much.

Buffett gets the rebound away from Pellam and sinks another.

"Hell with this," Pellam says. "Let's see a slam-dunk."

They play for a half hour and take a break for beer.

In response to a question Buffett tells Pellam he isn't seeing Nina anymore. "That's over with. It was just a fluke thing. I never knew what to make of her. She was moody a lot. It was like she had some big secret or something."

"I picked that up, too." Pellam wipes his mouth with his sleeve and thinks they're crazy to be drinking beer in December.

And crazy to be playing basketball now, too.

"Did I tell you?" Buffett asks.

"What?"

"Penny's moved out. We're getting a divorce."

"You're going to what?"

"A divorce. Get one."

"God," Pellam says.

"Well—"

"I think that's awful."

Buffett looks away, inordinately embarrassed, and swallows a lot of beer. "It happens."

"Did she find out about Nina?"

"No. She still doesn't know."

Pellam shakes his head and starts to wave his arm at Buffett's legs but changes the motion to encompass the entire court. "All this and she decides to leave you?"

"No, Pellam. Uh-uh. *I'm* the one getting the divorce. It's my idea. She's going to live with her parents."

"Oh." This, too, Pellam thinks is crazy. He looks at Buffett for a moment. "All this and *you* leave *her?*"

"Yep."

"Why?"

"You were over to the house. You really have to ask?"

"But you'll be living by yourself? A time like this?"

Buffett shrugs. "I guess, yeah."

Pellam gives him a more-power-to-you shrug and practices dribbling. The ball gets away from him. He hops in front and stops it, then asks, "You see Dr Wendy lately?"

"Th'other day."

"So?"

"Nothing new. Same old prognosis."

"You want to talk about it?"

"No."

They drink beer for a few minutes, talking about the Knicks and the Lakers. Then Buffett says, "They've tried these new drugs on me. They don't have any effect."

"You gonna kill yourself?"

"I don't think so. Someday maybe." Buffett is neither joking nor serious when he says this.

"I just thought of something. You play poker?"

Buffett laughs at the idiocy of the question. "Of course I play poker."

"You like chili?"

"No. I hate chili."

A breeze comes up and it's too cold to sit still and drink beer so they head back toward the basket and begin to play again. Pellam comes up fast and gets the ball away from Buffett. He dribbles fiercely and lobs a long one, a three-pointer, which he knows isn't going to go in, but it hits the rim, reverberates back and forth madly and finally drops through the rusty metal hoop into Buffett's waiting hands.

About the Author

A former journalist, folksinger and attorney, Jeffery Deaver is the international number-one bestselling author of thirty-seven novels, three collections of short stories and a non-fiction law book, and a lyricist of a country-western album. His novels have appeared on bestseller lists around the world and are sold in 150 countries and translated into twenty-five languages.

His most recent novels are *Solitude Creek*, a Kathryn Dance novel; *The October List*, a thriller told in reverse; and *The Steel Kiss*, a Lincoln Rhyme novel. For his Dance novel *XO* Deaver wrote an album of country-western songs, available on iTunes and as a CD; and before that, *Carte Blanche*, a James Bond continuation novel, a number-one international bestseller.

Deaver has been nominated for seven Edgar Awards, an Anthony, a Shamus and a Gumshoe. He was shortlisted for the ITV3 Crime Thriller Award and for the Prix Polar International 2013.

His novel *A Maiden's Grave* was made into an HBO movie, and *The Bone Collector* was a feature release from Universal Pictures, starring Denzel Washington and Angelina Jolie. Lifetime aired an adaptation of his *The Devil's Teardrop*. And, yes, the rumours are true; he did appear as a corrupt reporter on his favourite soap opera, *As the World Turns*. He was born outside Chicago and has a bachelor of journalism degree from the University of Missouri and a law degree from Fordham University.

Readers can visit his website at www.jefferydeaver.com.

John Pellam returns in

JEFFERY DEAVER

HELL'S KITCHEN

Every New York City neighbourhood has a story, but what John
Pellam uncovers in Hell's Kitchen has a darkness all its own.

The Hollywood location scout was hoping to capture the
unvarnished memories of longtime residents in a no-budget
documentary film. But when a suspicious fire ravages an elderly
woman's crumbling tenement, Pellam realises that someone
might want the past to stay buried. As more buildings and lives
go up in flames, he takes to the streets, seeking the twisted
pyromaniac who sells his services to the highest bidder.

But Pellam is unaware that the fires are merely preludes
to the arsonist's ultimate masterpiece – a conflagration of
nearly unimaginable proportions. With Pellam at its
blackened and searing centre . . .

Out now in paperback and ebook.

HODDER

Discover the first Kathryn Dance thriller

JEFFERY DEAVER

THE SLEEPING DOLL

YOU CAN TELL A LIAR BY HIS EYES.

Special Agent Kathryn Dance reads people
the way other investigators read crime scenes.
But she's never seen eyes like Daniel Pell's.

YOU CAN CATCH A KILLER BY HIS SMILE.

In 1999, Daniel Pell murdered an entire family. Only one
little girl survived, asleep in her bed and hidden by her dolls.

When Kathryn Dance interrogates Pell, he's serving
a life sentence for the murders. Moments later, he's on
the run, a trail of death and mayhem in his wake.

To catch him, Dance must draw on every clue from their
brief meeting. And her fear that they share a common aim:
to find the girl they call the Sleeping Doll . . .

Out now in paperback and ebook.

HODDER